THE
TAKER

ALMA KATSU

C

Century · London

Published by Century 2011

2 4 6 8 10 9 7 5 3 1

First published in Great Britain in 2011 by
Century
Random House, 20 Vauxhall Bridge Road,
London SW1V 2SA

www.randomhouse.co.uk

Addresses for companies within The Random House Group Limited can be found at:
www.randomhouse.co.uk

The Random House Group Limited Reg. No. 954009

A CIP catalogue record for this book
is available from the British Library

ISBN 9781846058172

The Random House Group Limited supports The Forest Stewardship
Council (FSC), the leading international forest certification organisation.
All our titles that are printed on Greenpeace approved FSC certified paper
carry the FSC logo. Our paper procurement policy can be found at:
www.rbooks.co.uk/environment

For my husband Bruce

AUTHOR'S NOTE

s *The Taker* is a work of fantasy, I don't imagine readers come to it expecting historical authenticity, but there is one liberty I've taken with history that must be pointed out. While there is no town of St. Andrew in the state of Maine, if the reader attempts to triangulate the fictional village's location based on clues in the text, you'll see that if it were to exist, it would fall about where the town of Allagash stands today. Truth be told, this exact area of Maine wasn't settled until the 1860s. However, the Acadian town of Madawaska, not far away, was settled in 1785, and so in my mind it didn't seem too much of a stretch to have Charles St. Andrew found his outpost around this time.

PART I

ONE

Goddamned freezing cold. Luke Findley's breath hangs in the air, nearly a solid thing shaped like a frozen wasp's nest, wrung of all its oxygen. His hands are heavy on the steering wheel; he is groggy, having woken just in time to make the drive to the hospital for the night shift. The snow-covered fields to either side of the road are ghostly sweeps of blue in the moonlight, the blue of lips about to go numb from hypothermia. The snow is so deep it covers all traces of the stumps of stalks and brambles that normally choke the fields, and gives the land a deceptively calm appearance. He often wonders why his neighbors remain in this northernmost corner of Maine. It's lonely and frigid, a tough place to farm. Winter reigns half the year, snow piles to the windowsills, and a serious biting cold whips over the empty potato fields.

Occasionally, someone does freeze solid, and because Luke is one of the few doctors in the area, he's seen a number of them. A drunk (and there is no shortage of them in St. Andrew) falls asleep against a snow-bank and by morning has become a human Popsicle. A boy, skating on the Allagash River, plunges through a weak spot in the ice. Sometimes the body is discovered halfway to Canada, at the junction where the Allagash meets up with the St. John. A hunter goes snow blind and can't make his way out of the Great North Woods, his body found sitting with its back against a stump, shotgun lying uselessly across his lap.

That weren't no accident, Joe Duchesne, the sheriff, told Luke in disgust when the hunter's body was brought to the hospital. *Old Ollie Ostergaard, he wanted to die. That's just his way of committing suicide.* But Luke suspects if this were true, Ostergaard would have shot himself in the head. Hypothermia is a slow way to go, plenty of time to think better of it.

Luke eases his truck into an empty parking space at the Aroostook County Hospital, cuts the engine, and promises himself, again, that he is going to get out of St. Andrew. He just has to sell his parents' farm and then he is going to move, even if he's not sure where. Luke sighs from habit, yanks the keys out of the ignition, and heads to the entrance to the emergency room.

The duty nurse nods as Luke walks in, pulling off his gloves. He hangs up his parka in the tiny doctors' lounge and returns to the admitting area. Judy says, "Joe called. He's bringing in a disorderly he wants you to look at. Should be here any minute."

"Trucker?" When there is trouble, usually it involves one of the drivers for the logging companies. They are notorious for getting drunk and picking fights at the Blue Moon.

"No." Judy is absorbed in something she's doing on the computer. Light from the monitor glints off her bifocals.

Luke clears his throat for her attention. "Who is it then? Someone local?" Luke is tired of patching up his neighbors. It seems only fighters, drinkers, and misfits can tolerate the hard-bitten town.

Judy looks up from the monitor, fist planted on her hip. "No. A woman. And not from around here, either."

That is unusual. Women are rarely brought in by the police except when they're the victim. Occasionally a local wife will be brought in after a brawl with her husband, or in the summer, a female tourist may get out of hand at the Blue Moon. But this time of year, there's not a tourist to be found.

Something different to look forward to tonight. He picks up a chart. "Okay. What else we got?" He half-listens as Judy runs down the activity from the previous shift. It was a fairly busy evening but right now, ten P.M., it's quiet. Luke goes back to the lounge to wait for the sheriff. He can't endure another update of Judy's daughter's impending wedding, an endless lecture on the cost of bridal gowns, caterers, florists. *Tell her to elope,* Luke said to Judy once, and she looked at him as though he'd professed to being a member of a terrorist organization. *A girl's wedding is the most important day of her life,* Judy scoffed in reply. *You don't have a romantic bone in your body. No wonder Tricia divorced you.* He has stopped retorting, *Tricia didn't divorce me, I divorced her,* because nobody listens anymore.

Luke sits on the battered couch in the lounge and tries to distract himself with a Sudoku puzzle. He thinks instead of the drive to the hospital that evening, the houses he passed on the lonely roads, solitary lights burning into the night. What do people do, stuck inside their houses for long hours during the winter evenings? As the town doctor, there are no secrets kept from Luke. He knows all the vices: who beats his wife; who gets heavy-handed with his children; who drinks and ends up putting his truck into a snowbank; who is chronically depressed from another bad year for the crops and no prospects on the horizon. The woods of St. Andrew are thick and dark with secrets. It reminds Luke of why he wants to get away from this town; he's tired of knowing their secrets and of them knowing his.

Then there is the other thing, the thing he thinks about every time he steps into the hospital lately. It hasn't been so long since his mother died and he recalls vividly the night they moved her to the ward euphemistically called "the hospice," the rooms for patients whose ends are too close to warrant moving them to the rehab center in Fort Kent. Her heart function had dropped below 10 percent and she fought for every breath, even wearing an oxygen mask. He sat with her that night, alone, because it was late and her other visitors had gone home. When she went into arrest for the last time, he was holding her hand. She was exhausted by then and stirred only a little, then her grip went slack and she slipped away as quietly as sunset falling into dusk. The patient monitor sounded its alarm at nearly the same time the duty nurse rushed in, but Luke hit the switch and waved off the nurse without even thinking. He took the stethoscope from around his neck and checked her pulse and breathing. She was gone.

The duty nurse asked if he wanted a minute alone and he said yes. Most of the week had been spent in intensive care with his mother, and it seemed inconceivable that he could just walk away now. So he sat at her bedside and stared at nothing, certainly not at the body, and tried to think of what he had to do next. Call the relatives; they were all farmers living in the southern part of the county . . . Call Father Lymon over at the Catholic church Luke couldn't bring himself to attend . . . Pick out a coffin . . . So many details required his attention. He knew what needed to be done because he'd been through it all just seven months earlier when his father died, but the thought of going through this again was just exhausting. It was at times like these that he most missed his ex-wife. Tricia, a nurse, had been good to have around during difficult times. She wasn't one to lose her head, practical even in the face of grief.

This was no time to wish things were different. He was alone now and would have to manage by himself. He blushed with embarrassment, knowing how his mother had wanted him and Tricia to stay together, how she lectured him for letting her go. He glanced at the dead woman, a guilty reflex.

Her eyes were open. They had been closed a minute ago. He felt his chest squeeze with hope even though he knew it meant nothing. Just an electrical impulse running through nerves as her synapses stopped firing, like a car sputtering as the last fumes of gas passed through the engine. He reached up and lowered her eyelids.

They opened a second time, naturally, as though his mother was waking up. Luke almost jumped backward but managed to control his fright. No, not fright—surprise. Instead, he slipped on his stethoscope and leaned over her, pressing the diaphragm to her chest. Silent, no sluicing of blood through veins, no rasp of breath. He picked up her wrist. No pulse. He checked his watch: fifteen minutes had passed since he had pronounced his mother dead. He lowered her cold hand, unable to stop watching her. He swore she was looking back at him, her eyes trained on him.

And then her hand lifted from the bedsheet and reached for him. Stretched toward him, palm up, beckoning him to take it. He did, calling her by name, but as soon as he grasped her hand, he dropped it. It was cold and lifeless. Luke took five paces away from the bed, rubbing his forehead, wondering if he was hallucinating. When he turned around, her eyes were closed and her body was still. He could scarcely breathe for his heart thumping in his throat.

It took three days before he could bring himself to talk to another doctor about what had happened. He chose old John Mueller, a pragmatic GP who was known for delivering calves for his rancher neighbor. Mueller had given him a skeptical look, as though he suspected Luke might have been drinking. *Twitching of fingers and toes, yeah that happens*, he'd said, *but fifteen minutes later? Musculorskeletal movement?* Mueller eyed Luke again, as though the fact that they were even talking about it was shameful. *You think you saw it because you wanted to. You didn't want her to be gone.*

Luke knew that wasn't it. But he wouldn't raise it again, not among doctors.

Besides, Mueller had wanted to know, *what difference does it make? So the body may have moved a little—you think she was trying to tell you something? You believe in that life-after-death stuff?*

Thinking about it now, four months later, still gives Luke a slight chill, running down both arms. He puts the Sudoku book on the side table and works his fingers over his skull, trying to massage out the confusion. The door to the lounge pushes back a crack: it's Judy. "Joe's pulling in up front."

Luke goes outside without his parka so the cold will slap him awake. He watches Duchesne pull up to the curb in a big SUV painted black and white, a decal of the Maine state seal on the front doors and a low-profile light bar strapped to the roof. Luke has known Duchesne since they were boys. They were not in the same grade but they overlapped at school, so he's seen Duchesne's narrow, ferret-like face with the beady eyes and the slightly sinister nose for more than twenty years.

Hands tucked into his armpits for warmth, Luke watches Duchesne open the back door and reach for the prisoner's arm. He's curious to see the disorderly. He's expecting a big, mannish biker woman, red-faced and with a split lip, and is surprised to see that the woman is small and young. She could be a teenager. Slender and boyish except for the pretty face and mass of yellow corkscrew curls, a cherub's hair.

Looking at the woman (girl?) Luke feels a strange tingle, a buzz behind his eyes. His pulse picks up with something almost like—recognition. *I know you*, he thinks. Not her name, perhaps, but something more fundamental. What is it? Luke squints, studying her more closely. Have I seen her somewhere before? No, he realizes he's mistaken.

As Duchesne pulls the woman along by the elbow, her hands tied together with a flexicuff, a second police vehicle pulls up and a deputy, Clay Henderson, gets out and takes over escorting the prisoner into the emergency ward. As they pass, Luke sees the prisoner's shirt is wet, stained black, and she smells of a familiar blend of iron and salt, the smell of blood.

Duchesne steps close to Luke, nodding in the pair's direction. "We found her like that walking along the logging road to Fort Kent."

"No coat?" Coatless in this weather? She couldn't have been out for long.

"Nope. Listen, I need you to tell me if she's hurt, or if I can take her back to the station and lock her up."

As far as law enforcement officers went, Luke's always suspected Duchesne of being heavy-handed; he's seen too many drunks brought in with lumps on their skulls or facial bruising. This girl, she's only a kid—what in the world could she have done? "Why is she in custody? For not wearing a coat in this weather?"

Duchesne gives Luke a sharp look, unaccustomed to being mocked. "That girl is a killer. She told us she stabbed a man to death and left his body out in the woods."

Luke goes through the motions of examining the prisoner, but he can barely think for the strange pulsing in his head. He shines a penlight into her eyes—they are the palest blue eyes he's ever seen, like two shards of compressed ice—to see if her pupils are dilated. Her skin is clammy to the touch, her pulse low and her breathing ragged.

"She's very pale," he says to Duchesne as they step away from the gurney to which the prisoner has been strapped at the wrists. "That could mean she's going cyanotic. Going into shock."

"Does that mean she's injured?" Duchesne asks, skeptical.

"Not necessarily. She could be in psychological trauma. Could be from an argument. Maybe from fighting with this man she says she killed. How do you know it's not self-defense?"

Duchesne, hands on hips, stares at the prisoner on the gurney as though he can discern the truth just by looking at her. He shifts his weight from one foot to the other. "We don't know anything . . . she hasn't said much. Can't you tell if she's wounded? 'Cause if she's not hurt I'll just take her in . . ."

"I have to get that shirt off, clean off the blood . . ."

"Get to it. I can't stay here all night. I left Boucher in the woods, looking for that body."

Even with the full moon, the woods are dark and vast, and Luke knows the deputy, Boucher, has little chance of finding a body by himself.

Luke picks at the edge of his latex glove. "So go help Boucher while I do the examination . . ."

"I can't leave the prisoner here."

"For Chrissakes," Luke says, jerking his head in the slight young woman's direction. "She's hardly going to overpower me and escape. If you're that worried about it, have Henderson stay." They both glance at Henderson tentatively. The big deputy leans against a counter, leafing through an old *Sports Illustrated* left in the waiting room, a cup of vending machine coffee in his hand. He's shaped like a cartoon bear and is, appropriately, amicably dim. "He won't be of much help to you in the woods . . . Nothing is going to happen," Luke says impatiently, turning away from the sheriff as though the matter is already settled. He feels Duchesne's stare bore into his back, unsure if he should argue with Luke.

And then the sheriff lurches away, heading for the double set of sliding doors. "Stay here with the prisoner," he yells at Henderson as he jams the heavy, fur-lined hat onto his head. "I'm going back to help Boucher. Idiot couldn't find his own ass with both hands and a map."

Luke and the nurse attend to the woman strapped to the gurney. He hefts a pair of scissors. "I'm going to have to cut your shirt away," he warns her.

"You might as well. It's ruined," she says in a soft voice with an accent Luke can't place. The shirt is obviously expensive. It's the kind of clothing you see in fashion magazines and that you would never find someone wearing in St. Andrew.

"You're not from around here, are you?" Luke says, small talk to loosen her up.

She studies his face, evaluating whether to trust him—or so Luke assumes. "I was born here, actually. That was a long time ago."

Luke snorts. "A long time ago for you, maybe. If you were born here, I'd know you. I've lived in this area almost my entire life. What's your name?"

She doesn't fall for his little trick. "You don't know me," she says flatly.

For a few minutes there's only the sound of wet fabric being cut and it is hard going, the scissors' tiny beak moving sluggishly through the sodden material. After it's done, Luke stands back to let Judy swab the girl with gauze soaked in warm water. The bloody red streaks dissolve, revealing a pale, thin chest without a scratch on it. The nurse drops the forceps holding the gauze into a metal pan noisily and hustles out of the examination room as though she knew all along that they'd find nothing, and yet again, Luke has proven his incompetence.

He averts his eyes as he drapes a paper sheet over the girl's naked torso.

"I'd have told you I wasn't hurt if you'd asked," she says to Luke in a low whisper.

"You didn't tell the sheriff though," Luke says, reaching for a stool.

"No. But I'd have told *you*." She nods at the doctor. "Do you have a cigarette? I'm dying for a smoke."

"I'm sorry. Don't have any. I don't smoke," Luke replies.

The girl looks at him, those ice blue eyes scanning his face. "You gave them up a while ago, but you started again. Not that I blame you, given everything you've been through lately. But you have a couple of cigarettes in your lab coat, if I'm not mistaken."

His hand goes to the pocket, out of instinct, and he feels the papery touch of the cigarettes right where he had left them. Was that a lucky guess, or did she see them in his pocket?

And what did she mean by *given everything you've been through lately*? She's just pretending to read his mind, trying to get inside his head like any clever girl who finds herself in a fix would do. He *has* been wearing his troubles on his face lately. He just hasn't seen a way to fix his life yet; his problems are interconnected, all stacked up. He'd have to know how to fix all of them to take care of even one.

"There's no smoking in the building, and in case you've forgotten, you're strapped to a gurney." Luke clicks the top of his pen and reaches for a clipboard. "We're a little shorthanded tonight, so I'm going to need to get some information from you for the hospital records. Name?"

She regards the clipboard warily. "I'd rather not say."

"Why? Are you a runaway? Is that why you don't want to give me your name?" He studies her: she's tense, guarded, but under control. He's been around patients involved in accidental deaths and they're usually hysterical—crying, shaking, screaming. This young woman is trembling slightly under the paper sheet and she jiggles her legs nervously, but by her face Luke can tell she's in shock.

He feels, too, that she is warming toward him; he senses a chemistry between them, as though she is willing him to ask her about the terrible thing that happened in the forest. "Do you want to tell me what went on tonight?" he asks, rolling closer to the gurney. "Were you hitchhiking? Maybe you got picked up by someone, the guy in the woods . . . He attacks you, you defend yourself?"

She sighs and presses back into the pillow, staring at the ceiling. "It was nothing like that. We knew each other. We came to town together. He"—she stops, choking on the words—"he asked me to help him die."

"Euthanasia? Was he already dying? Cancer?" Luke is skeptical. The ones looking to kill themselves usually pick something quiet and surefire: poison, pills, an idling car engine and a length of garden hose. They don't ask to be stabbed to death. If this friend really wanted to die, he could have just sat under the stars all night until he froze.

He glances at the woman, trembling under the paper sheet. "Let me get a hospital gown and a blanket for you. You must be cold."

"Thank you," she says, dropping her gaze.

He comes back with a much-laundered flannel gown edged in pink and a pilling acrylic blanket, baby blue. Maternity colors. He looks down at her hands, bound to the gurney with nylon strap restraints. "Here, we'll do this one hand at a time," Luke says, undoing the restraint on the hand closest to the side table where the examination tools are laid out: forceps, bloodied scissors, scalpel.

Quick as a rabbit, she lunges for the scalpel, her slender hand closing around it. She points it at him, wild eyed, her nostrils pink and flaring.

"Take it easy," Luke says, stepping backward off the stool, out of her arm's reach. "There's a deputy just down the hall. If I call for him, it's over, you know? You can't get both of us with that little knife. So why don't you put down the scalpel—"

"Don't call him," she says, but her arm is still outstretched. "I need you to listen to me."

"I'm listening." The gurney is between Luke and the door. She can cut her other hand free in the time it takes him to make it across the room.

"I need your help. I can't let him arrest me. You have to help me escape."

"Escape?" Suddenly, Luke isn't worried that the young woman with the scalpel will hurt him. He's feeling embarrassed for having let his guard down, allowing her to get the drop on him. "Are you out of your mind? I'm not going to help you escape."

"Listen to me—"

"You killed someone tonight. You said so yourself."

"It wasn't murder. He wanted to die, I told you that."

"And he came here to die because he grew up here, too?"

"Yes," she says, a little relieved.

"Then tell me who he is. Maybe I know him . . ."

She shakes her head. "I told you—you don't know us. Nobody here knows us."

"You don't know that for sure. Maybe some of your relatives . . ." Luke's obstinacy comes out when he gets angry.

"My family hasn't lived in St. Andrew for a long, long time." She sounds tired. Then she snaps, "You think you know, do you? Okay— my name is McIlvrae. Do you know that name? And the man in the woods? His name is St. Andrew."

"St. Andrew, like the town?" Luke asks.

"Exactly, like the town," she replies almost smugly.

Luke feels funny bubbles percolating behind his eyes. Not recognition, exactly . . . where has he seen that name, McIlvrae? He knows he has seen it or heard it somewhere, but that knowledge is just out of reach.

"There hasn't been a St. Andrew in this town for, oh, at least a hundred years," Luke says, matter-of-fact, stung at being upbraided by a girl pretending to have been born here, lying about a meaningless fact that won't do her a bit of good. "Since the Civil War. Or so I've been told."

She jabs the scalpel at him to get his attention. "Look—it's not like I'm dangerous. If you help me get away, I'm not going to hurt anyone else." She speaks to him as though he's the one being unreasonable. "Let me show you something."

Then, with no warning, she points the scalpel at herself and cuts into her chest. A long, broad line that catches her left breast and runs all the way to the rib area under her right breast. Luke is frozen in place for a moment as the line blooms red across her white skin. Blood oozes from the cut, pulpy red tissue starting to peep from the opening.

"Oh my god!" he says. What the hell is wrong with this girl—is she crazy? Does she have some kind of death wish? He snaps out of his baffled inertia and starts toward the gurney.

"Stay back!" she says, jabbing the scalpel at him again. "Just watch. Look."

She lifts her chest, arms outstretched, as though to give him a better view, but Luke can see fine, only he can't believe what he is seeing. The two sides of the cut are creeping toward each other like the tendrils of a plant, rejoining, knitting together. The cut has stopped bleeding and is starting to heal. Through it, the girl's breathing is rough but she betrays no sign of pain.

Luke can't be sure his feet are on the floor. He is watching the impossible—the impossible! What is he supposed to think? Has he gone crazy, or is he dreaming, asleep on the couch in the doctors' lounge? Whatever he's seen, his mind refuses to accept it and starts to shut down.

"What the hell—," he says, barely a whisper. Now he is breathing again, his chest heaving up and down, his face flushing. He feels like he is going to vomit.

"Don't call for the policeman. I'll explain it to you, I swear, just don't yell for help. Okay?"

As Luke sways on his feet, it strikes him that the ER has fallen silent. Is there even anyone around to hear him if he did call out? Where is Judy, where is the deputy? It's as if Sleeping Beauty's fairy godmother drifted into the ward and cast a spell, putting everyone to sleep. Outside the door to the examination room, it's dark, lights dimmed as usual for the night shift. The habitual noises—the far-off laugh track of a television program, the metallic ticking from inside the soda vending machine—have disappeared. There is no whir from a floor buffer wending its way laboriously down the empty halls. It's just Luke and his patient and the muffled sound of the wind beating against the side of the hospital, trying to get in.

"What was that? How did you do that?" Luke asks, unable to keep the horror from his voice. He slides back onto the stool to keep from dropping to the floor. "*What* are you?"

The last question seems to hit her like a punch to the sternum. She hangs her head, flossy blond curls covering her face. "That—that's the one thing I can't tell you. I don't know what I am anymore. I have no idea."

This is impossible. Things like this don't happen. There is no explanation—what, is she a mutant? Made of synthetic self-healing materials? Is she some kind of monster?

And yet she looks normal, the doctor thinks, as his heart rate picks up again and blood pounds in his ears. The linoleum tiles start to sway underfoot.

"We came back—he and I—because we missed the place. We knew everything here would be different—everyone would be gone— but we missed what we once had," the young woman says wistfully, staring past the doctor, speaking to no one in particular.

The feeling he had when he first saw her this evening—the tingle, the buzz—arcs between them, thin and electric. He wants to *know*. "Okay," he says, shakily, hands on his knees. "This is crazy—but go ahead. I'm listening."

She takes a deep breath and closes her eyes momentarily, like she is about to dive underwater. And then she begins.

TWO

I'll start at the beginning, because that is the part that makes sense to me and which I've inscribed in my memory, afraid that otherwise it will be lost in the course of my journey, in the endless unraveling of time.

My first clear, vivid memory of Jonathan St. Andrew is of a bright Sunday morning in church. He was sitting at the end of his family's box at the front of the congregation hall. He was fourteen years old at the time and already as tall as any man in the village. Nearly as tall as his father, Charles, the man who had founded our little settlement. Charles St. Andrew was once a dashing militia captain, I was told, but at the time was middle-aged, with a patrician's soft belly.

Jonathan wasn't paying attention to the service, but then again, probably few of us in attendance were. A Sunday service could be counted on to run for four hours—up to eight if the minister fancied himself an elocutionist—so who could honestly say they remained fixed on the preacher's every word? Jonathan's mother, Ruth, perhaps, who sat next to him on the plain, upright bench. She came from a line

of Boston theologians and would give Pastor Gilbert a good dressing-
down if she felt his service wasn't rigorous enough. Souls were at
stake, and no doubt she felt the souls in this isolated wilderness town,
far from civilizing influences, were at particular risk. Gilbert was no
fanatic, however, and four hours was generally his limit, so we all knew
we would be released soon to the glory of a beautiful afternoon.

Watching Jonathan was a favorite pastime of the girls in the village,
but on that particular Sunday it was Jonathan who was the one watching—he made no secret of staring at Tenebraes Poirier. His gaze hadn't
wavered from her for a good ten minutes, his sly brown eyes fixated on
Tenebraes's lovely face and her swanlike neck, but mostly on her bosom,
pressing against the tight calico of her bodice with every breath. Apparently it didn't matter to him that Tenebraes was several years his senior
and had been betrothed to Matthew Comstock since she was six.

Was it love? I wondered as I watched him from high up in the
loft, where my father and I sat with the other poor families. That Sunday it was just me and my father, the balance of my family at the
Catholic church on the other side of town, practicing the faith of my
mother, who came from an Acadian colony to the northeast. Resting
my cheek against my forearm, I watched Jonathan intently, as only a
lovesick young girl will do. At one point, Jonathan looked as though
he was ill, swallowing with difficulty and finally turning away from
Tenebraes, who seemed oblivious to the effect she was having on the
town's favorite son.

If Jonathan was in love with Tenebraes, then I might as well throw
myself from the balcony of the congregation hall in full sight of everyone in town. Because I knew with absolute clarity at age twelve that I
loved Jonathan with all my heart and that if I could not spend my life
with him, I might as well be dead. I sat next to my father through the
end of the service, my heart hammering in my throat, tears welling
behind my eyes even though I told myself I was a ninny to get carried
away over something that was probably meaningless.

When the service ended, my father, Kieran, took my hand and led me down the stairs to join our neighbors on the common green. This was the reward for sitting through the service: the opportunity to talk to your neighbors, to have some relief after six days of hard, tedious work. For some, it was the only contact they'd had outside their family in a week, the only chance to hear the latest news and any bits of gossip. I stood behind my father as he spoke to a couple of our neighbors, peeking from behind him to find Jonathan, hoping he would not be with Tenebraes. He was standing behind his parents, alone, staring stonily into the backs of their heads. He clearly wished to leave, but he might as well have wished for snow in July: socializing after services typically lasted for at least an hour, more if the weather was as pleasant as it was that day, and the stalwarts would practically have to be carried away. His father was doubly encumbered because there were plenty of men in town who saw Sundays as an opportunity to speak to the man who was their landlord or in a position to improve their fortune in some way. Poor Charles St. Andrew; I didn't realize till many years later the burden he had to endure.

Where did I find the courage to do what I did next? Maybe it was desperation and the determination not to lose Jonathan to Tenebraes that compelled me to slip away from my father. Once I was sure he hadn't noticed my absence, I made haste across the lawn, toward Jonathan, weaving between the knots of adults talking. I was a tiny thing at that age, easily hidden from my father's view by the voluminous skirts of the ladies, until I went up to Jonathan.

"Jonathan. Jonathan St. Andrew," I said but my voice came out as a squeak.

Those beautiful dark eyes looked on me and me alone for the first time and my heart did a little flip. "Yes? What do you want?"

What did I want? Now that I had his attention, I had no idea what to say.

"You're one of the McIlvraes, aren't you?" Jonathan said, suspiciously. "Nevin is your brother."

My cheeks colored as I remembered the incident. Why hadn't I thought of the incident before I came over? Last spring, Nevin had ambushed Jonathan outside the provisioner's store and bloodied his nose before adults pulled them apart. Nevin had an abiding hatred of Jonathan, for reasons unknown to all but Nevin. My father apologized to Charles St. Andrew for what was seen as nothing more than the sort of skirmish boys get into routinely, nothing sinister attached to it. What neither father knew was that Nevin would undoubtedly kill Jonathan if he ever saw the chance.

"What do you want? Is this one of Nevin's tricks?"

I blinked at him. "I—I have something I wish to ask you." But I couldn't speak in the presence of all these adults. It was only a matter of time before Jonathan's parents realized there was a girl in their midst, and they would wonder what the devil Kieran McIlvrae's oldest daughter was doing, if indeed the McIlvrae children harbored some strange intent toward their son.

I took his hand in both of mine. "Come with me." I led him through the crowd, back into the empty vestibule of the church, and, for reasons I will never know, he obeyed me. Strangely, no one noticed our exit, no one cried out to stop us from going off together by ourselves. No one broke away to chaperone us. It was as though fate conspired, too, for Jonathan and I to have our first moment together.

We went into the cloakroom with its cool slate floor and darkened recess. The sound of voices seemed a long way off, only murmurs and snippets of talk drifting in from the common. Jonathan fidgeted, confused.

"So—what is it you wish to tell me?" he asked, an edge of impatience in his tone.

I had intended to ask him about Tenebraes. I wanted to ask him about all the girls in the village and which ones he cared for and if he had been promised to one of them. But I couldn't; these questions choked in my throat and brought me to the edge of tears.

And so in desperation I leaned forward and pressed my lips against his. I could tell he was surprised by the way he drew back, slightly, before regaining his wits. And then he did something unexpected: he returned the kiss. He leaned into me, groping for my lips with his mouth, feeding his breath into me. It was a forceful kiss, hungry and clumsy and so much more than I knew to expect. Before I had the chance to be frightened, he backed me against the wall, his mouth still over mine, and pressed into me until I bumped against the spot hidden beneath the front of his breeches and below the folds of his jacket. A moan escaped him, the first time I heard a moan of pleasure come from another person. Without a word, he took my hand and brought it to the front of his breeches and I felt a shudder run through him as he uttered another moan.

I drew my hand back. It tingled. I could still feel his hardness in my palm.

He was panting, trying to get himself under control, confused that I'd pulled away from him. "Isn't that what you wanted?" he asked, studying my face, more than a little worried. "You did kiss me."

"I did . . ." Words tumbled out of me. "I meant to ask . . . Tenebraes . . ."

"Tenebraes?" He stood back, smoothing the front of his waistcoat. "What of Tenebraes? What difference—" He trailed off, perhaps realizing he had been watched in church. He shook his head as though brushing aside the very notion of Tenebraes Poirier. "And what is your name? Which McIlvrae sister are you?"

I couldn't blame him for being uncertain: there were three of us. "Lanore," I answered.

"Not a very pretty name, is it?" he said, not realizing that every little word can bruise a young girl's heart. "I will call you Lanny, if you don't mind. Now, Lanny, you know you are a very wicked girl." There was a playfulness in his voice to let me know he wasn't seriously angry with me. "Didn't anyone ever tell you that you should not tease a boy so, especially boys you do not know?"

"But I know you. Everyone knows you," I said, somewhat alarmed that he would think me frivolous. He was the eldest son of the wealthiest man in town, the owner of the logging business around which the entire settlement revolved—of course everyone knew who he was. "And—and I believe that I love you. I mean to be your wife one day."

Jonathan lifted a cynical eyebrow. "To know my name is one thing, but how can you possibly know you love me? How can you set your heart on me? You don't know me at all, Lanny, and yet you've declared yourself mine." He smoothed his jacket one more time. "We should go back outside before someone comes looking for us. It would be best if we were not seen together, don't you agree? You should go first."

I stood there for a second, shocked. I was confused, still possessed of phantom traces of his desire, his kiss and the memory of his hardness in my hand. In any case, he'd misunderstood me: I hadn't given myself to him. I had declared that he was mine. "All right," I said, and the disappointment must have been evident in my voice because Jonathan gave me his handsomest smile.

"Don't worry, Lanny. There is next Sunday—we will see each other after service, I promise. Perhaps I can persuade you to give me another kiss."

Shall I tell you about Jonathan, my Jonathan, and then you will understand how I could be so sure of my devotion? He was the firstborn of Charles and Ruth St. Andrew and they were so thrilled to have a son that they named him on the spot, had him christened within the month, recklessly exulting in him in an age when most parents would not even name a child until it had lived for some time and proved it had a chance of survival. His father threw a great party while Ruth was still recuperating in her bed; had everyone from the town come in for rum punch and sugared tea, plum cake and molasses cookies; hired an Acadian fiddler, had laughter and music so close after the boy's birth, it seemed the father was daring the devil—just try to come and take my boy! Just try and see what you will get!

It was apparent, from the earliest days, that Jonathan was uncommon: he was exceptionally clever, exceptionally strong, exceptionally healthy, and above all, exceptionally beautiful. Women would sit rapt beside the cradle, beg for turns to hold him and pretend that the well-formed bundle of flesh and swirling tendrils of black gossamer was their own. Even men, down to the hardiest axman working for St. Andrew in the logging operation, would get uncharacteristically misty when brought in proximity to the babe.

By the time Jonathan reached his twelfth birthday, there was no denying that there was something preternatural about him, and it seemed just as obvious to attribute this to his beauty. He was a wonder. He was perfection. That could not be said of many at the time; it was an age in which people were disfigured by any number of causes— smallpox or accident, burned at the hearth, spindly from malnutrition, toothless by thirty, lumpy from a broken bone set improperly, scarified, palsied, scabbed from lack of hygiene, and, in our stretch of the woods, missing parts from frostbite. But there wasn't a disfiguring mark on Jonathan. He'd grown tall, straight, and broad shouldered, as majestic as the trees on his property. His skin was as flawless as poured cream. He had straight black hair as glossy as a raven's wing and his eyes were dark and bottomless, like the deepest recess of the Allagash. He was simply beautiful to look upon.

Is it a blessing or a curse to have a boy like Jonathan living in your midst? Pity us girls, I say; consider the effect a boy like Jonathan can have on the girls in a small village, in a town so limited there are few other distractions and it is impossible to avoid all contact with him. He was a constant, inescapable temptation. There was always the chance you might see him, coming out of the provisioner's shop or as he rode across a field seemingly on some errand but really sent by the devil to weaken our reserve. He didn't even have to be present to dominate our thoughts: as you sat with your sisters or friends to take up needlework, one of them would whisper about a recent glimpse of Jonathan, and then, he would be all we could talk about. Perhaps we had a part in our own bedevilment, for the girls could not stop obsessing about him, whether on the occasion of a casual meeting (did he speak to you, the girls would want to know; what did he say?), or a mere sighting in town, when even a detail as trifling as the color of his waistcoat was discussed. But what we were really thinking, all of us, was: how he could look you over with an impertinent eye or the way the very corner of his mouth turned up in speculation, and how any of us would die to be in his arms, just once. And it was not just the young girls who felt this way about him; especially as he reached his teenage years, fifteen, sixteen, he already made the other men in the village seem spent, coarse, overfed, or scrawny, and the good wives started to consider Jonathan differently. You could tell by the way they'd stare at him, their feverish looks, flushed cheeks, bitten lips, and the eternal hope in a quick drawing in of breath.

There was the aspect about him of slight danger, too, of wanting to touch him the way a mad voice in your head tells you to touch a hot iron. You know you cannot help but be hurt, but you cannot resist. You must just experience it for yourself. You ignore what you know will come next, the unbearable pain of seared flesh, the sharp bite of the burn all over again every time the wound is touched. The scar you will carry for the rest of your life. The scar that will mark your heart. Inured to love, you will never be quite so foolish in the same way again.

In that respect, I was envied and ridiculed at the same time: envied for all the time I spent in Jonathan's presence, ridiculed because I had made it plain that there was no romance of any sort between us. This only confirmed in the eyes of the other girls that I lacked the necessary feminine wiles to pique a man's interest. But I was no different from them. I knew Jonathan had the ability to burn me up with the brilliance of his attention, like a flame to paper. A girl could be destroyed in an instant of divine love. The question was, was it worth it?

You might ask if I loved Jonathan for his beauty, and I would answer: that is a pointless question, for his great, uncommon beauty was an irreducible part of the whole. It gave him his quiet confidence—which some might have called aloof arrogance—and his easy, disarming way with the fairer sex. And if his beauty drew my eye from the first, I'll not apologize for it, nor will I apologize for my desire to claim Jonathan for my own. To behold such beauty is to wish to possess it; it's desire that drives every collector. And I was hardly alone. Nearly every person who came to know Jonathan tried to possess him. This was his curse, and the curse of every person who loved him. But it was like being in love with the sun: brilliant and intoxicating to be near, but impossible to keep to oneself. It was hopeless to love him and yet it was hopeless not to.

And so I was afflicted by Jonathan's curse, caught up in his terrible attraction, and both of us were doomed to suffer for it.

THREE

A friendship progressed between us—Jonathan and I—in this way through childhood. We met after services on Sundays and at social events such as weddings and even funerals, whispering together on the fringe of the mourners, or giving up on propriety altogether and wandering off to the woods so we could concentrate all our attention on each other. Heads shook in disapproval, and without a doubt, some tongues gave in to gossip, but our families did nothing to stop our friendship—at least, I was not made aware of it if they had.

It was during this time that I realized that Jonathan was lonelier than I imagined. The other boys sought his company far less than I'd assumed and, for Jonathan's part, when a group approached us at a social, he often skirted them. I recall one time, at a spring church gathering, that Jonathan steered me to another path when he saw a group of boys his age heading in our direction. I had no idea what to make of it and, after a few minutes of anxious contemplation, decided to ask.

"Why is it that you choose to walk this way?" I asked. "Is it because you are embarrassed to be seen with me?"

He made a derisive sound. "Don't be daft, Lanny. I am seen with you now. Anyone can see us walking together."

That was true enough, and a relief. But I could not give up my inquiry. "Then is it because you don't like them, those boys?"

"I don't *dislike* them," he said, peevishly.

"Then why—"

He cut me off. "Why are you questioning me? Take my word for it: it's different for boys, Lanny, and that's all there is to it." He began to walk faster, and I had to lift my skirts a bit to keep up with him. He hadn't explained what the mysterious "it" was that he referred to: *what* was different for boys? I wondered. Nearly everything, from what I could see. Boys were allowed to go to school, if their families could afford to pay the tutor's fee, whereas girls got no more schooling than their mothers could impart—the household arts of sewing, cleaning, and cooking, maybe a little reading from the Bible. Boys could tussle with each other for amusement, run and play tag without the encumbrance of long skirts, ride horseback. True, they drew hard chores and had to master all manner of skills—once, Jonathan told me, his father made him repair the foundation of their icehouse, stone and mortar, just so he would know a bit about masonry—but to my way of thinking, a boy's life was much freer. And here Jonathan was complaining about it.

"I wish I were a boy," I muttered, nearly out of breath from trying to keep up with him.

"No, you don't," he said over his shoulder.

"I don't see what—"

He whirled on me. "What about your brother, Nevin, then? He doesn't much like me, does he?" I stopped, dumbstruck. No, Nevin didn't like Jonathan and hadn't for as long as I could remember. I remembered the fight with Jonathan, how Nevin had come home spangled with a crust of dried blood on his face, and how Father was quietly proud of him.

"Why do you think your brother hates me?" he demanded.

"I don't know."

"I've never given him reason, but he hates me just the same," Jonathan said, straining not to betray the hurt in his voice. "It's that way with all the boys. They hate me. Some of the adults, too. I know it, I can feel it. That's why I avoid them, Lanny." His chest heaved, tired from explaining it to me. "There, now you know," he said and then hurried away, leaving me to stare after him in surprise.

I thought about what he'd said all week. I could have spoken to Nevin about his hatred of Jonathan, but to do so would restart an old argument between us; he couldn't stand that I'd befriended Jonathan, of course, and I knew the reasons well enough without having to ask. My brother thought Jonathan was proud and arrogant, that he flaunted his wealth, and that he expected, and received, special treatment. I knew Jonathan better than anyone outside his family—perhaps even within his family—so I knew all of this to be untrue, except the latter, but it was hardly Jonathan's fault if others treated him differently. And, though Nevin wouldn't admit to it, I saw in his hateful eye the wish to spoil Jonathan's beauty, to leave his mark on that handsome face and bring down the town's favorite son. In his own way, Nevin wanted to defy God, to right what he saw as an injustice God had deliberately meted out to him, that he should have to live in Jonathan's shadow in every regard.

That was why Jonathan had rushed away from me at the church gathering, because he had been forced to share his shame with me, and perhaps he thought that once I knew his secret I would abandon him. How strongly we hold on to our fears in childhood! As if there was any power on earth or in heaven that would stop me from loving Jonathan. If anything, it made me see that he, too, had his enemies and detractors, that he, too, was constantly judged, and that he needed me. I was the one friend with whom he could be free. And it was not one sided: to speak plainly, Jonathan was the only person who treated me as though I mattered. And to have the attention of the most desired, most important boy in town is no small thing to a girl nearly invisible among her peers. How could that help but make me love him even more?

And I told Jonathan as much the following Sunday, when I went up to him and slipped my arm under his as he paced about on the far side of the green. "My brother is a fool," was all I said, and we continued walking together without another word between us.

The one thing I did not take back from our conversation at the church social was that I'd rather have been born a boy. I still believed that. It had been drummed into my head, by the things my parents did and the very rules by which we lived, that girls were not as valuable as boys and that our lives were destined to be far less consequential. For instance, Nevin would inherit the farm from my father, but if he hadn't the temperament or inclination to raise cattle, he might be apprenticed to the blacksmith or sent to work as a logger for the St. Andrews—he had choices, albeit limited ones. As a woman, my options were fewer: marry and start my own household, remain at home and assist my parents, or work as a servant in someone else's home. If Nevin rejected the farm for some reason, conceivably my parents could pass it along to one of their daughters' husbands, but that, too, would depend on the husband's preferences. A good husband would take his wife's wishes into consideration, but not all of them did.

The other reason—the more important one, in my view—was that if I were a boy, it would be so much easier to be Jonathan's friend. The things we could do together if I were not a girl! We could ride horseback and go off on adventures without chaperones. We could spend lots of time in each other's company without anyone raising an eyebrow or finding it a fit topic to remark upon. Our friendship would be so banal and so ordinary that it would merit no scrutiny and would be allowed to proceed on its own.

Looking back, I understand now that this was a difficult time for me, still caught up in adolescence but stumbling toward maturity. There were things I wanted from Jonathan, but I could not yet put a name to them and had only the clumsy framework of childhood to measure them against. I was close to him but wanted to be closer in a way I didn't understand. I saw the way he looked at the older girls, and that he behaved differently with them than he did with me, and I thought I might die of jealousy. Partly, this was due to the intensity of Jonathan's attention, his great charm; when he was with you, he had a way of making you feel that you were the center of his world. His eyes, those bottomless dark eyes, would settle on your face, and it was as though he was there for you and you alone. Perhaps that was an illusion, perhaps it was merely the joy of having Jonathan to oneself. In any case, the result was the same: when Jonathan withdrew his attention, it was as though the sun slipped behind a cloud and a cold, sharp wind blew at your back. All you wanted was for Jonathan to come back, to enjoy his attention again.

And he was changing with every year. When his guard was down, I saw aspects of him that I hadn't seen (or noticed) before. He could act crudely, particularly if he thought no woman was observing him. He would display some of the rough behavior of the axmen who worked for his father, speak coarsely of women as though he was already acquainted with the full range of intimacies possible between the sexes. Later I would learn that by age sixteen he had been seduced and gone on to seduce others, a participant (comparatively early in his life) in this secret waltz of illicit lovers going on in St. Andrew, a hidden world if you did not know to look for it. But these were secrets he couldn't bring himself to share with me.

All I know is that my hunger for Jonathan grew, and it felt, at times, that it was nearly beyond my control. That there was something about his smoldering eye or half smile, or the way he knowingly caressed a young woman's silk sleeve when he thought no one was watching, that made me want him to look at and caress me in the same way. Or when I thought of the rough things I'd overheard him say, I wanted him to be rough with me, too. I understand now that I was a lonely and confused young girl who yearned for intimacy and craved physical passion (even though it was a mystery to me) and—I know this now—my ignorance would be the means of my ruin. I was in a mad rush to be loved. I cannot blame Jonathan alone. So often we bring about our own downfall.

FOUR

Smoke swirls in two down spots of light in the examination room. By now, the wrist restraints are undone and the prisoner sits with the gurney adjusted upright, like a chair, a cigarette smoldering between her fingers. Two butts, burned down to the filters, sit squashed at the bottom of a bedpan on the gurney between them. Luke leans back in his chair and coughs, his throat rough from the smoke, and his head cottony, as though he's been partaking of a narcotic all night.

A one-knuckle rap sounds at the door and Luke is on his feet quicker than a squirrel can run up a tree, because he knows that's the mandatory, perfunctory knock a hospital worker gives before stepping into an examination room. He blocks the door with his body, allowing it to open only about an inch.

Judy's cold eye, distorted by the lens of her glasses, sizes him up. "Morgue called. The body just came in. Joe wants you to call the medical examiner."

"It's late. Tell Joe there's no reason to call the medical examiner now. It can certainly wait until morning."

The nurse folds her arms. "He also wanted me to ask about his prisoner. Is she ready to go or isn't she?"

This is a test, he realizes. He's always thought of himself as an honest person, and yet he can't bring himself to let her go just yet. "No, he can't take her yet."

Judy stares so hard that it feels like it could go right through him. "Why not? There isn't a scratch on her."

A lie springs nimbly to mind. "She became agitated. I had to sedate her. I need to make sure she doesn't have an adverse reaction to the sedative." The nurse sighs audibly, as though she knows—doesn't suspect but *knows*—that he is doing something disgusting to the body of the unconscious girl. "Just leave me alone, Judy. Tell Joe I'll call him when she's stabilized." He pushes the door shut in her face.

Lanny pushes ash around the bedpan with her burning cigarette, deliberately not making eye contact with him. "Jonathan's here. Now you don't have to take my word for it," she says, tapping ash into the bedpan and motioning to the door with her head. "Go down to the morgue. Take a look for yourself."

Luke shifts uncomfortably on the stool. "So there's a dead man in the morgue—all that proves is that you really *did* kill a man tonight."

"No, there's something else. Let me show you," she says, pushing aside the cap sleeve of the hospital gown to reveal a small line drawing on the white underside of her upper arm. He leans in to look more closely and sees that it's a crude tattoo done in black ink, the outline of a heraldic shield with a reptilian figure inside. "You'll see on Jonathan's arm, in this spot—"

"The same tattoo?"

"No," she says, giving the tattoo a swipe with her thumb. "But it's the same size and it was done by the same person, so it will look similar, like it was done with pins dipped in ink, because it was. His looks like two comets circling each other, with the tails extended."

"What does it mean? The comets?" Luke asks.

"Damned if I know," she replies, rearranging the gown and bedding. "Just go look at Jonathan, and then tell me if you don't believe me."

After he ties her up again—inefficiently, with rarely used straps kept on hand for unruly patients—Luke Findley rises from the stool. He slips through the swinging doors, checking first to make sure no one sees him leave. The hospital is still dark and quiet, with only faint movement in the distant pools of light illuminating the nurses' station down the hall. His shoes squeak against the clean linoleum floor as he hurries down the staircase, heading north through a basement corridor that leads to the morgue.

The whole way his nerves jangle. If someone stops him and asks what he's doing out of the ER, why he's going to the morgue, he'll just tell them . . . His mind goes blank. Luke has never been a good liar. He sees himself as a fundamentally honest person, for whatever good that has done him. Despite his honesty and his fear of getting caught, though, he has agreed to the prisoner's outlandish suggestion because he is curious as to whether this dead person is the most beautiful man ever put on the planet and what the most beautiful man would look like.

He pushes open the heavy swinging door to the morgue. Luke hears music—the evening morgue attendant, a young man named Marcus, likes to have the radio playing at all times—but sees no one. His desk shows signs of occupation (the lamp glows brightly, papers are strewn about, a gum wrapper, an uncapped pen), but no Marcus.

The morgue is small, in keeping with the town's modest needs. There is a refrigerated examination room farther back, but the bodies are stored in four cold vaults in the wall just past the entryway. Luke takes a deep breath and reaches for one of the latches, big and heavy like the latches on old-fashioned frozen food trucks.

In the first vault he finds the body of an elderly woman, unknown to him, which means she probably came from one of the towns farther out in the county. The woman's short, thick body and white hair make him think of his mother, and for a moment he's brought back to the last lucid conversation they had. He'd sat at her bedside in the intensive care unit while her unfocused eyes searched in his direction and her hand sought his out for comfort. "I'm sorry you had to come home to take care of us," she'd said to him, his mother who never apologized because she never allowed herself to do anything that needed excusing. "Maybe we stayed on the farm a little too long. But your father, he wouldn't give it up . . ." She stopped herself, unable to be disloyal to the old man so stubborn that he had hobbled out to the barn to milk the cows the morning of the day he died. "I'm sorry for what it did to your family . . ." Luke recalls trying to explain that his marriage was already coming apart long before he moved his family back to St. Andrew but his mother wouldn't hear any of it. "You never wanted to stay in St. Andrew, from when you were little. You can't be happy here now. Once I'm gone, don't let yourself get stuck here. You go and find a new life." She started crying and kept trying to squeeze his hand, slipping into unconsciousness a few hours later.

It takes Luke a minute to realize the vault is still open and that he's been standing there so long a chill has settled in his chest. It's as if he can hear his mother's voice in his head. He shivers and slides the tray back into the locker, then stands another minute until he remembers why he came to the morgue in the first place.

He finds a black body bag in the second vault and, with a grunt of exertion, pulls the tray out. The zipper slides down with a satisfying tearing sound, like the unpeeling of Velcro.

Luke opens the bag and stares. He's seen many dead people over the years, and death does nothing to enhance appearance. Depending on how they died, the deceased may be bloated. There may be bruising or discoloration or they may be pale and bluing. There is always the unmistakable lack of animation to the features. This man's face is nearly white and spotted with flecks of dark, wet leaves. His black hair is plastered to his forehead, his eyes closed. It doesn't matter. Luke could stare at him all night. He is exquisite, even in death. He is breathtakingly, achingly beautiful.

Luke is about to push the tray back into the wall when he remembers the tattoo. He looks over his shoulder first in case Marcus might have returned, and then hurries, unzipping the bag farther and rearranging the clothing, to get to the dead man's upper arm. And there it is, as Lanny had said it would be, two interlocked spheres with tails trailing off in opposite directions, and the dots look similar, in size, in the hand-done quality, down to the slight wobble of the line.

Retracing his steps through the empty halls to the emergency ward, Luke struggles with the jumble of thoughts, mostly questions. They are like matter and antimatter, canceling each other out, two truths that cannot both exist. He knows what he saw in the emergency room when the girl cut herself: it cannot have happened, and yet it did. He had touched that very spot on her torso, before and after the slash, so he knows there was no trick. But what he saw couldn't have happened, not as he saw it.

Unless she is telling the truth. And now there is a handsome man in the morgue, and the tattoos . . . It all leaves him with the feeling that he needs to listen, to go along for a change. But he's stubborn because he's a man of science; he is not about to chuck everything he knows to be fact. He is, however, curious to learn more.

The doctor bursts through the door to the examination room in the darkened ER—his energy and nervousness in his chest like fireflies in a jar—to find the prisoner huddled on the gurney, caught in the downward shaft of light and the whirling motes of smoke. She could be an excommunicated angel, Luke thinks, her wings clipped.

Lanny looks at him hungrily. "So, did you see him? Wasn't he everything I said he'd be?"

Luke nods. Beauty like that is its own kind of narcotic. He rubs his face, takes a deep breath.

"So now you understand," Lanny says solemnly. "And if you believe me, Luke, help me. Untie me," she says, arching her back and holding out the restraints, her sweet child's face turned up to him. "I need you to help me escape."

FIVE

Perhaps Jonathan and I would both have been better off if I had been born male. I'd rather have let our friendship continue and always have Jonathan in that way. We'd have spent our entire lives within the confines of that tiny village; I'd never have gotten into the trouble I did, never have suffered this terrible ordeal put upon both of us. Our lives would have been so small, but full and rewarding and complete, and I would have been happy with that.

But I was a girl, and for all my wishing there was no changing that. Ahead of me loomed the mysterious transition from girl to woman, as unfathomable to me as a magic trick. Whose example was I to follow? My mother, Theresa, wouldn't be able to give me the kind of guidance I craved—she was too demure and quiet for my tastes; I did not want to be like her. I wanted more. I wanted to marry Jonathan, for instance, and it didn't seem as though my mother would be able to teach me to be the type of woman who could make Jonathan her own.

There were secrets, it seemed, that not every woman was allowed to know. Luckily, there was a woman in town who did, a woman about whom things were said, whose name prompted a smile from the men (if their wives were not nearby). She was a woman unlike any other in the village and I had to figure a way to get her to share her secrets with me.

On a well-worn path, hidden in the shadow of the blacksmith's forge, was a small cottage. If it was noticed at all, you might think it an out-building or a toolshed for the smithy, a place to store pig iron. It was far too ramshackle and tiny to be a house, yet it didn't appear to be abandoned and the path to the front door grew more worn with time. Certainly no more than one person could live there, and customary law against solitary living still prevailed at the dawn of the nineteenth century in our bleak Puritan outpost (for Puritans we were, make no mistake about that; the fathers of the town had grown up in the Mas-sachusetts territories and were accustomed to blending religion with governance). However, in this northernmost reach of what would be-come the state of Maine, the sole reason for the edict against solitary living was that of necessity: it was unthinkable that one person alone could perform the multitude of tasks it took to get by in this harsh environment. By contrast, in a more strictly Puritan town, no one was allowed to live alone because, in solitude, one might stray. One might do ungodly things. The edict against solitary living allowed for the po-licing of one's neighbors, but the citizens of St. Andrew valued their independence and guarded their privacy a shade more fiercely.

Someone did in fact live alone in that tiny house, a woman on the outer limit of her child-bearing years, beautiful still, though faded. She rarely went out, but whenever she did venture onto the street in daylight, the townspeople gave her a wide berth. The men would con-trive not to let their eyes meet hers, and the women would pull their long skirts aside. Some would glare outright at her.

But at night, it was a different story. Under the cover of darkness she had regular visitors. Men—one at a time, more rarely a pair— would scurry up the path and knock politely on the aged door. If no

one answered the knock, the visitor knew to take a seat on the step
and wait, his back to the door, pretending not to hear whatever sounds
came from within. Eventually, the sounds from the cottage would
fade into murmurs of conversation, then silence, and within a minute
the front door would open for the waiting visitor.

Those who knew of her existence called her Magdalena. It was the
name she'd given herself when she arrived in town seven years earlier.
No one questioned the odd appellation at the time. She arrived with
a small group of travelers from the French Canadian territory, and
when they moved on, she stayed. She said she was a widow and had
decided to relocate to more southerly climates, that is, if the townspeople of St. Andrew would let her stay.

The blacksmith offered to convert his old shed into a tidy little
abode and the good women of the village helped her to settle in,
bringing her whatever precious scraps they could spare: a wobbly
stool, an extra bit of tea, an old blanket. Husbands were sent over with
firewood and kindling. When asked what she would do to support
herself—needlework, spinning, weaving, perhaps? Was she a midwife,
skilled with healing and nursing?—she merely smiled demurely and
dropped her head as if to say, "Me? What skills could I have? My
husband treated me like a porcelain doll. How should a poor unskilled
widow make her way in the world?" The good wives walked away puz-
zled, clucking their tongues and shaking their heads, not knowing
what to say except that God would provide for all his children, including this innocent woman who seemed to think boundless charity was
to be found in this rugged, lonely town.

As it turned out, she did not have to depend on charity. Mysteriously, sustenance appeared at her doorstep, unbidden. A crock of
sweet butter, a bushel of potatoes, a jug of milk. Firewood piled outside the back door. And money—she was one of the few people in
town who had actual coin, would count it out at the provisioner's
when she ordered her supplies. And what curious supplies: bottles of
gin, tobacco. Neighbors noticed a lantern burning late, through the

one window of her tiny cottage—did she stay up all night smoking tobacco and drinking gin?

In the end, it was the axmen who gave her away, the lumberjacks who worked for Charles St. Andrew a year at a time and lived far from their wives. Men like this are capable of sniffing out women like Magdalena from across a town, across a valley if the wind is right and they are desperate enough. First one, then another, then each of them in turn found their way to Magdalena's doorstep once the sun went down. Not that the axmen were her only customers: they paid in coin, after all, not in eggs and cured ham. But through the axmen her reputation was spilled across town, like tainted water emptied from a rain barrel, and the ire was raised of many a good wife. Still Magdalena said nothing. Not while the sun was up. Not even when she was insulted to her face by an indignant spouse.

The wives, enjoined by the pastor, organized a movement to have her ejected from town. Her presence was the first sign of sinful city living to sprout up in St. Andrew, the sort of thing the settlers were trying to escape. Pastor Gilbert went to Charles St. Andrew, as he was the employer of the axmen, those customers who could be openly complained about.

Sympathetic as he was to the pastor's request, Charles pointed out that there was another side to Magdalena's services that the towns-folk were overlooking. The axmen were acting on completely natural urges—to which the pastor grudgingly agreed—separated by many miles from their legal spouses. Without Magdalena's services, what might the axmen get up to? Her presence actually made the town safer for its wives and daughters.

So an uneasy truce was struck between the whore and the virtuous womenfolk and had held for seven long years. In times of trouble and illness, she contributed her part, whether they liked it or not: she would tend to the sick and dying, feed the destitute traveler, slip coins in the church donation box when no one was around to see her enter. I couldn't help but think she must long for a small measure of female companionship, though she respectfully kept to herself and sought no discourse with the townswomen.

Magdalena's actual circumstances were a mystery to many children. We saw that our mothers avoided this puzzling figure. Most of the younger children believed her to be a witch or a supernatural creature of some kind. I remembered their taunting cries, the occasional handful of pebbles flung in her direction. Not by me—even at a tender age, I knew there was something compelling about her. By all rights, I should never have met her. My mother was not judgmental, but women such as she did not associate with prostitutes, nor would her daughters. And yet I did.

It happened during a long sermon one Sunday. I excused myself and slipped out to the privy. But instead of hurrying back to the balcony and to my father's side, I dawdled outside in the warmth of a beautiful early summer day. I meandered to Tinky Talbot's barn to look on the new litter of piglets, pink with black splotches, whirled with thin, coarse hair. I petted their curious snouts, listened to their gentle grunts.

Then I looked sideways down the path—it was the closest I had ever been to the mysterious singular cottage—and I saw Magdalena sitting in a chair on the narrow window box of a porch, a long, blackened pipe clenched between her teeth. She, too, was enjoying the sun, wrapped in a quilt, her hair scandalously loose around her shoulders. The parts of her not covered by the quilt were slender and delicate, the birdlike bones of her clavicle visible under papery skin. She had no powders on her face, just a trace of lampblack smudged at the corner of her eyes, a ghost of stain on her lips.

She was unlike the other women in town. You could tell as much by her very attitude: sitting by herself in the sunlight, enjoying her own company, and not apologizing for being idle. I was drawn to her immediately, though I was also frightened by her. There was something wicked about her. She didn't attend services, after all; here she was enjoying her Sunday, whereas everyone else in town was inside the church or the congregation hall.

She lifted her hand over her eyes against the sun. "Hello, who's there?"

I made my decision in that moment. I could have run back to church, but instead I took a few timid steps toward her. "You don't know me, ma'am. My name is Lanore McIlvrae."

"McIlvrae." She weighed the name, satisfying herself that she didn't know it and, hence, didn't count my father among her customers. "No, my dear, I do not think I have had the pleasure of making your acquaintance." She smiled when I curtsied.

"My name is Magdalena—though I suspect you may know that, yes? You may call me Magda." Up close, she was very pretty. She stood to rearrange the quilt and revealed that she was still in her night stays and a filmy shift of pale linen, drawn low on her chest with a thin pink ribbon. In a practical house such as ours, my mother owned not even one item of clothing as feminine as Magda's gently shabby shift. I was struck by the combination of her beauty and this pretty item of clothing; it was the first time I'd ever been really covetous of another person.

She noticed me staring at her shift and a knowing smile came to her face. "Wait here a minute," she said and went inside the house. When she came out, she held a ribbon of pink velvet out to me. You can't imagine what a treasure it was she offered; manufactured goods were rare in our hardscrabble town, fripperies such as ribbon rarer still. It was the softest fabric I'd ever touched and I held it lightly, like a baby rabbit.

"I couldn't accept such a gift," I said, though plainly I wished it weren't so.

"Nonsense," she laughed. "It's only a bit of trim from a dress. What would I do with it?" she lied. She watched me finger the ribbon, enjoying my pleasure. "Keep it. I insist."

"But my parents will ask where I got it—"

"You can tell them you found it," she offered, though we both knew I couldn't do that. It was an unlikely story. And yet I could not make myself give the ribbon back to Magda. She was pleased when my fist curled around her gift, and she smiled—but not in triumph, more in solidarity.

"You are most generous, Mistress Magda," I said, curtsying again. "I must return to the service or my father will worry that something has happened to me."

She tilted her chin up so she could look down her fine nose in the direction of the congregation hall. "Ah, so you are right. You mustn't worry your parents. I do hope you will visit me again, Miss McIlvrae."

"I will. I promise."

"Good. Then run along." I trotted down the path, lifting my skirts to avoid the muddy parts. Before I turned the corner, I looked back over my shoulder to the cottage to see that Magda had settled back in her chair and rocked contentedly, staring off into the woods.

I could hardly wait for next Sunday to steal out during service and visit Magda again. I'd hidden the ribbon in the pocket of my second set of petticoats where I could slip my hand in from time to time and give the velvet a surreptitious stroke. The ribbon reminded me of Magda herself; she was so unlike my mother and the other women in the village and that alone seemed reason to admire her.

One thing about her I thought worth admiring, but did not really understand, was that she did not have a man. No woman in the village lived without a man and the man was always the head of the household. Magda was the only woman in the village who spoke for herself, though from what I could tell, she did very little on that front. I doubted she went to town meetings. And yet she continued to live on her own terms and seemed to be successful at it, and for a young girl that was a very admirable thing indeed.

So the next Sunday I contrived to be excused from service again (though with stern looks from my father) and ran to Magda's cottage. And there was Magda, standing on her porch this time. Her casual air was gone. She was dressed in a pretty striped skirt and wore a fitted woolen jacket in purple heather, an unusual color. The entire effect seemed calculated to delight, as though it was her intent to impress me. I was flattered.

"Good day, Mistress Magda," I said as I ran up to her, slightly out of breath.

"Well, good Sabbath to you, Miss McIlvrae." Her green eyes sparkled. We chatted; she asked about my family, I pointed in the direction of our farm. Just as I was thinking I should return to service, she said shyly, "I would ask you in to see my home—but I suppose that your parents would not approve. Seeing as who I am. It wouldn't be proper."

She must have known I'd be curious to see the inside of her cottage. Her own place, the seat of her independence! I felt a tug to return to church, to my waiting father . . . but how could I turn this down? "I have but a minute . . . ," I said as I followed her up the steps and through the door.

It seemed to me like the inside of a jewel box, but in actuality, it was probably quite tumbledown and makeshift. The tiny room was dominated by a narrow bed covered with a beautifully embroidered quilt of yellow and red. Glass bottles lined the sill of the one window, sending slivers of green and brown light to the floor. A few pieces of jewelry rested in a ceramic bowl painted with tiny pink roses. Her clothing hung on pegs by the back door, an assortment of full skirts in a variety of colors, trailing sashes, the frill of petticoats. Not one but two pairs of delicate women's boots were lined up by the door. My only disappointment was that the room was stuffy, the air heavy with a musky scent I didn't yet recognize.

"I would love to live in a place such as this," I said, making her laugh.

"I've lived in nicer places, but this will do," she said as she sank into a chair.

Before I left, Magda gave me two pieces of advice, woman to woman. The first was that a woman should always put by some money of her own. "Money is very important," she said to me, showing me where she kept a pouch full of coin. "Money is the only way for a woman to have any true power over her own life." The second was that a woman should never betray another woman over a man. "It happens time and again," she said, sounding sad. "And it is understandable, seeing that men are given all the worth in the world. We are made to believe that a woman's only worth is that of the man in her life, but that's not true. In any case, we women must stand by each other, for to depend on a man is folly. He will disappoint you every time." She ducked her head but I swear I saw tears in her eyes.

I was rising from the floor to leave when there was a knock at the door. A burly man stepped in before Magda could answer; I recognized him as one of St. Andrew's axmen.

"Hullo, Magda, I figured you'd be alone and wanting company, as everyone else is in church this morning . . . Who's this?" He stopped short when he saw me and an unpleasant smile spread over his wind-burned face. "You have a new girl, Magda? An apprentice?" He put his hand on my arm as though I were not a person but a possession.

Magda stepped between us and deftly ushered me toward the back door. "She's a friend, Lars Holmstrom, and none of your business. You can keep your clumsy hands off her. Get along, now," she said to me as she pushed me out the door. "Perhaps I will see you again next week." And before I knew it I was standing in a pile of dead leaves, fallen branches crackling under my feet, the plank door shut tight in my face as Magda went about her business, the price of her independence. I crashed through the underbrush and onto the path, running back to the congregation hall as parishioners were spilling out into the sunlight. There would be hell to pay with Father this time, but I calculated it was worth it; Magda was the custodian of the mysteries of life and I sensed that whatever it took to continue learning at her knee was worth it.

SIX

One summer afternoon in my fifteenth year, the entire town gathered in the McDougals' pasture to hear a traveling preacher speak. I can still see my neighbors making their way to the golden field, tall grass glinting in the sun, plumes of dust rising from the winding trail. By foot, horseback, and wagon nearly everyone in St. Andrew made their way to the McDougals' that day, though not from any excess feelings of piety, I assure you. Even itinerant preachers were a rarity in our neck of the woods; we would take what entertainment we could get to fill the dreariness of a long summer day in that desolate place.

This particular preacher had come from out of nowhere, apparently, and in a few short years had built a following, as well as a reputation for fiery speech and rebellious talk. There were rumors he'd divided churchgoers in the nearest town—Fort Kent, a day's ride to the north—setting traditional Congregationalists against a new wave of reformists. There was also talk of Maine becoming a state and freeing itself from Massachusetts's proprietorship, so there was a frisson in the air—religious and political—pointing to possible revolt against the religion the settlers had brought with them from Massachusetts.

It was my mother who'd convinced my father to come, though she would brook no notion of converting from Catholicism: she'd only wanted an afternoon out of the kitchen. She spread a blanket on the ground and waited for the preaching to commence. My father took the spot next to her, hanging his head with a suspicious air, glancing about to see who else might be there. My sisters remained close to my mother, tucking their skirts primly under their legs, while Nevin had taken off almost as soon as the wagon came to a halt, eager to find the boys who lived on the farms neighboring ours.

I stood, shielding my eyes against the strong sunlight with one hand, surveying the crowd. Everyone in town was there, some with blankets, like my mother, some with dinner packed in baskets. I was looking for Jonathan, as usual, but he didn't seem to be there. His absence was no surprise; his mother was probably the most hardened Congregationalist in town, and Ruth Bennet St. Andrew's family would have no part of this reformist nonsense.

But then I spied a shimmer of black hide between the trees—yes, Jonathan, skirting the edge of the field on his distinctive stallion. I wasn't the only one to see him; a palpable ripple went through parts of the crowd. What must it be like to know dozens of people are watching you raptly, eyes following the line of your long leg against the horse's flank, your strong hands holding the reins. So much suppressed lust smoldering in the bosom of many a female in that dry field that day, it's a wonder the grass didn't catch on fire.

He rode up to me, and kicking free of the stirrups, vaulted from the saddle. He smelled of leather and sun-baked earth and I longed to touch him. "What's going on?" he asked, taking off his hat and running that sleeve along his brow.

"You don't know? A visiting preacher's come to town. You haven't come to listen?"

Jonathan looked over my head, assessing the crowd. "No. I've been out surveying the next plot we're to harvest. Old Charles doesn't trust the new surveyor. Thinks he drinks too much." He squinted, all the better to see which girls were looking his way. "Is my family here?"

"No, and I doubt your mother would approve of your being here, either. The preacher has a terrible reputation. You could go to hell just for listening to him."

Jonathan grinned at me. "Is that why you're here? You have a desire to go to hell? You know there are much more pleasant paths to damnation than listening to devious preachers."

There was a message in the glimmer in his deep brown eyes, but one I couldn't interpret. Before I could ask him to explain, he laughed and said, "Every soul in town looks to be here. More's the pity that I won't be staying, but as you say, there'll be hell to pay if my mother finds out." He steadied the stirrup and swung back into the saddle but then leaned over me, protectively. "What about you, Lanny? You've never been one for preaching. Why are you here? Are you hoping to find someone here, a particular boy? Has some young man caught your fancy?"

That was a complete surprise—the coy tone, the probing look. He'd never given the slightest indication that he cared if I was interested in another. "No," I said, breathless, barely able to stammer out a response.

He took up the reins slowly, seemingly weighing them as he might weigh his words. "I know the day will come when I'll see you with another boy, my Lanny with another boy, and I won't like it. But it's only fair." Before I could recover from shock and tell him it was within his power to prevent that—surely he knew!—he had turned the horse and cantered into the woods, leaving me to stare after him in confusion yet again. He was an enigma. For the most part he treated me as a favorite friend, his attitude toward me platonic, but then there were times I thought I saw an invitation in the way he looked at me or a wisp of—dare I hope?—desire in his restlessness. Now that he'd ridden away, I couldn't dwell on it or I'd go crazy.

I leaned against a tree and watched the preacher make his way to the center of a small clearing in front of the crowd. He was younger than I expected—Gilbert was the only pastor I'd ever known and had arrived in St. Andrew already white-haired and crotchety—and walked ramrod straight, assured that both God and righteousness were on his side. He was good looking in a way that was unexpected and even uncomfortable to see in a preacher, and the women sitting closest to him twittered like birds when he gave them a broad, white smile. And yet, watching as he gazed over the crowd, preparing to begin (as confident as though he *owned* them), I experienced a dark chill, as though something bad was in the offing.

He began speaking in a loud, clear voice, recalling his visits throughout the Maine territory and describing what he'd found there. The territory was becoming a copy of Massachusetts, with its elitist ways. A handful of wealthy men controlled the destiny of their neighbors. And what had this brought for the average man? Hard times. Common folk falling behind on their accounts. Honest men, fathers and husbands, jailed and land sold out from under the wives and children. I was surprised to see heads nod in the crowd.

What people wanted—what Americans wanted, he stressed, waving his Bible in the air—was freedom. We hadn't fought the British only to have new masters take the king's place. The landowners in Boston and the merchants who sold goods to the settlers were no more than robbers, demanding outrageous usury fees, and the law was their lapdog. His eyes glimmered as he surveyed the crowd, encouraged by their murmuring assent, and he paced within his circle of well-trod grass. I wasn't used to hearing dissent spoken aloud, in public, and I felt vaguely alarmed by the preacher's success.

Suddenly, Nevin was beside me, studying our neighbors' upturned faces. "Look at 'em, slack-jawed mopes . . . ," he said, derisively. There was no doubting that he'd gotten his critical temperament from our father. He folded his arms across his chest and snorted.

"They seem interested enough in what he has to say," I observed.

"Do you have the slightest idea what he's talking about?" Nevin squinted at me. "You don't know, do you? Of course not, you're just a stupid girl. You don't understand nothing."

I frowned but didn't reply because Nevin was right in one respect: I had no idea what the man was really talking about. I was ignorant of what went on in the world at large.

He pointed to a group of men standing to the side of the crowded field. "See them men?" he asked, indicating Tobey Ostergaard, Daniel Daughtery, and Olaf Olmstrom. The three were among the poorer men in town, although the less charitable might say they were among the more shiftless, too.

"They're talking trouble," Nevin said. "Do you know what a 'white Indian' is?"

Even the stupidest girl in the village would have attested to knowing the term: news had come up months ago of an uprising in Fairfax, when townsmen dressed as Indians had overpowered the town clerk when he tried to serve a writ to a farmer delinquent in his payments.

"The same business is afoot here," Nevin said, nodding. "I heard Olmstrom and Daughtery and some others talk to Father about it. Complaining about the Watfords unfairly charging too much . . ." The details would have been beyond Nevin's comprehension; no one explained to children about accounts and charges at the provisioner's store. "Daughtery says it's a conspiracy against the common man," Nevin recited, sounding as though he wasn't sure Daughtery might not speak the truth.

"So? What do I care if Daughtery won't pay his debt to the Watfords?" I sniffed, pretending I didn't care. Inside, however, I was shocked to think someone would willingly default on an obligation, having been taught by our father that such behavior was disgraceful and something only a person with no self-respect would consider.

"It could mean ill for your boy Jonathan," Nevin sneered, delighted to have the opportunity to tease me about Jonathan. "It's not just the Watfords who stand to be hurt if things go bad. The captain holds the paper to their property . . . What would happen if they refused to pay their rents? Them men fought for three days in Fairfax. I heard they stripped the constable and beat him with sticks, and made him return home on foot, naked as he was born."

"We don't even have a town clerk in St. Andrew," I said, alarmed by my brother's story.

"Most likely the captain would send his biggest, strongest axmen to Daughtery and demand he pay up." There was a touch of awe in Nevin's voice; his respect for authority and a desire to see justice prevail—our father's traits, surely—outweighed his desire to see Jonathan suffer some ill fortune.

Daughtery and Olmstrom . . . the captain and Jonathan . . . even prim Miss Watford and her equally supercilious brother . . . I was humbled by my ignorance, and felt a grudging respect for my brother's ability to see the world in its complexity. I wondered what else went on that I didn't know about.

"Do you think Father will join them? Will he be arrested?" I whispered, worried.

"The captain don't hold paper on our place," Nevin informed me, a tad disgusted that I didn't know this already. "Father owns it outright. But I think he agrees with this fellow here." He nodded at the preacher. "Father came to the territory same as everybody else, thinking they would be free, but it hasn't worked out that way. Some are having a hard time of it, while the St. Andrews are getting rich. Like I said."—he kicked at the dirt, raising a cloud of dry dust—"your boy could be in for trouble."

"He's not my boy," I shot back.

"You want him to be your boy," my brother said, teasingly. "Though God in heaven only knows why. You must have a backward streak in you, Lanore, to be taken with the nelly bastard."

"You're just jealous, that's why you don't like him."

"Jealous?" Nevin sputtered. "Of that peacock?" He scoffed and walked away, not wanting to admit I was right.

*   *   *

About thirty townsfolk followed the preacher to the Dales' place on the other side of the ridge where he would continue speaking to all who were interested. They had a good-size house but we were still packed in tightly, eager to hear more from this captivating speaker. Mrs. Dale lit a fire in the big kitchen fireplace, for even in the summer a chill came on in the evening. Outside the sky had darkened to a deep periwinkle with a bright band of pink at the horizon.

How angry Nevin must've been with me—I begged my parents to allow me to hear the preacher, which meant I needed a chaperone, so my father told Nevin he must accompany me. My brother fumed and turned red in the face, but could refuse my father nothing, so he stomped behind me all the way to the Dales'. But Nevin, for all his traditional sensibilities, had a streak of the rebel in him and I had to think he was secretly pleased to witness the rest of the gathering.

The preacher stood by the kitchen fire and studied us all, a wild grin on his face. This close, I saw that the preacher was less like a man of the cloth than he'd seemed in the big field. He filled up the room with his presence, made the air feel tight and thin, like at the top of a mountain. He started by thanking us for staying with him. For he had saved the greatest secret to share with us now, those who had demonstrated that we were seeking the truth. And that truth was that the church—whatever faith you followed, which in the territory was mostly Congregationalist—was the biggest problem of them all, the most elitist institution, and only served to reinforce the status quo. His last statement drew a sneer of contempt and agreement from Nevin, who prided himself on going to the Catholic service with Mother and not rubbing elbows on Sundays with the town fathers and more privileged families in the meeting hall.

What we must do is throw off the precepts of the church—the preacher said with that fiery glint in his eyes again, a glint that looked less peaceable up close—and embrace new precepts that were more in keeping with the needs of the common man. First and foremost among these outdated conventions was the institution of marriage, he said.

In the close room, with thirty bodies nestled snugly, you could hear a pin drop.

Before us, the preacher stalked his small circle like a wolf. It wasn't the natural affection between men and women that he objected to, the preacher assured the group. No—it was the legal constraints of marriage, the bondage, that he railed against. It went against our human nature, he protested, gaining confidence as no one had tried to shout him down. We were meant to express our feelings with those with whom we felt a natural affinity. As God's children, we should practice "spiritual wifery," he insisted: choosing partners with whom we felt a spiritual bond.

Partners? a young woman asked, raising her hand. More than one husband? Or wife?

The preacher's eyes danced. Yes, we'd heard right—partners, for a man should have as many wives as he felt spiritually drawn to, as a woman should be allowed to have more than one husband. He himself had two wives, he said, and had found spiritual wives in every town he had visited.

A titter ran through the group and the room became charged with suppressed lust.

He tucked his thumbs under his coat lapels. He didn't expect the enlightened here in St. Andrew to take up spiritual wifery right away, on his advice alone. No, he expected we'd have to think about the idea, think about the extent to which we let the law dictate our lives. We'd know in our hearts if he spoke the truth.

Then he clapped his hands and dropped the serious expression from his face, and his entire demeanor changed as he smiled. But enough of this talk! We'd spent the entire afternoon listening to him and it was time for a little enjoyment! Let's sing some hymns, lively ones, and get to our feet, and dance! That was a revolutionary change from our regular church service—lively singing? Dancing? The concept was heretical. After a moment's hesitation, several people got to their feet and began clapping their hands, and before long, had started singing a tune that resembled more a shanty than a hymn.

I nudged my brother. "Take me home, Nevin."

"Heard enough, have you?" he said, clambering to his feet. "Me, too. I'm tired of listening to that man's nonsense. Wait while I trouble the Dales for a light; the road is sure to be dark."

I stood conspicuously by the door, wishing Nevin would hurry. Still, the preacher's words thrummed in my ears. I saw the looks of the women in the crowd when he turned his powerful gaze on them, the smiles that lit their faces. They were imagining themselves with him, or perhaps another man in town with whom they felt a spiritual bond . . . and could only wish that such desires could be acted upon. The preacher had professed the most alien concept imaginable, moral turpitude—and yet, he was a man of the Bible, a preacher. He'd spoken in some of the most august churches in the coastal area, from the gossip that had arrived in town before him. Surely that gave him some sort of authority?

I felt alit under my clothes with heat and shame, for if truth be told, I, too, would like the freedom to share my affection with any man I desired. Of course, at that moment, the only man I desired was Jonathan, but who was to say another wouldn't cross my path one day? Someone perhaps as charming and attractive as, say, the preacher himself? I could see how a woman would find him intriguing; how many spiritual wives had the itinerant preacher known? I wondered.

As I stood by the door lost in my thoughts, watching my neighbors dance a reel (was it my imagination or were some desirous glances being exchanged between men and women as they spun past each other on the dance floor?), I became aware of the preacher's sudden presence before me. With his piercing eyes and sharp features, he was beguiling and seemed aware of this advantage, and grinned so that I could see his incisors, sharp and white.

"I thank you for joining me and your neighbors this evening," he said, bowing his head. "I take it you are a spiritual seeker, looking for greater enlightenment, Miss . . . ?"

"McIlvrae," I said, edging back a half step. "Lanore."

"Reverend Judah Van der Meer." He reached for my hand and gave my fingertips a squeeze. "What did you think of my sermon, Miss McIlvrae? I trust you weren't too shocked"—here his eyes danced again, as though he was teasing me for his enjoyment—"by the frankness with which I present my beliefs?"

"Shocked?" I could barely choke out the word. "By what, sir?"

"By the idea of spiritual wifery. I'm sure a young woman like your-self can sympathize with the principle behind it, the idea of being true to one's passions—for if I'm not mistaken, you seem a woman of great, deep passion."

He picked up vehemence as he spoke, his eyes—and I do not believe I imagined this—running over my body as surely as if he'd used his own hands. "And tell me, Miss Lanore, you look a mar-riageable age. Has your family already bonded you in the slavery of betrothal? It would be a pity for a fine young woman such as yourself to spend the rest of her life in a marriage bed with a man for whom she feels no attraction. What shame to go through one's entire life without feeling true physical passion"—here his eyes glinted again, as though he were about to pounce—"which is a gift from God to his children!"

My heart was near to bursting from my chest and I was like a rab-bit drawn up in the wolf's sights. But then he laughed, placed a hand on my arm, sending a tingle straight to my head, and drew close to me, close enough for me to feel his breath on my face and for an errant lock of his hair to brush my cheek.

"Why, you look as though you are about to faint! I think you need some air . . . will you step outside with me?" He had my arm already and didn't wait for me to answer, but whisked me to the porch. The night air was much cooler than the stuffy confines of the house and I took deep breaths until my stays wouldn't let me draw in any more.

"Better?" When I nodded, he continued, "I must tell you, Miss McIlvrae, I was so happy that you joined us in this more intimate setting. I hoped that you would. I noticed you in the field this afternoon and I knew right away that I had to meet you. I felt a bond with you immediately—did you feel it, too?" Before I had a chance to answer, he took my hand in his. "I've spent most of my life traveling all over the world. I have a thirst to meet people. Every so often I meet someone extraordinary. Someone whose singularity can be seen, even across a field full of people. Someone like you."

He had the glittery-eyed look of a man with a high fever, the wild look of someone chasing a thought but unable to focus, and I started to become frightened. Why had he singled me out? Or perhaps I hadn't been singled out, perhaps this was an enticement he made to any girl impressionable enough to consider his offer of spiritual wifery. He pressed against me in a way too familiar to be polite, seeming to enjoy my distress.

"Extraordinary? Sir, you do not know me at all." I tried to push him aside, but he continued to stand stubbornly in front of me. "There is nothing extraordinary about me."

"Oh, but there is. I can feel it. You must feel it, too. You have a special sensibility, a remarkably *primal* nature. I can see it in your lovely, delicate face." His hand hovered near my cheek as though he might touch me, as though he was compelled to do so. "You are full of *want*, Lanore. You are a sensual creature. You burn to know of this physical bond between man and woman . . . It is in the forefront of your thoughts. You *hunger* for it. Perhaps there is a particular man . . . ?"

Of course there was—Jonathan—but I thought the preacher was angling to see if I fancied *him*. "This talk is not proper between us, sir." I stepped sideways and started to dart around him. "I should go inside . . ."

He put a hand on my arm again. "I didn't mean to make you uncomfortable. I apologize. I'll speak of it no more . . . but please, indulge me for one more minute. I have a question I must ask of you, Lanore. As I took the field this afternoon, and I noticed you, I saw you were speaking to a young man on horseback. An exceptionally good-looking fellow."

"Jonathan."

"Yes, that's the name I was told. Jonathan." The preacher licked his lips. "I have since been told by your neighbors that this young man might be sympathetic to my philosophies. Do you think you might arrange an audience for me with Jonathan?"

I felt prickling along the back of my neck. "Why do you wish to meet Jonathan?"

He laughed in his throat, nervously. "Well, as I said, from what I've been told he seems a natural disciple, the kind of man who can appreciate the *truth* of what I say. Could take up the cause and, perhaps, be an outpost of my church up here in the wilderness." I looked into his eyes and saw for the first time a true wickedness about him, a love of chaos and disruption. He meant to sow this wickedness in Jonathan, too, as he tried to sow it in this town. As he'd hoped to sow it in me.

"My neighbors are amusing themselves at your expense, sir, since you don't know Jonathan as I do. I doubt he would have much interest in what you have to say." Why I felt I had to protect Jonathan from this man, I don't know. But there was something ominous about his interest.

The preacher didn't like my answer. Perhaps he knew I was lying or he didn't appreciate being thwarted. He gave me a long, intimidating stare, as though thinking about what to do next to get what he wanted, and I felt for the first time in his presence true danger, a sense that this man was capable of anything. Just then, Nevin appeared in front of us with a blazing torch in hand—and for once, I was glad to see him.

"Lanore! I was looking for you. I'm ready. Let's go!" he bellowed.

"Good night," I said, breaking away from the preacher, whom I hoped to never see again. His fiery stare bored into my back as Nevin and I left.

"Satisfied with your little outing?" Nevin grunted at me as we headed down the road.

"It wasn't what I expected."

"I would say so. The man's daft, probably made so by the diseases he undoubtedly carries," Nevin said, meaning syphilis. "Still, I hear he's had followers down in Saco. Wonder what he's doing this far north?" It didn't occur to Nevin that the man might have been driven out by the authorities, that he might be on the run. That in his madness he could be given to visions and grandiose predictions, putting ideas into the heads of gullible young girls and threatening those less than willing to do as he wished.

I hugged my shawl tightly around my shoulders. "I would appreciate it if you'd not tell Father what the preacher said . . ."

Nevin laughed blackly. "I should think not. I can barely bring myself to recall his blasphemous talk, let alone repeat it to Father! Multiple wives! 'Spiritual wifery'! I don't know what Father would do—take to me with a whipping rod and lock you in the barn until you were twenty-one for even *listening* to the heathen's words." He shook his head as we walked on. "I tell you what, though—that preacher's teachings sure would suit your boy Jonathan. He's made spiritual wives out of half the girls in town already."

"Enough about Jonathan," I said, keeping the preacher's strange interest in Jonathan to myself so as not to confirm Nevin's poor opinion of him. "Let us talk no more about it."

We fell quiet for the rest of the long walk home. Despite the cool night air, I still tingled from the dark look on the preacher's face and the glimpse into his true nature. I didn't know what to make of his interest in Jonathan nor what he meant by my "special sensibility." Was my longing to experience what went on between a man and a woman so obvious? Surely that mystery was at the heart of the human experience; could it truly be unnatural, or especially evil, for a young woman to be curious about it? My parents and Pastor Gilbert would probably think so.

I walked down the lonesome road agitated inside and titillated by all of this open talk of desire. The thought of knowing Jonathan—of knowing other men in the village the way Magda knew them—left me hot and liquid inside. This evening I had awakened to my true nature, though I was too inexperienced to know it, too innocent to realize I should be alarmed by the ease with which desire could be sparked within me. I should have fought against it more staunchly, but perhaps there was no use, as one's true nature always wins out.

SEVEN

Years passed in the way they do, with each year seeming no different than its predecessor. But little differences were evident: I was less willing to follow my parents' rules and longed for a measure of independence, and I'd grown weary of my judgmental neighbors. The charismatic preacher was arrested down in Saco, tried, and imprisoned, then escaped and disappeared mysteriously. But his absence from the scene did little to quell the unrest gurgling just beneath the surface. There was an undercurrent of sedition in the air, even in a town as isolated as St. Andrew; talk of independence from Massachusetts and statehood. If landowners such as Charles St. Andrew were worried that their fortunes would be adversely affected, they made no show of it and kept their concerns to themselves.

I grew more interested in such important matters, though I still had few opportunities to exercise my curiosity. The only fit topics of interest for a young woman, it seemed, were her domestic domain: how to make a tender loaf of molasses bread or coax milk from an aging cow, how well you could sew or the best way to cure a child's fever. Tests to prove our suitability as wives, but I had little interest in competition of this sort. There was only one man I wanted for my husband and he cared little for the tenderness of a bread crumb.

One of the household tasks I cared for the least was laundry. Lightweight clothing could be taken down to the creek for rinsing and wringing. But several times a year, we'd have to do a thorough washing, which meant setting a large cauldron over a fire in the yard for a full day of boiling, scrubbing, and drying. It was a miserable job—arms plunged in boiling water and lye, wringing out voluminous wool garments, spreading them to dry on bushes or over tree limbs. Laundry day had to be chosen carefully, for it required a stretch of good weather when no other laborious household task needed doing.

I remember one such day in the early autumn of my twentieth year. Oddly, my mother had sent Maeve and Glynnis to help my father with the haying, insistent that she and I could handle the washing by ourselves. She was strangely quiet that morning, too. As we waited for the water to boil, she fussed with the washing things—the bag of lye, the dried lavender, the sticks we used to push the clothing around in the pot.

"The time has come for us to have an important conversation," my mother said at last, as we stood beside the cauldron, watching bubbles rise to the surface of the water. "It's time to think about getting you started on a life of your own, Lanore. You're not a child any longer. You are well into a marrying age . . ."

Truth be told, I was nearly past a good age for marriage and had been wondering what my parents intended to do about the situation. They'd arranged betrothals for none of their children.

". . . and so we must address what to do about Master St. Andrew." She held her breath and blinked at me.

My heart fluttered at her words. What other reason would she have to bring up Jonathan's name in the context of marriage if she and my father didn't intend to seek an arrangement for me? I was speechless from joy and surprise—the latter for knowing Father didn't approve of the St. Andrew family, not anymore. Many things had changed since the families followed Charles St. Andrew north. His relationship with the rest of the town—with the men who'd trusted him—was strained.

Mother looked at me squarely. "I tell you this as a mother who loves you, Lanore: you must cease your friendship with Master Jonathan. The two of you are children no longer. To continue in this way will do you no good."

I didn't feel the flecks of boiling water alighting on my skin or the heat from the cauldron dampening my face. I stared back at her.

She rushed to cover my horror-struck silence. "You must understand, Lanore—what other boy will want you when you are so obviously in love with Jonathan?"

"I'm not in love with Jonathan. We're only friends," I croaked.

She laughed gently, but it stabbed at my heart all the same. "You cannot deny your love for Jonathan. It's quite evident, my dear, as it is just as evident that he does not feel the same way toward you."

"There's nothing for him to show," I protested. "We are just friends, I assure you."

"His flirtations are the talk of the village . . ."

I brushed a hand over my sweaty brow. "I know of these. He tells me everything."

"Listen to me, Lanore," she implored, turning to me even as I turned away. "It is easy to fall in love with a man as handsome as Jonathan, or as wealthy, but you must resist. Jonathan is not to be your destiny."

"How can you say that?" The protest broke from my lips though I hadn't meant to say anything of the kind. "You cannot know what lies ahead for me, or Jonathan."

"Oh, silly girl, do not tell me you've set your heart on him." She took me by the shoulders and gave me a shake. "You cannot hope to wed the captain's boy. Jonathan's family would never allow it, never, nor would your father abide it. I am sorry to be the one to tell you this hard, hard truth . . ."

She didn't have to. Logically, I knew that our families were unequal and I knew that Jonathan's mother had high hopes as far as her children's marriages were concerned. But a girl's dreams are near impossible to kill and I'd harbored this one for as long as I could remember; it seemed I was born with the desire to be with Jonathan. I'd always secretly believed that a love as fierce and true as mine would be rewarded in the end, and now I was being forced to accept the bitter truth.

My mother returned to her work, picking up the long stick to stir the clothing in the boiling water. "Your father means to begin searching for a match for you, and so you see why you must end your friendship. We have to find your match before we make matches for your sisters," she continued, "so you understand the importance of this, don't you, Lanore? You do not want your sisters to end up unwed, do you?"

"No, Mother," I said, dispirited. I was still turned away from her, looking off in the distance, willing myself not to cry, when I noticed movement in the forest beyond our house. It could be anything, benign or dangerous—my father and siblings returning from the hay field, someone traveling between farms, deer picking at greenery. My eyes followed the figure until I could make it out, large and dark, a graceful shimmering blackness. Not a bear. A horse and rider. There was only one true black horse in the village and it belonged to Jonathan. Why would Jonathan be riding out this way if not to see me, but he had passed beyond our house and was headed in the direction of our neighbors, the recently wed Jeremiah and Sophia Jacobs. I could think of no reason for Jonathan to call upon Jeremiah, none at all.

I raised a hand to tuck a few loose curls under my cap. "Mother, didn't you say Jeremiah Jacobs was not at home this week? Has he gone away?"

"Yes, he has," she said absently, stirring the pot. "He has gone to Fort Kent to look at a pair of draft horses and told your father he would return next week."

"And he's left Sophia by herself, has he?" The shimmering figure had slipped beyond my vision into the darkness of the woods.

My mother murmured in agreement. "Yes, but he knows there's no reason to worry. Sophia is safe on her own for a week." She lifted the wet garment out of the pot by the stick, a steaming, dripping mass. I took it from her and carried it under the tree, where we wrung the wool out together. "Promise me you will give up on Jonathan and will seek his company no more," was the last she said on the matter. But my mind was on our neighbor's tiny saltbox, Jonathan's horse waiting restlessly outside.

"I promise," I said to my mother, lying glibly, as though it meant nothing at all.

EIGHT

s autumn deepened and the leaves turned russet and gold, the love affair between Jonathan and Sophia Jacobs did not abate. During those weeks, my encounters with Jonathan were rarer than ever and painfully brief. While it wasn't all Sophia's fault—Jonathan and I each suffered demands on our time—I blamed Sophia entirely. What right had she to get so much of his attention? As far as I could see, she didn't deserve his company. Her worst sin was that she was married, and by pursuing this relationship, she was forcing Jonathan to compromise his Christian morals. She was condemning him to hell along with herself.

But the reasons she didn't deserve him did not stop there. Sophia was hardly the prettiest girl in the village; by my count, there were at least twenty girls comparable in age who were prettier than she, even if I excluded myself from this group on the basis of modesty. Further, she had neither the social position nor the wealth that would make her a suitable companion for a man of Jonathan's status. Her housekeeping skills were lacking: her sewing was passable, but the pies she brought to church socials were pasty and unevenly cooked. Sophia was clever, without a doubt, but if one were pressed to pick the smartest woman in town, her name would not be among those to spring to mind. So what exactly was the basis for her claim over Jonathan, who should have only the best?

I spun the late summer flax contemplating this queer development, cursing him for being inconstant. After all, that day in the McDougals' field, hadn't he said he'd be jealous if I was to become attached to another boy in the village, and yet here he was secretly courting Sophia Jacobs. A less heartsick girl might have drawn conclusions from his behavior, but I wouldn't, preferring to believe that Jonathan would still choose me if he only knew my feelings. I wandered by myself after church services on Sundays, casting unanswered glances in Jonathan's direction, hoping to tell him how badly I wanted him. I walked the trails that led to the St. Andrews' house and wondered what Jonathan might be doing at that moment, and in my daydreams I tried to imagine the feel of Jonathan's hands on my body, what it would be like to be pressed beneath him, raw from his kisses. I blush to think how innocent my view of love was then! I had a virgin's conception of love as chaste and courtly.

Without Jonathan, I was lonely. It was a preview of what my life would be like once Jonathan was wed and took over his family's business and I was married to another. Each of us would be drawn increasingly into our own orbits, paths destined never to cross. But that day had not come yet—and Sophia Jacobs was *not* Jonathan's lawful wife. She was an interloper who'd staked a claim on his heart.

It was just after the first frost when Jonathan came out to see me one day. How different he looked, as though he'd aged years. Or maybe it was only that the gaiety in his demeanor had gone; he seemed serious, very adult. He found me in the hay field with my sisters, pitching the last of the hay left to dry in the summer sun into the barn, where we stored the alfalfa that would feed the cattle through the long winter.

"Let me help you," he said, springing down from his horse. My sisters—dressed as was I in old clothes and with kerchiefs tied around our heads to keep our hair back—looked askance at him and giggled.

"Don't be ridiculous," I said, taking in his fine wool coat and doeskin breeches. Haying was miserable, sweaty work. Anyway, I was still smarting from his desertion and told myself I wanted nothing from him. "Just tell me what brings you out here," I said.

"I'm afraid my words are meant for your ears only. May we at least walk a ways by ourselves . . . ?" he asked, nodding at my sisters to show that he meant no disrespect. I threw my pitchfork to the ground and pulled off the gloves and started meandering in the direction of the woods.

He fell into step beside me, leading his horse by a slack rein. "Well, we haven't seen each other in a while, have we?" he began in an unconvincing manner.

"I've no time for niceties," I told him. "I have work to do."

He abandoned his pretext altogether. "Ah, Lanny. I have never been able to fool you. I have missed your company, but that's not why I've come out here today. I need your advice; I'm no good at judging my own problems and you always seem to see a way clear, no matter what's at issue."

"You can stop trying to flatter me," I said, wiping my brow against a dirty sleeve. "I'm hardly King Solomon. There are far wiser people in this town you could turn to, so the fact that you have come to me means you are in trouble of some kind that you don't dare share with anyone else. So, out with it—what have you done now?"

"You're right. There's no one I can confide in, except you." Jonathan turned his handsome face from me, embarrassed. "It's Sophia—you've guessed that much, I'm sure, and I know hers is the last name you wish to hear—"

"You've no idea," I muttered, tucking a fold of my skirt into my waist to lift the hem from the ground.

"It's been a happy enough union between us, Lanny. I never would have guessed as much. We are so different and yet I've come to enjoy her company immensely. She has an independent mind and isn't afraid to speak it." He spoke, oblivious to the fact that I'd stopped dead in my tracks, mouth agape. Hadn't I spoken my mind to him? Well, perhaps I hadn't spoken my mind plainly to him on all matters, but hadn't we conversed as equals, friends? It was maddening that he thought Sophia's demeanor so singular and remarkable. "It's all the more extraordinary considering the family she comes from. She tells stories of her father, that he is a drunkard and a gambler, and beats his wife and his daughters."

"Tobey Ostergaard," I said. It surprised me that Jonathan had not known of Tobey's poor reputation, but it only went to show how sheltered he was from the rest of the village. Ostergaard's problems were well known. No one thought much of him as a father or a provider. A poor farmer, Tobey dug graves on the weekends to earn extra coin, which he usually wasted on drink. "Her brother ran away a year ago," I said to Jonathan. "He fought with his father, and Tobey hit him in the face with his gravedigger's shovel."

Jonathan seemed genuinely horrified. "This rough upbringing has toughened Sophia, and yet she has not become hardened and bitter, not even after her grievous marriage. She regrets very much having agreed to the match, especially now that . . ." He trailed off.

"Now—what?" I prodded, fear rising in my throat.

"She tells me she is pregnant," Jonathan blurted out, turning back to me. "She swears the baby is mine. I don't know what to do."

His expression was a sheet of terror and, yes, trepidation that he'd had to tell me this. I would have slapped him if it weren't so plain that he truly didn't wish to hurt me. Still, I wanted to throw it back in his face: he'd been carrying on with this woman for weeks, what did he expect? He'd been lucky that it hadn't happened sooner. "What are you going to do?" I asked.

"Sophia's wish is plain: she wants us to be married and to raise the babe together."

A bitter laugh burst from my lips. "She must be mad. Your family would never allow it."

He gave me a quick, angry look that made me regret my outburst. "What is it," I tried again in a more conciliatory tone, "that *you* wish to do?"

Jonathan shook his head. "I tell you, Lanny, I do not know my own mind on this matter." I wasn't sure I believed him, however. There was a hesitancy in his tone, as though he held thoughts that he didn't dare speak. He seemed much changed from the Jonathan I knew, the scoundrel who'd planned to remain unfettered as long as possible.

If he only knew how conflicted I was by his dilemma. On one hand, he seemed so miserable and helpless to see his way clear that I was moved to pity. On the other hand, my pride stung like newly flayed skin. I paced around him, a knuckle pressed to my lips. "Well, let's think this through. You know as well as I that there are remedies for this sort of predicament. She needs to make a trip to the midwife . . ." I thought of Magda: surely she would know how to deal with this calamity, an eventuality in her line of work. "A tincture of herbs or some procedure, I've heard, will take care of the problem."

Face flushed, Jonathan shook his head again. "She won't. She means to have the baby."

"But she cannot! It would be madness to flaunt her wrongdoing so."

"If such behavior would be madness, then she is indeed not in her right mind."

"What about . . . your father? Have you thought of going to him for advice?" The suggestion wasn't completely ridiculous: Charles St. Andrew was known for chasing his servant girls and had probably been in Jonathan's position once or twice himself.

Jonathan snorted like a shying horse. "I suppose I will have to tell old Charles, though I don't look forward to it. He will know how to deal with Sophia, but I fear what the outcome might be." Meaning, I guessed, that Charles St. Andrew would make his son break all ties with Sophia and, baby or no, they'd not see each other again. Or worse, he might insist Jeremiah be told, and Jeremiah might demand a divorce from his adulterous wife and start proceedings against Jonathan. Or he could extort hush money from the St. Andrews, agreeing to raise the babe as his own if he was paid for his silence. What might happen once St. Andrew stepped in was anyone's guess.

"My dear Jonathan," I murmured, my mind scrabbling for a piece of advice to give him, "I am sorry for your misfortune. But before you go to your father, let me think on it a day. Perhaps a solution will come to me."

He looked over his shoulder at my sisters, who were now obscured from us behind a pitched stack of hay. "As always, you are my salvation." Before I knew what was happening, he clasped me by the shoulders and pulled me to him, fairly lifting me to my toes to kiss me. But it was no brotherly peck; the forcefulness of his kiss was a reminder that he could conjure up my desire at will, that I was his. He held me tight to him and yet he trembled, too; we were both panting when he released me. "You are my angel," he whispered hoarsely in my ear. "Without you, I would be lost."

Did he know what he was doing, saying such things to someone desperately in love with him? It made me wonder if he had meant to set me to take care of this unsavory business of his, or if he had merely come seeking reassurances from the one girl he could depend on to love him no matter what he did. I liked to think that a part of him loved me purely and was sorry to have disappointed me. I cannot honestly say I knew Jonathan's true intentions then; I doubt if he himself knew. After all, he was a young man in serious trouble for the first time; perhaps Jonathan wishfully believed that, if God would forgive him this indiscretion, he would mend his ways and be satisfied with one girl who would love him completely.

He climbed back in the saddle and nodded politely to my sisters before turning his horse in the direction of home. And before he had ridden to the edge of the field and disappeared from my sight, a thought came to me, for I was a clever girl and never more focused in intent than when it involved Jonathan.

I decided to visit Sophia the next day and speak to her in private. I waited until I had shut our chickens in the coop for the night, so my absence wouldn't be noticed, before setting out for the Jacobses' farm. Their property was much quieter than ours, mainly because they owned fewer livestock and there were no children to help tend to all the chores. I crept into the barn, hoping I would not run into Jeremiah, and found Sophia penning their three raggedy sheep in a stall for the evening.

"Lanore!" She started in surprise, hands flying up to cover her heart. She was lightly dressed for being outside, with only a woolly shawl over her shoulders instead of a cloak to ward off the cold. Sophia had to know of my friendship with Jonathan and God knows what he might have said to her about me (or perhaps I was foolish to believe that he gave a thought to me once he'd left my presence). She gave me an icy look, undoubtedly worried about why I'd come. I must have seemed a child to her for being not yet wed and still living under my parents' roof although, I was only a few years younger.

"Forgive me for coming to see you unannounced, but I had to speak to you alone," I said, looking over my shoulder to be sure her husband wasn't close by. "I will speak plainly, as there is no time for niceties. I think you know what I have come to discuss with you. Jonathan shared with me—"

She crossed her arms and gave me a steely look. "He told you, did he? He had to boast to someone that he has made me with child?"

"Nothing of the sort! If you think he is pleased that you are going to have a baby—"

"*His* baby," she insisted. "And I know he's not pleased."

I saw my opening. I'd been thinking about what I would say to Sophia from the moment Jonathan had ridden away from me the day before. Jonathan had come to me because he needed someone who could be ruthless with Sophia on his behalf. Someone who could make clear to her the weakness of her position. Sophia would know that I understood what she faced; there would be less room for conjecture and appeal to emotion. I wasn't doing this because I hated Sophia, I assured myself, nor because I resented that she'd usurped my place in Jonathan's life. No, I knew Sophia for what she was. I was saving Jonathan from this wily harridan's trap.

"With all due respect, I must ask you what proof you have that the baby is Jonathan's? We have only your word, and . . ." I trailed off, letting my implication linger in the air.

"What are you, Jonathan's solicitor now?" Her face reddened when I didn't rise to the bait. "Aye, you're right, it could be either Jeremiah's or Jonathan's, but I know it's Jonathan's. I *know*." Her hands wrapped around her belly though she showed no sign of pregnancy.

"You expect Jonathan to ruin his life on your *assurances*—"

"Ruin his life?" she shrieked. "What about my life?"

"Yes, what about your life," I said, drawing myself up as tall as I could. "Have you thought what will happen if you publicly accuse Jonathan of fathering your baby? All you will accomplish is to let it be known that you are a loose woman—"

Sophia chuffed, spinning on her heel away from me, as though she couldn't bear to hear another word.

"—and he will deny the affair. Deny that he could be the father of the child. And who will believe you, Sophia? Who would believe that Jonathan St. Andrew would choose to dally with you when he can have his pick of any woman in the village?"

"Jonathan will deny me?" she asked, incredulous. "Don't waste your breath, Lanore. You'll not convince me that my Jonathan would ever deny me."

My Jonathan, she'd said. My cheeks burned, my heart hammered. I do not know where I found the nerve to say the evil things to Sophia that I said next. It was as though another person was hidden inside me, one with qualities I'd never dreamed I possessed, and this hidden person had been summoned from inside me as easily as a genie is conjured from a lamp. I was blind with rage; all I knew was that Sophia was threatening Jonathan, threatening to ruin his future, and I would never let anyone harm him. He wasn't *her* Jonathan, he was mine. I'd claimed him years ago in the vestibule of the church, and foolish as it may seem, I felt that possessiveness rise in me, fierce and primordial. "You'll make yourself a laughingstock—the homeliest woman in St. Andrew claiming that the most eligible man in town is the father of her child, not the oaf who is her husband. The oaf she despises."

"But it *is* his child," she said, defiant. "Jonathan *knows* that. Does he not care what would happen to his own flesh and blood?"

That gave me pause; I felt a guilty twinge. "Do yourself a favor, Sophia, and forget your mad scheme. You have a husband—tell him the child is his. He'll be glad for the news. I'm sure Jeremiah has wished for children."

"He has—for children of his *own*," she hissed. "I cannot lie to Jeremiah about the child's lineage."

"Why not? You've lied to him about your fidelity, no doubt," I said ruthlessly. Her hatred was so palpable at that moment, I thought she might strike at me like a snake.

The time had come to drive the stake through her heart. I looked her up and down with hooded eyes. "You know, the punishment for adultery for the female partner, if she is married, is death. That is still the position of the church. Consider this, if you insist on going through with your decision. You will seal your own fate." It was a hollow threat: no woman would be put to death for being an adulteress in St. Andrew, nor in any frontier town where women of child-bearing years were scarce. The punishment for Jonathan, if the townspeople decided by some wild chance that he was guilty, would be to pay the bastardy tax and perhaps be ostracized by some of the town's most pious for a short while. Without a doubt, Sophia would bear most of the burden.

Sophia whirled around in circles as though searching for unseen tormentors. "Jonathan!" she cried, though not loudly enough for her husband to hear her. "How could you treat me like this? I expected you to behave honorably . . . I thought that was the kind of man you were . . . Instead, you visit upon me this viper"—she shot me another venomous look through teary eyes—"to do your evil work for you. Don't think I don't know why you do this," she hissed, pointing a finger at me. "Everyone in town knows you're in love with him but that he will not have you. It's jealousy, I say. Jonathan would never send you to deal with me in this way."

I had prepared myself to be cool. I backed a few steps away from her as though she was mad or dangerous. "Of course he told me to see you—otherwise, how would I know you are with child? He has despaired of being able to make you see reason and has asked me to speak to you, as a woman. And as a woman, I tell you: I know what you are up to. You are using this misfortune to better your lot, to trade in your husband for someone with means. Perhaps there is not even a baby. You look the same as always to me. As for my relationship with Jonathan, we have a special friendship, pure and chaste and stronger than that of brother and sister, not that I would expect you to understand it," I said, haughtily. "You don't seem to be able to comprehend a relationship with a man that doesn't involve lifting your skirts. Think hard on it, Sophia Jacobs. It is your dilemma and the outcome is in your hands. Choose the easiest path. Give Jeremiah a child. And do not approach Jonathan again: he doesn't wish to see you," I said firmly, then left the barn. On the path home, I trembled with fear and with triumph, burning from spent nerves despite the cold air. I had summoned all my courage to defend Jonathan and had done so with a single-mindedness I didn't know I possessed. I had rarely ever raised my voice and had never forced my position so vehemently on anyone. To know I had such an inner power was frightening, and yet also thrilling. I walked home through the woods, light-headed and flushed, confident that I could do anything.

NINE

It was the noise that woke me the next morning, a musket fired, ball and powder. A musket shot at this hour meant trouble: a fire at a neighbor's house, a raiding party, a terrible accident. This shot came from the direction of the Jacobses' farm; I knew it as soon as I heard it.

I pulled the blanket over my head, pretending to be asleep, listening to the murmurs coming from my parents' bed below. I heard my father rise and dress, and go out the door. My mother followed, probably wrapping a quilt around her shoulders as she went about the tasks she did every morning, stoking the fire and starting a pot of water to boil. I swung around to sit upright, reluctant to put the soles of my feet on the cold plank floor and start what seemed heralded to be a strange and ill-fortuned day.

My father came back inside, his expression grim. "Get dressed, Nevin. You must come with me," he said to the groaning lump in the bed downstairs.

"Must I?" I heard my brother ask in a voice heavy with sleep. "There's the cattle to feed—"

"I'll go with you, Father," I called down from the loft, pulling on my clothing hastily. My heart was already beating so hard that it would be impossible to remain in the house and wait for news of what had happened. I had to go with my father.

A snow had fallen in the night, the first of the season, and I tried to clear my mind as I walked behind Father, concentrating only on stepping into the footsteps he made in the fresh snow. My breath hung in the crisp air and a drop of mucus beaded on the tip of my nose.

Sitting in the hollow before us was the Jacobses' farm, a brown saltbox on the broad expanse of white snow. People had begun to congregate, distant small dark shapes against the snow, and more were coming to the farm from every direction, on foot and on horseback; the sight made my heart start to race again.

"We're going to the Jacobses'?" I asked of my father's back.

"Yes, Lanore." A taciturn reply, with his customary economy of words.

I could barely contain my anxiety. "What do you think has happened?"

"I expect we'll find out," he said patiently.

There was a representative present from every family—except the St. Andrews, but they lived at the farthest reach of town and could scarcely have heard the shot—everyone in mismatching layers of dress: dressing gowns, uneven hems of a nightshirt peeking out from beneath a coat, hair uncombed. I followed my father through the small crowd until we'd nudged our way to the front door, where Jeremiah knelt in the muddied, chopped snow. He'd obviously shoved himself hastily into breeches, boots unlaced on his feet, and a quilt draped over his shoulders. His ancient blunderbuss, the gun that had fired the alarm, leaned against the clapboard siding. His great ugly face contorted in agony, his eyes red, his lips cracked and bleeding. He was usually such an emotionless man that the sight was unnerving.

Pastor Gilbert pushed his way to the front, then crouched low so he could speak softly into Jeremiah's ear. "What is it, Jeremiah? Why did you sound the alarm?"

"She's missing, Pastor . . ."

"Missing?"

"Sophia, Pastor. She's gone."

The hush of his voice sent a wave of murmurs through the crowd, everyone whispering to the person on either side of them, except for me and my father.

"Gone?" Gilbert placed his hands on Jeremiah's cheeks, cradling his face. "What do you mean, she is gone?"

"She is gone, or someone has taken her. When I awoke, she was not in our home. Not in the farmyard, not in the barn. Her cloak is gone but her other things are still here."

Hearing that Sophia—angry, perhaps feeling she had naught to lose—had not revealed my visit to Jeremiah eased a tightness in my chest that I hadn't realized was there. At that moment, may God forgive me, I was worried not so much for a woman wandering bereft in the great woods as I was for my own part in her undoing.

Gilbert shook his white head. "Jeremiah, surely she has just stepped out for a bit, a walk perhaps. She will be home soon and sorry to have caused her husband worry." But even as he spoke, we all knew he was mistaken. No one went walking for recreation in weather this cold, first thing in the morning.

"Calm yourself, Jeremiah. Let us take you inside, to warm yourself before you get a bone chill . . . Stay here with Mrs. Gilbert and Miss Hibbins, they'll see to you while the rest of us search for Sophia— won't we, neighbors?" Gilbert said with false enthusiasm as he helped the big man to his feet and turned to the rest of us. Speculation passed in the sideways glances of husband to wife, neighbor to neighbor—so the new bride has left her husband?—but no one had the heart to do anything but take up the pastor's suggestion. The two women escorted Jeremiah, stumbling and dazed, into his house and the rest of us broke up into groups. We looked for a line of footprints in the snow leading away from the house, hoping that Sophia's path had not been trampled by those who had answered Jeremiah's shot.

My father found one set of tiny footprints that could have been Sophia's and the two of us began to trace her steps. With my eyes trained on the snow, my mind raced ahead, wondering what had drawn Sophia from her house. Perhaps Sophia had stewed over my words all night and woke with her mind made up, to have it out with Jonathan. How could our confrontation not have something to do with her disappearance? My heart beat fiercely as we followed the footprints that I feared would lead to the St. Andrews' house, until the snow disappeared in the deeper woods and with it, Sophia's tracks.

Now we followed no discernible path, my father and I, the forest floor a dizzying patchwork of bare, hard ground and thinly scattered scabs of snow and dead leaves. I had no idea if my father was picking up telltale signs of Sophia's path—snapped branches, crushed leaves—or if he pushed on out of a sense of duty. We traveled parallel to the river, the sound of the Allagash to my left. Usually I thought the sound of water rushing over rock comforting, but not today.

Sophia had to have been moved strongly by something to venture into the woods by herself. Only the hardiest villagers went into the forest alone because it was easy to lose your way in the sameness. Acre after acre of forest unfurled in a repetition of birch and spruce and pine, and the regularity of boulders pushing their way up through the forest floor, all covered with extravagant mosses or crackled with celadon lichens.

Maybe I should have spoken to my father earlier, to let him know that his neighborly sacrifice was unnecessary and that in all likelihood Sophia had gone to see a man, a man whose company she should not keep. She could be safe and warm in a room with this man while we tramped through the cold and damp. I pictured Sophia rushing along the trail, stealing away from her unhappy home to Jonathan, tender-hearted and confused, who would undoubtedly take her in. My stomach twisted at the thought of her tucked in Jonathan's bed, the thought that she had won and I had lost and that Jonathan was now hers.

Eventually we turned toward the river and walked a ways, following its contours. My father paused at one point, breaking a hole through a thin patch of ice to dip his hand in for a drink. Between sips, he eyed me not without curiosity.

"I don't know how much longer we will need to search. You can go home now, Lanore. This is no place for a girl. You must be freezing with cold."

I shook my head. "No, no, Father, I'd like to keep on a while longer . . ." It would be impossible to wait at home for news. I would go out of my mind or abandon all propriety to race to Jonathan's house and confront Sophia. I could picture her, smug, triumphant. At that moment, I don't think I'd hated anyone as much as I hated her.

It was Father who spotted her first. He had been scanning the way ahead while I had kept my eyes trained on the dizzying ground underfoot. He found the frozen body trapped in an eddy formed by a fallen tree, almost hidden in a tangle of reeds and wild vines. She floated prone, caught in a mass of frozen cattails, her delicate body outstretched, the folds of her skirt and her long hair bobbing on the surface of the water. Her cloak sat on the riverbank, neatly folded.

"Look away, girl," my father said as he tried to turn me by the shoulders. I couldn't tear my eyes from her.

Father sounded the call while I stared dumbly at her corpse. Other searchers came crashing through the woods, following my father's voice. Two of the men waded into the frigid water to pull her body from the embrace of the frozen grasses and the thin shelf of ice that had started to claim her. We spread her cape on the ground and laid her body on it, the sodden fabric clinging to her legs and torso. Her skin was blue all over and her eyes, mercifully, were closed.

The men wrapped her in her cloak and took turns holding the edges, using it as a sling to carry Sophia's body back home, while I walked behind them. My teeth chattered and my father came up to me to rub my arms in an attempt to warm me, but it did no good, for I shook and shivered from fear, not cold. I held my arms tight to my stomach, afraid I would be ill in front of my father. My presence dampened the discussion among the men and they refrained from speculating as to why Sophia had taken her life. They generally agreed, however, that Pastor Gilbert would not be told about the cape set deliberately aside. He would not know that she had been a suicide.

When my father and I made it home, I ran straight to the fireplace and stood so close that the fire toasted my face, but even that heat could not stop my shaking. "Not so close," my mother chided as she helped me take off my cloak, afraid no doubt that the cape might catch on a spitting ember. I would have welcomed it. I deserved to burn like a witch for what I'd done.

A few hours later, my mother came up to me, squared her shoulders, and said, "I'm going to the Gilberts' to help with the preparations for Sophia. I think you should come with me. It's time you started taking your place among the women in this town and learned some of the duties that will be expected of you."

By now I had changed into a heavy nightgown, curled by the fire, and had drunk a mug of hot cider with rum. The drink helped to numb me, to tamp down the urge to cry out loud and confess, but I knew that I would come undone if I had to confront Sophia's body, even in the presence of the other women in town.

I rose up from the floor on an elbow. "I couldn't . . . I don't feel well. Still cold . . ."

My mother pressed the back of her fingers to my forehead, then my throat. "If anything, I'd say you were burning with fever . . ." She looked at me cautiously, skeptically, then rose from the floor, tossing her cloak over her shoulders. "All right, this one time, seeing what you went through earlier . . ." Her words trailed off. She looked me over one more time, in a way I couldn't quite figure out, and then slipped out the door.

She told me later what had happened at the pastor's house, how the women prepared Sophia's body for burial. First, they set it by the fire to thaw, then they rinsed the river silt from her mouth and nose and gently combed out her hair. My mother described how white her skin had become from the time in the river, and how she'd been scraped with thin, red scratches after the current had dragged her corpse over submerged rocks. They dressed her in her finest dress, a yellow so pale as to be almost ivory, embellished with embroidery by her own needle and tailored to her slender frame with pin tucks. No mention was made of Sophia's body, no abnormality, no remark of the faintest swell to the dead woman's abdomen. If anyone noticed anything, it would be attributed to bloat, no doubt, water the poor girl had ingested as she drowned. And then a linen shroud was tucked into a plain panel coffin. A couple of men who had waited while the women completed their work loaded the coffin into a wagon and escorted it to Jeremiah's house, where it would lie in wait for the funeral.

As my mother calmly described the state of Sophia's body, I felt as though nails were being driven into me, exhorting me to confess my wickedness. But I held on to my wits, if barely, and cried as my mother spoke, my hand shielding my eyes. My mother rubbed my back as though I were a child again. "Whatever is it, Lanore dear? Why are you so upset for Sophia? It is a terrible thing and she was our neighbor, yes, but I didn't think you even knew her very well . . ." She sent me up to the loft with a goatskin filled with warm water and went to chide my father for taking me with him into the woods. I lay with the goatskin pressed against my stomach though it brought me no comfort. I lay awake, listening to all the sounds of the night—the wind, the shaking trees, the dying embers—whisper Sophia's name.

As had been the case at her wedding, Sophia Jacobs's funeral was a mean affair, attended by her husband, her mother and a few of her siblings, and not many others. The day was cold and overcast, snowfall promising to drift down from the sky as it had every day since Sophia had killed herself.

We stood and watched from a hilltop overlooking the cemetery, Jonathan and I. We watched the mourners press around the dark, hollow plot. Somehow they had managed to excavate a grave site though the ground was beginning to freeze, and I could not help but wonder if it had been her father, Tobey, who had dug the grave. The mourners, specks of black against a white field far in the distance, shifted to and fro restlessly, as Pastor Gilbert pronounced words over the deceased. My face was tight, swollen from days of crying, but now, in Jonathan's presence, no tears came. It felt surreal to be spying on Sophia's funeral—I, who should be down there on my knees, begging Jeremiah for forgiveness, for I was responsible for his wife's death as surely as if I'd pushed her into the river myself.

Next to me, Jonathan stood silently. Snow began to fall at last, like the release of a long-pent-up tension, tiny flakes swirling on the cold air before landing on the dark wool of Jonathan's greatcoat and in his hair.

"I cannot believe she is gone," he said, for the twentieth time that morning. "I can't believe she took her life."

I choked on my words. Anything I could say would be too weak, too palliative and altogether untrue.

"It is my fault," he croaked, raising a hand to his face.

"You mustn't blame yourself for this." I rushed to comfort him with the words I had said to myself over and over the past few days, as I'd hidden in feverish guilt in bed. "You knew her life was miserable, from when she was a child. Who knows what unhappy thoughts she carried with her, and for how long? She finally acted on them. It's hardly your fault."

He took two steps forward, as though longing to be down in the graveyard. "I can't believe she had been carrying thoughts of self-injury, Lanny. She had been happy—with me. It seems inconceivable that the Sophia I knew was fighting the desire to kill herself."

"One never knows. Maybe she had an argument with Jeremiah . . . perhaps after the last time you saw her . . ."

He squeezed his eyes shut. "If she was troubled by anything, it was my reaction when she told me of the baby. That is why I blame myself, Lanny, for my thoughtless reaction to her news. You said"—Jonathan lifted his head, suddenly, looking in my direction—"that you might think of a way to dissuade her from keeping the baby. I pray, Lanny, that you didn't approach Sophia with any such plan—"

Startled, I jerked back. I'd thought these past few days about telling him everything, as I'd struggled with my guilt. I had to tell someone—it was not the kind of secret a body can keep without doing irreparable harm to the soul—and if anyone would understand, it would be Jonathan. I'd done it for him, after all. He'd come to me for help and I had done what was required. Now I needed to be absolved for what I had done; he owed me that absolution, didn't he?

But as he searched me with those dark, willful eyes, I realized I could not tell him. Not now, not while he was raw with grief and capable of being carried away by emotion. He would not understand. "What? No, I came up with no plan. Why would I approach Sophia on my own, anyway?" I lied. I hadn't intended to lie to Jonathan, but he surprised me, his guess like an arrow shot with uncanny precision. I would tell him one day, I resolved.

Jonathan turned his three-cornered hat in his hands. "Do you suppose I should tell Jeremiah the truth?"

I rushed up to Jonathan and shook him by the shoulders. "That would be a terrible thing to do, for yourself as well as poor Sophia. What good would it do to tell Jeremiah now, except to appease your conscience? All you would accomplish would be to ruin Jeremiah's illusion of her. Let him bury Sophia thinking her a good wife who honored him."

He looked at my small hands clasping his shoulders—it was unusual for us to touch each other now that we were no longer children—and then looked into my eyes with such sorrow that I couldn't help myself. I collapsed against his chest and pulled him toward me, thinking only that he needed comfort from a woman at that moment, even if it wasn't Sophia. I will not lie and say I didn't find the feeling of his strong, warm body against mine comforting, too, though I had no right to comfort. I nearly wept with happiness at the touch of him. Holding his body against mine, I could pretend that he had forgiven me for my terrible sin against Sophia, although, of course, he knew nothing of it.

I'd kept my cheek against his chest, listening to his heart beat beneath layers of wool and linen and breathing in his scent. I didn't want to release my hold of Jonathan, but I sensed he was looking down at me, and so I looked up at him, too, ready for him to tell me again of his love for Sophia. And if he did, if he said her name, I resolved, I would tell him what I had done. But he didn't; instead, his mouth hovered over mine for an instant before he kissed me.

The moment for which I'd waited went by in a blur. We slipped into the protection of the woods, steps away. I remember the wonderful heat of his mouth on mine, its hunger and forcefulness. I remember his hands pulling on the ribbon that closed my blouse over my breasts. He pressed my back against a tree and bit into my neck as he fumbled with the fall of his breeches. I lifted my skirts so he could claim me, his hands on my hips. I regret that I didn't have even a glimpse of his manhood for all the clothing between us, coats and cloaks, skirts and petticoats. But I felt him in me, suddenly, a great firm hotness pushed up inside me, and him bucking against me, grinding me into the bark of the tree. And at the end, his groan in my ear sent a shiver through me, for it meant he had found pleasure with me, and I had never been so happy and feared I would never be so again.

We rode together on his horse through the woods with me holding tight around his waist, as we had as children. We took the least-traveled trails lest we be seen together without a chaperone. We didn't exchange a word and I kept my hot face buried in his coat, still trying to come to grips with what we'd done. I knew of plenty of other girls in town who had given themselves over to a man before marriage—with Jonathan often the recipient—and had looked down on them.

Now I was one of them. A part of me felt that I had disgraced myself. But another part of me believed I'd had no choice: it might have been my only chance to capture Jonathan's heart and prove that we were meant to be together. I couldn't let it pass.

I slipped from the back of his horse and, after a squeeze of his hand, hiked the short distance to my family's cabin. As I walked, however, doubts began to set in as to what our tryst had meant to him. He swived girls with no thought to any consequences: why did I imagine he would attach consequences this time? And what of his feelings for Sophia—or my obligation, for that matter, to the woman I had driven to take her own life? I had as good as murdered her and here I was fornicating with her lover. Surely a more wicked soul did not exist.

I took a few minutes before proceeding to my home, to compose myself with deep breaths of cold air. I couldn't go to pieces in front of my family. I had no one with whom I could talk this over. I would have to keep this secret hidden inside until I was calm enough to think on it rationally. I pushed it down, all of it, the guilt, the shame, the self-hatred. And yet, at the same time, I was filled with tremulous excitement, for though I didn't deserve as much, I'd gotten what I'd wanted. I exhaled, dusted the fresh snow from the front of my cloak, squared my shoulders, and trudged the rest of the way to my family's cottage.

TEN

S ounds are heard out in the hall.

Luke looks at his wristwatch: 4 A.M. The hospital will come to life before long. The mornings are busy with injuries common to farm country—a rib shattered by a kick from a dairy cow, a slip on a patch of ice while lugging a bale of hay—followed at six by the shift change.

The girl looks at him the way a dog might regard an unreliable master. "Will you help me? Or are you going to let that sheriff take me to the police station?"

"What else can I do?"

Her face glows pink. "You can let me go. Close your eyes while I slip out. No one will blame you. You can tell them you went down to the lab, left me alone for just a second, and I was gone by the time you returned."

Joe says she's a murderer, Luke thinks. *Can I let a murderer walk out the door?*

Lanny reaches for his hand. "Have you ever been in love with someone so badly that you'd do anything for them? That no matter what you want, you want their happiness more?"

Luke is glad she can't see into his heart because he has never been that selfless. He's been dutiful, yes, but he's never been able to give without a tug of resentment and he doesn't like how that makes him feel.

"I'm not a threat to anyone. I told you why I . . . did what I did to Jonathan."

Luke looks into those ice blue eyes filling with tears and he tingles from his scalp to his gut. The pain from loss overcomes him quickly, as it tends to since his parents' deaths. He knows she is feeling the same sadness as he, and for a moment they are together in this bottomless grief. And he's so tired of being imprisoned by grief—the loss of his parents, his marriage, his entire life—that he knows he must do something to break free of it, do it now or he never will. He's not sure why he's going to do what he's about to do, but he knows he can't think about it in advance or he won't do it.

"Wait here. I'll be right back."

Luke slips down the narrow corridor to the doctors' locker room. Inside his dented gray locker he finds a pair of scrubs, wadded up and forgotten. He rummages through a couple of other lockers and comes up with a white lab coat, a surgical cap, and, from the pediatrician's locker, a pair of women's running shoes so old that they curl at the toes. Luke brings these back to the examination room.

"Here, put these on."

They take the shortest route to the back of the hospital, pushing through janitors' passages to the loading dock in the service area. An orderly coming in for the day shift waves as they cross the parking lot, but when Luke waves back his arm feels rusted tight with anxiety. It isn't until they're in the parking lot, standing beside his pickup truck, that Luke remembers he's left his keys in his parka back in the doctors' lounge.

"Damn it. I have to go back. Don't have my keys. Hide in the trees. I'll be right back."

Lanny says nothing but nods, hunched against the cold in her thin cotton scrubs.

The walk from the parking lot to the ambulance entrance is the longest of his life. Luke hustles because of the cold and his nerves. Judy or Clay may have already noticed he is gone. And if Clay is still asleep on the couch, Luke might wake him when he goes into the lounge to retrieve his keys and then he'd be caught. Each step gets harder and harder, until he feels like a water-skier being dragged under the surface after something has gone horribly wrong with the tow line.

He pushes back the heavy glass door, so on edge that his shoulders are pinched high around his ears. Judy, at the nurses' station, frowns at her computer, not even looking up when Luke walks by. "Where have you been?"

"Having a smoke."

Now Judy is paying attention, fixing Luke with the beady eyes of a crow. "When did you start smoking again?"

Luke feels like he smoked two packs last night, so what he's told Judy doesn't feel like a lie. He decides to ignore her. "Is Clay up?"

"I haven't seen him. The door to the lounge is still closed. Maybe you ought to wake him up. He can't sleep here all day. His wife will be wondering what happened to him."

Luke freezes; he wants to make a joke, to act as though everything is normal in front of Judy, but then of course, Luke has never joked with Judy in the past and that in itself would seem abnormal. His inability to lie and cover his tracks only makes him more self-conscious. He feels like he's fallen through the frozen skin of a pond and is drowning, sucking frigid water into every crevice of his lungs, and Judy sees nothing. "I need coffee," Luke mumbles as he heads off.

The door to the lounge is just a couple of steps away. He sees immediately that it is slightly ajar and dark within. He nudges it open another ten degrees and plainly sees the empty sag on the couch where the policeman should be.

Blood rises to his ears, the glands in his throat swell to four times their normal size. He can't breathe. It's worse than drowning: it feels as if he's being strangled.

His parka hangs to the right from a hook on the wall, waiting for him to reach into the pocket. The jingle tells him that the keys are right where he expected them to be.

On the way back, his walk is direct and purposeful. Head down, hands pushed deep into the pockets of his lab coat, he decides not to take the service hallway, it's too indirect, and marches toward the ambulance entrance instead. Judy's head jerks up as Luke passes the duty station.

"I thought you were getting coffee."

"Left my wallet in the car," he tosses over his shoulder. He's almost at the door.

"Did you wake Clay?"

"He's already up," Luke says, backing into the door to push it open. And at the far end of the hall, there is the deputy, seemingly having materialized at the mention of his name. He sees Luke in return and raises his arm the way he'd hail a bus. Clay wants to talk to him and starts jogging down the hall in Luke's direction, hand waving . . . *Stop, Luke.* But Luke doesn't. Throwing all his weight into the hip check, Luke knocks the door back.

Cold slaps his face as he bursts out on the other side, bobbing to the surface of his real life. *What am I doing? This is the hospital where I work. I know every tile and plastic chair and gurney as well as I know my own house. What am I doing, throwing away my life by helping a suspected murderer escape? Have I lost my mind?* But he continues, compelled by a strange itching in his blood, ricocheting through his veins like a pinball, driving him forward. He speed-walks across the parking lot, frantic and off-kilter, like a person trying to remain upright while descending a steep hill, knowing he must look like a lunatic.

Luke squints anxiously at his truck, but the girl is gone, not a speck of the telltale aqua of hospital scrubs to be seen. At first, he panics—how could he have been so stupid, leaving her outside unattended? But a small kernel of hope expands in his chest as he realizes that if the prisoner is gone, so are his worries.

The next minute she is there, wispy, ethereal, an angel dressed in hospital clothing . . . And his heart leaps at the sight of her.

Luke fumbles with the ignition while Lanny slouches low, trying not to watch and further the doctor's nervousness. Finally, the engine turns over and the truck leaps out of the parking lot, launching recklessly onto the road.

The passenger stares directly ahead, as though her concentration alone is keeping them from being discovered. "I'm at Dunratty's hunting lodge. Do you know where that is?"

Luke is incredulous. "Do you think it's smart to go there? I'd think the police would have tracked you to your hotel by now. We don't get many strangers this time of year."

"Please, just swing by. If it looks suspicious, we'll keep going, but all my things are there. My passport. Money. Clothing. I bet you don't have anything that would fit me."

She is smaller than Tricia but larger than the girls. "You'd win that bet," he confirms. "Passport?"

"I came over from France, where I live." She curls on her end of the bench seat like a cat trying to conserve its warmth. Suddenly, Luke's hands on the steering wheel feel large, outlandishly huge and clumsy. He's having an out-of-body experience from the stress and has to concentrate not to jerk the wheel and send them hurtling off the road.

"You should see my house in Paris. It's like a museum, filled with all the things I've collected over many, many years. Want to go there?" Her tone is sweet and as warming as liquor, and the invitation is intriguing. He wonders if she's telling the truth. Who wouldn't like to go to Paris, stay in a magical house. Luke feels his tension start to melt, his spine and neck begin to relax.

There are hunting lodges like Dunratty's all over this part of the woods. Luke has never stayed in one but remembers seeing the inside of a couple when he was a kid, for some reason he can't recall now.

Cheap cabins dating back to the 1950s, nailed together from plywood and filled with thrift shop furniture and mold, cheap linoleum and mouse droppings. The girl directs Luke to the last cottage on Dunratty's gravel driveway, and the cabin's windows are dark and empty. She extends a hand to Luke. "Give me one of your credit cards and I'll see if I can open the lock."

Once inside, they draw the shades and Lanny snaps on a light. There is a chill on every surface they touch. Personal belongings are strewn about, left out, as though the inhabitants had been forced to flee in the night. There are two beds but only one is unmade, the crumpled sheets and dimpled pillows looking wanton and incriminating. A laptop with a digital camera attached to it via a cord sits on a shaky table that was once part of a kitchenette set. Open bottles of wine litter the side table, two tumblers smudged with fingerprints, lip prints.

Two bags, open, rest on the floor. Lanny crouches next to one, stuffing loose items into it, including the laptop and camera.

Luke jingles his keys, nervous and impatient.

The girl zips the bag shut, stands upright, then turns to the second suitcase. She fishes out an item of men's clothing and holds it to her nose, breathing in deeply.

"Okay. Let's go."

As they go down the drive past the front office (surely closed at this hour of the morning, Dunratty Junior upstairs asleep), Luke thinks he sees the red gingham curtains move, as though someone might have been watching them. He imagines Dunratty, in his bathrobe, coffee cup in hand, hearing the sound of tires on gravel and going to see who's driving by; would he recognize my truck? Luke wonders. Forget it, it's nothing, just a cat going by the window, or so Luke tells himself. No sense in looking for trouble.

Luke is a little unnerved as the girl changes clothing while he drives, until he remembers that he's already seen her naked. She slips on blue jeans and a cashmere sweater more luxurious than anything his wife had ever worn. She drops the scrubs to the car floor.

"Do you have a passport?" she asks Luke.

"At home, sure."

"Let's go get it."

"What—we're going to fly off to Paris, just like that?"

"Why not? I'll buy the tickets, pay for everything. Money is not a problem."

"I think we should get you to Canada, now, before the police put out a bulletin on you. We're fifteen minutes from the border."

"Will you need your passport to cross the border? They've changed the regulations, haven't they?" the girl asks, a note of panic in her voice.

Luke tightens his grip again on the wheel. "I don't know . . . I haven't crossed the border in a while . . . Oh, okay, we'll go to my house. But only for a minute."

The farmhouse stands in the middle of an open field, like a child too stupid to know to come in from the cold. His truck climbs and bucks over the churned mud, now frozen into peaks like cake frosting.

They enter through the back door into a sad, shabby kitchen that hasn't been changed in the past fifty years. Luke flips on the overhead light and notices it makes no appreciable difference in the level of light in the room. Used coffee mugs sit on the dinette table and crumbs crunch underfoot. He is disproportionately embarrassed by the disarray.

"This was my parents' house. I've been living here since they died," he explains. "I didn't like the idea of the farm going to a stranger, but I can't run it like they did. Sold the livestock a few months ago. Have someone lined up to rent the fields, to plant next spring. Seems a waste to let them go fallow."

Lanny drifts around the kitchen, running a finger over the chipped Formica countertop, the back of a vinyl-cushioned kitchen chair. She stops at a drawing hanging from a magnet on the refrigerator, made by one of his daughters when she was in preschool. A princess on a pony; the pony is recognizable as some type of horselike creature but the princess is an approximation, with bushy blond hair and blue eyes, wearing a pink gown to go horseback riding. Except for the long gown, it could be Lanny.

"Who drew this? Do you have children at home?"

"Not anymore."

"Gone, with your wife?" she guesses. "No one taking care of the place for you?"

He shrugs.

"You don't have any reason to stay," she says, stating a fact.

"I still have obligations," he says, because that is how he's used to thinking about his life. A farm he won't be able to sell in this economy. He has his practice, mostly elderly as their children and grandchildren move out of town. His caseload shrinks every month.

Luke goes up the stairs and to his bedroom, and finds his passport in the drawer of a bedside table. He moved into his parents' old bedroom after his wife left him: the bedroom of his childhood had also been his marital bed and he wants no part of that anymore.

He flips the passport open. Never used. He's never had the time to travel, not since his residency, and even then it was only in the U.S. He's never been to even one of the faraway places he used to dream about seeing when he was a teenager, spending long hours on the tractor, his daydreaming time. His empty passport makes him feel a little ashamed in front of somebody who has been to all these exotic places. His life was supposed to turn out differently.

He finds Lanny in the dining room inspecting the family pictures, placed on a low bookcase. His mother had the photos out for as long as Luke could remember and he didn't have the heart to put them away, but his mother was the only one who knew who these people were and how they were related to him. Old black-and-white photographs, with stern, long-gone Scandinavians staring back, strangers to one another. There's one color picture in a thick wood frame, a photo of a woman and her two daughters nestled among the relatives as though they belong there.

Luke turns off the lights and sets the thermostat very low, just enough to keep the pipes from freezing. He checks the locks on the doors, though he doesn't know why he is being so careful. He plans to come right back after dropping this girl off over the border, but the touch of his hand on the light switch makes a lump rise in his throat. It feels like he is saying good-bye—which he hopes to do one day, for which he's planned and pictured in his more sensible moments, maybe in the spring when he can think more clearly—but right now he's just helping a girl in trouble, a girl with no one else to turn to. As for today, he's coming right back.

"Ready?" Luke asks, jingling the keys once more, but Lanny reaches into the bookcase and pulls out a small book, barely larger than her hand. The dust jacket is missing and the hard covers are worn at the corners, so that the cardboard is visible, like a bud among the fraying yellow fabric. It takes a minute before Luke recognizes the book: it had been his favorite as a boy and his mother must have kept it all these years. *The Jade Pagoda,* a classic child's tale, like Kipling but not Kipling, a British expatriate's story set in a faraway locale, a story with a Chinese prince and a European princess, or a Caucasian girl in any case, set with pen-and-ink illustrations done by the author's own hand. Lanny flips through the pages.

"Do you know the book?" he asks. "I used to love it . . . Well, you can see the use it got. The binding is just about shot. I don't think it's in print anymore."

She is holding it out to him now, open, pointing to one of the illustrations. And he'll be damned if it isn't her. She's in a period dress and her hair is pinned up like a Gibson girl's, but that is her heart-shaped face and her slightly haughty, bemused eyes. "I met Oliver, the author, when we both lived in Hong Kong. He was just a British civil servant then, and known as a drinker, begging the officers' wives to pose for his 'little project,' as he called it. I was the only one who would do it; they all thought it was scandalous and some kind of ruse, just an excuse to get one of us alone with him in his apartment."

There's a stirring in his diaphragm. He feels his heart leap posses-sively. The girl in the illustration stands before him in the flesh, and it is like the strangest kind of magic to have something he's known only as incorporeal suddenly manifest itself before him. He is afraid, for a moment, that he might faint.

In an instant, she is at his side, hurrying to the door. "I'm ready. Let's go."

ELEVEN

I'd gotten my heart's one desire—for Jonathan to behold me as a woman and his lover—but nothing more. I lived in a state of uncertainty because I hadn't been able to communicate with him since that thrilling, frightening afternoon.

Winter had intervened.

Winter was not to be denied in our part of Maine. We would endure blizzard after blizzard, snow piled waist deep within a day or two, negating any possibility of travel. All attention and energy was directed toward keeping warm and fed, and taking care of the livestock. Every common task outdoors required wading in snow, an exhausting prospect. By the time a path to the barn and pasture was cleared, a clearing chopped through the icy surface of the stream for both livestock and household use, and the cattle had gotten used to negotiating the snowdrifts in the field, and it looked as if life might return to normal (or, at least, routine), another storm would descend on the valley.

I sat by the window and stared down the wagon trail, unsullied snow standing nearly two feet deep. I prayed fervently for the snow to settle and become compact enough for us to be able to travel on it, so that we could go to services on Sunday, my only opportunity to see Jonathan. I needed him to assuage my fears, to tell me he had not swived me only because he could not have Sophia but because he desired me. Perhaps because he loved me.

Finally, after several weeks of being housebound, the snow had condensed to a passable depth and Father said we would go into town on Sunday. While any other time of year such news would be met with mere tolerance if not indifference, this time you would have thought Father had told us we were going to a ball. Maeve, Glynnis, and I spent the days in a tizzy, deciding what we would wear, how to scrub a stain out of a beloved chemise, and which of us would fix the others' hair. Even Nevin seemed anxious for Sunday to come so he could escape from our tiny cabin.

My father and I deposited my sisters, brother, and mother at the Catholic church and then drove to the congregation hall. Father knew why I went to service with him, so he must have had an inkling of why I was more anxious than usual as we approached the hall. And after service, as the snow was too deep on the common for socializing, the congregation remained indoors, packing the aisles, hallways, and staircases. The air was loud with the bright chatter of people who had been confined with their families for too long and were anxious to speak to someone new.

I squeezed through the crowds, searching for Jonathan. My ears caught snippets of my neighbors' conversations—how dreary it had been, how boring, how sick everyone was of dried peas in molasses and salt pork—and they bounced off me like pellets of sleet. Through a narrow window, I caught sight of the churchyard and Sophia's grave. The recently turned ground had settled and sunk, and the snow over the grave dipped a good inch or two lower than the rest of the cover, leaving an irregularity on the landscape.

Finally, I saw Jonathan weaving through the crowd, too, looking as though he might be searching for me. We met at the foot of the staircase to the balcony, packed shoulder to shoulder with our neighbors, aware that we couldn't speak freely. Someone was bound to overhear.

"How charming you look today, Lanny," Jonathan said, politely. A harmless statement, the casual eavesdropper might think, but the Jonathan of my childhood had never remarked on my appearance, any more than he would remark on the appearance of another boy.

I couldn't return the compliment; I could only blush.

He leaned forward and whispered in my ear, "The past three weeks have been unbearable. Go out to your barn an hour before sundown tonight and I will contrive to meet you there."

Of course, under the circumstances I could ask him no questions nor seek any reassurances for my uncertain heart. And, to be honest, I don't think anything he could have said would have kept me from going to him. I burned to be with him.

That afternoon, my fears were assuaged. For an hour, I felt I was the epicenter of his world, all I could wish for. The whole of his being was in his every touch, from the way he fumbled with the tapes and ties that bound my clothing, to his fingers pulling gently through my hair and his kisses on my bare, goose-prickled shoulders. Afterward, we nestled together as we returned to our bodies and it was bliss to be encircled in his arms, to feel him pressed tight against me, as though he, too, wanted nothing to come between us. No happiness can compare to the happiness of getting what you have begged and prayed for. I was exactly where I'd longed to be, but now was aware of every second ticking by and how my family would be wondering after me.

Reluctantly, I pried his arms from my waist. "I can't stay. I must go back . . . though sometimes I wish there was somewhere else for me . . . a place I could go rather than home."

I had meant to say only that I wished I didn't have to leave the sweet harbor of his company but this truth slipped out, a truth I'd kept smothered inside me. It felt shameful, a secret fear to which I should not admit, but the words had escaped and there was no taking them back. Jonathan looked at me quizzically. "Why is that, Lanny?"

"Well, sometimes I feel—I have no place within my family." I felt a fool having to explain it to Jonathan, perhaps the one person in the village who had never gone unloved or had ever felt undeserving of happiness. "Nevin's the only son, so he's invaluable to my parents. And he'll inherit the farm one day. Then there are my sisters . . . well, they're so pretty, everyone in town admires them for their prettiness. Their prospects are good. But me . . ." I couldn't say, even to Jonathan, the heart of my secret fear—that my happiness mattered to no one, that I mattered to no one, not even to my father or mother.

He pulled me down next to him in the hay and drew me into his arms, holding me fast as I tried to pull away, not from him but from my shame. "I can't bear to hear you say these things, Lanny . . . well, you're the one I choose to be with, aren't you? The only one I seem to feel comfortable with, the only person I reveal myself to. I would spend all my time in your company, if I could. Father, Mother, my sisters, Benjamin . . . I'd give them up, all of them, for it to be just you, just the two of us, together forever."

I ate up his pretty tribute, of course; it cut through my shame and went straight to my head like a draft of strong whiskey. Don't mistake what I am saying: at the time, he believed he loved me and I was sure of his sincerity. But now, with hard-earned wisdom, I understand how foolish we were to say such dangerous words to each other! We were arrogant and naive, thinking we knew what we felt then was love. Love can be a cheap emotion, lightly given, though it didn't seem so to me at the time. Looking back, I know we were only filling in the holes in our souls, the way the tide rushes sand to fill in the crevices of a rocky shore. We—or maybe it was just I—bandaged our needs with what we declared was love. But, eventually, the tide draws out what it has swept in.

It was impossible for Jonathan to give me what he'd claimed to wish for; he couldn't give up his family or his responsibilities. He didn't have to tell me that his parents would never let him settle for me as a wife. But that late afternoon, in that cold barn, I possessed Jonathan's love, and having it, I was all the more ferocious to hold on to it. He'd declared his love for me, I was assured of mine for him, proof that we were meant to be together and that, of all the souls in God's universe, we were bound to each other. Bound in love.

We met that way only twice more over the next two months, a sorry record for lovers. On each occasion, we spoke very little (except for him to confess how he'd missed me), rushing to lovemaking, our haste owing to the fear that we would be discovered as well as due to the cold. We stripped each other as bare as we dared go, and used mouths and hands to knead, caress, and kiss. Each time, we coupled as though it would be the last time for either of us—perhaps we intuited an unhappy future, hovering at our elbow, counting down the seconds until it would wrap us in a dread embrace. Both times, we parted in haste, too, the scent of him slithering up from under my clothes, wetness between my legs and a burn on my cheeks that I hoped would be mistaken by my family for a nip from the cold.

Each time we parted, however, doubt began to nibble at the back of my mind. I had Jonathan's love—for now—but what did that mean? I knew Jonathan's past better than anyone. Hadn't he loved Sophia, too, and yet I had made him forget about her—or so it seemed. I could pretend that he would be true and faithful to me, choose to be willfully blind, as many women do, and hope that in time this would come to pass. My blindness was aided by a stubborn conviction that a bond of love was ordained by God, and no matter how inconvenient, how unlikely or painful, it could not be changed by man. I had to have faith that my love would triumph over any imperfection in Jonathan's love for me; love, after all, is faith, and all faith is meant to be tested.

Now I know only a fool looks for assurances in love. Love demands so much of us that in return we try to get a guarantee that it will last. We demand permanence, but who can make such promises? I should have been happy with the love—companionable, abiding— that Jonathan had had for me since childhood. That love was eternal.

Instead, I tried to make his feelings for me into what they were not and, in trying, I ruined the beautiful eternal thing that I had.

Sometimes the worst tidings come as an absence. A friend who does not visit at the usual time, and who quickly thereafter withdraws from the friendship. An awaited letter that does not arrive, followed at some distance by news of an untimely death. And, in my case that winter, the cessation of my monthly flowers. First, one month. Then a second.

I prayed there might be another cause. I cursed Sophia's spirit, sure that she was paying me back. Once bidden, however, Sophia's spirit was not so easy to contain.

Sophia began visiting me in my dreams. In some, her face would merely appear in a crowd, jarring and accusatory, then disappear. In one recurring dream, I would be with Jonathan only to have him leave me abruptly, turning from me as though by silent command, ignoring my pleas that he stay. He'd then reappear with Sophia, the two walking hand in hand in the distance, Jonathan without even a thought for me. I'd always wake from these dreams feeling hurt and abandoned.

The worst dream would throw me out of sleep like a bucking horse and I'd have to stifle my cries or risk waking my sisters. The other dreams might have been my guilty mind playing tricks, but this dream could be nothing else but a message from the dead girl herself. In this dream, I walk through an empty village, the wind rippling at my back as I travel down the main carriage trail. There's not another person to be seen, no voice or sound of life, no chopping of wood or clanging of the blacksmith's anvil. Soon, I'm in the woods, white with snow, following the half-frozen Allagash. I stop at a narrows in the river and see Sophia standing on the opposite shore. She is the Sophia who committed suicide, blue, her hair frozen in clumps, heavy wet clothing weighing on her. She is the forgotten lover, moldering in the grave, at whose expense I have made my happiness. Her dead eyes settle on me and then she points to the water. No words are spoken but I know what she is telling me: jump into the river and end your life and the life of your child.

I dared not speak to anyone in my family about my condition, not even my sisters, with whom I was normally close. My mother commented once or twice that I seemed moody and preoccupied, though she jested that I must be suffering greatly from the monthly curse, to judge by my behavior. If only I could have spoken to her about my situation, but alas, my loyalties were to Jonathan; I could not reveal our relationship to my parents without consulting him first.

I waited to meet with Jonathan at Sunday services, while again nature intervened. Several weeks elapsed before the trails into town were passable again. By then, I felt the press of time upon me: if I were forced to wait much longer, I would not be able to keep my secret to myself. I prayed during every waking moment for God to give me the opportunity to speak to Jonathan, soon.

The Lord must have heard my prayers, for at last the winter sun came out in its fullness for several days running, melting a goodly portion of the last snowfall. Finally, that Sunday we were able to hitch up the horse, bundle ourselves in cloaks, scarves, gloves, and blankets, and pack ourselves together, tightly, in the back of the wagon for our trip into town.

In the congregation hall, I felt conspicuous. God knew of my condition, of course, but I fancied everyone else in town did, too. I feared that my abdomen had begun to swell and all eyes were upon the unsightly bulge under my skirt—though surely it was too soon for that, and in any case it was doubtful that anyone could find anything amiss, given the layers of winter clothing. I pressed near my father and cowered behind a post throughout the service, wishing to be invisible, waiting for the opportunity to speak to Jonathan afterward.

As soon as Pastor Gilbert dismissed us for the day, I hurried down the stairs, not waiting for my father. I stood on the last step, searching for Jonathan. He emerged, soon enough, and made his way through the crowd toward me. Without a word, I took his hand firmly and drew him behind the staircase where we'd have more privacy.

The bold move made him nervous, and he glanced over his shoulder to see if anyone had taken notice that we'd stolen away. "Good God, Lanny, if you are thinking I should kiss you here—"

"Listen to me. I am with child," I blurted out.

He dropped my hand, and his handsome face shifted through a series of expressions: shock, a flush of surprise, a creeping realization that brought on pallor. Although I hadn't expected Jonathan to be happy with my news, his silence frightened me.

"Jonathan, speak to me. I do not know what to do." I tugged at his arm.

He took a sidelong glance at me, then cleared his throat. "Dear Lanny, I am at a loss to know what to say—"

"That is not what a girl wants to hear at a time like this!" Tears strained at my eyes. "Tell me I am not alone, tell me you will not desert me. Tell me that you will help me figure out what to do next."

He continued to behold me with great reluctance but said, stiffly, "You are not alone."

"You cannot imagine how frightened I've been, confined with this secret at home, unable to speak of it with anyone. I knew I had to tell you first, Jonathan. I owed you that." *Speak, speak*, I willed him; *tell me that you will confess your part in my downfall to our parents and that you will do right by me. Tell me that you still love me. That you will marry me.* I held my breath, tears rolling down my cheeks, almost faint with wishing to hear him speak those words.

But Jonathan could look at me no longer. His gaze fell to the floor. "Lanny, I have something I must tell you, but believe me when I say I would rather die than have to share this news with you right now."

I felt light-headed and a chill of fear broke over me like sweat. "What could be more important than what I have just told you—"

"I've been engaged. It was settled this week. My father is in the hall making the announcement now, but I had to find you and tell you myself. I didn't want you to hear from anyone else . . ." His words trailed off as he realized how little his courtesy meant to me now.

As we were growing up, we'd sometimes made light of the fact that Jonathan had not been betrothed. This business of betrothal was difficult in a village as small as St. Andrew. The best prospective brides and husbands were snapped up early, marriages arranged for children as young as six, so if your family hadn't acted promptly, there might not be a good choice to be had. One would think a boy of Jonathan's means and social stature would be an attractive candidate for any of the families in town with daughters. And he was, but a match had never been made, nor for his sisters, either. Jonathan said it was due to his mother's social aspirations: she didn't think any family in town would be advantageous enough for her children. They would surely do better among his father's business associates or through her own family's network in Boston. There had been flurries of inquiries over the years, some looking more solid than others, but they all seemed to peter out and Jonathan had approached his twentieth birthday with no bride in sight.

I felt as though my stomach had been opened with a butcher's knife. "To whom?"

He shook his head. "Now is not the time to speak of these things. It is your condition we should be talking about—"

"Who is it? I demand to know," I cried.

There was hesitation in his eyes. "It's one of the McDougal girls. Evangeline."

Even though my sisters were close to the McDougal girls, I struggled to recall which of them was Evangeline, because there was no shortage of them. The McDougals had seven daughters in all, a gaggle, all very pretty in a hardy Scots way, tall and sturdy, with ginger hair in coarse curls, and skin that freckled like copper trout in the summer. I could picture Mrs. McDougal, too, practical and good-natured, with her shrewd eye, perhaps more capable than her husband, who made a passing living as a farmer, but everyone knew it was Mrs. McDougal who made the farm turn a nice profit and had raised their standing in the town. I tried to see Jonathan with a woman like Mrs. McDougal at his side, and it made me want to fall in a heap at his feet.

"And you intend to proceed with the engagement?" I demanded.

"Lanny, I don't know what to say . . . I don't know that I *cannot* . . ." He took my hand and drew me back farther into a dusty corner. "The contract with the McDougals has been signed, the announcements made. I don't know what my parents will make of our—situation."

I could argue with him but knew that it would be futile. Marriage was a business arrangement, meant to enhance the prosperity of both families. An opportunity such as allegiance to a family like the St. Andrews would not just be given away, not for something as common as a pregnancy out of wedlock.

"It pains me to say this, but there would be objections to our marriage," Jonathan said as kindly as possible. I shook my head wearily; he did not have to tell me. My father may have been respected by his neighbors for his quiet good judgment, but we McIlvraes did not have much to recommend us to prospective spouses, being poor and half the family practicing Catholics.

After a while, I asked hoarsely, "And Evangeline—is she the one after Maureen?"

"She's the youngest," Jonathan replied. Then, after hesitating, he added, "She is fourteen."

The youngest—I could only picture the toddler brought by her sisters when they came to visit our house and work with Maeve and Glynnis on cross-stitch samplers. She had been a small pink-white thing, a pretty doll with gossamer gold tendrils and an unfortunate tendency to cry.

"So, the betrothal is set but the wedding date, if she is fourteen, that must be far off . . ."

Jonathan shook his head. "Old Charles wants us to wed this fall, if possible. By the end of the year, without fail."

I gave voice to the obvious. "He is desperate for you to continue the family name."

Jonathan wrapped his arm around my shoulders, holding me up, and I wished to cling to his strength and warmth forever. "Tell me, Lanny, what would you have us do? Tell me and I will do my best to make it so. Do you want me to tell my parents and ask them to release me from the marriage contract?"

A cold sadness washed over me. He said what I wanted to hear but I could tell that he was afraid of my answer. Although he had no desire to wed Evangeline, now that the inevitable had been arranged, he had reconciled himself to it. He didn't want me to take him up on his offer. And in all likelihood it would be unsuccessful anyway: I was unacceptable. His father may have wanted an heir, but his mother would insist on an heir who had been conceived in wedlock, a boy born free of scandal. Jonathan's parents would insist he go ahead with the marriage to Evangeline McDougal, and once word of my pregnancy got out, I would be ruined.

There was another way. Hadn't I said as much to Sophia, those few months ago?

I squeezed Jonathan's hand. "I could go to the midwife."

A look of gratitude lit up his face. "If that is what you want."

"I will—find a way to visit her as soon as possible."

"I can help with the expense," he said, fumbling at his pocket. He pressed a large coin into my hand. I was sickened, and resisted the urge to slap him, but I knew it was only out of anger. After staring at the coin for a second, I slipped it inside my glove.

"I am sorry," he whispered, kissing me on the forehead.

They were calling for Jonathan, his name echoing from the cavernous congregation hall. He left to answer the summons before we were discovered together, and I crept back up the stairs to the loft so I could see what was going on.

Jonathan's family stood in the aisle outside their box, the one closest to the pulpit as the place of honor. Charles St. Andrew was at the top of the aisle, arms raised as he made an announcement, but he looked more piqued than usual. He had been this way since the autumn, said it was exhaustion or too much wine (if anything, it would be a combination of too much wine and too much dallying with the servant girls). But it had been as though one day he suddenly turned older, grayer, and sagging of flesh. He tired easily, falling asleep in congregation as soon as Pastor Gilbert opened the Bible. He soon couldn't be bothered to attend the town council meetings and sent Jonathan in his place. None of us guessed at the time that he could be dying. He had forged the town with his own hands; he was indestructible, the courageous frontiersman, the prescient businessman. Looking back, that was probably why he'd pressed Jonathan to marry and start producing heirs: Charles St. Andrew sensed his time was running out.

The McDougals rushed down the aisle to join him in the formal announcement, Mr. and Mrs. McDougal like a pair of harried ducks followed by their ducklings, in a row, more or less descending in age. Seven girls, some properly tied and bowed, others windblown and tousled, with a hem or lace peeking from their garments.

And, at the very end, the baby of the family, Evangeline. A lump formed in my throat at the sight of her, she was that beautiful. No sturdy farm girl, Evangeline was just beginning to cross from child to woman. She was graceful and willowy, with modestly budding breasts and hips, and a cherub's lips. Her hair was golden still, and fell down her back in long ringlets. It was evident why Jonathan's mother had picked Evangeline: she was an angel sent to earth, a heavenly figure worthy of her eldest son's attentions.

I could have wept, there in the church. Instead, I bit my lip and watched as she brushed by Jonathan, giving him the faintest nod, stealing a glance up at him from under her bonnet. And he, pale-faced, nodded back. The entire congregation followed this minute exchange and understood what had transpired between the two young people in the fluttering of an eye.

"It's about time they found a wife for 'im," someone behind me muttered. "Now mebbe he'll quit chasin' after the girls like a dog in heat."

"A scandal, I say! The girl is but a child—"

"Hush now, the difference 'tween their years is but six, and a good many husbands are older than their women by more'n that . . ."

"True, in a few years' time it will make no difference, when the girl is eighteen or twenty. But fourteen! Think of our own daughter, Sarabeth; would you wish to see her married off to the St. Andrew boy?"

"Good heavens, no!"

Below, the rest of the McDougal girls formed a loose chain around Jonathan and their parents, while Evangeline stood shyly a pace behind her father. *Now is no time to be coy*, I thought at the time, straining to hear what was being said below. *You are the one he will wed. That handsome man is to be your husband, the one who will take you to his bed every night. He is a hard man to give your heart to, and you must prove yourself up to the challenge. Go stand next to him.* Eventually, with much urging from her parents, she stepped out awkwardly from behind her father, like a newborn foal trying out its legs. It wasn't until they stood side by side that it struck me: she *was* still a child. He towered over her, so much larger than she was. I pictured them lying together in bed, and he looked as though he could crush her. She was small and trembled like a leaf at his slightest attention.

He took her hand and stepped closer to her. There was something gallant about the gesture, almost protective. But then Jonathan leaned over and kissed her. It was not his usual kiss, the one I had memorized, the one so powerful that you'd feel it down to your toes. But he'd signaled that he'd accepted the marriage contract by kissing her in full sight of their families and the congregation. And in front of me.

I understood Sophia's message to me, then, from the dream. She wasn't exhorting me to kill myself in recompense for what I had done to her. She was telling me that I had a life of disappointment before me if I continued to love Jonathan as I did, as she had. A love that is too strong can turn poisonous and bring great unhappiness. And then, what is the remedy? Can you unlearn your heart's desire? Can you stop loving someone? Easier to drown yourself, Sophia seemed to be telling me; easier to take the lover's leap.

All this reverberated in my mind as I watched from the balcony, tears forming, my fingers digging into the soft pine railing. I was high above the congregation floor, high enough to take the lover's leap. But I didn't; even then I was mindful of the baby inside. Instead, I turned and ran down the steps and away from the wrenching scene before me.

TWELVE

I rode home from church in silence in the wagon with my father. He kept an eye on me, wrapped in my cloak and scarf but shivering and with teeth chattering, even though the winter sun had come out and painted us both in sunlight. He said nothing, undoubtedly attributing my ill appearance and reticence to the news of Jonathan's betrothal. We stopped at the tumbledown Catholic church and found my mother, sisters, and Nevin waiting in the snow, blue-lipped and chiding us for being late as they climbed into the wagon.

"Hush now, we have good reason for the delay," my father said to them in a tone that meant he would brook no nonsense. "Jonathan's betrothal was announced after the service today." Considerately, there was no merrymaking among the rest of them, only glances from my sisters and a sneer of "Pity the girl, whoever she be!" from my brother.

When we arrived at our farm, Nevin unharnessed the horse while Father went to check on the cattle, and my sisters took advantage of the sunny day to see to the chickens. I followed my mother desultorily into the house. She bustled around the kitchen, getting ready to work on the evening meal, while I sat on a chair in front of a window, still in my cloak.

My mother was no fool. "Would you like a cup of tea, Lanore?" she called from the hearth.

"I do not care," I said, careful to keep a warble of sadness out of my voice. My back to her, I listened to the clatter of a heavy pot hung on the hook over the fire and the splash of water poured from the bucket of drawn water.

"I see you are upset, Lanore. But you knew this day would come," she said at length, firmly but kindly. "You knew one day Master Jonathan would marry, as will you. We told you having such a strong friendship with a boy was inadvisable. Now you see what we meant."

I let a tear dribble down my face since she couldn't see me. I felt weak, as though I'd been trampled on and battered by one of the bulls in the field. I needed to turn to someone; I knew at that moment, sitting there, that I would die if I had to keep this secret to myself any longer. The question was, who could I trust in my family?

My mother had always been kind to us children, defending us when my father's upright sensibility got the better of him and his scolding grew too harsh. She was a woman and had been pregnant six times, with two babes buried in the churchyard; surely she would understand how I felt and would protect me.

"Mother, I have something I must tell you, but I am terrified of how you might react, you and Father. Please promise me that you will still love me after I have said what I must," I said, my voice quaking.

I heard a muffled cry escape my mother, followed by the sound of a mixing spoon clattering to the floor, and I knew I had to say no more. For all her advice to me, for all her pleading and nagging, her worst fear had come true.

Nevin was made to hitch the horse up to the wagon again and go with my sisters to the Dales' house on the other side of the valley, and stay there until our father fetched them. I was left alone with my parents in the darkening house, sitting on a stool in the middle of the room as my mother cried softly to herself by the fire and my father paced around me.

I'd never seen my father so enraged. His face was red and bloated, his hands white from clenching them into fists. The only thing that kept him from striking me, I believe, were the tears flowing down my face.

"How could you do it?" my father railed at me. "How could you give yourself to the St. Andrew boy? Are you no better than a common harlot? Whatever possessed you?"

"He loves me, Father—"

My words were too much provocation for my father; he lashed out and struck me hard across my cheek. Even my mother sucked in her breath in surprise. The pain radiated sharply from my jaw, but it was the rawness of his anger that stunned me.

"Is that what he told you? Are you stupid enough to believe him, Lanore?"

"You're wrong. He really does love me—"

He drew his hand back to hit me a second time but stopped himself. "Do you not think he's said as much to every girl who'd listen to him, to get them to give in to his desire? If his feelings for you are true, why is he betrothed to the McDougal girl?"

"I don't know," I gasped, wiping tears from my cheeks.

"Kieran," my mother said sharply, "don't be cruel."

"It's a hard lesson," my father said back to her, looking over his shoulder. "The McDougals have my pity, and 'tis a shame for the wee Evangeline, but I'd not have St. Andrew for a son-in-law."

"Jonathan is not a bad man," I protested.

"Listen to yourself! Defending the man who made ye pregnant and hasn't the decency to be standing here beside ye, giving your family the news!" my father bellowed. "I take it the bastard knows about your state—"

"He does."

"And what about the captain? Do you think he had the spine to tell his father?"

"I—don't know."

"I doubt it," my father said, resuming his pacing, his heels clattering loudly against the pine floorboards. "And it's just as well. I want no part of that family. Do you hear me? No part. I've made my decision, Lanore: you will be sent away to have your baby. Far away." He stared straight ahead, not even a glance in my direction. "We will send you to Boston in a few weeks, when the road is passable, to a place where you can have your child. A convent." He looked to my mother, who stared at her hands as she nodded. "The sisters will find a home for it, a good Catholic home, to ease your mother's heart."

"You're going to take my child away from me?" I started to rise from the stool but my father pushed me back down.

"Of course. You cannot bring your shame back with you to St. Andrew. I won't have our neighbors knowing you are another of the St. Andrew boy's conquests."

I started crying again, violently. The baby would be all I had of Jonathan; how could I give it away?

My mother crept over to me and took my hands in hers. "You must think of your family, Lanore. Think of your sisters. Think of the shame if word were to get out in town. Who would want their sons to marry your sisters after such a disgrace?"

"I would think my failings should be no reflection on my sisters," I said, hoarsely, but I knew the truth. The righteous townsfolk would make my sisters—and my parents—suffer for my misdeeds. I lifted my head. "So . . . will you not tell the captain of my condition?"

My father stopped pacing and turned to face me. "I'll not give the old bastard the satisfaction of knowing that my daughter could not resist his son." He shook his head. "You may think the worst of me, Lanore. I pray that I am doing the right thing by you. I only know that I must try to save you from complete ruin."

I felt no gratitude. Selfish as I was, my first thought was not of my family and their hurt but of Jonathan. I would be forced to leave my home and I would never see Jonathan again. The thought was a blade pushed into my heart.

"Must I leave?" I asked, misery breaking my voice. "Why can't I go to the midwife? Then I could stay. No one would know."

My father's cold stare wounded me more deeply than another blow. "*I* would know, Lanore. I would know and your mother would know. Some families may condone it but . . . we cannot let you. It would be a monstrous sin, even worse than the one you've already committed."

So I was not only a bad daughter and a helpless puppet for Jonathan's desires, but I had it in my heart to be a godless murderer as well. I wanted to die at that moment, but shame alone was insufficient. "I see," I said, wiping at the cold wetness on my cheeks, determined to cry no more in front of my father.

Oh, the shame and the terror I felt that night. Today, looking back, it seems ridiculous to be so ashamed, so terrified. But then, I was just another victim of propriety, shaking and crying in my parents' house, crushed under the weight of my father's demands. A helpless soul about to be exiled to the cruel world. It would take many years for me to forgive myself. At the time, I thought my life was over. My father knew me for a harlot and a monster, and he was taking me away from the only thing that mattered to me. I couldn't imagine going on.

The worst of winter passed; the short, dark days lengthening and skies that had been perpetually overcast, the color of old flannel, beginning to lighten. I wondered if I, too, was changing incrementally with the baby inside me or if any changes to my body were all in my head. After all, I'd always been slender, and in my predicament had lost my appetite. My clothing did not bind me, as I'd expected it would, but perhaps that was only guilt fanning my imagination. In odd moments, too, I wondered if Jonathan thought about me, if he knew I was being sent away and was sorry for having abandoned me. Perhaps he assumed I'd done as promised, seen the midwife and gotten purged.

Perhaps he was distracted by his impending wedding. I had no way of knowing: I was no longer allowed to go to Sunday services and so my only chance to see Jonathan was taken away from me.

The days passed in dreary sameness. My father kept me employed every minute, from when we woke in the semidarkness of a new day until I laid my head on my pillow at night. Sleep brought no respite, for I frequently dreamed of Sophia: rising from the frigid Allagash, standing like a plume of smoke in the graveyard, circling my house in the darkness as a restless ghost. Perhaps her ghost found some comfort in my suffering.

I knelt at my bedside before retiring in the evening and wondered if it would be blasphemous to ask God to extricate me from this predicament. If banishment was to be my punishment for my grievous sins, oughtn't I accept my lot rather than petition God for clemency?

My sisters grew sad as winter waned and the day of my leaving grew closer. They spent as much time as they could with me, not speaking of my departure, but sitting with me, hugging me, pressing their foreheads against mine. They worked furiously with my mother to mend my wardrobe, not wanting to send me away looking so rustic, and even made me a new cloak of last year's spring wool.

The inevitable would not be delayed forever, and one night, when the thaw had settled on the valley in earnest, my father told me that the arrangements had been made. I would leave the next Sunday on the provisioner's wagon, escorted by the town tutor, Titus Abercrombie. From Presque Isle, we would ride in a coach to Camden, then travel by ship to Boston. The family's one trunk was packed with my belongings and left by the door, a paper with the name of all my contacts—ship's captain, mother superior of the convent—sewn into the lining of a petticoat along with all the coin my family could spare. My sisters spent that night huddled against me in our wide bed, unwilling to let go of me.

"I don't understand why Father is sending you away."

"He wouldn't listen, no matter how we begged."

"We shall miss you."

"Will we see you again? Will you come to our weddings? Will you stand beside us at our babies' baptisms?" Their questions brought tears to my eyes, too. I kissed them gently on their foreheads and held them tightly.

"Of course you'll see me again. I'll only be gone a short while. No more tears, eh? So much will happen while I'm away, you won't notice my absence at all." They cried out in denial, promising to think of me every day. I let them cry themselves to exhaustion before lying awake the rest of the night, trying to find peace in the last few hours before dawn.

When we arrived, the drivers were hitching the horses to the wagons, now empty, having delivered loads of dry goods—milled flour, bolts of fabric, fine needles, tea—to the Watfords' store the day before. Three large wagons, and six brawny men made the last adjustments to the harnesses and doubletrees, and watched sheepishly as my family huddled around me. My sisters and mother were pressed tight, tears streaming down their faces. My father and Nevin stood to the side, gruff and emotionless.

One of the drivers coughed, reluctant to impose but anxious to depart on schedule.

"Time to be going," Father said. "Into the carriage with you, girls." He waited while my mother embraced me a last time, as Nevin helped the driver load my trunk into the empty wagon bed. My father turned to me.

"This is your opportunity to redeem yourself, Lanore. God has seen fit to give you another chance, so do not be frivolous with his beneficence. Your mother and I will pray that you safely deliver your child, but do not think about refusing the sisters' assistance in placing the baby with another family. I am ordering you to not keep the child, and if you see fit not to heed my orders, you would do just as well to not return to St. Andrew. If you do not transform yourself into a proper God-fearing Christian, I wish never to hear from you again."

Stunned, I went to the wagon, where Titus waited for me. With a chivalrous dignity, he helped me climb onto the bench next to him. "My dear, it is my pleasure to chaperone you as far as Camden," he said in the stiffly formal, though friendly, tone I'd heard Jonathan mock. I didn't know Titus well as I'd never taken a class with him and only had stories from Jonathan by which to judge him. He was an older gentleman, on the delicate side, with the constitution of a scholar: bandy arms and legs, a little potbelly that had grown over the years. He'd lost most of his hair, and what was left had turned gray, leaving his bald pate with a wispy fringe in the style of Benjamin Franklin. He was one of the few men in town to wear spectacles, a spindly pair of wire frames that made his pale gray eyes seem smaller and even more watery. Titus spent the summer months in Camden tutoring his cousin's children in Latin in exchange for his keep, since all of his students in St. Andrew worked on their family farms until school began in the fall.

As the wagon lurched to life, I cried copiously, returning my mother's and sisters' frantic waves through my tears.

As the town rolled by, the aching in my throat and heart intensified as I watched the only place I'd ever known shrink into the distance and said good-bye to everyone—and to the only one—I'd ever loved.

THIRTEEN

FORT KENT ROAD, PRESENT DAY

The border crossing is not far away. Although Luke hasn't driven there in years, not since taking the family on some half-assed vacation to the Appalachain Range trail, he's pretty sure he can still find it without looking at a map. He takes back roads, which are slower and will take longer, but he figures they'll be less likely to run into any state troopers or other police officers; there are too few of them to watch secondary roads or bother with small towns. The highway, that's where the trouble is, speeders and overweight long-haul truckers, the money offenses that will bring in revenue for the state.

He grips the steering wheel in the dead center and steers with one hand. His passenger stares doggedly at the road in front of them, biting her lower lip. She looks even more like a teenager, burying concern under a veil of impatience.

"So," he says, trying to warm the air between them. "Do you mind if I ask you a couple of questions?"

"Be my guest."

"Well, can you tell me what it feels like to be—what you are?"

"It doesn't feel like anything special."

"Really?"

She leans back in her seat and puts her elbow on the armrest. "I don't feel any different, not that I can remember anyway. I don't notice change on a day-to-day basis and not in the ways that matter. It's not like I have superpowers or anything. I'm not a character in a comic book." She smiles to let him know that she doesn't think it's a stupid question.

"That thing you did in the ER, cutting yourself? Did that hurt?"

"Not really. The pain is very minor, just feels sort of dull, maybe like how surgery would feel if you got a low dose of anesthesia. Only the person who made you like this can hurt you, can really make you feel pain. It's been so long I've forgotten what pain feels like—almost."

"A *person* did this to you?" Luke asks, incredulous. "How did it happen?"

"I'm getting to that," she answers, still smiling. "Be patient."

The revelation that this miracle is man-made almost makes Luke dizzy, like suddenly looking at a landscape from a different perspective. It seems all the more impossible—more the chance that this is a deception by a pretty and manipulative young woman.

"Anyway," she continues, "I'm pretty much the same as I was before except I don't really get tired. I don't get exhausted physically. But I get emotionally tired."

"Depressed?"

"Yeah, that's probably what it is. There are a lot of reasons, I suppose. Mostly, it just gets to me every once in a while, the futility of my life, having no choice but to live through every day, day after day. What is the point of enduring all this time alone, I wonder, except to make me suffer, to be reminded of the bad things I've done or the way I might have treated people? It's not like I can do anything about it. I can't go back in time and undo the mistakes I've made."

This is not the answer he expected. He repositions his hand on the wheel while it vibrates hard in his palm as they travel over a rough patch of macadam. "Do you want me to prescribe something for you?"

She laughs. "Antidepressants, you mean? I don't think it would do much good."

"Medications have no effect on you?"

"Let's just say I've built up a pretty high tolerance." She shifts away from him now, facing the window. "Obliteration is the only way out of your head, sometimes."

"Obliteration—you mean alcohol? Drugs?"

"Can we stop talking about this?" Her voice wavers at the end.

"Sure. Are you hungry? It's probably been a while since you've eaten . . . Want to stop for a bite? There's a place that makes good doughnuts over near Fort Kent . . ."

She shakes her head noncommittally. "I'm never hungry anymore. I can go for weeks before I think about eating. Or drinking, for that matter."

"And what about sleeping? Do you want to take a nap?"

"Don't sleep much, either. I just forget about it. After all, the best part of sleeping is having someone next to you, isn't it? A warm body, a heavy weight leaning against you. It's very comforting, don't you think? How your breathing falls into a rhythm together, gets synchronized. It's heavenly." Did that mean there hadn't been a man in her bed in a while? Luke wondered. Then what of the dead man in the morgue, the mussed sheets at the cabin—what did it all mean? Or maybe she was playing him, covering up what she is really like.

"Do you miss having your wife with you in bed?" she asks, after a beat, prodding him.

Of course he did, even though his ex-wife had been a light, restless sleeper and frequently jolted him awake when she tried to get comfortable or acted out in a dream. By the same token, he loved seeing her asleep in their bed when he came home from a late evening at the hospital, her long, elegant body draped by the covers, all gently rising and falling curves. The crush of golden hair looped about her head, her mouth slightly open; there was something about seeing her, unaware, that made her beautiful to him, the memory of those intimate scenes forcing a knot to rise in his throat. That is too much to confide to a stranger, his loneliness and regret, so he says nothing.

"How long has she been gone? Your wife?" Lanny asks.

He shrugs. "Nearly a year now. She's going to marry her childhood sweetheart. She moved back to Michigan. Took our two daughters."

"That's—terrible. I'm sorry."

"Don't waste your sympathy on me. It sounds as though you're dealing with something much, much worse." He has that feeling again, the same one he had outside the morgue, disorientation at the clash of her story with the world as he knows it. How could she possibly be telling the truth?

Just then, he thinks he sees the flash of a black-and-white patrol car in the rearview mirror as he makes a right turn. Had it been following them the whole time, Luke wonders, and he hadn't noticed? Could the police be after them? The thought carries a special kind of discomfort for a man who has never been in trouble with the law.

"What is it?" Lanny asks suddenly, straightening up. "Something's happened, I can tell by the look on your face."

Luke keeps his eye on the rearview mirror. "Take it easy. I don't want you to be alarmed, but I think we're being followed."

PART II

FOURTEEN

The trip south in the provisioner's wagon took two weeks. It skirted the eastern edge of the Great North Woods, went wide enough of Mount Katahdin to keep us from seeing the snow-capped mountaintop, then picked up the Kennebec River, which we followed down to Camden. It was a lonely trip through that part of the state; not widely settled now, it was practically empty then. We'd passed trappers and occasionally camped with them for the night, the wagon drivers anxious to have someone to share a bottle of whiskey with.

The trappers we met were generally French Canadians and were often either stoic or strange, the trade suiting those who were hermits or fierce independents at heart. A few of them seemed to me to be half mad, gibbering to themselves in an unsettling way as they cleaned and oiled their tools before settling down to work on the game they'd caught. Frozen animals would be set by the campfire until they'd thawed enough to be malleable, and then the trappers would take out their narrow-bladed knives and set to skinning. Watching the men peel back the skin and reveal the wet, red bodies made me nauseous and uneasy. Having no desire to sit with them, I'd slink away to the wagons with Titus and leave the drivers to pass the bottle with the trappers in the warm embrace of the campfire.

While unhappy about my exile, I'd always wanted to see something of the world outside my village. St. Andrew might not have been sophisticated, but I had assumed it was civilized in comparison with most parts of the territory, which were largely unsettled. Aside from the trappers, we saw few other people on our journey to Camden. The Indians who were native to the area had moved on years before, though there were a few living in the white settlements or working with the trappers. There were tales of settlers who'd gone native, leaving their towns to set up camps in imitation of the Indians, but they were few and generally surrendered during their first winter.

The trip through the Great North Woods promised to be dark and mysterious. Pastor Gilbert warned of evil spirits that lay in wait for travelers. The axmen claimed to have seen trolls and goblins—to be expected, as most of them were from Scandinavian lands where such folklore was common. The Great North Woods represented the wild, the part of the land that had resisted man's influence. To enter was to risk being swallowed up, reverting to the wild man who was still inside each of us. Most of the people of St. Andrew would claim not to put much stock in this talk in public, but it was a rare soul who went into the woods by himself at night.

Some of the drivers liked to try to frighten one another by telling tales around the campfire, stories of ghosts seen in graveyards or demons encountered in the woods while driving a route. I tried to avoid them at such times but often there was nothing for it, as we'd have only one fire burning and all the men were hungry for entertainment. Judging from the drivers' frightening stories, I suppose they were either very brave or terrible liars, because despite their tales of wandering ghosts and banshees and such, they were still willing to drive a wagon through lonely stretches of wilderness.

Most of the stories were about ghosts, and as I listened, it struck me that all the ghosts seemed to have one trait in common: they haunted the living because they had unfinished business on this earth. Whether they were murdered or died by their own hands, the ghosts refused to move on to the afterlife because they felt they belonged in this world rather than the next. Whether to exact vengeance on the person responsible for their death or because they couldn't bear to leave a loved one, the ghost remained close to the people from its last days. Naturally I thought of Sophia. If anyone had a right to come back as a ghost, it was she. Would Sophia be angered when she came back and found that the person most responsible for her suicide had left town? Or would she follow me? Perhaps she had cursed me from the grave and was responsible for my current unhappy situation. Listening to the drivers' stories only reinforced my belief that I was damned for my wickedness.

And so I was cheered and relieved when we started to come across small settlements with more frequency: it meant we were approaching the more populated southern part of the territory and I would not be at the mercy of the wagon drivers much longer. Indeed, within a few days of finding the Kennebec River, we arrived in Camden, a big town on the sea coast. It was the first time I would see the ocean.

The wagon dropped me and Titus off at the harbor, as that was the agreement with my father, and I ran out on the longest pier and stood staring at the green water for a long time. What a singular smell, the smell of the ocean, salty and dirty and coarse. The wind was very cold and very strong, so strong that it was almost impossible to catch my breath. It buffeted my face and tangled my hair, as though it were challenging me. Then, too, I was taken with the vastness of the ocean. I'd known water, yes, but only the Allagash River. Wide as it was, you could see the riverbank on the far side and the trees beyond that. In contrast, with its never-ending horizon the flat expanse of ocean looked like the very end of the world.

"You know, the first explorers to travel to America believed they might fall off the edge of the world," Titus said, reminding me that he was at my elbow.

I found the raking green tide frightening but mesmerizing as well, and I couldn't tear myself away until I was nearly frozen to the bone.

The tutor escorted me to the harbormaster's office, where we found an old man with frightening leathery skin. He pointed the way to the small ship that would take me down to Boston, but cautioned me that it wasn't sailing until near midnight, when the tide would be going out. I wouldn't be welcome onboard until shortly before it would make sail. He suggested I spend the time in a public house, get something to eat and perhaps convince the innkeeper to let me pass the hours napping on a spare bed. He even gave me directions to a tavern close to the harbor, taking pity on me, I suspect, because I could barely make myself understood, tongue-tied from nerves and so obviously unsophisticated. If Camden were this big and intimidating, how in the world would I find my way in Boston?

"Miss McIlvrae, I must protest. You cannot stay unescorted in a public house, nor can you walk the streets of Camden by yourself at midnight to find your ship," Titus said. "But I am expected at my cousin's house and can scarcely remain with you the rest of the day."

"What other choice do I have?" I asked. "If it would ease your conscience, walk me to the public house and see for yourself if it is respectable, and then do as your mind dictates. That way, you won't feel as though you've betrayed your assurances to my father."

The only public house I knew was Daughtery's tiny homespun place in St. Andrew, and this public house in Camden dwarfed Daughtery's, with two barmaids and long tables with benches, and hot food for purchase. The beer was considerably tastier, too, and I realized with a pang that the people back home were deprived of so many things. The unfairness of it struck me, although I didn't feel privileged for being introduced to it now. Mostly, I felt homesick and sorry for myself, but I hid this from Titus who, anxious to be on his way, agreed that it didn't seem to be a place of ill repute and left me to the innkeeper's care.

After I'd eaten and had my fill of gawking at strangers who came into the pub, I accepted the invitation of the innkeeper to nap on a cot in the storage room until my ship was ready for boarding. Apparently it was common for passengers to pass the time at this particular inn and the innkeeper was used to providing this service. He promised to wake me after the sun set, in plenty of time for me to get to the harbor.

I lay on the cot in the windowless storage room and took stock of my situation. It was then—curled up in the dark, arms hugged tight around my chest—that I became aware of how alone I was. I had grown up in a place where I was known to all and there was no question of where I belonged or who would take care of me. No one here or in Boston knew me or cared to know me. Heavy tears rolled down my face in self-pity; I didn't imagine, at the time, that my father could have come up with a more brutal punishment.

I awoke in darkness to the rapping of the innkeeper's knuckles on the door. "It's time you got up," he called from the other side of the door, "or you'll be missing your ship." I paid with a few coins I pried out of the lining of my cloak, took his offer of an escort as far as the harbormaster's office, and retraced my steps down the waterfront to the pier.

Evening had fallen quickly, along with the temperature, and a fog started to roll in from the ocean. There were few people on the street and the ones who were about hurried home to get out of the chill and the fog. The overall effect was eerie, as though I was walking through a town of the dead. The innkeeper was friendly enough despite the late hour and we followed the sound of the lapping ocean to the harbor.

Through the fog I saw the ship that would take me to Boston. Its deck was dotted with lanterns, illuminating the preparations being made to set sail: seamen clambered on the masts, unfurling some of the sails; casks were rolled up a gangplank for storage in the hold, the ship buoying gently under its shifting weight.

I know now that it was a common cargo ship, but at the time it was as exotic as a full-masted British ship-of-the-line, or an Araby *baghlah*, the first real seagoing vessel I'd ever seen up close. Fear and excitement rose up in my throat—they would be my ever-constant companions now, fear of the unknown and an irrepressible willingness for adventure—as I strode up the gangplank to the ship, another step further away from all I knew and loved, and another step closer to my mysterious new life.

FIFTEEN

Several days later, the ship closed in on Boston's harbor. By afternoon we had docked, but I waited until dusk to creep out on the ship's deck. It was quiet now: the other passengers had disembarked as soon as the ship was made fast in its berth and most of the cargo, it appeared, had been unloaded. The crew members, at least those faces I remembered, were nowhere to be seen, probably out rediscovering the benefits of being on land by visiting one of the taverns that faced the harbor. To judge by the number of such establishments on the street, taverns were an integral part of the business of shipping, more important than timber or sailcloth.

We had docked far ahead of schedule owing to good winds, but it was only a matter of time before the convent was notified and dispatched someone to fetch me. As a matter of fact, the captain had eyed me curiously once or twice as I lingered belowdecks, wondering why I hadn't left already, and even offered to find transportation to take me to my destination if I was unsure of the way.

I didn't want to go to the convent. In my mind, I'd built it up to be something between a workhouse and a prison. It was to be my punishment, a place designed to "correct" me by any means possible, to cure me of being in love with Jonathan. They would take my baby away from me, my last and only connection to my beloved. How could I allow such a thing?

On the other hand, I was terrified of striking out on my own. The uncertainties I'd faced in Camden were a hundred times worse in Boston, which seemed like a vast, teeming city. How would I find my way about? To whom would I turn for help, a place to stay, particularly in my condition? I suddenly felt every inch the unschooled country girl from the wilderness, completely out of her depth.

Cowardice and indecision had kept me from fleeing the ship immediately, but in the end, it was the thought of losing my child that made me decide to leave. I would rather sleep in a filthy alley and earn my keep scrubbing floors than let someone take this baby away from me. Thoroughly worked into a frenzy, I took to the streets of Boston with only my little satchel, abandoning the trunk to the harbormaster's office. Hopefully I would find it later when I had secured a residence. That is, if the convent didn't confiscate it on my behalf when they found out I was missing.

Even though I'd waited till dusk to sneak off the ship, I was surprised and frightened by the amount of activity still going on. People spilled out of public houses and into the streets, they packed the sidewalks, or rattled by in carriages. Wagons loaded with barrels and boxes as big as coffins rolled through the busy streets. I trudged up one street and down another, sidestepping other pedestrians, ducking wagons, unable to absorb the layout of the roads in any meaningful way, unable to tell after fifteen minutes of walking which way the harbor lay. I began to think Boston a cheerless and harsh place: hundreds of people had streamed past me that night but not one took notice of my fearstruck expression, the lost look in my eye, my aimless wandering. No one asked if I needed help.

Dusk gave way to darkness. Streetlamps were lit. Traffic began to thin as people hurried home for the evening, while shopkeepers drew curtains and locked doors. Panic bloomed in my chest again: where would I sleep that night? And the next night, and the night after that, for that matter? No, I told myself, I mustn't think too far ahead or else I'd fall into despair. Getting through that first night was worry enough. I needed a good plan or I would start to wish I'd surrendered to the convent.

The answer was a public house or an inn. The cheapest possible, I thought, fingering the few coins I had left. The neighborhood I had stumbled into seemed residential and I struggled to recall where I had last passed a public establishment. Had it been closer to the docks? Probably, yet I hesitated to backtrack, thinking that would only confirm that I didn't know what I was doing and that I'd put myself in the worst possible situation. I was unsure of which direction I'd come from, anyway. Psychologically, it was best to keep moving into new territory.

So frazzled was I that I stood in the middle of the road pondering my next move, oblivious to the traffic that in a busier part of the city would have run me over. In my preoccupation it took me a minute to realize a carriage had pulled beside me and that I was being hailed.

"Miss! Hello, miss," a voice called from inside the coach. And a handsome coach it was, finer by degrees than any coarse country wagon I'd ever seen. The dark wood glistened with oil and all its appointments were extremely delicate and well crafted. It was drawn by a pair of heavy bays, groomed as ornately as circus horses but fitted with black harnesses like a funeral trap.

"I say, don't you speak English?" A man appeared at the window of the coach, wearing an extraordinarily fancy three-cornered hat, edged with burgundy plumes. He was pale and blond with a long, aristocratic face, but had a withering, pinched set to his mouth, as though he was eternally displeased. I looked up at him, surprised that such a fine stranger was addressing me.

"Oh, let me try," a woman said from within the coach. The man in the hat withdrew from the window and a woman took his place. If the first man was pale, she was far paler, her skin the color of snow. She wore a very dark dress of maroon moiré taffeta, which was perhaps what gave her skin its bloodless quality. She was lovely but frightening, with pointed teeth concealed behind lips stretched in a tight, insincere smile. Her eyes were of a blue so pale that they appeared lavender. And what I could see of her hair—she, too, sported an ornate hat, riding high on her head at a daring angle—was the color of buttercups, but heavily dressed and worn close to the skull.

"Don't be frightened," she said before I even realized that I *was*, a little. I stood back as she opened the carriage door and descended to the street, rustling as she moved owing to the stiffness of the fabric and the fullness of her skirt. Her dress was the fanciest garment I'd ever seen, adorned with miniature ruffles and bows, drawn tightly around her tiny wasp's waist. She wore black gloves and reached a hand toward me slowly, as though she was afraid of scaring away a timid dog. The hatted man was joined by a second man who took her place in the carriage window.

"Are you all right? My friends and I couldn't help but notice as we passed that you seem at a loss." Her smile warmed by a degree.

"I—well, that is . . . ," I hemmed, embarrassed that someone had found me out, while at the same time desperate for any assistance and a touch of human kindness.

"Are you newly arrived in Boston?" the second man in the carriage asked from his perch. He seemed infinitely nicer than the first, with dark features and exquisitely kind eyes and a gentleness that invited trust.

I nodded.

"And do you have a place to stay? Forgive me for presuming, but you have the air of an orphan about you. Homeless, friendless?" The woman stroked my arm while he asked this.

"Thank you for your concern. Perhaps you could point me in the direction of the nearest public house," I began, shifting the weight of the satchel in my hand.

By then, the tall, haughty man had descended from the carriage, too, and snatched my bag away from me. "We'll do better than that. We'll give you a place to stay. Tonight."

The woman took my arm and steered me toward the coach. "We're going to a party. You like parties, don't you?"

"I—don't know," I stammered, my senses tingling in warning. How could three people of means just come from out of nowhere to rescue me? It seemed natural—prudent, even—to be skeptical.

"Don't speak nonsense. How can you not know if you like to go to parties? Everyone likes parties. There will be food and plenty of drink, and fun. And at the end of it, there will be a warm bed for you." The haughty man heaved my satchel into the coach. "Besides, do you have a better offer? Would you rather sleep on the street? I think not."

He was right and, intuition aside, I had no choice except to obey. I even convinced myself that this chance meeting was a matter of good fortune. My needs had been answered, at least for the time being. They were expensively dressed and it stood to reason, well off; they could hardly be planning to rob me. Nor did they look like murderers. Why they were so eager to take a stranger to a party with them was a complete mystery, however, but it seemed risky to question my good fortune too strenuously.

We rode along in tense silence for a few minutes. I sat between the woman and the convivial dark-haired man and tried not to notice as the blond man picked me over with his eyes. When I couldn't contain my curiosity any longer I asked, "Excuse me, but why is it, exactly, that you require my attendance at this party? Won't the host be annoyed to receive an unexpected guest?"

The woman and the haughty man snorted, as though I'd told a joke. "Oh, don't worry about that. The host is our friend, you see, and we happen to know for a fact that he enjoys entertaining pretty young women," the blond man said with another snort. The woman rapped her fan across the back of his hand.

"Don't mind these two," the dark-haired man said. "They are making merry at your expense. You have my word that you will be entirely welcome. As you said, you need a place to stay the night and, I suspect, to put your troubles aside for one evening. Perhaps you'll find something else you need there as well," he said, and he had such a gentle way about him that I softened. There were many things I needed, but most of all I wanted to trust him. Trust that he knew what would be best for me when I myself didn't know.

We rattled up and down streets in the dark trap. I kept watch out the window and tried to memorize the route, like a child in a fairy tale who might need to find her way home. It was a waste of time; I couldn't hope to retrace my journey, not in the state I was in. Eventually, the carriage pulled up in front of a mansion of brick and stone, lit up for a party, so grand it took the breath from me. But apparently the party hadn't started; there was no activity to be seen, no men and women in evening dress, no other carriages pulling up to the curb.

Footmen opened the doors to the mansion and the woman led the way as though she was the mistress of the house, pulling her gloves off finger by finger. "Where is he?" she snapped at a liveried butler.

His eyes briefly rolled skyward. "Upstairs, ma'am."

As we climbed the stairs, I felt more and more self-conscious. Here I was, dressed in a shabby, homemade frock. I reeked of the ship and of seawater and my hair was tangled and tossed with salt spray. I looked down at my feet to see my simple, rustic shoes crusted with mud from the streets, the toes curling up from hard use.

I touched the woman's arm. "I shouldn't be here. I'm in no state for a fancy affair. I'm not even fit to be a kitchen girl in this fine house. I will take my leave—"

"You will stay until we give you permission to leave." She whirled and dug her fingernails into my forearm, making me gasp at the pain. "Now stop being a ninny and come along. I guarantee you will enjoy yourself tonight." Her tone told me that my enjoyment was the last thing on her mind.

The four of us burst through a set of doors into a bedchamber, a massive room as big as my family's entire house back in St. Andrew.

The woman led us straight into the dressing room where a man stood with his back to us. He was obviously the master of the house, a valet waiting at his side. The master was dressed in bright blue velvet breeches and white silk stockings, fancy slippers on his feet. He wore a lace-edged shirt and waistcoat to match the breeches. He hadn't donned his frock coat, so I had a clear view of his true form without a tailor's tricks to enhance his build. He wasn't as tall and athletic as Jonathan—my yardstick for the masculine ideal—but nonetheless possessed a magnificent physique. A broad back and shoulders blossomed from his narrow hips. He'd be terrifically strong, judging from those shoulders, like some of the axmen back in St. Andrew, stocky and powerful. And then he turned around and I tried not to show my surprise.

He was much younger than I expected, in his twenties I would have guessed, older than I by only a few years. And he was good looking in an unfamiliar way, vaguely savage. He had an olive complexion, which I'd never seen before in our village of Scots and Scandinavians. His dark mustache and beard were wispy along a square jaw, as though they'd not been growing in for long. But his strangest feature was his eyes, olive colored and struck through with gray and gold. They were like two jewels in their beauty, and yet his stare was wolfish and mesmerizing.

"We've brought another entertainment for your party," the woman announced.

His appraising gaze was as rough as a pair of hands; after one look, I felt I had no secrets from him. My throat went dry, my knees soft.

"This is our host." The woman's voice drifted over my shoulder. "Curtsy, you simpleton. You are in the presence of royalty. This is the Count cel Rau."

"My name is Adair." He stretched a hand toward me, as though to keep me from bowing. "We are in America, Tilde. I understand Americans will not have royalty in their country and so they will not bow to anyone. We must not expect Americans to bow to us."

"You've just arrived in America?" Somehow I found the courage to speak to him.

"A fortnight ago." He dropped my hand and turned back to his valet.

"From Hungary," the short, dark man added. "Do you know where that is?"

My head swam. "No, I'm afraid not." More snorts of laughter sounded behind my back.

"It's not important," this Adair, the master of the house, snapped at his minions. "We cannot expect anyone to know of our homeland. Home is farther away than the miles of land and sea we have put behind us. It is another world from this place. That is why I have come here—because it is another world." He gestured toward me. "You—do you have a name?"

"Lanore."

"You are from here?"

"From Boston? No, I just arrived today. My family"—I stumbled over a hitch in my throat—"lives in the Maine territory, to the north. Have you heard of it?"

"No," he answered.

"Then we are even." I don't know where I found the nerve to joke with him.

"Perhaps we are." He let the valet adjust his cravat, eyeing me curiously before addressing the trio. "Don't just stand there," he said. "Get her ready for the party."

I was led to another room, this one filled with trunks stacked on more trunks. They threw back lids, rummaging until they found clothing that would fit me, a nice dress in a red cotton and a pair of satin slippers. It made for a mismatched outfit but the clothing was still much finer than anything I'd ever worn. A servant had been ordered to prepare a hasty bath and I was instructed to scrub thoroughly, but quickly. "We'll burn these," the blond man said, nodding at my homemade clothes, now lying discarded on the floor. Before leaving me to my bath, the frightening blond woman pressed a goblet in my hand, good red wine sloshing inside. "Drink up," she said. "You must be thirsty." I drained it in two gulps.

I could tell the wine had been drugged by the time I left the washroom. The floors and walls seemed to shift and I needed all my powers of concentration to make it down the hall. By then, guests had begun to arrive, mostly well-dressed, bewigged men with masks obscuring their faces. The trio had vanished and I had been left alone. In my daze, I went from room to room, trying to grasp what was going on, the raucous bacchanalia spilling all around me. I remember seeing card games in a huge room, men sitting four or five to a table, amid roars of laughter and anger as coins flashed as they were tossed in the pot. I continued to roam, randomly drifting in and out of room after room. As I stumbled through the halls, a stranger would try to take my hand but I would pull away and run off as best I could, given my disorientation. There were confused young men or women without masks, all very pretty, being led off by partygoers in all directions.

I began to hallucinate. I was convinced I was dreaming, and that I'd dreamed myself into a maze. I couldn't make myself understood; words came out in mumbles and no one seemed inclined to listen to me, anyway. There seemed to be no way out of this hellish party, no way to the relative safety of the street. Just then, I felt a hand alight on my elbow and then I passed out.

When I woke up, I was lying on a bed on my back, and I was nearly being suffocated by the man hovering over me. His face was unnaturally close to mine, his hot breath raking my face. I shuddered under his weight and the insistent slamming of his body against mine, and heard myself moan and cry in pain, but the pain was detached, blunted for now by the drug. I knew, instinctively, that it would all come back to me later. I tried to call out for help and a sweaty hand covered my mouth, salty fingers pushed past my lips. "Quiet, pet," the man on top of me grunted, eyes half closed.

Over his shoulder, I saw we were being watched. Masked men sat in chairs pulled up to the foot of the bed, goblets in hand, laughing and urging the man on. Sitting in the middle of the group, one leg crossed over the other, was the host. The count. Adair.

I awoke with a start. I was in a large bed in a dark, quiet room. Just the act of waking sent bright sparks of pain shooting through my body. I felt as though I'd been turned inside out, stretched and raw and stiff, numb from the waist down. My stomach churned, a sea of bile. My face was puffy, my mouth, too, with lips dry and cracked. I knew what had happened to me last night, my pain all the evidence I needed. What I needed now was to survive it.

Then I saw him lying next to me on the bed. Adair. His face was almost beatific in sleep. From what I could see, he was naked though covered by sheets from the waist down. His back was exposed to me and mottled with old scars, hinting of a horrific beating once upon a time.

I leaned over the edge of the bed and, clutching the mattress, threw up on the floor.

My retching woke the host. He moaned at his hangover, or so I assumed, and raised a hand to his temple. His green-gold eyes blinked uncertainly.

"Good God, you're still here," he said to me.

I lunged at him in anger, raising a fist to strike him, but he knocked me aside with a lazy, powerful arm. "Don't behave stupidly," he warned me, "or I'll break you in half like a stick."

I thought of the other young men and women I'd seen last night. "Where are they? The others?" I demanded.

"Paid and gone, I hope," Adair muttered, running a hand through tangled hair. He wrinkled his nose at the smell of my fresh vomit. "Get someone in here to clean that up," he said as he lurched off the bed.

"I'm not your servant. And I'm not a—" I groped for a word I didn't know existed.

"Not a whore?" He pulled a blanket off the bed and wrapped it around his body. "You were not a virgin, either."

"That doesn't mean I want to be drugged and savaged by a group of men."

Adair said nothing. He held the blanket closed at his hip, walked to the door, and bellowed for a servant. Then he turned to face me. "So, you think I wronged you? What will you do about it? You could tell your story to the constable and he will lock you up for being a prostitute. So I suggest you take your pay and get a meal from the cook before you go." Then he cocked his head as he looked me over a second time. "You're the one Tilde found on the street, the one with no place to go. Well . . . let it never be said that I am not a generous man. You can stay a few days with us. Rest up and get your bearings, if you like."

"And am I to sing for my supper the same as last night?" I asked tartly.

"You are impertinent, aren't you, to speak to me like this? All alone in the world—no one knows you're here, I could eat you up like a little rabbit, a little rabbit in a stew. Doesn't that frighten you in the least?" He smirked at me but with a glimmer of approval. "We'll see what comes to mind." He sank onto a sofa, wrapping the blanket around him. For an aristocrat, he had the manners of a ruffian.

I tried to stand and search for my clothes, but my head went light and the room swirled. I fell back onto the bed as a servant came in with rags and a bucket. He paid no attention to me as he got down on his knees to attend to my puddle of sick. It wasn't until then that I felt the throbbing pain at my gut, just one sensation lost amid an ocean of hurt. I was covered, head to toe, in scratches, welts, and bruises. The pain inside had undoubtedly come the same way as the pain outside: at the hands of a brute.

I intended to flee the mansion if I had to crawl on my hands and knees. But I didn't make it beyond the foot of the bed; I collapsed dead away in a faint of exhaustion.

Months would pass before I'd leave the house.

SIXTEEN

The dawn this time of year has a characteristic hue, the dusty yellow-gray like the rime on the yolk of a boiled egg. Luke could swear it hangs over the land like a miasma or a ghost's curse but knows it's probably nothing more than a trick of light playing on the water molecules in the morning air. Whether it is light waves or an ancient curse, it gives the morning a peculiar appearance: the yellow sky a low ceiling of clouds in ominous shades against which nearly bare trees stand in grays and browns.

After seeing the police car in the rearview mirror, Luke decided that they can't continue the trip to the Canadian border in his truck. It's too recognizable, with its MD plates and bumper sticker from Jolene's former school proclaiming the driver's child to be an honor-roll student at Allagash River Elementary. (Since when, Luke had wondered when Tricia insisted they put the sticker on his old truck, were there honor rolls in elementary schools?) So they have spent the past half hour backtracking to St. Andrew, hurtling over single-lane roads to get to the house of someone he believes he can trust. He called on his cell phone first to see about borrowing a car, but mostly he wants to see if the police have been asking around about him.

He stops in front of a large reconditioned farmhouse outside the St. Andrew city limits. The house is a beauty, one of the biggest and best kept, with touches like pussywillow wreaths decorating the wraparound porch and solar lanterns lining the driveway. The house belongs to a new doctor at the hospital, an anesthesiologist named Peter, who moved up from the city so he could raise his children in the country, where he believes there is no crime or drugs. He is a pathologically nice guy, even to Luke who, prickly and still grieving from all his recent trouble, had withdrawn from everyone in the past few months.

When Luke knocks at the front door, Peter answers it in bathrobe and slippers, a grave look on his face. He seems to have been rousted out of bed by Luke's phone call, for which Luke is inwardly embarrassed.

Peter puts a hand on Luke's arm as they stand in the doorway. "Is everything all right?"

"I'm sorry to ask, it's a strange request, I know," Luke says, shuffling from foot to foot, head down. He's practiced this lie in his head for the last ten minutes. "It's just . . . my cousin's daughter has been staying with me for a few days and I promised her mother I'd get her home in time to make the bus for some school trip. Only my truck is acting up and I'm afraid it won't make it up there and back . . ." Luke's tone blends the right amounts of ineptitude and apology for inconveniencing a friend, projecting a sort of bumble-headed, well-intentioned haplessness that only an ogre would refuse.

Peter looks over Luke's shoulder at the truck parked at the end of the long driveway, where—Luke knows—he will see Lanny standing beside the truck, her suitcase at her feet. She is too far away for Peter to get a good look at her, in case the police come by later with questions. She gives Peter a little wave.

"Didn't you just get off shift?" Peter peers back at Luke, so closely that he might be inspecting him for fleas. "Aren't you tired?"

"Yeah, but I'm okay. It was a quiet night. I got a little sleep," he lies. "I'll be careful."

Peter pulls the keys from a pocket and drops them in Luke's hand. When Luke tries to give him the keys to the truck in return, Peter balks.

"You don't need to leave your keys with me. You're not going to be gone long, are you?"

Luke shrugs, trying to appear nonchalant. "Just in case you have to move it or something. You never know."

The door to the three-bay garage rises slowly and Luke checks the key fob to find that Peter is entrusting him with a new luxury SUV, gleaming steel gray. Heated leather seats and a DVD player for the second row to keep the children appeased on long road trips. He recalls how people at the hospital gave Peter a hard time the first day he drove up in it, as the vehicle was so uncharacteristic for the area, its shiny coat likely to be eaten up by road salt by the end of its third winter.

Luke backs the car out of the garage and waits at the mouth of the driveway for Lanny to scramble into the passenger seat. "Nice car," she says as she reaches for the seat belt. "You know how to trade up, don't you?"

She hums to herself as Luke guides the car down the road, once again headed for the Canadian border-crossing station—this time, half hidden behind darkly tinted windows. He feels guilty for what he's done. He can't quite put his finger on why, but he suspects he will not be turning right around once they've crossed the border, which is why he left the keys to his dented old pickup with his friend. Not that Peter needs the truck; he obviously has other vehicles if he must go somewhere. Still, it makes Luke feel better, as if he has posted bond or left a token in good faith, because he knows Peter will think less of him soon enough.

Lanny catches Luke's eye as they coast into an empty intersection. "Thank you," she says with heartfelt gratitude. "You seem like the kind of man who doesn't like to ask for favors, so . . . I want you to know that I appreciate what you're doing for me."

Luke just nods, wondering how far he will go and at what cost to help her escape.

SEVENTEEN

BOSTON, 1817

I woke in a different bed in a different room, the dark-haired man from the carriage sitting at the bedside with a bowl of water and a cold compress for my forehead.

"Ah, you're back among the living," he said when I'd opened my eyes. He lifted the compress from my brow and dropped it into the water to soak.

A cold light was visible through the window behind him, so I knew it was day, but which day? I checked under the coverlet to see that I was dressed in a plain night shift. They had given me a room to myself that was clearly meant for a senior member of the household staff, small and dutifully appointed.

"Why am I still here?" I asked, groggy.

He ignored my question. "How are you feeling?"

The pain came on dully, sour and hot in my abdomen. "Like I've been stabbed with a rusty blade."

He frowned slightly, then reached for a soup bowl sitting on the floor. "The best thing for you is rest, complete rest. You've likely got a puncture in you somewhere, in there"—he pointed obliquely to my stomach—"and you need to heal as quickly as possible, before infection sets in. I've seen it before. It can become serious."

The babe. I pulled myself upright. "I want to see a physician. Or a midwife."

He pushed a spoon through clear broth, metal ringing against china. "Too soon for that. We'll watch awhile, to see if it gets worse."

Between daubs of the compress and spoonfuls of clear soup, he answered my questions. First, he told me about himself. His name was Alejandro and he was the youngest son of a fine Spanish family from Toledo. Being the youngest son, he had no hope of inheriting the family's property. The second oldest had joined the military and was captain of a fierce Spanish galleon. The third oldest served in the court of the Spanish king and would shortly be sent as an emissary to a foreign land. Thus, the family had fulfilled its customary obligations to king and country; Alejandro was free to decide his own way in the world, and through various incidents and twists of fate, he eventually found himself with Adair.

Adair, he explained, was bona fide royalty from the old world, as wealthy as some minor princes, having managed to hold on to property that had belonged to his family for centuries. Tired of the old world, he'd come to Boston for the novelty, to experience the new world for himself. Alejandro and the other two from the carriage—Tilde, the woman, and Donatello, the blond man—were Adair's courtiers. "Every royal keeps a court," Alejandro said, the first of many circular arguments. "He must be surrounded by educated people of breeding, who can see that his needs are met. We are the buffer between him and the world."

Donatello, he explained, had come from Italy, where he had been an assistant and muse to a great artist whose name I'd never heard. And Tilde—her background was a mystery, Alejandro confessed. The only thing he knew about her was that she'd come from a northern land as snowy and cold as mine. Tilde had already been with Adair when Alejandro joined the court. "She has his ear and her temper can be formidable, so be careful around her at all times," he warned, dipping the spoon for more broth.

"It's not like I'll be here a minute longer than I need to," I said, reaching with my mouth for the spoon. "I'll be gone as soon as I'm feeling better." Alejandro made no comment, appearing to be concentrating on conveying the next spoonful of broth to my open mouth.

"There is one more member of Adair's court," he said, then hastened to add, "but you probably won't meet her. She is—reclusive. Just don't be surprised if you think you see a ghost flit by."

"A ghost?" The hairs rose on the back of my neck, memories of the wagon drivers' ghost stories rushing back to mind, the sad dead looking for loved ones.

"Not a real ghost," he chided. "Though she might as well be one. She keeps to herself, and the only way you'll see her is to stumble across her, like coming upon a deer in the wood. She doesn't speak and she won't pay any attention to you if you try to talk to her. Her name is Uzra."

As grateful as I was to Alejandro for sharing his knowledge, each bit of his information sat uncomfortably with me, as each was further evidence of my ignorance and isolated upbringing. I'd never been told about any of these foreign lands, didn't know the name of one famous artist. Most unsettling was this Uzra—I didn't want to meet a woman who had made herself a ghost. And what had Adair done to keep her from speaking? Cut out her tongue? I didn't doubt he was cruel enough to do it.

"I don't know why you bother to tell me these things," I said. "I'm not staying."

Alejandro observed me with the beautiful smile of an altar boy and a glittering eye. "Oh, it's just a way to pass the time. Shall I get you more soup?"

That night, when I heard Adair and his minions sweep down the hallway, preparing to depart for the evening, I crept out of my bed and to the landing to watch. How beautiful they were, swathed in velvets and brocades, powdered and coiffed by servants who had spent hours fussing over them. Tilde, with jewels pinned in her yellow hair, her lips painted red; Dona, with a spotless white cravat wound up to his jaw, accentuating his aristocratic neck and his long chin; Alejandro, in a black frock coat and forever sorrowful look—nattering at one another in their sharp-tongued way and aflutter like regally plumed birds.

But mostly I gazed at Adair, for he was captivating. A savage buttoned up in a gentleman's finery. Then it struck me: he was a wolf in sheep's clothing, going hunting tonight with his pack of jackals to flush out the quarry. They hunted for fun, as they'd hunted for me. He had been the wolf, I the rabbit with the tender, downy neck easily snapped by that remorseless maw. The valet placed the cloak on Adair's shoulders, and as Adair turned to leave, he glanced up at me, as though he'd known I'd been there all along, and flashed me a look and a slight smile that sent me staggering backward. I should have been afraid of him—I *was* afraid of him—and yet I was transfixed. A part of me wanted to be one of them, wanted to be on Adair's arm as he and his minions went out to enjoy themselves, to be fawned on by admirers as was their due.

That night, I was half awakened by the party as they returned home and not surprised when Adair came into my room and carried me to his bed. Despite my illness, he had me that evening and I let him, surrendered to the thrill of his weight over me, his thickness in me, and the feel of his mouth on my skin. He whispered in my ear as we coupled, more moans than words, and I couldn't make out what he was saying aside from "cannot deny me" and "mine," as though he was staking a claim to me that night. Afterward, I lay next to him, shaking as the thrall passed through me.

The next morning, when I awoke in my quiet little room, the pain in my lower body was markedly worse. I tried to walk, but each step was punctuated with a sharp jab in my abdomen and I leaked blood and feces; I couldn't imagine getting as far as to the front door, let alone finding someone to take me in. By evening I became consumed by a fever and over the next few days dropped in and out of sleep, each time waking up weaker than before. My skin grew pale and tender, my eyes rimmed in pink. If my bruises and scratches were healing, it happened more slowly than could be perceived. Alejandro, the only person who came to my bedside, delivered his prognosis with a shake of his head. "A puncture of the bowels."

"Surely that is a trifling illness?" I asked, hopefully.

"Not if it goes septic."

Ignorant as I was of the complexities of anatomy, if pain was an indication of the severity of the problem, the baby had to be in peril. "A physician," I begged, squeezing his hand.

"I'll speak to Adair," he promised.

A few hours later, Adair burst into the room. I didn't see even a flicker of acknowledgment of the pleasure we'd shared the previous night. He dragged a stool beside the bed and began examining me, pressing fingers to my forehead and cheeks to judge my temperature.

"Alejandro said your condition has not improved."

"Please, send for a physician. I'll pay you back someday, as soon as I am able . . ."

He clicked his tongue as though to say that the cost was of no consequence. He lifted one of my eyelids, then felt the pouches of flesh under my jaw. After he finished, he rose from the stool.

"I'll return in a moment," he said and swept out of the room.

I'd nodded off by the time he returned with an old, pitted tankard in his hands. He pulled me into a sitting position before handing me the tankard. The contents smelled like dirt and weeds stewed in warm liquid and looked like swamp water.

"Drink it," he said.

"What is it?"

"It will help you feel better."

"Are you a doctor?"

Adair gave me a look of mild disgust. "Not what you'd consider a doctor, no. You might say I've made a study of traditional medicine. If that had simmered longer, it would be much more palatable, but there was no time for it," he added, as though he didn't want me to think less of his prowess because of the taste.

"You mean you're like a midwife?" It should go without saying that midwives—though they were often the only practitioners of medicine in any village—had no training, as women were not allowed to attend medical classes at college. The women who became midwives learned about child birthing and ways with herbs and berries through apprenticeship, often learning from their mothers or other relatives.

"Not quite," he said sourly, apparently not taking midwives any more seriously than doctors. "Now drink up."

I did as he ordered, thinking he wouldn't agree to bring in a doctor if he was piqued at me for not trying his remedy. I thought I would throw it all up in front of him; the concoction was so grassy and bitter, with a grit that I couldn't clear from my mouth. "Now, get some more rest, then we'll see how you are doing," he said, reaching for the tankard.

I put my hand on his wrist. "Tell me, Adair . . ." But then I was at a loss.

"Tell you what?"

"I don't know what to make of your behavior toward me last night . . ."

He twisted his handsome mouth into a cruel smile. "Is it so hard to understand?" He helped me to ease back against the pillows, and then he drew the blanket up to my chin. He smoothed the blanket down across my chest and touched my hair, very gently. His mocking expression softened, and so for a moment all I saw was his boyish face and a trace of kindness in his green eyes. "Did you not think that I have grown a little bit fond of you, Lanore? You have turned out to be a bit of a surprise, not just a ragamuffin Tilde dragged in from the street. I sense something about you . . . you're a kindred spirit in some way that I haven't figured out yet. But, I will. First, you must get well. Let's see if that elixir does any good. Try to rest now. Someone will check on you later."

I was surprised by his revelation. To judge from that one night, what existed between us was mutual attraction. Lust, to put it simply. On one hand, it went to my head that a nobleman, a man with wealth and a title, might be interested in me, but on the other hand, he was also a sadist and egotist. Despite the warning signs, I accepted Adair's affection, even if it was a substitute for that which I desired from another man.

My stomach calmed, the taste of the bitter elixir forgotten. I had a new conundrum to puzzle over. My curiosity was no match for Adair's curative, though, and before too long I'd fallen peacefully asleep.

Another night and day dragged by but no doctor came to see me and I began to wonder what game Adair was playing. He hadn't been back since his confession of interest in me; he sent servants to my room with additional servings of the elixir but no doctor materialized at my door. After thirty-six hours had passed, I'd become suspicious, again, of his motives.

I had to get out of this house. If I stayed, I would die in this bed, the baby dying with me. I had to try to find a doctor or someone else who would bring me back to health or at the very least, keep me alive until the baby could be delivered. This child would be the only proof of Jonathan's love for me and I was adamant that this proof should live on after my own death.

I stumbled out of bed to search for my satchel, but as I groped under the bedstead and in a cupboard, I became aware of the icy wetness of my underclothes, clinging to my legs. They'd taken away my linen and swaddled me in a length of fabric instead, to catch the foul discharge coming out of me. The fabric was soiled and evil smelling; there was no way I could travel on the streets like this without being mistaken for a lunatic and taken to an asylum. I needed clothing, my cloak, but they had taken everything away.

Of course, I knew where I might find something to wear. The room full of trunks, where they'd taken me on the first fateful night.

Outside my room, it was quiet, only the murmur of a conversation between a couple of servants wafting up the stairwell. The hallway was empty. I staggered to the stairs but was so weak and feverish in my limbs that I had to resort to my hands and knees to climb to the next floor. Once there, I leaned against the wall to catch my breath and regain my bearings. Which corridor led to the room of trunks? The corridors looked all the same and there were so many doors . . . I didn't have the strength or time to try them all. And as I stood there, near tears from frustration and pain, struggling to hang on to my resolve to escape, I saw her. I saw the ghost.

I saw movement from the corner of my eye. I assumed it was a kitchen girl on her way to the servants' loft, in the highest part of the attic, but the figure who stood on the landing was no common servant.

She was very small. If not for her full bosom and curvy hips, you might mistake her for a child. Her womanly shape was draped in an exotic costume made of tissue-thin silk, billowing pantaloons, and a sleeveless tunic too small to fully cover her breasts. And gorgeous breasts they were, perfectly round and firm and high. You could tell by looking at them how heavy they'd be in your hand, the kind of breasts that could make any man's mouth water.

In addition to her luscious form, she was aesthetically beautiful. Her almond-shaped eyes were made to look all the bigger by a ring of kohl. Her hair was a multitude of shades of copper, auburn, and gold, and hung in untamed ringlets all the way to the small of her back. Alejandro had described the color of her skin perfectly: cinnamon, seemingly flecked with mica to make her glisten, as though she was made of some precious stone. I recall all this now with the benefit of having seen her many times after this episode and knowing she was made of flesh and blood, but at the time, truly, she could have been an apparition, conjured up by the male mind as the perfect sexual fantasy. The sight of her was startling and breathtaking. I feared that if

I moved, she'd dart away. She stared back at me cautiously as I stared at her.

"Please don't go. I need your help." Tired from standing, I leaned on the banister. She took one step backward, her bare feet silent on the carpet.

"No, no, please, don't leave me. I'm ill and I need to get out of this house. Please, I need your help if I'm going to stay alive. Your name is Uzra, right?" At the sound of her name, she danced backward a few steps more, turned, and disappeared in the gloom at the top of the attic stairs. I don't know if my strength gave out at that moment or if it was my resolve that faltered as she ran away from me, but I slipped to the floor. The ceiling spun overhead, like a lantern twirling free on a twisted cord: first spinning in this direction, then in the other direction. Then everything went dark.

Then, murmuring and the touch of fingers.

"What is she doing out of her room?" It was Adair's voice, gruff and low. "You said she wouldn't be able to leave her bed."

"Apparently she is stronger than she looks," Alejandro muttered. Someone lifted me and I felt weightless, buoyed.

"Put her back in there and lock the door this time. She's not to leave this house." Adair's voice began to drift away. "Is she going to die?"

"How the bloody hell should I know?" Alejandro muttered under his breath, then called out, much stronger, so Adair could hear, "I suppose that's up to you."

Up to him? I wondered, even as I was slipping back into unconsciousness. How could it be up to him whether I lived or died? I had no time to further contemplate this perplexing conversation, however, as I sank back into the vacuum of a lightless, soundless oblivion.

EIGHTEEN

"She's dying. She won't make it through the day."

It was Alejandro's voice, his words not meant for my ears. My eyelids fluttered. He stood next to Adair at my bedside. Both had their arms crossed over their chests in resignation, grave looks on their faces.

Here it was, the absolute end, and I still had no idea what they meant to do with me, why Adair had bothered to mislead me with a declaration of affection, or ply me with homeopathic potions but refuse me a doctor's care. At that point, his strange behavior made no difference: I was about to die. If it was my body they were after—for medical dissection or experimentation, to use in a satanic ritual—there would be no one to stop them. After all, what was I but a penniless and friendless vagrant? I wasn't even their servant; I was less than that, a woman who let strangers do what they pleased with her in exchange for shelter and a meal. I would have cried for what I'd become but the fever had dried me up, leaving me without tears.

I couldn't help agreeing with Alejandro's conclusion: I had to be dying. A body could not feel this bad and live. Inside I was on fire, every muscle burning. I ached. With each breath, my rib cage creaked like a rusty bellows. If I weren't sorry to be taking Jonathan's baby with me and so afraid of the heavy weight of the sins for which I would be judged, I would have prayed for God to show me mercy by letting me die.

I had only one regret, which was that I'd never see Jonathan again. I'd believed so strongly we were destined to be together that it seemed inconceivable we could be separated, that I would die without being able to reach out and touch his face, that he would not be holding my hand as the last breath escaped me. The gravity of my situation became real to me at that moment: my end was here, there was nothing I could do, no entreaty to God that would change that. And the thing I wanted above all else was to see Jonathan.

"It's your decision," Alejandro said to Adair, who hadn't spoken a word. "If she pleases you. Dona and Tilde have made their positions clear—"

"It's not up for a vote," he growled. "None of you has a say in who joins our household. You all continue to exist at my pleasure"—did I hear him correctly? I thought not; his words slurred and boomed in my head—"you continue to serve me at my pleasure."

Adair stepped beside me and ran a hand over my sweaty brow. "See the look on her face, Alejandro? She knows she is dying and yet she fights. I saw that look on your face, on Tilde's . . . it is always the same." He cupped my cheek. "Listen to me, Lanore. I am about to give you a rare gift. Do you understand? If I do not intervene, you will die. So this is to be our bargain . . . I am ready to catch you as you die and bring your soul back to this world. But that means you will belong to me entirely, more than just your body. To own your body, that is an easy thing, I can do that now. I want more from you; I want your fiery soul. Do you agree to this?" he asked, searching my eyes for a reaction. "Prepare yourself," he said to me. I had no idea what he was talking about.

He leaned close, like a priest about to hear my confession. He held a silver vial as slender as a hummingbird's beak and pulled a stopper out—more like a needle than a stopper. "Open your mouth," he commanded, but I was frozen with fright. "Open your damn mouth," he repeated, "or I will crack your jaw in two."

In my confusion I thought he might be offering last rites—I was from a Catholic family, for all intents and purposes—and I wanted absolution for my sins. So I opened my mouth and closed my eyes, waiting.

He smeared the stopper against my tongue. I didn't even feel it— the instrument was minute—but my tongue immediately went numb and was seized with the most vile taste. My mouth watered and I began to convulse; he pushed my mouth shut and held it, pinning me to the bed as I was wracked with seizures. Blood welled in my mouth, made bitter and sour by the potion he had put on my tongue. Had he poisoned me to hasten my dying? I was lost in my own blood and could feel nothing else. In the back of my mind, I heard Adair mumble, words that made no sense. But panic had replaced all else, especially logic. I didn't care what he was saying or why he was doing this, I was completely in shock.

My chest squeezed, the pain and panic excruciating. My lungs no longer worked—pump rusted bellows, for God's sake. I couldn't breathe. I know now that my heart was stopping and was unable to make my lungs work. My brain flailed. I was dying, but I wouldn't die alone. My hands went instinctively to my belly, cupping the small mound that had just begun making itself undeniably evident.

Adair froze, realization breaking on his face. "My God, she is pregnant. Did no one know she was with child?" he roared as he spun around, flinging an arm at Alejandro behind him. My body was shutting down, piece by piece, and my soul was terrified, searching for a place to go.

And then it ceased to be.

I woke up.

Of course, the first thing I thought was that the terrible episode had been a dream or that I'd passed the peak of my illness and was recovering. I found momentary comfort in these explanations, but I couldn't deny that something terrible and irrevocable had happened to me. If I concentrated very hard, I remembered blurred visions, of being held against the mattress, of someone carrying away a large copper basin filled with thick, foul-smelling blood.

I woke in my pauper's bed in the tiny room, but the room was ghastly cold, the fire long since died out. The curtains over the sole window were drawn, but there was a sliver of overcast sky visible where the panels met. The sky had that gray cast of a New England autumn to it, but even those tiny chinks of light were bright and chalky, and painful to look at.

My throat burned as though I'd been forced to drink acid. I decided to go searching for a draft of water, but when I sat up, I was thrown immediately to my back as the room circled and spun. The light, my equilibrium . . . I felt terribly sensitive, like an invalid altered by a prolonged illness.

Aside from my throat and my fiery head, the rest of me was cold. My muscles no longer burned with fever. Instead, I moved sluggishly, as though I'd been left to float in cold water for days. One very important thing had changed and I didn't need anyone to tell me what it was: I no longer carried my baby with me. It was gone.

It took me about a half hour to leave the room, slowly acclimating to standing, then walking. As I inched down the hall toward the courtiers' bedchambers, I heard the quotidian noises of the household quite precisely, with an animal's keenness: whispered conversations between lovers in bed; the snoring of the head butler napping in the linen closet; the sound of water being drawn from the giant cauldron, perhaps for someone's bath.

I stopped in front of Alejandro's door, swaying on my feet, steeling myself to go in and demand that he explain what had happened to me and to my unborn child. I raised my hand to knock, but stopped. Whatever had happened to me was serious and irrevocable. I knew who had the answers and I decided to go right to the source: the one who had placed poison on my tongue, spoken magical words in my ear, and made everything change. The one who, in all likelihood, had taken my child from me. For my lost child's sake, I had to be strong.

I turned and strode to the end of the hall. I raised my hand to knock and again thought better of it. I wouldn't come to Adair as a servant, asking for permission to speak with him.

The doors parted with one push. I knew the room and the habits of its occupant, and went straight to the bower of cushions where Adair slept. He lay under a sable blanket, unmoving as a corpse, his eyes wide open, staring at the ceiling.

"You've rejoined us," he said, more a declaration than an observation. "You're back among the living."

I was afraid of him. I couldn't explain the things he'd done to me, or why I hadn't run from Tilde's invitation at the carriage, or why I'd let any of this happen. But the time had come to confront him.

"What did you do to me? And what happened to my baby?"

His eyes shifted, settling on me, as baleful as a wolf's. "You were dying from infection and I decided not to let you leave, not yet. And you didn't want to die. I saw it in your eyes. As for the baby—we didn't know you were with child. Once you'd been given the unction, there was nothing to be done for the child."

My eyes welled with tears, that after everything—the exile from St. Andrew, surviving despite the hellish infection—my baby had been taken away from me so thoughtlessly. "What did you do . . . how did you keep me from dying? You said you were not a doctor . . ."

He rose from the bed and slipped on a silk robe. He grabbed my wrist, and before I knew what was happening, whisked me out of the room and down the stairs. "What has happened to you cannot be explained. It can only be—shown."

He dragged me to the common rooms in the back of the house. As we passed Dona in the hall, Adair snapped his fingers at him and said, "Come with us." He took me to the room behind the kitchen where the giant cauldrons used to cook for crowds and the other pantry oddities were kept: fish grills, shaped to fit a fish like an iron maiden; cake tins and forms; and the half barrel of water drawn from the cistern for household use. The water glinted, black and cold, in the barrel.

Adair shoved me into Dona's arms and gestured to the barrel with a toss of his head. Dona rolled his eyes as he yanked up the sleeve on his right arm and then, as swiftly as a housewife snatching up the chicken that is to be the evening's supper, he grabbed the back of my neck and plunged my head into the water. I had no time to prepare and swallowed a lungful of water immediately. By the strength of his grip, I could tell he didn't mean to let me go. All I could do was thrash and struggle in the hope I might knock the barrel over or that he'd relent out of pity. Why had Adair saved me from infection and a fever if he meant to have me drowned now?

He shouted at me; I heard his voice through the splashing but couldn't make out his words. A long stretch of time seemed to pass, but I knew this must be an illusion. The dying were said in their panic to experience each of their last seconds clearly and distinctly. But I had depleted the air in my lungs; surely death would come at any moment. I hung from Dona's hand in the water, numb with cold and terror, waiting for my end. Wanting to join the lost child, wanting—after all that had happened to me—to give up. To be at peace.

Dona yanked my head from the barrel and water coursed from my hair, down my face, and over my shoulders, spattering all over the floor. He held me upright.

"So, what do you think?" Adair asked.

"You tried to kill me just now!"

"But you didn't drown, did you?" He handed Dona a towel, which he used to wipe his wet arm, disdainfully. "Dona held you under for a good five minutes, and here you stand, alive. The water didn't kill you. And why do you think that is?"

I blinked the frigid water from my eyes. "I—don't know."

His grin was like a skeleton's. "That's because you're immortal. You can never die."

I crouched by the fire in Adair's bedchamber. He gave me a glass and a bottle of brandy, and lay on his bed while I stared at the flames and avoided the hospitality of his alcohol. I didn't want to believe him and I didn't want anything he might give me. If I couldn't kill him for taking my baby from me, then I wanted to run away from him and out of the house. Again, however, fear kept me from thinking clearly, and the last shreds of my common sense warned me that I shouldn't leave. I had to hear him out.

Next to the bed was a curious instrument, with tubes and chambers made of brass and glass. I now know it to be a hookah, but at the time it was only an exotic contraption that bellowed sweet smoke. Adair drew on the pipe and exhaled a long stream toward the ceiling, until his eyes grew glassy and his limbs were languid.

"Do you understand now?" he asked. "You are no longer mortal. You are beyond life and death. You cannot die." He offered the hookah's mouthpiece to me, then pulled it back when I didn't take it. "It doesn't matter how someone might try to kill you—neither bow nor rifle, knife nor poison, fire nor water. A mound of earth piled on top of you. Neither disease nor famine."

"How can that be?"

He took another long draft on the pipe, holding in its narcotic smoke for a moment before releasing it in a thick cloud. "How this came to be, I cannot tell you. I've thought on it, prayed on it, tried to dream on it using all manner of drugs. No answer has come to me. I can't explain it and have come to stop looking for answers."

"You're saying you cannot die?"

"I'm saying I've been alive for hundreds of years."

"Who in God's universe is immortal?" I asked of myself. "Angels are immortal."

Adair snorted. "Always the angels, always God. Why is it that when one hears a voice speak to them, they always assume it is God talking?"

"Are you saying it's the work of the devil?"

He scratched his flat stomach. "I'm saying I have searched for answers, and no voice has spoken to me. Neither God nor Satan has taken the trouble to explain to me how this—miracle—fits into his plans. No one has commanded me to do his bidding. From this, I can only deduce that I am no one's minion. I have no master. We are all immortal—Alejandro, Uzra, and the rest. I have made all of you, understand?" Another long draw on the pipe, a gurgle of water, and his booming voice lowered. "You have transcended death."

"Please stop saying that. You're frightening me."

"You will get used to this, and very soon, you'll never be frightened again. There will be nothing to be frightened of. There is only one rule for you to follow now, one person you must obey, and that person is me. Because I have your soul now, Lanore. Your soul and your life."

"I must obey you now? Does that mean you are God?" I snorted, too, being as brazen as I felt I could be with him.

"The God you were raised on has given you up. Do you remember what I said before you received the gift? You are my possession now and forever. I *am* your god and if you do not believe me and care to test what I tell you, I invite you to try to defy me."

By then, I had let him lead me to the bed and didn't protest as he lay beside me. He fed me the mouthpiece and stroked my damp hair as I sucked in the heavy fumes. The narcotic wrapped around me, cradled me, and my fear collapsed like an exhausted child. Now that I was worn down and sleepy, Adair was almost tender. "I have no explanation to give you, Lanore, but there is a story. I'll tell you that story, *my* story. I'll tell you how I came to be, and perhaps then you'll understand."

NINETEEN

HUNGARIAN TERRITORY, A.D. 1349

As soon as Adair saw the stranger, he knew with the unmistakable chill of premonition that the old man had come for him.

The end of the day was the time when they celebrated, the nomadic laborers with whom Adair's family traveled. As night descended, they built giant campfires to enjoy the one piece of the day they could call their own. Their long hours working in the fields were over and so they gathered to share food and drink and entertain one another. His uncle would not yet be drunk and so would play folk tunes on his peasant's violin, accompanying Adair's mother and the other women as they sang. Someone would bring a tambourine, another would bring a balalaika. Adair sat with his whole family, his five brothers and two sisters, along with the older brothers' wives. His happiness that night was complete when he saw, on the far side of the leaping fire, Katarina approach the circle with her family.

He and his family were wanderers, as were Katarina's family and everyone in the caravan. Once upon a time they had been serfs to a

Magyar lord, but he had deserted them, leaving them to bandits. They fled from the villages in their wagons and had lived in their wagons ever since, following the harvest as itinerant workers, digging ditches, tending fields, taking whatever work they could find. The Magyar and Romanian kingdoms were fighting then, and there were too few Magyar nobles spread over the countryside to protect the vagabonds, should they even be inclined.

Still, it hadn't been so long ago that they had been forced from their home that Adair couldn't remember what it was like to sleep inside a house at night, to have that small bit of security. His brothers Istvan and Radu had been babies, though, and had no recollection of the earlier, happier life. Adair felt bad that his younger brothers had never known those times, but then they seemed in their own way to be happier than the rest of the family and were perplexed by the melancholy that haunted their siblings and parents.

The stranger had appeared suddenly, at the edge of the gathering that evening. The first thing Adair noticed about him was that he was very old, practically a shrunken corpse leaning on his walking stick, and as he got closer, he looked older still. His skin was papery and wrinkled, and dotted with age spots. His eyes were coated with a milky film but nevertheless had a strange sharpness to them. He had a thick head of snow white hair, so long that it trailed down his back in a plait. But most notable were his clothes, which were of Romanian cut and made of costly fabrics. Whoever he was, he was wealthy and, even though an old man, had no fear of stepping into a gypsy camp alone at night.

He pushed through the ring of people and stood in the center of the circle, next to the bonfire. As his gaze rippled over the crowd, Adair's blood stood in his veins. Adair was no different from every other boy in the encampment: uneducated, unwashed, underfed. He knew there was no reason for the old man to single him out, but his sense of foreboding was so strong that he would have leaped to his feet and run from the circle if his youthful pride hadn't stopped him— he hadn't done anything to this old man, so why should he run?

After a silent search of the faces illuminated in the fire's lambent glow, the old man smiled unpleasantly, lifted his hand, and pointed directly at Adair. Then he looked over at the group of elders. By now, all activity had stopped, the music, the laughter. All eyes fell on the stranger and then moved to Adair.

His father broke the silence. He pushed through Adair's brothers and sisters and grabbed Adair by the forearm, nearly yanking it from its socket. "What have you done, boy?" he hissed through his gaping teeth. "Do not just sit there—come with me!" He pulled his son to his feet. "The rest of you—what are you staring at? Go back to your storytelling and your foolish singing!" And as he dragged Adair away, Adair felt the stares of his family, and Katarina, on his back.

The two went to a dark overhang under a tree, out of earshot of the campfire, followed by the stranger.

Adair tried to deflect whatever trouble had found him. "Whoever you are looking for, I swear it is not me. You've mistaken me for another."

His father slapped him. "What did you do? Steal a chicken? Take some potatoes or onions from the fields?"

"I swear," Adair sputtered, holding the fiery spot on his cheek and pointing at the old man. "I don't know him."

"Do not let your guilty imagination run away with you. I'm not accusing the boy of any crime," the old man said to Adair's father. He beheld both Adair and his father with contempt, as he might beggars or thieves. "I have chosen your son to come work for me."

To his credit, Adair's father was suspicious of the offer. "What use could you have for him? He has no skills. He is a field hand."

"I need a servant. A boy with a strong back and sturdy legs."

Adair saw his life taking an abrupt, unwelcome turn. "I've never been a house servant. I wouldn't know what to do—"

A second slap from his father stopped Adair short. "Do not make yourself out to be more worthless than you are," his father snapped. "You can learn, even if learning is not among your strengths."

"He will do, I can tell." The stranger walked around Adair slowly, appraising him like a horse for sale in the thieves' market. He trailed a scent in his wake, smoky and dry, like incense. "I do not need someone with a strong mind, just someone to help a fragile old man with the demands of life. But . . ." Here his eyes narrowed, and his countenance became fierce again. "I live a distance away and will not make this trip again. If your son wants the position, he must leave with me tonight."

"Tonight?" Adair's throat tightened.

"I am prepared to pay for the loss of your son's contribution to your family," the stranger said to Adair's father. With those words, Adair knew he was lost, for his father would not turn down money. By this time, his mother was approaching them, keeping to the tree's shadow, wringing her skirts in her hands. She waited with Adair, as his father and the stranger haggled over a price. Once a sum was settled upon and the old man left to ready his horse, Adair's mother flew to her husband.

"What are you doing?" she cried, even though she knew her husband would not change his mind. There would be no arguing with him.

But there was more at stake for Adair and he had nothing to lose, so he turned on his father. "What have you done to me? A stranger walks into camp and you sell one of your children to him! What do you know of him?"

"How dare you question me!" he said, lashing out, knocking Adair to the ground. The rest of the family had come down from the bonfire by now, and stood beyond their father's reach. It was nothing new for them to watch a sibling being beaten, but it was unsettling all the same. "You are too stupid to know a good opportunity when you see it. Obviously, this man is wealthy. You'll be the servant of a rich man. You'll live in a house, not a wagon, and you will not have to work in the fields. If I thought the strange man would agree to it, I'd ask him to take one of the others as well. Maybe Radu, he is not so blind that he cannot see when a good thing falls in his lap."

Adair picked himself off the ground, shamefaced. His father cuffed him again on the back of the head for good measure. "Now, pack your things and say your good-byes. Do not make this man wait for you."

His mother searched her husband's face. "Ferenc, what do you know of this man you are entrusting with our son? What has he told you of himself?"

"I know enough. He is a physic to a count. He lives in a house on the count's estate. Adair will be indentured to him for seven years. At the end of seven years, Adair can choose whether to leave or remain in the physic's employ."

Adair calculated the figures in his mind: in seven years, he would be twenty-one, halfway through his life. As it was, he was just coming into marrying age and was impatient to follow in his older brothers' footsteps and take a bride, start a family, be accepted as a man. As a house servant, he wouldn't marry or be allowed have children; his life would go into suspension during this most crucial time. By the time he was free, he would be old. What woman would want him then?

And what about his family? Where would they be in seven years? They were itinerants, moving to find work, shelter, to escape the bad weather. Not one of them could read or write. He would never be able to find them. To lose his family was unthinkable. They were the lowest class of society, shunned by everyone else. When he left the stranger's employ, how would he survive without them?

A cry broke in his mother's throat. She knew as well as Adair what this meant. But his father stood firm in his decision. "It is for the best! You know it is. Look at us—we can barely earn enough to feed our children. It is better if Adair took his burden on himself."

"You mean that we are all burdens to you!" Radu wailed. Two years younger than Adair, Radu was the sensitive one in the family. He ran up to Adair and wrapped his thin arms around his brother's waist, blotting his tears on Adair's ragged shirt.

"Adair is a man now and has to make his own way in the world," their father said to Radu, then to all of them. "Now, enough of these hysterics. Adair must pack his things."

*   *   *

Adair traveled all that night, riding behind the stranger, as instructed. He was surprised to find that the old man had a magnificent horse, the sort of horse a knight would own, heavy enough for its hoofbeats to shake the ground. Adair could tell they were headed west, deeper into Romanian territory.

Toward morning, they passed the castle of the count by whom the physic was employed. There was nothing lyrical about it. It was meant for siege—squat and solid, foursquare, surrounded by a scattering of dwellings and pens of sheep and cattle. Cultivated fields stretched off in all directions. The two rode for another twenty minutes through a dense forest before coming upon a small stone keep, almost hidden by trees. The keep itself looked dank, overgrown with moss that ran wild without sunlight to keep it in check. To Adair, the keep appeared more dungeon than house, seemingly without even a door cut into its daunting facade.

The old man dismounted and instructed Adair to take care of the horse before joining him inside. Adair lingered as long as he could with the giant equine, stripping off the saddle and bridle, fetching water for it, rubbing its sweaty back with dry straw. When he could avoid it no longer, he picked up the saddle and went into the keep.

Inside, it was almost too smoky to see, a small fire burning in the fire pit and only a miserly narrow window to let the smoke escape. Looking around, Adair saw that the keep was one large, circular room. A woman slept next to the door on a bed of straw. She was easily ten years older than Adair and matronly, with large florid hands and almost sexless features. She slept surrounded by the tools of her gender: mixing bowls and clumsy wooden spoons, pots and buckets; a slab of a wooden table, worn and greasy; stacks of wooden chargers that served as plates; crocks of wine and ale. Garlands of peppers and garlic hung from hooks in the stone walls, along with ropes of sausage and a string of hard circlets of rye bread.

On the far side of the room was a desk covered with bottles and jars, sheaves of paper, an inkstand and quills and an oddity Adair had never laid eyes on before: books, bound with wooden covers. Baskets holding strange artifacts from the forest stood ready behind the desk: dusty dried roots, cones, handfuls of nettles, tangles of weeds. Beyond the desk, Adair spied a staircase leading downward, possibly to a cold cellar.

The old man was suddenly at Adair's side, peering at the peasant boy. "I suppose you want to know my name. I am Ivor cel Rau, but you shall refer to me as 'master.'" As he took off his heavy cape and warmed his hands at the fire, the physic explained that he came from a line of landed Romanian nobles, the last male in his family. Although he would one day inherit the family's castle and property, as a young man he decided to pursue a career and had gone to Venice to study medicine. In his decades as a physician, he'd served several counts and even kings. He was now at the end of a long career, in the service of Count cel Batrin, the Romanian nobleman who owned the castle they had passed. The physic explained that he had not hired Adair to teach him the healing arts, but expected Adair to assist him by gathering herbs and other ingredients for salves and elixirs, in addition to doing chores and helping the housekeeper, Marguerite.

The old man rummaged through an open chest until he found a tatty old blanket of rough woven wool. "Make up a bed of straw by the fire. When Marguerite awakes, she will give you food and your orders for the day. Try to rest some, too, because I will want you to be ready tonight when I awaken. Oh, and do not be surprised when Marguerite neither heeds you nor speaks to you—she is deaf and dumb, and has been since birth." And then the old man took a candle, which had been burning on the kitchen table in wait for him, and hobbled toward the dark stairwell. Adair followed his orders and curled by the fire, and was asleep before the light from the physic's candle had faded down the stairs.

He woke to the stirrings of the housekeeper. She stopped what she was doing to stare at Adair openly as he rose from the floor. Adair found her a disappointment, more so than when she'd been asleep:

worse than plain, she was ugly, with a mannish face and the broad body of a field worker. She gave Adair a meal of cold gruel and water, and when he'd finished, led him to the well and gave him a bucket, pantomiming her instructions. In this way, she had him chop firewood, as well as haul water for the kitchen and the livestock. Later, when she went to scrub clothing in a big wooden tub, Adair tried to nap, remembering the old man's admonition.

The next thing Adair knew, Marguerite was shaking him by the shoulder and pointing to the stairway. Evening had fallen and the old man was rising downstairs in his chamber. The housekeeper went about lighting candles around the main room, and presently, the old man came up the stairs, carrying the same stubby candle from the early morning hours.

"You have risen—good," the physic said as he shuffled by Adair. He went straight to his desk and riffled through pages of indecipherable writing. "Build up that fire," he ordered, "and fetch a cauldron. I must make a potion tonight and you will help me." Ignoring his new servant, the physic started searching the rows of jars, each covered with waxed cloth and string, and turned each in the firelight to read its label, putting a few aside. After the cauldron had been hung and heated above the flames, Adair helped the old man carry the jars to the fire pit. Sitting to the side, he watched the physic measure ingredients in his withered hand, then toss them into the pot. Adair recognized some plants and herbs, now dried to ash, but others were more mysterious. A bat's claw, or was it a mouse's paw? A rooster's comb? Three black feathers, but from what bird? From one tightly lidded jar, the physic poured an oozing, dark syrup that emitted a foul smell as soon as it was exposed to air. Lastly, he poured in a pitcher of water, and then he turned to Adair.

"Watch this carefully. Let it come to a full boil, but then knock the fire down and take care that the unction does not seize up. It must be thick, like pitch. Do you understand?"

Adair nodded. "May I ask, what is this potion for?"

"No, you may not ask," he answered, then seemed to think better of it. "In time, you will learn, when you have earned such wisdom. Now, I am going out. Mind the pot as I instructed you. Do not leave the keep, and do not fall asleep." Adair watched as the old man took his cloak from a peg and slipped outside.

He did as he was told, sitting close enough to inhale the foul fumes coming off the bubbling liquid. The keep was quiet except for Marguerite's snores, and Adair watched her for a while, the rise and fall of her broad stomach under the blanket, straw crackling as she turned in her sleep. When he tired of this miserly entertainment, he went to the physic's desk and studied the pages of handwriting, wishing he had the ability to read them. He thought about trying to persuade the old man to teach him to read; surely the physic would find it helpful for his servant to have this skill.

From time to time, Adair poked at the contents of the pot with a wooden spoon, gauging its consistency, and when it seemed right, he took the poker and knocked down the burning logs, scattering them to the edges of the pit so only the embers remained under the cauldron. At that point, Adair felt it was safe to relax, so he wrapped himself in the threadbare blanket and leaned against the wall. Sleep nibbled at his ear, a delicious ale of which he'd been given a sip but knew he could drink no more. He tried everything he could think of to keep awake: he paced the floor, gulped cold water, did handstands. After an hour of this, he was more exhausted than ever and on the verge of falling to the floor in a stupor when, suddenly, the door was pushed open and the old man entered. He appeared invigorated by his excursion, his milky eyes almost bright.

He peered into the cauldron. "Very good. The unction looks fine. Take the cauldron off the spit and let it cool on the hearth. In the morning, you will pour the unction into that urn and cover it with paper. Now you may rest. It's almost dawn."

Several weeks passed like this. Adair was glad for the routine to keep his mind off the loss of his family and his lovely Katarina. Mornings he assisted Marguerite, and the afternoons he rested. Evenings were spent preparing potions or salves, or being taught by the old man to recognize and gather ingredients. He would lead Adair into the woods to hunt for a specific plant or seed by moonlight. Other evenings, Adair bundled cuttings and hung them from the rafters near the fire pit. Almost every night, the physic would disappear for a few hours, always returning before daybreak, only to withdraw to his chamber underground.

After a month or two had passed, the physic began to send Adair into the village that surrounded the castle walls to exchange a crock of ointment for goods, some cloth or ironwork or pottery. By this time, Adair was desperate for the company of people, even to hear his own voice. But the villagers invariably kept their distance once they learned he worked for the physic. If they saw that Adair was lonely and desperate for company and a few kind words, they were unmoved and kept the transactions curt and unfriendly.

Around the same time, a change occurred between Adair and Marguerite, to his shame. One afternoon, when he'd woken from a nap and started to dress, she came up to his bed and put her hands on him. Without waiting for encouragement, she pushed him on his back onto the straw, feeling his chest under his tunic, then went to his breeches and searched for Adair's manhood. Once she'd gotten it sufficiently engaged, she lifted her dusty skirts and squatted over him. There was no tenderness in her movements, nor in Adair's, no pretense that it was anything other than a physical release for them both. As Adair grasped handfuls of her flesh, he thought of Katarina, but there was no way to pretend that this great bear of a woman was his delicate, dark-eyed love. When it was over, Marguerite made a guttural noise in her throat as she rolled away from Adair, lowered her skirt, and went about her business.

He lay back against his straw bed, looking up at the ceiling and wondering if the physic might have heard them, and if so, what he would do. Perhaps he took his own pleasures with Marguerite—no, that didn't seem possible, and Adair figured the old man visited a wench in the village to satisfy that itch during his nocturnal prowling. Perhaps in time, he would be able to do the same. For now, he seemed to have fallen into a strange way of life, but it wasn't as difficult as working in the fields had been and there was the promise of betterment, perhaps, if he could persuade the old man to teach him about the healing arts. Though Adair still missed his family terribly, he took comfort from these facts and decided to stay a while longer and see what his fortune might hold.

TWENTY

After months had passed in the physic's employ with only the sparest contact with anyone besides the old man and Marguerite, the night came for Adair's first visit to the castle. Not that Adair wanted to go to the stronghold of a Romanian nobleman. He had nothing but hatred for the devils who raided Magyar villages, destroyed their homes and captured their land. He couldn't easily dismiss his curiosity, however; Adair had never been in the abode of a rich man, never been inside castle walls. He'd only worked the fields. He figured he would be able to bear it if he pretended the owner of the castle was Magyar, not Romanian. Then he could marvel at the grand rooms and finery all the same.

His job that night was to carry a huge jar of a potion they had worked on the previous evening. As usual, the potion's purpose was kept secret from him. Adair waited by the door as the physic fussed over his appearance, finally choosing to dress in a fine tunic embroidered with gold threads and studded with colored cabochons, signifying that it was a special occasion. The physic rode his charger and Adair trudged behind, lugging the urn on his back like an old grandmother who could no longer walk upright. The drawbridge over the moat was lowered for them, and they were escorted into the great hall by a squad of the count's soldiers. Guards lined the walls.

A feast was in progress in the great hall. The physic joined the count at the head table and Adair squatted in the back of the room against the wall, still hugging the jar. He recognized some of the emblems on the shields decorating the walls; they were from the estates where he'd worked. The count's dialect sounded familiar, but Adair couldn't understand what they were talking about because the conversation was peppered with Romanian. Even a simple boy like Adair understood what this combination of facts meant: this count was originally a Magyar, but he had allied himself with the Romanian oppressors to save his own skin and preserve his fortune. That had to be why the villagers shunned him: they figured Adair was a Romanian sympathizer as well.

He'd just stumbled on this realization when the old man summoned him over with the urn. Dismissed with a wave of the physic's hand, Adair went back to his place at the wall. The physic removed the oiled cloth cover so the count could inspect the contents. The nobleman closed his eyes and inhaled deeply, as though the foul-smelling stuff was as sweet as a field of wildflowers. The count's courtiers laughed with anticipation, as though they knew something exciting was about to happen. Adair was holding his breath at the prospect of learning the purpose of at least one of the physic's mystical potions, when the old man's sharp gaze fell on him.

"This is not the place for the boy, I think," he said, motioning to a guard. "Perhaps you can find something better to occupy his time, teach him a thing or two about soldiering. He may have to help defend this castle one day, or at the very least, save my old and worthless head." Adair was led away amid mocking laughter from the onlookers, and taken to a courtyard where a handful of guards lazed about.

These were not knights or even professional soldiers, just simple guards, though far more experienced with a sword or a spear than Adair. Under the guise of "training," they took brutal pleasure in abusing Adair for two hours as he tried to defend himself with these unfamiliar weapons. By the time he was allowed back into the great hall, his arms ached from swinging a dull broadsword, the heaviest one the guards could find, and he was nicked and bruised.

The scene in the great hall was not what he'd expected. The count and his vassals seemed to be merely intoxicated, lolling in their seats or fallen to the floor, eyes closed, childish smiles on their faces, ropy muscles gone slack. They paid little notice as the physic made his farewells, leading Adair through the courtyard. In the gray predawn, they picked their way over the drawbridge and through the forest. Adair trudged behind the old man's horse, and exhausted as he was, was grateful not to be carrying the urn.

The mystery of the physic's ways slowly began to coalesce in Adair's mind. On one hand, Adair was grateful for the warm, dry place to sleep and not to be working himself to daily exhaustion and an early grave as a field hand. Unlike his family, he had three meals a day, nearly all he could eat: stew, eggs, the occasional strip of roasted meat. He had sexual companionship, so he would not go insane with unsatisfied desire. On the other hand, Adair could not help but see it as a deal with the devil, even if it had been made against his will: there was a price to pay for a life of relative ease, and he sensed he would be given the bill eventually.

He received the first hint of the payment due one evening, when the physic took Adair and Marguerite to the woods. They walked for a long time, and since they were engaged in nothing more than putting one foot in front of the other, Adair saw the opportunity to ask a few questions of the old man.

"May I ask, master, why it is that you do all your work at night?" he asked, careful to sound as timid and guileless as possible.

At first the old man harrumphed, as though he wouldn't dignify the question with an answer. But after a few moments—for who doesn't like to talk about himself, no matter how trivial the questions—he cleared his throat to answer. "It is a habit, I suppose . . . It is the sort of work best done away from the prying eyes of others." The physic breathed heavily as they went up a slight incline, and it wasn't until they reached a level path that he continued. "The fact of the matter is, Adair, that this work is best done at night, for there is a power in the darkness, you know. It is from the darkness that these potions draw their strength." He said this so matter-of-factly that Adair felt it would only reveal his ignorance to ask the old man to explain, and so he resumed his silence.

Eventually, they came to a place so wild and overgrown that it looked as if it had never been seen by human eyes. Around the roots of the poplars and larches was a proliferation of a strange plant, the broad and fan-shaped leaves standing on willowy stems high above the ground cover, waving to the trio of visitors.

The physic motioned for Marguerite to follow him. He led her to one of the plants, wrapped her hands around it, and then signaled for her to wait. Then he walked away from her, calling Adair to come with him. They walked until the maidservant had almost disappeared in the dimness, her white smock glowing in the moonlight.

"Cover your ears and be sharp about it, or you will be the worse for it," he instructed Adair. Then he pantomimed for Marguerite to pull, which she did, throwing all her weight into one jerking movement. Despite having his hands clasped tight over his ears, Adair swore he heard a muffled noise erupt from the plant as it was ripped from the ground. Adair looked at the physic and lowered his hands, feeling conspicuous.

Marguerite trotted up like a dog following its master, carrying the plant in her hands. The physic took it from her, brushing away the dirt clinging to the hair roots. "Do you know what this is?" he asked Adair as he inspected the thick, five-pointed knob, bigger than the span of a man's hand. "This is a mandrake root. See how it's shaped like a man? Here are the arms, the legs, the head. Did you hear it scream just now, as it was pulled from the ground? The sound will kill any man who hears it." The physic shook the root at Adair. It did look like a stubby, misshapen man. "This is what you need to do to gather more man- drake root—remember this well when I send you out for more. Some physics use a pure black dog to pull up the root, but the dog will die when he hears the scream, like any man. We don't have to bother with killing dogs since we have Marguerite, do we?"

Adair didn't like that the physic had included him in his comment about Marguerite. He wondered, ashamed, if the old man knew about their trysts and condoned Adair's casual treatment of her. Indeed, the physic might liken it to his own brusque treatment of the housekeeper, using her like an ox to pull a stump from a field and, though she was deaf and dumb, he clearly had so little regard for human life that it didn't matter to him if she lived or died by pulling out the root. Of course, it was possible that the mandrake's shriek wouldn't really kill her even if she had been able to hear it, and that the old man had only told Adair the story to frighten him. But Adair filed the tidbit of knowledge about the mandrake away in his memory, with the other morsels of wisdom the physic had shared with him, for use another day.

What little enjoyment Adair took from his new life began to fade as he grew increasingly unhappy with his solitary routine. Boredom gave way to curiosity. He made a thorough inspection of the bottles and jars in the physic's study, then took inventory of the wider room, until he knew every inch of the upper floor of the keep. He had enough common sense not to venture into the cellar.

Without asking the physic's permission, Adair started taking the horse on afternoon rides into the countryside. He reasoned that it was good for the horse to be exercised between the physic's infrequent rides. But sometimes, when he'd put many miles between him and the keep, a voice would tempt him to flee, to keep riding and never return. After all, how would that old man find Adair without a horse to carry him? However, Adair also knew that with the time that had elapsed since he'd arrived at the keep, he wouldn't be able to find his family, and without a family to return to, there was no point in leaving. Here he had food and shelter. If he ran away, he'd have nothing and would be a fugitive for the time he still owed the physic. After a long moment looking at any road that led away from his prison, he would reluctantly turn the horse around and ride back to the keep.

Over time, Adair thought the physic was beginning to warm to him. At night as they worked on a potion, he'd catch the old man staring at him less harshly than usual. The physic started to tell Adair a little bit about the things in the jars as he crushed dried seeds or separated the herbs for storage, such as the names of the more obscure plants and how they might be put to use. There was to be a second visit to the castle over which the old man was practically ebullient, rubbing his hands as he paced around the keep.

"We have a new order from the count, for which we shall start preparations tonight," he chortled, as Adair hung up the old man's cloak on a peg by the door.

"Start what, master?" Adair asked.

"A special request from the count. A very difficult task, but one I have performed before." He scurried back and forth across the timber floor, gathering jars of ingredients on the worktable. "Fetch the large cauldron, and build up the fire—it has almost gone out."

Adair watched from the hearth. First, the physic selected a sheet from his handwritten recipes and read it over quickly before propping it against a jar to consult. He glanced at the paper from time to time as he measured ingredients into the warming pot. He took down things from the shelves that he'd never troubled with before: mysterious bits of animals—snouts, leathery pieces of skin, mummified nubs of flesh. Powders, shiny crystals of white and copper. He poured in an exact amount of water, and then had Adair hang the heavy pot from the spit. As the water began to boil, the physic took a handful of yellow powder from a vial and threw it on the fire: it flamed in a puff of smoke, emitting the unmistakable stench of brimstone.

"I've never seen this mixture before, have I, master?" Adair asked.

"No, you have not." He paused. "It is a potion that makes anyone who drinks it invisible." He searched Adair's face for a reaction. "What do you think of that, boy? Do you believe that can truly happen?"

"I have never heard of such a thing." He knew better than to disagree with the old man.

"Perhaps you will get to see it with your own eyes. The count will have some of his best men drink this potion, and they will become invisible for one night. Can you imagine what an army can do when it cannot be seen?"

"Yes, master," Adair replied, and from that moment, he began to think of the physic's spells and potions in a different way.

"Now, you must watch this cauldron, and let the water boil down, as you have done before. When it has boiled down, you must take it off the fire and let it cool. When you've done that, you may go to sleep, but not before. These ingredients are rare, and that is the last of a few of them, so we cannot afford to ruin this batch. Watch the pot carefully," he said over his shoulder as he descended the staircase. "I will see how well you've done at dusk tonight."

Adair had no trouble staying awake that night. He sat bolt upright against the hard stone wall, realizing that the old man had lied to him and his father. The old man was not a physic, but an alchemist, maybe a necromancer. No wonder the people in the village avoided him. It wasn't just because of the turncoat noble. They were frightened of the old man, and with good reason: he was very likely in league with the devil. God knew what they suspected of Adair.

This potion was not like the previous ones and took forever to shed its moisture. Dawn started to break before an appreciable amount had evaporated. But through the last hours of the night, as he watched a slow vapor rise from the cauldron's depths, Adair's gaze kept wandering back to the stack of handwritten papers on the desk. Surely there were formulas in that pile more intriguing—and more profitable—than the ability to turn men invisible for one night. The old man probably knew how to make fail-safe love potions and talismans to bring great wealth and power to the owner. And surely any alchemist should know how to turn base metal into gold. Even though Adair couldn't read the recipes, he didn't doubt that he could find someone who would, for a piece of the profits.

The longer he thought about it, the more restless he became. He could hide the papers in the sleeve of his tunic and sneak past Marguerite, who would rise at any minute. Then he'd walk all day and get as far from the keep as he could. He thought fleetingly about taking the horse, but there his courage failed. To steal property as valuable as a horse was a death offense. The old man could justifiably seek Adair's life. But the recipes . . . even if the old man could track his servant down, he probably wouldn't dare take Adair before the count. The physic wouldn't want the villagers to know how powerful he really was, or that his mystical knowledge was written down where it could be stolen or destroyed.

Adair's heart pounded, until he could no longer ignore its wild exhortation. It was almost a relief, giving in to this desire.

Adair tightly rolled as many papers as he dared take at once and slid them up his sleeve just as Marguerite began stirring. Before leaving, he hoisted the cauldron off the spit and left it to cool on the hearth. Once outside, he chose a path he knew, one that would take him to Hungarian territory, to a stronghold where Romanian sympathizers would hesitate to go. He walked for hours, cursing his impetuousness, for he hadn't thought to bring provisions. When he started to get light-headed, and the sun had started to slip on the horizon, Adair figured he'd traveled far enough and took refuge in a barn in the middle of a hayfield. It was a desolate place with nothing about, not even livestock, so Adair felt he'd traveled a safe distance and no one would search for him here. He fell asleep in the hay a free man.

He was jarred awake by a hand at his throat, jerking him to his feet and then, inexplicably, off the ground. Adair couldn't see at first who had him, the air thick with night, but as his eyes adjusted, he refused to believe them. The figure holding him was slight . . . wizened . . . but in less than a minute Adair knew it was the old man by the smell of him, the stink of brimstone and decay.

"Thief! This is how you reward my patronage and trust!" the physic roared with outrage, and threw Adair to the ground with such force that he skidded all the way to the back of the barn. Before he could regain his breath, the old man was on him again, clutching him by the shoulder and again lifting him off the ground. Adair was aflame with pain and confusion: the physic was ancient, how could a weak old man lift him so easily? It had to be an illusion, or a fantasy induced by a blow to the head. Adair had only a minute to ponder this before the old man threw him to the ground a second time, then began hitting and kicking him. The blows were tremendously powerful. Adair's head chattered in pain, and he was sure he would black out. He felt himself carried, felt the movement of air all around. They were traveling at a great rate of speed, by horseback, but it seemed unlikely that the old charger would be capable of such speed. Surely it must all be a delusion, he told himself, produced by some elixir the old man had forced on him in his sleep. It was too magical and frightening to be real.

Still in a stupor, Adair felt the air slow, their bodies again take on a human weight. Then the smells came to him: the musty dankness of the keep, the residue of burning herbs and brimstone hanging in the air. He felt curdled with fear. Dropping to the floor, he opened his eyes a crack and was crushed to see that he was indeed back in the keep, returned to his prison.

The old man walked toward him. He had changed: perhaps it was a trick of angle and perception, but he seemed tall and foreboding, not the old physic at all. The physic's hand snaked out for the poker, and then he leaned over to fish the ratty blanket from Adair's straw pallet. Slowly, deliberately, he wound the blanket around the poker as he advanced on Adair.

Adair watched the arm rise, but averted his gaze as the poker came down. The blanket cushioned the blow, kept the iron from breaking the boy's bones outright. But the blows were like nothing he'd felt before, not the punches and slaps he'd endured from his father, not like willow switches or the lash of a leather strap. The iron bar compressed muscle, smashed the flesh until the bar came in contact with bone. It came down again and again, across his back, shoulders, and spine. He rolled to escape the blows, but the weapon caught him anyway, striking his ribs, his stomach, his legs. Soon Adair was beyond pain, no longer able to move or even to flinch as the poker continued to rain down. It hurt to breathe; white-hot lashings of flame laced his sides with every breath, his insides awash in runny, hot liquid. He was dying. The old man was going to beat him to death.

"I could cut off your hand, you know, that is the punishment for thieves. But what good would you be to me then, with only one hand?" The physic stood upright stiffly, throwing the poker to the floor. "Maybe I'll chop off your hand when your service is over, so that everyone will know what you are. Or perhaps I won't release you, when your seven years are over. Perhaps I'll take another seven years, as punishment for your crime. How could you ever think you'd escape me, and steal from me what is mine?"

His words made little difference. The old man was deluded, Adair decided, to think his servant would live. He'd not see the sunrise, let alone seven years. Hot liquid worked its way around his intestines and organs, up Adair's throat, into his mouth. Blood seeped over his lips and onto the wooden floor, oozing toward the old man's feet in a dark, trickling stream. Blood was escaping from every orifice in Adair's body.

Adair's eyes flickered. The old man had stopped talking and was staring at him again in that intense way of his. He began creeping on the floor toward the boy, like a snake or lizard, close to the ground, until he was very near Adair, his mouth open, his tongue inching forward, straining. He took one long, bony finger and dipped it in the stream of blood flowing from Adair's mouth. A long red trail dribbled down his finger as he brought it to his face and wiped it over his tongue. He rolled his tongue in his mouth and a faint, excited sigh passed over his lips. At that point, Adair passed out and was relieved for it. But the last thing he discerned, as consciousness left for what he was sure would be the last time, was the old man's fingers stroking the side of his face, and running through Adair's sweat-soaked hair.

TWENTY-ONE

Marguerite found Adair in the morning in a terrible state. In the night, his body had prepared for death: his bowels evacuated, his blood-soaked clothing had stuck to the floor so stubbornly that the housekeeper had to swab the spot with rags steeped in warm water to pry him loose.

He lay on his straw pallet, unconscious, for several days, and when he awoke, he found he was covered with large patches of black and violet edged with yellow and green, his skin hot and tender to the touch. But somehow Marguerite had cleaned away all outward traces of blood and dressed him in a fresh linen nightshirt.

Adair drifted in and out of consciousness, his thoughts incoherent as they danced in his head. In the worst of the twilight moments, he imagined someone was touching him, that fingertips glided over his face and lips. Another time he fancied he was being rolled onto his stomach and his clothing disturbed. The latter could be explained if Marguerite was cleaning him, as he was unable to move with sufficient coordination to use the chamber pot. Incapacitated, he couldn't move or resist, could do nothing but accept this violation, real or imagined.

Smell was the first sense to return and then taste, the tang of iron from blood and the unctuousness of beef tallow. Once his eyes opened—and it took a few moments for his vision to focus and to be assured that he hadn't lost his sight—his surroundings became real again and the sensation of pain came back to him. His ribs ached, his gut went wobbly and loose, and every breath stabbed into splintered ribs. With pain came his voice. He flailed at the blanket, attempting futilely to rise.

Marguerite hurried to his side and felt Adair's forehead, and flexed his feet and hands, looking for signs of discomfort that foretold broken bones, to see which parts he could move by himself and which parts were injured. After all, what good was a laborer without the use of arms or legs?

She fetched broth and then ignored Adair for the rest of the afternoon while she moved through her chores. He had no alternative but to stare at the ceiling and watch time mark its passage as a square of sunlight working its way down the wall, counting off the hours until nightfall when the old man would awaken. Adair spent the time in fearful anticipation: it would have been better to have died that night, Adair decided, than to awake trapped in a wrecked body. How long would it take to recover, he wondered: Would he be whole when his bones had mended? Would the parts mesh correctly? Would he limp or be hunchbacked? At least his face seemed free of scar or disfiguration: the old man had spared his head—had he struck it with a poker, he would have split Adair's skull open.

When the square of light faded, signaling the end of daylight, Adair knew his time had run out. He decided to pretend to be asleep. Marguerite, too, sensed a confrontation was near and she tried to hurriedly prepare for bed as the old man came up the stairs, but the physic interrupted her, catching her arm and pointing toward Adair's bed inquisitively. But she had seen Adair close his eyes and settle into a pose of unconsciousness, so she only shook her head and withdrew into her bed, pulling a blanket over her shoulder.

The old man went to Adair's bed, crouching low. Adair tried to keep his breathing even and calm and to control his trembling, waiting to see what the old man was going to do. He didn't have to wait long: the old man's cold, bony hand touched the young man's cheek, then his Adam's apple, then slid down his chest, but only briefly before settling on Adair's flat stomach. He barely touched the bruised spots and yet it was all Adair could do to keep from curling up in pain.

The hand did not stop, but continued gliding downward: to the abdomen, then lower still, and the shock almost caused Adair to cry out. Somehow he managed to lie stoically while the old man's fingers found what they were looking for, caressing the irregular piece of flesh, massaging, kneading, coaxing. But before Adair's manhood could respond, the fingers withdrew, and without a backward look, the old man turned and drifted through the door and into the night.

The panic was almost enough to cause Adair to leap out of bed despite his condition. He was seized by the urge to flee but could not: he had little control of his arms and his legs were entirely unresponsive. The old man was considerably stronger than he appeared; Adair was defenseless against him in good health, never mind in his current state. He couldn't even crawl across the room to find a weapon to use to defend himself. Sour with despair, Adair realized there was nothing he could do for himself, not now. He could only endure whatever the physic wished to inflict upon him.

He passed the days by thinking of the work he'd done for the physic, the elixirs and salves he'd made, wondering if perhaps there might be something there he could use for his defense. Such thoughts were hopeless; though they served to strengthen his memory of the ingredients that went into these powerful things—as well as the proportions and smells and textures—he was still ignorant of their purpose, for all except the one that conferred invisibility.

*　　　*　　　*

He managed to keep up the charade for two more days before the physic realized Adair had regained consciousness. He tested his limbs and joints in the same way Marguerite had done, and prepared an elixir that he poured down the young man's throat. It was the elixir that gave Adair away, for the potion burned and stung, and he couldn't help but choke on it.

"I hope you have learned a lesson, so at least some good may come from your deceit," the physic growled as he stumped around the desk. "And that lesson is that you can never escape from me. I can find you no matter where you go. No journey would be far enough, no hiding spot deep enough to elude me. The next time you try to cheat me out of the service I have paid for or steal any of my things, this little episode will seem like the lightest of punishments. If I so much as *sense* you are being disloyal, I will chain you to the walls of this keep and you will never again see the light of day, do you understand?" The old man wasn't disturbed in the least by the hateful look Adair gave him.

Within a few weeks, Adair was able to rise from bed and hobble around the room with the use of a walking stick. As his ribs creaked with pain every time he lifted his arms, he was still worthless to Marguerite, but he could again assist the physic in the evening. However, all conversation between them ceased: the old man barked his orders and Adair slinked from his sight as soon as he had fulfilled them.

After a couple of months, with regular doses of the burning elixir, Adair had healed considerably, to the point where he could fetch water and chop wood. He could run, though not for long, and was sure he would be able to ride, if the chance arose. Sometimes, when he gathered herbs in the woods and strayed to the edge of the hill, he'd look over the valley and think about trying to escape again. He wished, fiercely, to be free of the old man and yet . . . A sickening feeling came over Adair at the prospect of punishment and, with near-suicidal thoughts, he would turn back to the keep.

"Tomorrow, you are to go to the village and find a young girl child. She must be a virgin. You are not to ask anyone for information, or draw attention to yourself in any way. Just find this child, return, and tell me where she lives."

Panic clawed at Adair's throat. "How am I to know if a child is unspoiled? Am I to examine—"

"Obviously you must find one who is very young. As for any examination, you will leave that to me," he said chillingly.

The old man gave no explanation, and by then, Adair needed none. He knew any order from the physic was surely a diabolical request and yet Adair was not in a position to refuse. Usually, he viewed trips to the village as rare treats, when he got to be around the familiar bustle of family life, even if not his own family, but this trip portended no good. In the village, Adair lingered near the houses as inconspicuously as he could to spy on the villagers, but the village was small and he was not unknown to them. As soon as he found some children playing or attending to chores, the parents would usher their children away or threaten Adair with menacing stares.

Afraid of the physic's reaction to his failure, he took an unfamiliar path on his way back to the keep, hoping it might bring him luck. The trail took him to a clearing where, to his surprise, a number of wagons stood, wagons not dissimilar to the one his own family had lived in. A troupe of Roma had come to the village and Adair's heart swelled with the hope that his family had come looking for him. As he searched through the itinerant workers, he soon realized that he recognized not one member of this group. There were children of every age, however, red-cheeked boys and sweet-faced girls. And because he was of the same descent, he could move freely among them, though he was obviously unknown.

Could he do such a terrible thing? he asked himself, heart pounding as he cast about, glancing from face to face. He was about to flee, overcome with self-hatred—how could he choose which one was to be delivered into the hands of that monster?—when he ran abruptly into a child, a little girl who reminded him so much of his own Katarina. The same creamy white skin, the same piercing dark eyes, the same winsome smile. It was as though fate had made the decision for him.

The physic was delighted with the news and instructed Adair to go to the Roma encampment that evening, when all were asleep, and bring the girl back to him. "It is fitting, is it not?" the old man cackled, perhaps thinking it would make Adair feel better for what he was about to do. "Your people cast you out, gave you away without a second thought. Now is your chance for revenge."

Instead of persuading Adair that it was within his rights to steal the child, it only made him bristle. "Why do you require this girl? What will you do with her?"

"It is not your place to think, only to obey," the old man growled. "You have just started to heal, haven't you? It would be a shame to break your bones all over again."

Adair thought to beg God to intervene, but at that moment prayers were useless. Adair had every reason to believe that he and the girl were doomed and that nothing would save either of them. So, late that evening he went back to the encampment. He went from wagon to wagon, peering through windows or through the tops of open Dutch doors until he found the girl, curled up like a kitten on a blanket. Holding his breath, he pushed back the door and scooped up the sleeping child, half wishing she would cry out and alert the mother and father, even if it meant he would be caught. But the child slept in his arms as though bewitched.

Adair heard nothing behind him as he ran off: no footsteps, no telltale noise of any kind coming from the parents' wagon, no cry of trespass from the encampment. The child grew restless and began to fuss, and Adair didn't know what to do except hold her closer to his wildly beating heart in hopes that it would calm her. As much as he wished for the courage to disobey the old man's ominous orders, Adair crashed through the woods, crying the entire way.

However, as he approached the keep, a desperate courage came to him. He simply could not fulfill the physic's wishes, no matter what it meant for his own safety. His feet slowed of their own accord and within steps, he had turned around. By the time he reached the edge of the clearing, the girl was awake though trustingly quiet. He set her on her feet and knelt next to her.

"Go back to your parents. Tell them they must leave this village immediately. There is great evil here and it will bring tragedy if they do not heed this warning," he said to the girl.

The girl reached up to his face and touched his tears. "Who should I tell them has given them this message?"

"My name is not important," he said, knowing that even if the Roma had his name and came for him, looking to exact punishment for stealing into their encampment and kidnapping a child, it wouldn't matter. He would be dead by then.

Adair remained kneeling in the grass as he watched the girl run toward the wagons. He wished he could run, too, run toward the open forest and keep running, but he knew that it would do no good. He might as well return to the keep and accept his punishment.

When Adair pushed back the door to the keep, the old man was sitting at his desk. The slight eagerness on the physic's face gave way quickly to the familiar expression of scorn and displeasure when he saw that Adair was alone.

The physic drew himself up, suddenly very tall, like a towering tree. "You've failed me, I see. I can't say I'm surprised."

"I may be a slave to you, but you can't make me a murderer. I will not do it!"

"You're still weak, fatally weak. Cowardly. I need you to be stronger. If I thought you were incapable of this, I would kill you tonight. But I am not convinced, not yet . . . so I will not kill you this evening, merely punish you." The physic struck his servant so hard that he fell to the floor and blacked out. When Adair came to, he realized the old man had lifted his head and was shoving a goblet to Adair's mouth. "Drink this."

"What is it—poison? Is this how you will kill me?"

"I said I would not kill you tonight. That doesn't mean I do not have other plans. Drink this"—he said, eyes glinting ruthlessly— "drink this and you will feel no pain."

Adair would have welcomed poison at that point, so he gulped the contents the physic fed into his mouth. A strange feeling overtook Adair quickly, not unlike the dizzy stupor brought on by the old man's healing elixirs. It started with a tingling in his limbs, then quickly overtook him. Unable to control his muscles, Adair fell slack, eyelids drooping like a victim of palsy, his breathing labored. By the time the tingling had reached the base of his skull, a numbing buzz foretold that something supernatural was about to take over.

The old man stood in front of his servant, appraising him in a cold, unsettling way. Adair felt himself be lifted and carried, felt his weight drop with every step. Down, down the stairs, to the cellar where he had never been, the old man's chamber, and the realization filled Adair with cold panic. It was dank and airless, a true dungeon, and filthy. Vermin crawled busily in the corners. The old man dropped the young man on a bed, a stinking old mattress of mildewed down. Adair wanted to crawl away but was trapped in a body that would not respond.

Unmoved, the old man climbed on the bed and began undressing his captive, pulling the tunic over his head, loosening the belt at his waist. "Tonight, you will cross the last threshold of your reserve. From tonight, there will be nothing I cannot make you do." He pushed the young man's breeches down, and reached for the thin linen covering his groin. Again, Adair closed his eyes as the physic searched with his fingers, digging through the pubic hair. Adair fought not to be aroused as the old man manipulated his penis. After what seemed a very long time, the old man released his plaything, but let his hands travel up to Adair's face. His fingers pressed against Adair's cheek-bones, then in the valley under his eyes. The young man fought as best he could, in this narcotic state, against this horrific trespass.

"Now, foolish boy. I'll smother you if you do not obey me. You have to breathe, do you not?" He closed a hand over Adair's nose, cutting off all air. Adair held out as long as he could, wondering in a disoriented state if he would die or black out . . . But in the end, reflex took over and he gasped for air. Once his mouth was open, the old man forced himself past his captive's slackened jaw. Mercifully, the drug began to pull the shade of incoherency over Adair's horror and humiliation, and the last thing he would recall was the old man saying that he knew about the trysts with Marguerite and that they would stop. He would not have Adair expending his energy and wasting his seed on another.

TWENTY-TWO

In the morning, Adair awoke on the upper floor on his skimpy pallet of straw, his clothes in disarray. Wracked with nausea and traces of the narcotic, he recalled the old man's warning but had no idea if other liberties had been taken. He was seized with the urge to rush downstairs and stab the old man to death in his bed, the idea flaming up in his mind for a dazzling second. He knew something mysterious and supernatural was afoot, however; the old man's strength and powers were beyond reasonable expectation and he would be powerful enough not to let himself be killed in his own lair.

He spent the day trying to summon the courage to flee. But a familiar fear chained Adair to the spot, the cold ache in his knitted bones a reminder of the price of disobedience. So, when the sun had traveled across the sky and darkness began to settle in, Adair sat in a corner, gaze fixed on the top of the staircase.

The old man wasn't surprised to find his servant still there. A sly smile crossed his face but he didn't try to approach Adair. He went about his business as before, retrieving his cloak from the peg. "I am going to the castle tonight, for a special function. If you know what is good for you, you will be here when I return." When he left, Adair collapsed by the fire, wishing he had the courage to throw himself into it.

Life continued like this for countless months. The beatings became routine, though the old man didn't use the poker again. Adair quickly saw that there were no reasons behind the beatings; he was so docile that there could be no excuse for them. The beatings merely served to keep him obedient and so there would never be an end to them. The molestations continued, unevenly. The physic had Marguerite drug Adair's food or drink to facilitate these sessions, until the young man became wise to this tactic and refused to eat. Then the old man would beat him and force him to swallow debilitating narcotics until he was in a helpless state.

The physic's decadence accelerated. Perhaps he'd opened some sort of floodgate: now that he'd indulged in these immoral acts, there was no stopping him. Or maybe this was how the old man had always been. Adair wondered if the old man had killed his last servant, and had sought out Adair to start over again. The count began to send a maid occasionally for the old man's enjoyment, some unfortunate young woman captured by the count's men during their raids into the Hungarian countryside. The young woman would be taken to the physic's chambers and chained to his bed. The maid's cries would waft upstairs during the day, haunting Adair, punishing him for not going down to the physic's lair to help her escape.

Occasionally, after the old man had left on his nightly wanderings, Marguerite would send Adair below with food for the poor prisoner. He remembered the first time, creeping reluctantly into the chamber to see the poor woman, naked under the bedding, shivering in shock and fear, and unable to acknowledge his presence. This first one didn't beg the young man to release her. Paralytic with fear, she didn't move toward the food. Adair was ashamed to find he was aroused, staring at her feminine form under the blanket, her flat stomach rising and falling with each terrified breath. His sympathy for her plight and his own horrible memories of what had happened to him in this bed were not enough to keep him from filling with lust. He didn't dare force himself on her, as she was the old man's property, and so, shaking with desire, left her untouched and retreated upstairs.

The maidens usually died within three days and the old man made Adair dispose of them, retrieving their cold bodies from the bed and carrying them into the woods. They would lie on the ground like toppled statues as he dug their graves, sprinkled them with lime, covered them over with dark earth. The first maiden's death filled him with shame, self-hatred, and despair, so much so that he couldn't look at her as she waited for her anonymous grave.

But after the first one, and the third, and the fourth, Adair found that something had changed within him and his yearning—which he knew to be abominable—outstripped his fear of trespass into the profane. His hands trembled as he surrendered to the desire to touch their breasts, now hard and inhuman, or run his hands over their curving bodies. Each time he lowered one of them into the ground, he brushed against the torso and thrilled at the stiffening in his body. But he never went further, never committed an act he found more repulsive than fascinating, and so the bodies were spared further molestation.

Several years passed like this. The beatings and rapes dwindled, perhaps because Adair had grown bigger and stronger and gave the old man pause. Or perhaps, because he was no longer a boy, he didn't appeal to the physic.

After one particularly brutal winter, the old man announced they were traveling to Romania to visit his estate. Word was sent ahead to the vassal who ran the property so the accounts could be put in order and everything made ready for the physic's review. Leave was secured from the count, and a second horse was purchased for Adair to ride on the journey. When it was time to go, only a few provisions were packed, some clothing and two small, locked trunks. They departed after the sun had set, riding eastward into the night.

At the end of seven nights of travel, they were deep in Romanian territory, having traveled through a pass in the foothills of the Carpathian Mountains to get to the old man's estate. "Our journey is over," the physic told Adair, nodding toward a light glowing faintly from a castle in the distance. The castle had high turrets at each corner, the forbidding shape sharply visible in the moonlight. The last stretch took them through fertile fields, vineyards clinging to the mountainside, cattle sleeping in the fields. The huge gates were thrown open as the pair approached and a coterie of servants waited in the courtyard, torches held overhead. An older man stood at the head of the group, holding a fur robe that he wrapped around the physic's shoulders as soon as he dismounted.

"I trust your lordship had a safe journey," he said with the solicitousness of a priest, following the physic up the broad stone steps.

"I am here, am I not?" the old man snapped.

Adair drank in details of the estate as they made their way inside. The castle was massive, old but well tended. Adair saw that the servants wore the same look of terror he fancied he did. One servant took his arm and led him to the kitchen, where Adair was given a meal of fancy roast meats and fowl, and afterward was taken to a small chamber. He sank into a real feather bed that night, nestled under a fur-edged blanket.

Adair came to love this time away, living more grandly than he ever imagined possible for anyone, let alone a peasant boy. Freed from the regime of life in the keep, he spent most days roaming the castle, as the physic was immersed in the running of the property and lost interest in Adair's whereabouts.

The overseer, Lactu, took a liking to Adair. He was a kind man, and seemed to recognize the unspoken burden the physic's servant carried. Because Lactu also spoke Hungarian, Adair was able to have a real conversation for the first time in all the years he'd worked for the physic. Lactu had come from a line of servants who had been in the physic's employ for generations. He explained that he didn't find it strange that the physic was away most of the time: the lords of this property had been absentee landowners for generations, traditionally taking up service to the Romanian king instead. In Lactu's experience, the physic returned only every seven years or so, to tend to important matters.

Through the overseer, Adair gained entrance to all the special chambers in the castle. He got to see the room that held the old man's ceremonial robes, packed away in chests, and the buttery, filled with stocks of all the foods made on the estate. The most eye-popping, however, was the treasure room, filled with the cel Rau family's share of conquest: crowns and scepters, gem-studded adornments, coins of strange mint. The sight of so much property and so many possessions put Adair in mind of the written alchemic recipes: the gigantic castle in the faraway land was such a waste. It was criminal to have such treasure and not put it to good use.

Weeks passed with Adair rarely seeing the physic, though one night the physic sent word for Adair to attend a ceremony in the great hall. The young man watched as the physic signed declarations that would have a binding effect on everyone who lived on the estate. Next to the old man's right hand stood a heavy seal. Lactu brought out each proclamation, read it aloud, and then laid the sheet before the physic for his signature. Then the overseer would drip scarlet wax below the physic's scrawl, into which the old man would press the seal with the family crest—a dragon wielding a sword. Later Lactu explained to Adair that it was the seal that conveyed the cel Rau rule of law: because the lords often died while away from the property and without their heirs properly introduced to the Romanian authorities or even the overseer, signatures were meaningless. Whoever held the seal was recognized as lord of the estate.

Weeks turned into months. Adair would have been happy never to return to Hungary. He enjoyed the dual benefit of being treated like a favored son while escaping the physic's attentions. In his free time, he practiced swordplay with the guards, or rode through the hamlets. He discussed what he saw with the overseer, deepening his understanding of the property and its many aspects, such as the cultivation of crops, the production of wine, the care of livestock. Adair believed Lactu came to hold him in regard, but the young man didn't dare share any details of life back in the keep. He returned Lactu's affection tenfold but greatly feared what the overseer would think of him if he knew what he had suffered, or that he helped the old man in his practice of the dark arts. He longed to tell Lactu of their master's evil nature, but couldn't think of a way to do so without implicating himself, and he was loath to lose the overseer's affection.

One night, late in the season, Adair was woken by a presence in his bedchamber. He knew as he lit a candle that he wasn't alone, but nonetheless was startled to find the physic standing at the foot of the bed.

His heart pounded at the memory of the horrors the man was capable of. "Master, you surprised me. Are you in need of my services?"

"I have not seen you in so long, Adair, I wanted to look upon you but, I swear, I would almost not recognize you," he said in his brittle rasp. "Life here has agreed with you. You've grown. You're taller— and stronger." There was a look, a flash of the old temptation in the physic's eyes that Adair didn't wish to see.

"I've learned much in my time here," Adair said, wanting to show the physic that he hadn't been idle while out of the old man's gaze. "Your estate is magnificent. I do not understand how you can bear to be away from it."

"Life here is too quiet for my tastes. I think you would find it so yourself, in time. But that is why I have come tonight, to tell you that we will not stay much longer. Summer is fast approaching, and I am needed back in Hungary."

The old man's words alarmed Adair. He'd known this time would end but somehow had deluded himself into believing that it would go on forever. Adair tried to keep the panic from showing on his face. In the meantime, the old man glided to his servant's bedside, searching his features. He reached over and drew the blanket away, exposing Adair's chest and abdomen. Adair steeled himself for the touch, but it did not come. Instead, the old man looked at the young man, his hunger palpable, but he seemed content with just the sight of Adair's body. Or maybe Adair's maturity gave him pause, for after a long minute, he turned and left the room.

TWENTY-THREE

Upon returning to the physic's keep, Adair expected that life would continue as it had before, but that proved to be impossible. Too much had happened to him. He was controlled by a notion that he could not expunge from his head, especially during the daylight hours when the physic wasn't around to dominate his thoughts. Adair could not forget what he'd seen at the old man's estate: the massive stronghold itself, the bountiful fields, the treasure, the servants, the serfs . . . The only part missing was a liege, and all that stood in his way were two simple things: the seal, now hidden somewhere in the keep, and the old man's death.

The seal could be found with a little persistence. Killing the old man was another matter. Adair had thought about it many times during his years of imprisonment, turned it over in his mind and tinkered with each detail, but dismissed it in the end as a mad dream. Every time the old man had laid a hand on Adair, either in anger or lust, the servant had smothered his humiliation by vowing that one day he'd make the physic pay. But it was the memory of that brutal attack with the poker and the months of agonizing recovery that had kept Adair from acting.

Years had passed since that beating, however, and Adair had grown considerably. The physic was no longer quick to raise his hand and, while he continued to look at Adair with desire, his approaches were few and calculated. And Adair's hatred of the old man had been with him for so long, it was as natural as breathing. His thoughts had grown more precise, the need for revenge more ferocious and undeniable. He hadn't realized how completely he had changed until one evening as he buried another dead wench. He looked on her lovely body and realized that this last taboo had fallen away. He could easily assault that empty form—but what he really wanted was to ravish the lifeless body of the physic before burying him in the wet ground. And, what's more, he would be glad for having done it. He felt no fear and no revulsion. He had forsaken the last shred of his humanity. All reserve had been stripped away, layer by layer, like an animal skinned by a hunter. He had become a ready match for the old man, and the thought made Adair happy for the first time in years.

The first step was to secure assistance. Adair needed allies, villagers who already hated the physic, who was in league with their Romanian oppressor. Adair had to find those villagers who held a grudge against their overlord and would be willing to take their fury out on the physic, an easier target than the count. If he could prove the physic had committed crimes against the villagers, crimes the count could not defend, then the count would be forced to look the other way if their vengeance took the form of murder. It was a matter of finding the right people, choosing the right trespass, and producing the necessary proof.

Adair went into the village one day to look for the religious authorities, who seemed a likely choice for his purpose. In the abbey, Adair found a young monk, spared from the rigors of the field and pink all over, like a newborn. The cleric seemed surprised to find the wicked physic's servant standing in his doorway, but when Adair fell to the cleric's feet, begging his counsel, the young monk could hardly refuse. They sat together in the solitude of the abbey and he listened as Adair poured out his remorse for being a servant of the village's oppressor. Adair explained that he was forced to serve against his will. Without dwelling on the circumstances, Adair went on to express repulsion for serving such a wicked and unrepentant despot. When the monk started to reassure him—hesitantly at first, but then the words coming more freely—Adair knew he'd found the ally he was looking for. As a final touch, Adair hinted at dark sins the physic and the count had committed. The monk assured Adair that he could return at any time to further unburden himself.

And so Adair did. The second time he went to see the monk, he described how he'd been sent by the physic to kidnap a child. The monk's face grew pale and he drew back, as though confronted with a viper, when Adair described the location of the gypsy wagons; the monk confirmed that the gypsies had fled without an explanation. "I assume he intended to use the child for one of his fiendish potions but to what effect, for what cause, I cannot say. It must be the devil's work, mustn't it, to require a human sacrifice?" Adair asked in an incredulous voice, making himself sound as innocent and repentant as he could muster.

At that point, the monk begged him to stop, not wanting to believe what he was being told. "I swear it's true," Adair said, dropping to his knees. "I can bring proof. The parchment on which the spells were written, would that be proof enough?" The monk, stricken, could only nod his head.

Adair knew it was a simple enough trick to smuggle the papers out of the keep during the day while the physic was asleep, but the next day as he went to gather his evidence, his hands still trembled as he reached for them. *Don't be foolish*, he chastised himself. *It's been years. Are you a man or still a frightened boy?* Tired of being haunted by fear and humiliation, he snatched up the papers with a certain ruthlessness, rolling them tightly before slipping them in his sleeve. Without a word to Marguerite, he set out for the abbey.

The young monk's eyes lit up when he read the faded words written on the parchment. He apologized to Adair for doubting him as he handed the papers back and instructed Adair to return them swiftly to the keep, and alert him should the physic begin planning another murderous crime. However, he needed time to work up a scheme to capture the heretic who was, after all, an ally of their liege. Adair protested: the physic was in league with the devil and didn't deserve one more day of freedom. But the monk's resolution was tottering; he was obviously having trouble screwing up his courage for so bold a move against the count. To shore up the monk's resolve, Adair promised to be back with more proof of witchcraft.

That evening, the physic's company was agony. Adair jumped whenever the old man gave him the slightest look askance, sure the physic could sense that Adair had touched his precious parchments. While the old man searched through his papers for the spell he needed, Adair fidgeted, certain that the physic would find something amiss: a bent corner, a smudge, the smell of burning lavender and incense from the abbey. But the old man continued calmly about his work.

Shortly after midnight, the old man looked up from the worktable.

"Do you still wish to read, boy?" he asked, pleasantly enough. It seemed strange to Adair that the old man would bring this up, so suddenly. Still, if Adair gave any other response, the old man would know something was wrong.

"Yes, of course."

"I suppose tonight is as good as any to begin. Come over here, and I will teach you some of the letters on this page." The physic crooked a finger at him. Chest squeezing, Adair rose from the floor and walked to the old man.

The physic eyed the small space left between them. "Closer, boy, you will not be able to see the paper from there." He pointed to the spot next to him on the floor. Sweat broke out across Adair's brow as he sidled closer. No sooner had he slid next to the old man and bowed toward the paper than the old man reached up and grasped Adair's throat with an iron claw. He couldn't breathe as the fist closed around his windpipe.

"Tonight will be a very important night for you, Adair, my fine boy. Very important," he crooned, rising from his seat, lifting the young man into the air by the throat. "I did not think I would keep you in my employ this long. I had planned to kill you long ago. But despite your one serious offense, you have grown on me. You've always had a certain savage beauty, but you have also been more loyal than I thought possible. Yes, you've done better than I would have guessed from that first night I saw you. And so I've decided to keep you as a servant—forever." He slammed Adair into the stone wall as though he were a rag doll, Adair's head cracking against the rocks. The strength left his body. The old man lifted him, carrying him down the stairs again, to the privacy of the subterranean chamber.

Adair fluttered in and out of consciousness as he lay on the bed, aware of the old man's hands on his face. "I have a precious gift to give you, my rebellious peasant boy. Did you think I could not see it in your eyes, but of course I could . . ." Adair panicked at the old man's words, worried that the physic could read his mind and knew of the pact with the monk. "But once you have received this gift, you will be unable to refuse me anything ever again. This gift will bind us together, you will see . . ."

The old man drew very close, studying his servant in a terrifying way. It was then that Adair noticed an amulet hanging from a leather cord on the physic's neck. The old man wrapped his hand around the amulet and snapped the cord, protecting the amulet with his two hands from Adair's view. But Adair had gotten a glimpse of it in the meager candlelight: it was a tiny silver vial, detailed with the minutest fretwork and its own miniature lid.

Somehow, with his withered fingertips, the physic managed to pull off the lid, revealing a long needle that served as a slender stopper. A viscous copper-colored fluid clung to the needle, forming a fat droplet on the tip. "Open your unworthy mouth," the physic ordered, holding the stopper over Adair's lips. "You are about to receive a precious gift. Most men would kill for this gift or would pay vast sums. And here I am about to waste it on a clod like you! Do as I tell you, you ungrateful dog, before I change my mind." He needn't have struggled: the needle was slight enough to force over Adair's lips, and he jabbed the needle into Adair's tongue.

It was more the shock than the pain that made Adair thrash against the physic, the shock of a strange numbness taking over his body. It froze the young man's heart in terror, and with the instantaneous appreciation that he was in the grasp of something demonic. As pressure dropped in his body, his heart began to beat more and more rapidly, desperate to push the dwindling supply of blood to his starving limbs, his brain, his heart. All the while, the old man pressed down on him, heavy as stone, mumbling unintelligibly and certainly in the devil's tongue as he performed another strange act on him, this time with needles and ink. Adair tried to throw off the old man but could not budge him, and within a minute no longer had the strength to try. His lungs collapsing, he could no longer draw breath. Convulsing, choking, bucking against the bedding in the throes of death and bluing cold . . . Adair felt as though he were being buried alive, locked inside a body that was spiraling downward, failing.

A fierce will inside Adair resisted death. If he died, the old man would never be punished, and more than anything else, Adair wanted to see that day.

The physic studied Adair's face in the throes of death. "So strong. You have a strong will to survive, that is good. Glower with hatred for me. That is what I expect, Adair. Your body will go through the final stages of dying; that will hold your attention for a while. Lie still."

When Adair's body could not save itself, it began dying. It started to stiffen, trapping Adair's consciousness inside. As he lay there, the physic spoke of how he'd been drawn into alchemy—he didn't expect Adair, a peasant, to understand the allure of science—how his training as a physic had opened the door. But beyond alchemy, he had joined the few, the most astute, who moved beyond the secrets of the natural world to the supernatural world. Changing base metals to gold was an allegory, did Adair understand? The true seers sought not to change materials of the earth into finer things, but to change the nature of man himself! Through mental purification and applying himself solely to the knowledge of alchemy, the physic had moved into the ranks of the most knowledgeable, the most powerful men on earth.

"I can command water, fire, earth, and wind. You've seen as much—you know it's true," he boasted. "I can make men invisible. I have the strength of my youth—that has surprised you, hasn't it? Actually, I am stronger than I used to be; sometimes, I feel as strong as twenty men! And I have command over time, too. The gift I've given you"—his face broke into a hideous display of superiority and self-satisfaction—"is immortality. You, my near-perfect servant, will never leave my employ. Will never fail me. Will never die."

Adair heard the words as he was dying and hoped he'd misunderstood. To serve the physic forever! He begged for death to take him away. In his panic, he blocked out the rest of what the physic was telling him, but it didn't matter.

There was a last thread he heard as the blackness swallowed him up. The physic was saying there was only one way to escape from eternity. There was only one way to be killed, and that was by the hand of the one who had transformed him. By his maker, the physic.

TWENTY-FOUR

When Adair awoke, he found he was still in the physic's bed, the old man lying close in a deathlike slumber. Adair sat up, feeling peculiar. It was as if everything had changed in his sleep, but he couldn't say precisely how. Some changes were evident: vision, for instance. He could see in the dark. He saw rats milling about in the corners of the room, climbing over one another as they ran the length of the wall. He could hear every single sound as though he were right beside the source of the noise, each sound separate and distinct. Smell was the most overpowering of all, though; odors clamored for his attention, most of all something sweet and rich, with a hint of copper, on the air. He couldn't identify it, no matter how it teased him.

Within a few minutes, the physic stirred, then bolted awake. He noticed Adair was in a stupor, and laughed. "Part of the gift, you see. Wonderful, isn't it? You have the senses of an animal."

"What is that smell? I smell it everywhere." Adair looked at his hands, the bedding.

"It is blood. The rats, they are fat with it, and they are all around you. Marguerite, sleeping above. You can also smell minerals in the rocks, in the walls surrounding you. The sweet dirt, the clear water—everything is better, cleaner. It is the gift. It elevates you above men."

Adair dropped to his knees on the floor. "And what about you? Are you also like me? Is that where you got your powers? Can you see everything?"

The old man smiled mysteriously. "Am I the same as you? No, Adair, I have not put myself through the transformation that you have gone through."

"Why not? Don't you wish to live forever?"

He shook his head as though he was talking to a fool. "It's not as simple as granting a wish. It might be beyond your comprehension. In any case, I am an old man and suffer the indignities of age. I would not wish to live through eternity in this form."

"If that is the case, then how do you propose to keep me now, old man? Now that you've made me strong, there will be no more beatings. God knows there will be no more violations. How can you hope to keep me in your company?"

The old man walked to the staircase, looking archly over his shoulder. "Nothing has changed between us, Adair. Do you think I would have given you the sort of power that would set you free? I am still stronger. I can extinguish your life like the flame of a candle. I am the only vehicle of your undoing. Remember that." The physic disappeared in the gloom.

Adair remained on his knees, shaking, not knowing at that moment if he believed what the old man had told him, if he believed the strange power that surged through his limbs. He looked at the spot on his arm where he'd seen the physic at work with needles and ink, thinking he might have dreamed it, but no, there was a curious design there, of two circles dancing around each other. The design had a strange familiarity to it, but he couldn't recall where he'd seen it.

Maybe the physic was right: perhaps Adair was too stupid to grasp something this complex. But eternal life—it was the last thing he cared about, at the moment. He didn't care if he lived or died. All he wanted was to convince the monk to carry out his plan, and it didn't matter if he perished in the bargain.

Adair found the monk praying by candlelight in the chapel. Standing in the doorway, he wondered if his seemingly supernatural condition would bar him from entering a sanctified place. If he tried to cross the threshold, would he be thrown back by angels and denied entry? After taking a deep breath, he slipped over the oak threshold with no ill effects. Apparently God had no domain over whatever creature he'd become.

The monk saw Adair and rushed over, taking his arm and hurrying him to a dark corner. "Come away from the doors, where we might be seen together," he said. "What's the matter? You seem agitated."

"I am. I've learned something even more terrifying than what I have told you already, something about the physic that I didn't know until last night." Adair wondered if he was playing with fire. Still, he was convinced that he was clever enough to take down the physic without incriminating himself.

"Worse than being a worshipper of Satan?"

"He is—not human. He is now one of Satan's creatures. He revealed himself to me, in all his evil. You have been trained by the church, you know of things not of this world—wicked creatures unleashed on poor mortals for Satan's amusement and our torment. What is the worst you can imagine, Friar?"

To his relief, Adair didn't see skepticism in the monk's round face. The cleric had gone pale and held his breath in fear, recalling perhaps the terrible stories he'd heard over the years, the unexplained deaths, the disappeared children.

"He has made himself a demon, Friar. You cannot think what it is like to have such evil up close, at your throat, the stink of hell on his breath. The strength of Lucifer in his hands."

"A demon! I've heard of demons who walk among men, that they take many forms. But never, never has anyone confronted one and lived to speak of it." The monk's eyes bulged in his pale face and he drew away from Adair. "And yet, here you are, alive. By what miracle?"

"He said he wasn't ready to take me. He said he still needed me as a servant, the same as with Marguerite. He warned me not to flee, that there would be severe penalties if I tried to escape, now that I knew . . ." Adair didn't have to pretend to flinch.

"The devil!"

"Yes. He may be the very devil himself."

"We must get you and Marguerite out of that house this instant! Your souls are in jeopardy, to say nothing of your lives."

"We can't risk it, not before a plan is in place. Marguerite is safe enough. I have never seen him raise a hand to her. As for me—there is little more he could do to me that he hasn't already done."

The monk drew in a breath. "My son, he can take your life."

"I would be one among many."

"You would risk your life to rid this village of such a fiend?" he asked.

Adair flushed with hatred. "Gladly."

Tears welled in the cleric's eyes. "Very well then, son, we will proceed. I will speak to the villagers—discreetly, I assure you—and see which can be counted on to move against the physic." He rose to escort Adair to the door. "Keep watch on this building. When we are ready to act, I will tie a white cloth to the lantern post. Be patient until then, and be strong."

A week passed, then two. At times Adair wondered if the monk had lost heart and fled the village, too cowardly to stand up to the physic. Adair spent as much time as he could searching the keep for the seal the old man had used to authorize documents back at his estate. After the ceremony at the physic's castle, it seemed to have vanished, though Adair knew the physic would not risk storing it where he wouldn't be able to get his hands on it when needed. At night, once Marguerite had gone to sleep and the old man had slipped out on his nightly excursions, Adair went through every box, basket, and trunk, but did not find the heavy gold stamp.

Just as Adair was afraid he'd not be able to contain his impatience any longer, the night came when the white cloth fluttered from the church's lantern post.

The cleric stood in the entrance to the abbey. He'd suffered since Adair had last seen him, and was feckless no more. His cheeks, once full as a squirrel's, were now hollow. His eyes, guileless and clear the first time he and Adair had met, were clouded and sorrowful because of the knowledge he now possessed.

"I have spoken to the men in the village and they are with us," the cleric said, as he took Adair's arm conspiratorially and drew him into the shadows of the vestibule.

Adair tried to hide his glee. "What is your plan?"

"We will gather tomorrow at midnight and march on the keep."

"No, no, not midnight," Adair interrupted, laying a hand on the cleric's arm. "To surprise the physic, it would be best to come at high noon. As with any fiend, the physic is active at night and sleeps during the day. Approach the keep by daylight for your best chance."

The cleric nodded, though the news seemed to trouble him. "Yes, I see. But what of the count's patrol? Do we not risk being discovered in the light of day?"

"The patrol never comes out to the keep. Unless an alarm is sounded, you have nothing to fear from the count's guards." This wasn't strictly true. The guards had visited the keep during the day several times but for one reason only: to deliver a wench for the old man. Such deliveries were infrequent, however. The count had not sent a maid for some time, so the chance was greater, but . . . Adair figured the odds were still against it and the risk was not worth mentioning to the monk, who might use it as an excuse not to proceed.

"Yes, yes . . ." The monk nodded, eyes glazed.

He is slipping away from me, Adair thought. "And what do you propose to do with the old man, when you have captured him?"

The cleric looked stricken. "It is not up to me to determine the man's future . . ."

"Yes, Father, it should be your duty as God's representative. Remember what the Lord says about witches: you shall not suffer them to live." He squeezed the man's arm firmly as he spoke, as though pushing courage along the man's veins.

After a long moment, the cleric cast his eyes down. "The crowd . . . I cannot vouchsafe that I will be able to control the crowd's anger. After all, there is much hatred of the old physic . . . ," he said, his voice stiff with resignation.

"That is right." Adair nodded, coaxing. "You cannot be responsible for what happens. It is God's will." He had to stifle the wild laughter that bubbled up within him. The hated old man would finally get his due! It might be beyond Adair's power alone to vanquish a man with the devil on his side, but surely the physic wouldn't be able to fend off half the village.

"I'll need another day to inform the men of the change in plans, that we'll go to the keep by daylight," the cleric added.

Adair nodded.

"The day after tomorrow then, at noon." The cleric gulped and crossed himself.

A day. Adair had a day to find the seal, or risk having it discovered by the villagers. He returned to the keep, fending off panic. Where could the object be? Adair had searched every shelf, every drawer, gone through every item of the physic's clothing, even going so far as to go through every trunk to be sure the seal hadn't been hidden among them. Failure only compounded Adair's despair and he saw all his plans fall apart, one after the other: he would never escape the physic, never live in the distant castle, never see his family or his beloved Katarina. He might as well be dead, he figured. So complete was his frustration that he might have asked the old man to end his existence out of pity, if his hatred for the physic were not so raw.

The old man was at his desk when Adair returned from his secret appointment, glancing up when his manservant entered the room.

"I will need to go to the village tomorrow, to get feed for the horses," Adair said to the old man, and a split second later a thought, a possibility, bloomed in his mind.

The old man drummed his fingers on the table. "Your errand must wait a day. I will make a poultice that you can take, to trade with the quartermaster for the oats . . ."

"My apologies, but due to my inattentiveness, the grain stores are depleted. There has been no feed for several days, and the grass is too sparse to satisfy the horses for much longer. It cannot wait. With your permission, I will purchase only a small amount, enough to get the horses through this week, and meet with the quartermaster next week when you have had time to make your poultice."

Adair held his breath, waiting to see what the old man would do, for if he refused him, it would be hard to come up with another way, in a short amount of time, to trick him into revealing where he hid his money and valuables. The old man shook his head at his servant's incompetence, then rose and went down the staircase. Adair knew better than to follow but listened with the attention of a hound, picking up every sound, every clue. Despite the thick timber floor, he heard digging, then the sound of something heavy being moved. The clink of coin, then the sound of movement again. Finally, the old man climbed back up the steps and threw a small deerskin pouch on the table. "Enough for the week. Make sure you get a fair bargain," he grunted in warning.

When the old man left for the night, Adair flew to the cellar. The filthy floor looked undisturbed and it was only after a careful search that Adair found the place where the old man had been working, along the wall, in a dank, mildewed spot littered with rat droppings.

Dirt had been scraped away from one of the stones. Adair dropped to his knees and gripped the stone's edges by his fingertips, pulling it out of the wall. In a small recess, he could just make out a burlap bundle, which he extracted and unrolled. There was a fat money bag and, wrapped in a square of velvet, the seal of the kingdom of his dreams.

Adair took it all and pushed the stone back into place. Kneeling in the dirt, he was flush with success, happy to have found the seal, happy to have one victory over his oppressor after all the injustices that had befallen him.

Adair should have killed his father rather than let him beat his mother or siblings.

He should not have let himself be sold into slavery.

He should have taken every chance to escape and never given up trying.

He should kill the wicked count. He deserved death as an enemy of the Magyar people, and a heathen in league with an emissary of Satan.

He should help Marguerite escape, take her to a kindly family or a convent, find someone to care for her.

The way Adair viewed the situation, it was not a matter of stealing. The physic *owed* Adair his kingdom. And the physic would either give it to Adair, or die.

On the appointed day, Adair watched the sun overhead as closely and covetously as a hawk eyes a field mouse. The cleric and his mob would be at the keep in an hour or two. The question for Adair was whether he should remain in place and bear witness to the physic's undoing.

It was tempting. To watch as the villagers dragged the old man from his filthy bed and into the sunlight, his face contorted with fear and surprise. To listen to his screams as they beat him to the ground, pummeled him with clubs, cut him to ribbons with scythes. To urge them on as they ransacked the keep, plundered his trunks, smashed the bottles and jars of precious ingredients to the floor and ground the contents underfoot, and then burned the unholy fortress to the earth.

Even though he was in possession of the seal, Adair could hardly go riding off to the estate without knowing for sure that the physic wouldn't come after him. But there was one good reason for disappearing before the mob arrived—what if the old man escaped death somehow? If the mob's courage failed or the old man had given himself immortal powers as well (a possibility—the physic had never said he *hadn't,* not outright), Adair might be implicated in the attack if he remained. There would be no denying it to the physic later if his alliance was discovered. It might be most prudent to preserve that last shadow of a doubt.

He went up to Marguerite as she stood scrubbing potatoes in a bucket of water, took the potatoes from her hand, and started to lead her to the door. She resisted, earnest soul that she was, but Adair prevailed, and had her wait beside him as he saddled the old man's aging charger. He would take Marguerite to safety in town. That way, she'd not be present during the melee. That would be best. He'd come back to see the outcome for himself.

The sun was fading by the time Adair retraced his way to the keep. He took his time, letting the charger meander on a loose rein down unfamiliar paths through the woods: he wasn't anxious to run into the party of villagers on their return, flush with excitement and bloodlust.

Adair noticed a plume of black smoke on the horizon, but by the time he drew close to the keep, it had thinned to a miasma. He urged the horse on, through the envelope of wood smoke, until he came to the familiar clearing before the stone keep.

The door was missing off its bolt and the ground in front was churned frightfully. The corral was knocked down and the second horse was missing. Adair slid off the old charger's back and cautiously approached the open door, black and ominous as a skull missing an eye from its socket.

Inside, streaks of soot ran up the walls as though clawing for escape. The ruin was as he'd imagined it: shards of glass and pottery underfoot everywhere; overturned cauldrons and pots and buckets; the desk broken into pieces. And all the recipes were gone, along with the old man's remains. Unless . . . Adair's blood ran cold instantly at the thought that perhaps the mob's courage *had* failed. He began to sift through the rubble, lifting furniture, searching through clothing left on the floor and the few items left from the ransacked trunks. But he found nothing of the old man, not even an ear. Surely there'd be some remains—a telltale piece of bone, a charred skull—had the villagers been successful in bringing about his demise.

Other, more frightening alternatives came to Adair: perhaps the physic had managed to escape to the woods or hide somewhere in the keep itself. After all, if there was a small vault behind a stone in the wall, who was to say there wasn't a bigger hidden chamber? Or perhaps— more dangerous still—he had delivered himself away by means of a spell, or been spared by the dark master himself, moved to intervene on behalf of a faithful servant.

Panic rising in his throat, Adair ran down the stairs into the old man's chamber. The scene below was even more horrific than upstairs. The air was thick still with black smoke—apparently the main fire had been set down here—and the room was completely empty, except for a smoldering bed of ash where the physic's mattress and bedstead had been.

But Adair could smell death hidden deep within the smoke and he went to the black pit of ash, crouched down, and raked his fingers through the remains. He found pieces of bone, slivers and nuggets, still hot to the touch. And finally, most of the skull, with a patch of charred flesh and long, wiry hair still attached in one spot.

Adair stood and dusted the soot from his hands as best he could. He took his time in leaving the keep, looking one last time on the place of his five years of misery. It was a pity the stone walls could not have burned down, too. He kept nothing except the clothes on his back and, of course, the seal and a pouch of coin in his pocket. At length, he left through the gaping doorway, gathered up the charger's reins, and headed east, to Romania.

Adair was able to live on the physic's estate for a good many years, though ownership did not pass directly to him as he'd hoped. When he arrived at the estate alone, without the physic, Adair presented himself to the caretaker, Lactu, and told him that the old man had died. The wife and son had been fabrications, Adair explained, a story to provide the physic with privacy for the true reason for his bachelorhood: his peculiar leanings. With no heir, the physic had left the estate to his faithful servant and companion, Adair said, and held out the seal for the caretaker to witness.

The caretaker's doubts were plain on his face, and he said the claim would have to be presented to the king of Romania. If Adair was not a blood descendant of the physic, the king had the right to decide the disposition of the property. The king's decision took years but ultimately was not resolved in Adair's favor. He was allowed to remain on the estate and to keep the family's title, but the king took ownership of the lands.

The day came when Adair was no longer able to remain. Lactu and everyone else had withered and aged with time, while Adair had remained the same as the day he'd returned to the castle. So as not to arouse suspicion, the time had come for Adair to disappear for a while, lay low, perhaps to return in a few decades' time pretending to be his own son, golden seal in hand.

He decided to go to Hungary, as his heart directed, to track down his family. Adair longed to see them—not his father, of course, whom he hated only second to the physic. By now his mother should be old and living with the eldest son, Petu. The rest would be grown, with children of their own. He burned to see them and to know what had happened to them.

It took Adair two years to find his family. He started at the estate where he'd been taken from them and painstakingly reconstructed their route based on threads and scraps of information from former neighbors or overlords. Finally, as the second winter was setting in, he stopped at Lake Balaton and rode through the village, searching for faces that were like his own.

As he came to a gathering of huts on the outskirts of the village, a feeling passed over him, a feeling that someone he knew was very close. Adair dismounted, crept through darkness toward the huts, and peered through the windows. Pressing an eye to a chink in the shutters, where candlelight was barely visible, he saw a few familiar faces.

Though they had changed with time, had gotten rounder, wrinkled, and worn, he recognized those faces. His brothers were gathered around the fireplace, drinking wine and playing the fiddle and the balalaika. With them were women Adair didn't recognize, their wives, he supposed, but no sign of his mother. Finally, he caught sight of Radu, grown up, barrel-chested, tall . . . How Adair wanted to rush into the cottage, throw his arms around Radu, and thank God he was still alive, that he'd been spared all the hell and torment Adair himself had been through. Then it struck him that Radu looked older than Adair did, that all his brothers had passed by him in time. And then he saw a woman come up to Radu and smile, and Radu slipped an arm around her shoulders and drew her tight. It was Katarina, a woman now and beautiful, and in love with Radu, the brother who looked just like Adair. Except older.

As he stood in the dark and cold, Adair still burned with the desire to see his family, to embrace them and speak to them, to let them know that he hadn't perished at the physic's hands—when the terrible truth settled on him in its fullness. This would be the last time he would look on them. How could he explain all that had happened to him and what lay ahead still? Why he would never age. That he was no longer mortal like them. That he had become something he could not explain.

Adair went to the front of the hut and slipped a bag of coin from his pocket, leaving it before their door. It was enough money to end their wandering. It would be hard for them to fully trust in this miracle, but in time they would accept their good fortune and thank God for his generosity and mercy. And by then, Adair would be several days to the north, losing himself in the crowds of Buda and Szentendre, learning to cope with his fate.

By the end of the story, I had withdrawn from Adair's arms, the narcotic smoke's effect worn off. I didn't know if I should be in awe of him, or fear.

"Why did you tell me this?" I asked, recoiling from his touch.

"Consider it a cautionary tale," he replied cryptically.

TWENTY-FIVE

Luke turns off the highway and onto a shaggy dirt road, letting the engine's low torque pull the SUV along over the ruts. When they come to a bend, he parks just off the access road but lets the engine run. Their view is clear owing to the nakedness of the winter trees, and both he and his passenger can see the U.S.-Canadian border crossing in the distance. It looks like a child's play set of a construction site: an enormous span of booths and bays clogged with trucks and cars, the air above it heavy with the fug of exhaust fumes.

"That's where we're going," he says, gesturing toward the windshield.

"It's huge," the girl replies. "I thought we'd be going to some backwater outpost—two guards and a bloodhound, inspecting cars with a flashlight."

"Are you sure you want to go through with this? There are other ways to get to Canada," Luke says, though he's not sure that he should encourage her to break the law any more than she already has.

The look she gives Luke goes straight to his heart, like a child turning to a parent for assurance. "No, you brought me this far. I trust you to get me over the border."

As they approach the checkpoint, Luke's nerves begin to falter. The traffic is light today but still, the prospect of sitting in a queue for an hour is daunting. There must be a police bulletin out on them by now, for the murder suspect and the doctor who helped her escape . . . He nearly jerks out of line, but stops himself, hands shaking on the wheel.

The girl glances over, nervous. "Are you okay?"

"It's taking too long," he mutters, sweating despite the chilly winter air outside the car.

"Everything's fine," she croons.

Suddenly, a green light snaps on over a booth the next lane over, and with surprising speed, Luke cuts the steering wheel and stomps on the gas, throwing the car toward the border police benignly waving traffic in. He cuts off a car that was waiting two vehicles ahead in line and the woman behind the wheel gives him the finger, but Luke doesn't care. He brakes hard in front of the border agent.

"In a hurry?" the official says, disguising his interest with nonchalance as he reaches for the doctor's identification. "We normally take the next person waiting in line when we open a new lane."

"Sorry," Luke says abruptly. "I didn't know . . ."

"Next time, okay?" he responds, amicably, not even looking up as he goes over the driver's license, then Lanny's passport. The agent is middle-aged, in a dark blue uniform, his utility vest bristling with a walkie-talkie and pens and whatnot. In his hands are a clipboard and an electronic device that seems to be some kind of scanner. His partner, a younger woman, walks the perimeter of the car with a mirror on the end of a long pole, as though they expect to find a bomb strapped to the underside of the SUV. Luke watches the female guard in the side-view mirror, a new round of nerves breaking over him.

Then it dawns on him: if they ask for the vehicle registration, he'll be in trouble. Because it's not registered in his name. *Don't you own this vehicle?* the agent will ask.

People borrow cars every day, Luke tries to tell himself. Nothing criminal there.

I'm just going to have to run this through the system to make sure it's not stolen . . .

Don't ask for the registration, don't ask for the registration, he thinks, as though by directing this mantra at the agent, he will keep the guard from thinking of it. If Luke's name is flagged in a database some-where—*wanted for questioning*—their chances for escape dwindle to nothing. This glitch makes Luke even more nervous because he has never been in trouble, never, not even as a kid, and so he is ill-suited to try to trick authority figures. He is afraid of turning red, and sweating, and appearing too anxious, and—

"So you're a doctor?" the agent at the window asks, jolting Luke to attention.

"Yes. A surgeon." *Stupid*, he catches himself; *he doesn't care about your specialty*. It's his doctor's vanity rearing up, demanding attention.

"Reason for traveling to Canada?"

Before Luke can answer, Lanny leans forward, to be seen by the border agent. "He's doing me a favor, actually. I've been staying with him and it's time for me to go sponge off the next relative for a while. And rather than put me on a bus, he generously insisted on driving me there himself."

"Oh, and where is the cousin?" the agent asks, a gentle prod hidden in the question.

"Baker Lake," the girl answers casually. "Well, we're meeting him in Baker Lake. He actually lives closer to Quebec." She knew the name of a nearby town, which seems like a miracle to Luke. The doc-tor relaxes a little.

The agent steps into the booth and, through the scratched Plexi-glass window, Luke watches him, hunched over a terminal, filling in a database no doubt. It's all he can do to keep from stomping on the gas. There's nothing to stop him, no striped automated arm or strip of metal teeth waiting to puncture the tires, blocking their escape.

The agent is suddenly at his window, the driver's license and passport in his extended hand. "There you go . . . have a nice stay," he says, waving them along, already looking to the next car in line.

Luke doesn't start breathing until the border-crossing station is shrunken in the rearview mirror. "Why were you so worried?" Lanny laughs, looking over her shoulder. "It's not like we're terrorists or trying to smuggle black-market cigarettes over the border. We're just nice American citizens going to Canada for lunch."

"No, we're not," Luke says, but he is laughing, too, in relief. "Sorry, I'm not used to this cloak-and-dagger stuff."

"I'm sorry, I didn't mean to laugh. I know you're not. You did great." She squeezes his hand.

They stop at a motel on the outskirts of Baker Lake, a nondescript place, not part of a chain. Luke waits in the car while Lanny is in the office. He watches her chat up the older gentleman behind the counter, who moves slowly, stretching out his one chance that morning to speak to a pretty young girl. Lanny climbs back into the SUV and they drive around to a unit in back, overlooking a stretch of trees and the tail end of a neighborhood baseball field. Theirs is the only vehicle in the parking lot.

Once inside the hotel room, Lanny is a blur of activity, unpacking her bag, checking out the bathroom, complaining about the quality of the towels. Luke sits on the bed, suddenly too tired to remain upright. He lies down on top of the polyester bedspread, staring up at the ceiling. His surroundings spin like a carnival ride.

"What's the matter?" Lanny sits next to him on the edge of the bed, touches his forehead.

"Exhaustion, I guess. On the midnight shift, I usually go to bed as soon as I get home."

"Then go ahead, take a nap." She eases the doctor's shoes off without untying the laces.

"No, I should head back. It's only a half hour away," he protests but doesn't move. "I have to return the car . . ."

"Nonsense. Besides, it will only arouse suspicion at the border station, turning right around and going home like that." She spreads a blanket over him, then digs around in her suitcase and pulls out a Ziploc bag filled the most voluptuous marijuana buds Luke has ever seen.

In less than a minute, she expertly rolls a generous doobie, lights it up, and takes a long, greedy hit. She closes her eyes as she exhales and her face relaxes with satisfaction. Luke thinks that he would like to bring such a look to this woman's face sometime.

Lanny holds the joint out to him. After a second's hesitation, Luke takes it, brings it to his lips. He inhales and holds the smoke, feels it spread into the lobes of his brain, feels his ears clog and stop up. Sweet Jesus, this stuff is potent. Fast.

He coughs and hands the joint back to Lanny. "I haven't done that in a while. Where'd you get that stuff?"

"In town. St. Andrew." Her answer both faintly alarms and surprises him, reminds him that there are other unseen worlds that exist right under his nose. He's just glad he didn't know she was holding when they crossed the border or he would have been even more nervous.

"You do this kind of thing a lot?" He nods at the joint.

"Couldn't get by without it. You don't know the memories I carry around in my head . . . Lifetime after lifetime of things you regret doing . . . things you've seen other people do. Stuff you can't get away from—without this." She regards the spliff in her hand. "There are times when I've wished I could knock myself out for, say, a decade. Go to sleep, make it all stop. No way to erase the bad memories. It's not *doing* that's so hard—it's living with what you've done."

"Like the man in the morgue—"

She presses a finger to Luke's mouth to keep him from saying another word. Time enough for that later, he imagines; in fact, she has nothing but time stretching out before her to realize the irreversible thing she has done to her true love. Not enough pot in all the world to wash that away. Hell on earth.

The things he's done seem small in comparison. Still, he reaches for the joint.

"I'm going back," he says, as though he has to convince her. "As soon as I take a nap. It'll be safer driving if I take a nap. But I have to get back . . . things to do, waiting for me . . . Peter's car . . ."

"Sure," she says.

When the doctor wakes, the hotel room is bathed in gray. The sun is setting but none of the lamps has been turned on. Luke lies still, not sitting up, trying to get his bearings. For a long minute, his head is stuffed with cotton, and he can't remember where he is and why everything is unfamiliar. He's hot and sweaty from lying under the blanket and feels like a kidnapping victim rushed out of a car, blind-folded, spun around.

Slowly, the room comes into focus. The stranger is sitting in one of the hard wooden chairs at the table, looking out the window. She sits absolutely still.

"Hey," Luke says, to let her know he's awake.

"Feeling better? Let me get you a glass of water." She rises from the chair and hurries through a doorway to the kitchenette. "It's only tap water. I put some in the refrigerator to get cold."

"How long have I been asleep?" Luke reaches for the glass; it feels deliciously cold, and he's tempted to press it to his forehead. He's burning up.

"Four, five hours."

"Oh Christ, I'd better get on the road. They'll be looking for me, if they aren't already." He pushes the blanket back, and sits up on the edge of the bed.

"What's the rush? You said there's no one at home to wait for you," the girl replies. "Besides, you don't look well. That shit might have been too much for you. It's strong. Maybe you should lie down for a little longer."

Lanny retrieves her laptop from the chipped veneered chest of drawers and walks over to him. "I downloaded these from the camera while you were asleep. I thought you would like to see him. I mean, I know you've *seen* him, you've seen his body, but you might be interested anyway . . ."

Luke winces at this macabre little speech, not happy to be reminded of the dead body in the morgue and its relation to Lanny, but accepts the laptop when she hands it to him. The images jump off the screen brightly in the dusky darkness of the room: it is the man in the body bag but there is no comparison. Here he is, vividly alive, vibrant and whole. The eyes, the face animated, electrified with life.

And he is so, so beautiful, the sight of him makes Luke strangely sad. The first picture must have been taken in a car, window down, his longish black hair swirling about his head and his eyes crinkled as he laughs at the woman taking the picture, laughs at something Lanny has said or done. In the next picture, he is in bed, the bed they must have shared at Dunratty's, his head on a white pillow, again his hair falling over his face, lashes brushing his cheeks, the perfect blush of pink across the high ridge of his cheekbone. A glimpse of throat and the protruding knob of a collarbone are visible beneath a creamy white fold of sheet.

After a minute, looking from picture to picture, it occurs to Luke that the beautiful thing about the man in the photos is not the pleasing quality of his face. It's not his handsomeness. It's something in his expression, an interplay between the delight in his eyes and the smile on his face. It's that he's happy to be with the person holding the camera and taking the pictures.

A lump forms in Luke's throat and he thrusts the laptop at Lanny. He doesn't want to look anymore.

"I know," the girl says, also choked up, giving in to tears. "It kills me to think he's gone. Forever gone. I feel his absence like a hole in my chest. A feeling I have carried with me for two hundred years has been ripped away. I don't know how I will go on. That's why I am asking you . . . please stay with me a little longer. I can't be alone. I'll go out of my mind." She puts the laptop on the floor, then reaches for Luke's hand. Hers is tiny and warm in his. The palm is damp, but Luke can't tell if the dampness is his or hers.

"I can't thank you enough for what you've done for me," she says as she looks through his eyes and into him, as though she can see what is swimming inside him. "I've— I've never— I mean, no one has ever been so good to me. Taken a risk like that for me."

Suddenly, her mouth is on his. He closes his eyes and sinks his entire being into the warm wetness of her mouth. He falls backward into the spot on the bed he had just left, her nearly insubstantial weight falling on him, and he feels a part of him tear in two. He is horrified by what he is doing, yet he's wanted to do this from the moment he first saw her. He's not going back to St. Andrew, not yet anyway; he's going to follow her—how can he walk away? Her need for him is like a hook planted in his chest, pulling him along effortlessly, and he cannot resist. He is diving off a cliff into black water; he can't see what's waiting below for him, but he knows there's not a force on earth that can stop him.

TWENTY-SIX

After hearing Adair's story, I withdrew to my room in fright. I crawled onto the bed and tucked my knees under my chin. I was afraid to recall the things he'd told me and I tried to push them away.

Alejandro knocked, and when there was no answer, nudged the door back so he could slip in bearing a tray of tea and biscuits. He lit several candles—"You can't sit in the dark, Lanore, it's ghoulish"— and then placed a cup and saucer quietly at my elbow, but I wanted none of his hospitality. I pretended to look out the window, but in truth I could see nothing, still blinded by fury and despair.

"Oh my dear, don't be so sad. I know it's scary. I was scared when it happened to me."

"But, Alej, what are we?" I asked, hugging the pillow to my chest.

"You are yourself, Lanore. You are not part of the magic world. You can't pass through walls like a ghost or visit God in his heaven like an angel. We sleep and wake, eat and drink, go through our day like anyone else. The only difference is that another person might ponder, from time to time, which day will be his last. But you and I, our days will never end. We go on, bearing witness to everything around us." He said all this dispassionately, as though the endless shuffle of days had washed all the excitement out of him. "When Adair explained what he'd done to me, I wanted to escape from him, even if it meant killing myself—the one thing I couldn't do.

"But to lose your baby on top of it . . . well, it is too terrible to contemplate. Poor Lanore. Your sadness will pass, you know," he continued in his singsong English, accented with Spanish. He took a sip of tea and then looked at me through steam rising from the cup. "Every day your past drifts farther and farther away and life with Adair grows more and more familiar. You become part of this family. Then, one day, you will remember something from your other life—a brother or a sister, a holiday, the house where you used to live, a toy you used to cherish— and you realize you no longer mourn its loss. It will seem like something from long ago. That's when you know the change is complete."

I glanced over my shoulder at him. "How long does it take for the pain to go away?"

Alejandro lifted a lump of sugar from the bowl with a tiny pair of tongs and dropped it into his tea. "It depends on how sentimental you are. Me, I am very tenderhearted. I loved my family and missed them for ages after the change. But Dona, for instance, he probably never looked back. His family had abandoned him when he was a little boy, for being a catamite," Alejandro said, dropping his voice to a whisper on the last few words, even though we were all sodomites in this house. "His life was full of deprivation and uncertainty. Lynchings. Starvation. Imprisonment. No, I don't imagine he has any regrets."

"I don't think my pain will ever fade. My child is gone! I want my child back. I want my life back."

"You can never have your child back, you know that," he said gently, stroking my arm. "But why, my dear, would you want your old life back? From what you have told me, you have nothing to return to: your family threw you out. They abandoned you in your time of need.

I see nothing to regret leaving behind." Alejandro stared into me with his dark, gentle eyes, as though he could summon the answer from my heart. "In times of trouble, we often want to go back to the familiar. That will go away."

"Well, there is one thing . . . ," I murmured.

He leaned forward, eager for my confession.

"A friend. I miss a particular friend."

Alejandro was, as he'd said, a tender soul who loved nostalgia. He squeezed his eyes shut, like a cat sitting in the warmth of the sun on a windowsill, eager to drink in my story. "It's always the people you miss the most. Tell me about this friend."

Since I'd left St. Andrew, I tried as hard as possible not to think about Jonathan. It was beyond my ability not to think of him at all, so I allowed myself only short indulgences, such as a few minutes before falling asleep, when I'd recall the feel of his warm, flushed cheek pressed against mine, the way my spine tingled when he circled his hands around my corseted waist, claiming me for his own. It was hard enough to control my emotions when Jonathan was only a ghost on the fringes of my memory: to recall him directly was painful. "I can't. I miss him too much," I told Alejandro.

Alejandro leaned back. "This friend means everything to you, doesn't he? He is the love of your life. He was the father of your child."

"Yes," I said. Alejandro waited for me to go on, his silence like a string tugging at me, until I obliged. "His name is Jonathan. I've been in love with him since we were children. Most people would say that he was too good to end up with me. His family owns the town where I lived—it's not big or wealthy, but everyone there depends on Jonathan's family to survive. And then there is his great beauty." I blushed. "You must think me a terribly shallow person . . ."

"Not at all!" he said amicably. "No one is immune to the sway of beauty. But truly, Lanore, how beautiful could he be? Think of Dona, for instance. So striking that he enchanted one of the greatest artists in Italy. Is he more beautiful than Dona?"

"If you met Jonathan, you'd understand. He would make Dona look like a troll."

That made Alejandro chuckle; none of us liked Dona very much—he was so vain he was nearly intolerable. "You must not let Dona hear you say that! Very well, then—what about Adair? Is he not a handsome fellow? Have you ever seen eyes like his? They are like a wolf's . . ."

"Adair has a certain charm." *An animal charm*, I thought, though I didn't say it aloud. "But there is no comparison, Alej. Believe me. But—it's of no consequence. I'll never see him again."

Alejandro patted my hand. "Don't say that. You don't know—you may."

"I can't imagine going home, not now. Isn't it as Adair said in his story? How would I explain it to them?" I scoffed.

"There are ways . . . You couldn't live among them again. No, that would be out of the question, but a brief visit . . . if you stayed only a short while . . ." He toyed with his lower lip, contemplative.

"Don't raise my hopes. It's too cruel." Tears pressed at my eyes. "Please, Alejandro, I need to rest. I have a terrible headache."

He pressed his fingers to my forehead briefly. "No fever . . . Tell me, this headache, does it feel like a constant prickling in the back of your mind?" I nodded. "Yes? Well, my dear, you'd best get used to it. That is not a headache: that is part of the gift. You are connected to Adair now."

"Connected to Adair?" I repeated.

"There is a bond between you two, and that sensation is a reminder of that bond." He leaned toward me conspiratorially. "Remember how I said that you were changed only in one way, that you were not magical? Well, we are a bit magical, just a little bit. Sometimes I think we are like animals, you know? You must have noticed how everything seems a little brighter, how you can hear the tiniest noise, how every odor stings so sharply at your nose? That is part of the gift: the transformation makes us *better*. We are enhanced. You will hear a voice from a long way away and know who is coming to visit, you can detect the aroma of sealing wax and know a person has a letter hidden on them. You will cease to notice these powers in time, but to others it will seem like you are a mind reader, that you are magic!

"The second thing you must know is that you will no longer feel pain. It has to do with the ability not to die, I think. You will not feel the sharpness of hunger or thirst. Oh, it takes time for the reflex, the expectation that one must eat and drink, to go away . . . But you could fast for weeks and not feel hunger gnawing at your stomach, or become weak and faint. You could be run over by a charging horse and feel little more than slight discomfort where you might have a broken bone, but the pain will go away in minutes as the bone heals itself. It's as though you are now made of earth and wind, and can repair yourself at will." His words made me shiver with recognition. "And this connection to Adair, the needling in your brain, is a reminder of this power because only he can make you like a mortal again. At his hands, and only his hands, you feel pain. But any damage he causes you to suffer will be temporary, unless he chooses otherwise. He can *will* anything on you, pain, disfigurement, death. *By his hand and intent.* Those are the words he uses in the spell. Those are the words that bind you to him."

I put a hand to my abdomen; he was right about pain. The muted throbbing I'd felt in my purged womb had disappeared entirely.

"He must have said as much to you. Believe him: he is your god now. You live or die at his whim. And"—his expression softened entirely for a moment, as though a shield was being lowered briefly—"you should be careful with Adair. He has given you everything a mortal could want, but only as long as you please him. He will not hesitate to take it away if you anger him. Never forget that."

I quickly realized that whether I wanted it or not, I was part of this strange household now and it would be to my benefit to figure out my place in it. My life had changed irrevocably and I wasn't at all sure how to survive. Adair, however, had hundreds of years of experience. The others he had chosen had all stayed with him, probably for good reason.

I also resolved to try to forget Jonathan. I believed I'd never see him again, despite what Alejandro had said. My old life was gone in every way: Boston was as different from St. Andrew as cream from water, and I was no longer a poor country girl with only a dreary future to look forward to. I'd lost the baby, the only thing that would have connected me to Jonathan. Better to put it behind me now, all at once.

Within a few days I saw that the house's rhythms were unlike anything I'd experienced in my Puritan hometown. First of all, no one in the household besides the servants rose before noon. Even then, the courtiers and their guests remained in their rooms until two or three in the afternoon, though you could hear low sounds behind the doors, murmurs or a shriek of laughter or the scrape of a chair leg as it was dragged across the floor. Alejandro explained that it was the European way: evenings, the most important part of the day, were given over to socializing—dinners, balls, gaming tables—and days were spent getting ready, to be properly appointed, with hair coiffed and the most fetching ensemble donned. They'd brought a few key servants with them from Europe, those skilled in styling hair and maintaining the wardrobes. I thought it a decadent way to live, but Alejandro assured me this was only because I was a misguided puritanical American. There was a reason the Puritans left England in search of a new world, he pointed out.

Which brings me to the second strange thing about Adair's household: no one seemed to have purpose to their lives. No business concerns or finances were ever discussed in front of me. No mention of the old country, no reminiscing about past lives (as Alejandro told me, "We let the dead sleep"). No letters arrived, only calling cards from members of Boston society eager to meet this mysterious European royal. The tray in the hall overflowed with invitations to parties and salons and teas.

The only subject that interested Adair and his entourage, the only endeavor they undertook with any seriousness, the preoccupation that filled their days, was sex. Each member of the entourage kept a playmate, whether for the evening or for a week; it could be a Brahmin met at a soiree or a comely footman co-opted for the night. There was a stream of women parading through the mansion, too, blowsy prostitutes, as well as daring society daughters. No one in the household ever slept alone. Neither Alejandro nor Donatello seemed interested in me at all, and when I asked Alej if he didn't find me attractive, he laughed and told me not to be obtuse.

The family was given over to seeking and experiencing pleasure, it was as simple as that. Everything about my surroundings was the antithesis of how I was raised and eventually their lack of industry would disgust me, but at first I was seduced by luxuries I'd had no idea existed. St. Andrew had been a town of homespun linen clothing and raw pine furniture. Now I lived surrounded by finery, each new temptation better than the last. I ate food and drink I had never known existed, wore dresses and gowns made from exotic European fabrics by a professional tailor. I learned to dance and play cards, was given novels to read that would expose me to even more worlds.

Adair was fond of parties, and since he was still a sensation in Boston, we went to one almost every night. He took his entourage with him everywhere, letting Alejandro, Dona, and Tilde charm the Bostonians with their continental ways, outrageous fashions from Paris and Vienna and London, and tales of decadent European aristocracy.

What really stunned the Brahmins, though, was when Adair forced Uzra to accompany us. She would venture outdoors wrapped in a swath of burgundy cloth that covered her from head to toe. Once we had arrived among the partygoers, the wrapping would fall to the floor to reveal Uzra in one of her costumes, tight organza bodice and a skirt of veils, her eyes rimmed thickly in kohl, adornments of brass ringlets circling her bare waist, hands, and ankles. The richly colored silks were pretty, but sheer; she was practically naked compared with the rest of us women in layers of petticoats and corsets and stockings. Uzra jingled softly as she walked, eyes downcast, aware that she was being ogled and leered at like a carnival animal. The women clapped hands over their mouths, now fallen open in shock, and the men—the air would become thick with the musk of their desire, frock coats hastily rearranged to cover their clumsy erections. Adair would laugh later about the propositions he received, men offering huge sums of money for an hour with his odalisque. They would part with their souls if he gave them the chance, Adair would say later, when we had decamped to our house after the party and sat around the cook's table in the kitchen, next to the still warm hearth, sharing a bottle.

"You could do the same," Adair said to me in private, as we walked up the stairs to our bedchambers, his voice soft as velvet. "A man's desire is a powerful thing. It can reduce a strong man to nothing. When he sees a woman who fascinates him, he will give up everything for her. Remember that, Lanore: everything."

"Give up everything for me? You are mad. No man has ever given up anything for my company," I scoffed, thinking of Jonathan's inability to give himself wholly to me. Deep in self-pity, I wasn't being fair to him, I know, but I had been stung by my faithless lover and was hurting.

Adair gave me a strangled look and said something I had never considered. "That is sad to hear said about any woman, but especially sad to hear said about you. Perhaps it's because you have never asked for anything in exchange for your attention. You don't know your own worth, Lanore."

"My worth? I understand my worth only too well—I am a plain girl from a poor family."

He took my arm and tucked it under his. "You are hardly plain. You have an appeal for certain men, the type of man who values a discreet freshness and disdains a vulgar display of womanly charms. Too much breast pouring out of a bodice, too prominent a bustle, too voluptuous—do you understand?" I didn't follow him; in my experience men seemed bedazzled by these very parts, and the fact that I did not possess them had seemed a detriment my entire life.

"Your description of 'vulgar' womanly charms sounds an awful lot like Uzra to me, and she never fails to render any man who sees her agog. She and I are as opposite as two women can be," I said, meaning to tease Adair.

"There is not only one measure of beauty, Lanore. Everyone adores the red rose, and yet it is a common sort of beauty. You are like a golden rose, a rare bloom but no less lovely," he said, meaning to flatter, but I nearly laughed out loud at his attempt. I was thin as a boy and nearly as flat-chested. My curly blond hair was as unruly as a thistle. I could only think he was flattering me for some purpose of his own, but his sweet words were appealing all the same.

"So if you trust me, let me guide you. I will teach you how to have power over ordinary men. Like Tilde, like Alej and Dona," he said, stroking my hand. Perhaps that was their purpose; maybe that was their industry. They did seem able to make most people—most men, and they were the ones with power—do what they wanted, and that seemed to be a good skill to have.

"It is not enough to be able to conquer your enemies; in order to control them, you must be able to seduce them as well."

"Consider me your pupil," I said, letting Adair lead me into his bedchamber.

"You will not regret it," he promised.

TWENTY-SEVEN

And so began my schooling in the business of seduction. It started with evenings in Adair's bed. After that night when Adair opened my eyes, he seemed determined to prove to me that I was worth a man's attention: his. We continued to go to parties, where he charmed the Bostonians, but he always returned home with me on his arm. He took me to his bed every night. He indulged me and gave me anything I asked for. I had beautiful undergarments made, corsets (though I hardly needed them to hold up my breasts, modest as they were) and stays of colored silks, trimmed with ribbon. Garters decorated with tiny silk roses. Delights for Adair to find when he peeled off my clothing. I devoted myself to becoming his golden rose.

I would be lying if I said I did not think of Jonathan during this time. He was my first lover, after all. Still, I tried to kill the love I felt for him by remembering the bad moments between us, the times he wounded me to the quick. The times I'd heard that he'd taken up with a new girl. Standing next to him on the hill as we looked down on

Sophia's funeral, knowing he was thinking of her. Kissing Evangeline in front of the entire congregation mere moments after I'd given him news of my pregnancy. I tried to see my love for Jonathan as a malady, a fever burning up my heart and brain, and these wrenching memories were the purgative, the cure.

And the attentions of my new lover would be my restorative. Comparing my experiences with the two men, it seemed that the act with Jonathan filled me with such happiness that I felt I would die. At those times, I was barely aware of my body, I could have floated to the ceiling in his arms. It was sublime. With Adair, it was all sensation, a neediness for flesh and the power to have that hunger satisfied. At the time, I wasn't afraid of this newfound hunger Adair had created in me. I delighted in it, and Adair, instead of judging me indulgent and sluttish, seemed pleased that he brought this out in me.

Adair confirmed as much one evening in his bed, lighting up the hookah after an acrobatic session. "I judge that you have a natural disposition for the business of pleasure," he said, grinning obscenely. "I'd daresay you *enjoy* your adventures in the bedroom. You've done everything I've asked, haven't you? Nothing I have done has frightened you?" When I gave a little shake of my head, he continued, "Then it is time to expand your experiences, because the art of love is such that the more expert lovers one has, the more expert one becomes. Do you understand?" I greeted this statement with a frown, sensing that something was amiss. Had he tired of me already? Was the bond that had developed between us an illusion? "Don't be cross," he said, feeding the narcotic smoke from his mouth to mine in a kiss. "I've made you jealous, haven't I? You must fight feelings like that, Lanore. They are beneath you now. You have a new life ahead of you, one filled with a richness of experience, if you aren't afraid."

He wasn't inclined to explain any more to me at the time, but I found out the next night when Dona slipped into the bedroom with us. And Tilde the night after that. When I objected, protesting that I was too self-conscious to enjoy myself in front of the others, I was given a blindfold. The next morning, when I glanced at Tilde shyly as we passed on the stairs, still dazzled by the pleasure she had given me in bed, she growled, "It was only a performance, you stupid cuny," and trotted away, dispelling any doubt that it had been anything more. I suppose I was naive, but the pleasures of the flesh were new to me, the sensations overwhelming. I would become numb to all of it, and numb to what it did to my soul, soon enough.

It was not long after this that a most notable event occurred, though I didn't gather its significance at the time. It started with a lecture on astronomy and navigational arts that we attended at Harvard College. Science was a bit of a fad in that day and sometimes the colleges would host public lectures. These were places to be seen as much as any party, a way to show that just because you were a socialite you still had a bit of brain, so Adair made it a point to attend. The lecture that day was of little interest to me, so I sat at Adair's side and borrowed his opera glasses to scan the audience. There were many faces I'd seen before even if I couldn't remember their names, and just as I was thinking the outing was a waste of time, I spied Tilde chatting up a man on the far side of the auditorium. I could see only a quarter profile of his face, and mostly my view was of his back, but I could tell he had a striking physique.

I handed the opera glasses to Adair. "It looks like Tilde has found herself a new man," I whispered and nodded in her direction.

"Hmm, I believe you're right," he said, peering through the glasses. "She is a born hunter, that Tilde."

It was common to meet up with other socialites after the lectures at a nearby public house. Adair had no patience that afternoon for the small talk over coffee and beer, however, and watched the door. Before long, Tilde came in on the arm of the young man we'd seen at the college. He was quite dashing, with a beautiful face (a trifle on the delicate side), a sharp little nose, a cleft in his chin, and glorious blond curls. He looked all the younger on Tilde's sophisticated arm, and while Tilde could hardly be mistaken for his mother, the disparity in their ages was hard to miss.

They joined us at our table and Adair spent the whole time peppering him with questions. Was he a student at Harvard? (Yes.) Did he have family in Boston? (No, he'd come from Philadelphia and had no family in this area.) What was he studying? (He had a passion for science, but his parents wished him to continue the family business, which was law.) How old was he? (Twenty.) At this last answer, Adair frowned as though displeased, a quizzical response to so straightforward an answer. Then Adair invited the young man to dine with us that evening at the mansion.

I will be blunt: the cook may have served a saddle of lamb, but it was clear that the flaxen-haired young man was the main course. Adair continued to ask him all sorts of personal questions (Any close friends here at college? A fiancée?) and when the young man became nonplussed, Alejandro would jump in and distract everyone around the table with self-deprecating stories and jokes. More wine than usual flowed, particularly into the young man's glass, and then after dinner the men were given snifters of cognac, and we all repaired to the game room. At the end of an evening of faro, Adair claimed we could not send the young man back to his rooms at the college in such a state—he would be reprimanded for drunkenness if caught by the tutors—and insisted he stay with us for the night. By that time the young scholar was almost unable to stand without assistance, so he was hardly in a position to refuse.

Adair had a footman help him up the stairs while we gathered outside Adair's bedchamber like jackals preening before dividing up the night's kill. In the end, Adair decided he and I would enjoy the young man's company and dismissed the others. Drunk as he was, he stripped gamely when commanded and followed me eagerly into bed. Here is the curious part: as the boy stripped, Adair watched him closely, not with enjoyment (as I had expected) but with a clinical eye. It wasn't until then that we learned the young man had a club foot;

it wasn't terribly misshapen and he had a specially made boot that helped him walk without much of a limp. But upon noticing it, Adair seemed visibly deflated.

Adair sat in a chair and watched as the young man swived me. I saw, over the boy's shoulder, disappointment on Adair's face, a detachment toward our guest that he fought to overcome. In the end, Adair took off his clothes and joined us, surprising the young man with his attentions, which were nevertheless accepted (he didn't resist in any case, though he did yelp a little when Adair got rough with him). And the three of us slept together, our guest relegated to the foot of the bed, succumbing to the effects of alcohol and the usual result of a man's amorous effusions.

The next morning, after the young man was sent off in a carriage, Adair and Tilde had heated words behind closed doors. Alejandro and I sat in the breakfast room and listened—or tried not to—over tea.

"What is that about?" I asked, nodding in the direction of the muffled argument.

"Adair has given us standing orders to be on the lookout for attractive men, but only the most attractive. We are to bring them to his attention. What can I say, Adair enjoys a pretty face. But he is only interested in perfection, you see? And I understand the man Tilde brought to Adair was less than perfect?"

"He had a club foot." I didn't see how that made any difference; his face was exquisite.

Alejandro shrugged. "Ah—there you go." He busied himself buttering a heel of bread and said no more, leaving me to stir my tea and wonder about Adair's strange obsessions. The thing was, he'd swived that boy as though it was punishment for disappointing him somehow. It made me uneasy to think about it.

I leaned across the table and clasped Alejandro's hand. "Remember the conversation we had a few weeks ago, about my friend? My handsome friend? Promise me, Alejandro, you will not tell Adair about him."

"Do you think I would do that to you?" he said, hurt. I know now that his offense was all pretend. He was a good actor, Alejandro was. We all had to be around Adair, but this was Alejandro's role in the group, to be the one to lull the distressed or uncertain, to assuage and calm the victim so she doesn't see the blow coming. At the time, I thought of him as the good one whereas Tilde and Dona were evil and bitter, the deceivers, but I see now they each had a role to play.

But at the time, I believed him.

TWENTY-EIGHT

I started to become more curious about my housemates. I had just begun to see them as a pack that worked together, each with a purpose, each performing his or her part with an ease that came from having done a job many times. Flushing out prey, distracting the quarry, running the unfortunate victim to ground, whether it was the club-footed young man or an easy mark at a card game. The three were like hounds held in check on slip collars; Adair had only to loosen them and they were off, each confident of what he or she must do. I was the fourth hound, new to the pack and unsure of my role. And, well-tuned instrument that they were together, they were reluctant to make room for me, sure that I would trip them up and detract from their cold grace and efficiency. It was just as well to me: I had no desire to join them.

I expected a backlash from the others regarding Adair's fondness for me and was surprised when there wasn't any. After all, I must have displaced one of them as Adair's favorite and confidante. But none of them was upset. There wasn't a spark of jealousy in the air. In truth, except for Alejandro, they had little to do with me. Now, all three gave me a wide berth but without malice. They skirted both me and Adair, except for when we traveled to and from parties, and during those times there was an air of forced joviality hanging over us like a fog. When Tilde and I caught sight of each other, for instance, I sometimes noticed the grim set of her mouth combined with a slight furrow to her brow, but what I saw did not seem like jealousy. The three of them drifted through the house like ghosts, haunted and powerless.

One night I decided to ask Adair about this. After all, he was more likely to tell me the truth than were they. I waited as Adair found a bottle of brandy and goblets to take to the bedroom, while the servants helped me slip out of my skirts and bodice and unpinned my hair. As Adair poured the drink into our glasses, I said, "There is something on my mind that I have been meaning to raise with you . . ."

He took a swig from his drink before handing a glass to me. "I expected as much. You've been distracted lately."

"It's . . . the others," I started, unsure of how to continue.

"Don't ask me to send them away. I won't. You may want us to spend all our time with each other, but I can't have them wandering loose. And besides, it's important that we stay together. You never know when you will need one of us to come to your aid, someone who understands the obligation. You'll understand someday," he rushed to say.

"I don't want them to be sent away. I've just been wondering, Adair, which of their hearts has been broken now that you spend all your time with me? Which of them most keenly feels the loss of your attention? I see them and feel sorry for—Why are you laughing at me? It wasn't my intention to amuse you."

I'd expected him to smile at my question, chide me perhaps for my foolish sensitivity and assure me that no one resented me, that the others had each had their turn as his favorite and knew that this pleasure wouldn't last forever, that the harmony of our household was intact.

That wasn't the reaction I got from Adair, however. His laugh wasn't one of appreciation: it was mocking. "'The loss of my attention'? Do you think they're upstairs, crying themselves to sleep at night, now that they no longer are the apple of my eye? Let me tell you a bit about the people with whom you share a home. You have a right to know since you are bound to them for eternity. It's best to keep your guard up around them, my dear. They're not going to look out for your best interests, not ever. You have no idea about them, do you?"

"Alej has told me a little," I murmured, dropping my eyes.

"I wager he's told you nothing of consequence and certainly nothing to make you think badly of him. What did he tell you about himself?"

I started to regret that I had brought this up. "Only that he comes from a good family in Spain . . ."

"A very good family. The Pinheiros. You might even say a grand family, but you will not find any Pinheiros in Toledo, Spain, today. Do you know why? Have you ever heard of the Inquisition? Alejandro and his family were rounded up by the Inquisition, by the grand inquisitor himself, Tomás de Torquemada. Alejandro's mother, his father, his grandmother, his little sister—all were thrown into prison. They were given two choices: they could confess their sins and convert to Catholicism—or they would remain in prison, where they would likely die."

"Why didn't he convert?" I cried out. "To spare his life, would it have been so terrible?"

"But he did." Adair poured more brandy for himself and then stood in front of the fire, his face lit by a flickering flame. "He did as they asked. He would have been a fool to refuse them, under the circumstances. The Inquisition was proud of its ability to break a man: they made it a science. They kept him in a cell so small he had to tuck into a ball in order to fit, and he had to listen to the screams and prayers of the other prisoners until the sun came up. Who would not go mad in these circumstances? Who would not do anything they asked, in order to save himself?"

For a moment, there was only the crackle and spit from the fire, and in my heart, I begged that Adair would not go on. I wanted to keep the Alejandro I knew, sweet and considerate, and remain ignorant of whatever evil he kept hidden inside.

Adair tossed back the last of his drink and stared again into the flames. "He gave them his sister. They wanted someone they could make an example of, evil in their midst. A reason to rid the country of Jews. So he told them his sister was a witch, an unrepentant witch. In exchange for his fourteen-year-old sister, the priests let him go. And that is when I found him, gibbering like a madman for what he'd done."

"That's horrible." Shivering, I pulled the sable blanket around my shoulders.

"Dona handed over his master to the authorities when he was arrested for being a sodomite. The man who had taken him in off the street, fed and clothed him, painted his likeness on the walls of Florence. A man who adored him, truly adored him, and Dona gave him up without a second's hesitation. I'd be a fool to expect any better treatment from him.

"And then there's Tilde. She's the most dangerous of all of them. She comes from a country very far north, where there are days in the winter when the sun is out for only a few hours. I came across Tilde one of those frigid nights, on the road. She had been doused with water and turned out in the cold winter evening by her own people. You see, she had set her heart on a rich man in the next village. There was only one obstacle in her way: she was already married. And how did she decide to solve her problem? By killing her husband and her two children. She poisoned them, thinking no one would ever figure out what she'd done. Only, the people in her village discovered her plot and put her to death. She was meant to freeze to death, and by the time I found her, she was already half frozen. Her hair was solid ice, her eyelashes and her skin were frosted with crystals. She was dying and yet she still managed to glare at me with an expression of pure hatred."

"Stop," I whimpered, burrowing completely under the heavy blanket of pelts. "I don't want to know any more."

"The true measure of a man is how he behaves when death is close." There was a sneer in Adair's voice.

"That's not fair. A person has a right to do anything to survive."

"Anything?" He raised an eyebrow and snorted. "In any case, I felt you had a right to know that sympathy is wasted on them. Beneath their beauty and their manners, they are monsters. There is a reason I chose each of them. They have their place in my plans . . . but not one of them is capable of love, except of themselves. They wouldn't think twice about giving you up if there was something to be gained in the bargain. They might even ignore their obligation to me, if they thought they could get away with such treachery." He slid beside me into the bed, cupping my body against his, and I fancied I felt a strange neediness in his touch. "That is what I find fascinating about you, Lanore. You have a great capacity for love. You long to give your heart to someone, and when you do, it is with impossible commitment, inexhaustible loyalty. I think you would go to any lengths for the man you love. It is a very lucky man who will win your heart one day. I would like to think that even I might be so lucky."

He petted my hair for a while before drifting into sleep, leaving me to wonder how much he knew about Jonathan, just how precisely Adair might have read my thoughts. The entire conversation gave me the shivers; I couldn't see the purpose of giving eternal life to such undeserving people, to surrounding himself for eternity with cowards and murderers, especially if what he sought was loyalty. His plans, for I didn't doubt he had them, eluded me.

And the worst part, the part that I couldn't bear to face, was the question of why he had chosen me to join his perverse family. He must have seen something in me that told him I was like the others; perhaps it was written on my soul that I was selfish enough to drive another woman to take her own life in order to have the one she loved.

And as for his invitation to love him, I wouldn't have thought someone like Adair would feel the need to be loved . . . or that I was the
type of woman capable of loving a monster. I lay shivering in Adair's
arms that night as he slept soundly.

What of Uzra? It didn't take a mystic to see that she didn't fit the pattern of the others in Adair's family. She floated above the rest of the
household. It wasn't that the others forgot about her, but she was not
discussed. She was not expected to join us when we gathered to drink
and talk late in the evening on returning from a party, she never sat
among us when we gathered around the table in the dining room for a
meal. But we might hear whispers of her pattering overhead or in the
walls, like a mouse climbing the battens.

Occasionally, Adair summoned her to the bedroom, where she
joined us, tight-lipped, eyes downcast, surrendering but not partici-
pating. But she'd seek me out later when I was alone, let me brush
her hair or read to her, which I took to be her way of letting me
know that she did not hold me responsible for what transpired in
Adair's bed or, at the least, forgave my allegiance to him. One time,
I sat still so she could paint my face in her native fashion, with thick
rings of kohl encircling my eyes and the line extended out toward my
temples. She wrapped me in one of her long, winding cloths so that
only my eyes were visible and I must say, the getup gave me a very
exotic look.

Sometimes, she'd give me a strange look, as though she were trying to talk to my soul, find some way to convey a message to me. A
warning. I didn't think I needed her to warn me; I knew Adair was a
dangerous man and that I risked grave damage to my soul or my san-
ity if I got too close to him. I thought I knew where the line of control
was and that I'd be able to stop myself in time. How stupid of me.

Sometimes Uzra came to my room and held me, as though she
was comforting me. A few times she pulled me out of bed, insisting I
follow her to one of her hiding spaces. Now I understand that she did

this so I would know where to go when the day came that I needed to hide from Adair.

Tilde, on the other hand, gave me no warning when she took me by the hand one afternoon with an irritated sigh and, ignoring my questions, led me firmly to a seldom used room. There, on a table next to the fire, stood a bottle of ink, a number of needles arrayed in a fan, and a much stained old handkerchief. Tilde settled in a chair, tucking stray hairs behind her ears and not regarding me in the least. "Take off your bodice and sleeves," she said, very matter-of-factly.

"What is this about?" I demanded.

"I'm not *asking* you, you stupid cuny," she said, taking the stopper out of the ink bottle and wiping the stain from her fingers. "This is by Adair's orders. Give me your bare arm."

Gritting my teeth, I did as I was told, knowing that Tilde delighted in bullying me, and then flounced onto the stool opposite her. She grabbed my right wrist and drew my arm to her, giving it a twist so that the underside was exposed to her, and then she pinned my arm under hers the way a blacksmith traps a horse's hoof between his knees in order to shoe it. I watched suspiciously as she selected a needle, dipped it into the ink, and then stabbed it into the delicate white skin of the inside of my upper arm.

I jumped even though I felt nothing more than the press of contact. "What are you doing?"

"I told you, it's on Adair's orders," she growled. "I'm pricking a mark into your skin. It's called a tattoo. I take it you've never seen one."

I stared at the black dots—three, now four; Tilde worked quickly. They looked like beauty marks, formed as the ink spread slightly beyond the puncture. After about an hour had passed, Tilde had completed the outline of a crest about the size of a dollar piece and was starting on an animal-like figure, a bit snakelike and fantastical. It took me a minute to realize that she was drawing a dragon. It was at this time that Adair strolled in. He tilted his head to watch Tilde at her work. He dragged a thumb over the site, now awash in both black ink and red blood, to get a clearer view.

"Do you know what this is?" he asked me, a little proudly. I shook my head. "It's the crest of my family. Or rather, the crest of my adopted lineage," he amended. "It's the emblem on the seal I told you of."

"Why are you doing this to me? What does this mean?" I asked.

He took the handkerchief and wiped at the tattoo, to better admire it. "What do you think it means? I am marking you—as mine."

"Is this really necessary?" I asked, trying to twist my arm free, which only earned me a mild slap from Tilde. "I suppose you do this to all your creatures. What about yours, Tilde? May I see it, so I'll know what it will look like when—"

"I don't have one," she said abruptly, not looking up from her work.

"You don't?" I faced Adair. "Then why me?"

"It is something special I have elected to give to you. It means you are mine forever."

I didn't like the proprietary gleam in his eye. "There are other ways of conveying such an intent to a girl. A ring, a necklace, some token of your devotion is the traditional method, I believe," I said, testily.

My feistiness seemed to please him. "Those are but tokens, trivial and transitory. You can take off a ring. You won't be able to do the same with this."

I stared at Tilde's handiwork. "What do you mean . . . my skin will be stained permanently?"

At this, he gave me the queer smile I had come to expect when he was about to do something hurtful. He jerked my arm away from Tilde and pinned it under his, took a deep breath, picked up one of the needles, and stabbed it through the center of Tilde's handiwork, careful to land in the middle of the design. A sharp pain suddenly bit into my upper arm, the stings of Tilde's needles coming alive all at once. "By my hand and intent," he said into the air like a proclamation, and then the wound stung as though salt had been rubbed into the open flesh. He twisted my arm sharply to get another look at the tattoo, and I winced in pain before he let go.

"Lanore, you surprise me," Adair said, though exaggerating for effect. "I thought it would please you to know I value you so highly that I would claim you for eternity."

The thing was, he was right: it did please the perverse part of me that wanted a man to desire me so badly he would burn his name into my skin. Though I was not so deluded that I wasn't alarmed, too, at being treated as though I were livestock.

Weeks passed in this way. I was content with Adair most days: he was attentive enough, kind enough, generous enough. We made love robustly. But there were times when he acted cruelly for no reason other than his own enjoyment. At those times, Alejandro, Tilde, Dona, myself—we became court jesters trying to appease a vindictive regent and coax him out of his terrible mood, or at least, trying to avoid being the object of his cruelty. At those times I felt trapped in a madhouse and was desperate to escape, only I didn't believe I could. The others were still with Adair, even after decades of such nerve-shattering treatment. I had been told that Uzra had tried to run away from him countless times. Surely, if there was a way to escape, they would have done so by now.

Also, despite my preoccupation with Adair, Jonathan began creeping back into my thoughts. At first, it was guilt that I felt, because there was another man in my life—as though I'd had a choice! Nonetheless, no matter how logically I tried to think about it, how vigorously I recalled his poor treatment of me, his callousness, I missed Jonathan and felt I was being unfaithful to him. It didn't matter that he was sworn to another woman and that he'd abdicated his claim to my heart—sleeping with one man, while loving another, seemed wrong.

And I did still love Jonathan. A thorough examination of my heart told me so. As flattered as I was by Adair's attention, pleased that a man who'd seen the world would find me intoxicating, I knew in my heart that if Jonathan arrived in town tomorrow, I would leave Adair without even saying good-bye. I was merely surviving. The only hope left to me was to one day see Jonathan again.

TWENTY-NINE

Time slipped past me, immeasurably. How long had I been with Adair—six weeks, six months? I'd lost count and was convinced it didn't matter; in my new circumstances, I'd never have to keep track of time again. Time in all its infinity was open to me now, like the ocean, and much like the first time I'd seen it, too great for me to grasp.

One blue and gold late summer afternoon, there was a knock at the front door. As I was happening by and there were no servants at hand (sleeping off a binge of purloined claret in the pantry, no doubt), I opened it, thinking it might be a tradesman or someone come to call on Adair. Instead, standing on the steps, satchel in hand, was the wild-eyed charismatic preacher from Saco.

His jaw dropped upon seeing me and his cunning face lit up with pleasure. "I *know* you, miss, do I not? I recognize your pretty face because a face like yours I would not be likely to forget," he said, sweeping into the front hall without an invitation. He brushed by me in his dusty cloak, removing the tricorner hat from his head.

"I know you too, sir," I replied, horrified, drawing back, unable to guess what in the world had brought him here.

"Well, don't keep me in suspense, then. What is your name and how did we meet?" he asked, still smiling but in a way meant to hide the calculations going on in his head, trying to recall where we had met and under what circumstances.

So instead of answering him, I asked, "Why have you come here? Do you know Adair?"

My guardedness seemed to amuse him. "Of course I know him, why else would I show up on his doorstep? I know him in the same way that *you* know him, I'll wager." So it was true—we were the same now, he and I. Adair's creations.

And then it came to him, his face lighting up with lurid delight. "Oh, I remember now! That little Maine village not far from the Acadian settlement! That's where I met you! Without the drab brown dress—you are barely recognizable in blue silk and French lace! It's an amazing transformation, upon my word. Left the Puritans behind without a regret, have you? It's always the quiet ones who turn out to be the most wild at heart," he said, narrowing his eyes to slits and leering, probably guessing that we stood a good chance of ending up in bed together. All he had to do was ask Adair and he was unlikely to be denied.

At that moment, we were interrupted by Adair's voice booming from the landing above us. "Look who has turned up at my door! Jude, come for a respite from your travels? Come in, come in, it has been too long since I last saw you," he said as he jogged down the stairs. After embracing Jude heartily, he noticed that Jude was staring at me in gleeful anticipation and so he asked, "What is it? Do you two know each other?"

"As a matter of fact, we do," Jude said, circling me, making a great show of drinking in the sight of me. "I wrote to you about this young woman some time back. Do you recall a letter describing a promising unspoiled beauty with a feral streak?"

I drew myself up, chin held high. "What do you mean by that?"

But Adair only chuckled and brushed my cheek to assuage my anger. "Come now, my dear. I think his meaning is plain, and you wouldn't be here at my side if it wasn't true."

The unwelcome visitor's eyes swept over me like a housewife's hands testing a piece of fruit. "Well, I'll wager she's unspoiled no more, eh? So, you've made this little spitfire your spiritual wife, have you?" Jude asked Adair in a mocking tone, and then he addressed me. "It must be your destiny, my dear, for you to turn up here, don't you think? And you are lucky, Adair, that you didn't have to make the journey all the way up there to get her—trust me, it's not a trip I would wish on anyone. She made a bit of trouble for me when I was there, too. Wouldn't introduce me to the fellow I wrote to you about."

He had to be referring to Jonathan. I held my tongue.

"I wish you would refrain from that 'spiritual wife' nonsense, at least when you're around me. I've no use for that religious mumbo-jumbo," Adair said as he threw an arm around Jude's shoulder and led him into the drawing room, where our visitor made a beeline for the decanters of wine. "Now, who is this you're talking about? What fellow?"

The preacher poured a full glass for himself. "Didn't you read my letters? Why ask me to write about my observations if you aren't going to pay any attention to them? It was all in my report to you, about what I found in this godforsaken little backwater village way up in the northernmost corner of the territory. Your latest acquisition here"— he nodded at me as he took a gulp of wine—"kept me from meeting a remarkable young man. She guarded him most jealously, from what I could see. This man is exactly what you've been looking for, if the stories I heard about him were accurate."

My skin crawled; something terrible was afoot. I stood paralyzed with apprehension.

Adair poured wine for himself, offering none to me. "Is this true, Lanore?" I didn't know how to respond and, in any case, common sense deserted me at that moment. "I see by your silence that it is. When were you going to tell me about him?" he asked.

"Your spy has it all wrong. This man is not worth your attention." These were words I never thought I'd say about Jonathan. "He's just a friend from home."

"Oh, hardly unworthy of attention. We are talking about Jonathan, the man you bragged of to Alej? Don't be surprised; of course Alejandro told me. He knows not to keep secrets from me. So, to be clear, this Jonathan, this paragon of beauty, he is the man you love? I am disappointed, Lanore, to find that you are so easily led by a handsome face—"

"Who are you to speak!" I said, outraged. "When it comes to love of beauty, who is the one who gathers pretty creatures to him like an art collector? If love of beauty is shallowness, you are far more guilty than I—"

"Oh, do not be so quick to take offense. I'm only teasing you. The fact that this Jonathan is the man you believe you love is reason enough for me to want to meet him, don't you think?"

Jude raised his eyebrows. "If I didn't know better, Adair, I'd say you sound a trifle jealous."

In a panic to change Adair's mind, I pleaded, "Spare Jonathan. He has a family who depends on him. I don't want him drawn into this. As for loving him . . . you're right, but he is gone from my life. I loved him once but no longer."

Adair cocked his head, and appraised me. "Oh, my dear, you lie. You would have given up on him by now, if that were the case. But you love him still. I feel it here," he said, as he touched my breast above my heart. His sparkling eyes, flecked with a note of pain, bored into me. "Bring him to me. I want to meet the man of amazing beauty who has fascinated our Lanore."

"If this is about bedding him, it won't do you any good. He's not— like Alejandro or Dona."

Jude blurted out a rude laugh, then covered his mouth quickly, and it seemed for a moment that Adair, bubbling with a spike of rage, might strike me. "You think I am only interested in this man to swive him? You think that is my only use for a man such as your Jonathan? No, Lanore, I want to meet him. I want to see why he is so deserving of your love. Perhaps we are like souls, he and I. I could use a new companion, a friend. I am sick of being surrounded by fawning syco-phants. You're all little more than servants—treacherous, scheming, demanding. I am sick of all of you." Adair stepped away and slammed his empty glass down on the sideboard. "Besides, what complaints could you have about your life here? Your days are spent in pleasure and comfort. I've given you everything you could want, treated you as a princess. I've opened your world, haven't I? Freed your mind from the limitations put there by those ignorant priests and ministers, and introduced you to secrets that learned men spend their lives seeking. All these things I've given you freely, my dear, haven't I? Frankly, your ingratitude offends me."

I bit my tongue, knowing nothing good would come of pointing out all that he'd put me through. What could I do except bow my head and murmur, "I'm sorry, Adair."

He clenched and unclenched his jaw and pressed his knuckles against the table, using the silence between us to show that he was coming down from his rage. "If this Jonathan is truly your friend, I would think you'd want to share your good fortune with him."

That may have been Adair's view of my life with him, but it only demonstrated the extent of his delusion. The truth was more compli-cated; grateful as I was, I was also afraid of him and felt like a prisoner in his house. I'd been made into a prostitute and didn't want Jonathan to see me like this, let alone draw him into this predicament with me.

As he left the room, Adair smirked over his shoulder at me. "Don't think for a moment that you fool me, Lanore. You protest, but in your heart you want this, too."

I could not let Jonathan suffer the same fate as me—ever. "Jude is not exaggerating; Jonathan lives far, far away," I continued, ignoring his slander. "You'd have to travel for three weeks by boat and carriage and have nothing at the end of it but forest and field. No parties, no gaming. Not even a public house to put you up."

Adair studied me for a second. "Very well, then. I will not make this trip, if it is as tedious as you say. You will go and fetch him for me. That is a fine test of your loyalty, don't you think?"

My heart sank.

During his stay at the mansion, Jude went with us to parties, but at the end of a night's carousing, as the group of us made our way to our chambers, Adair would block Jude from following us into the bedroom, throwing a shoulder against the door with a cold smirk and a cheery good night.

Jude's stay was short. He spent an afternoon behind closed doors with Adair in the study, after which I saw Jude dropping coins into his purse; clearly Adair was compensating him for something.

The day Jude was to leave us, he sought me out as I sat sewing in the morning room, taking advantage of the light. He bowed before me as though I was the lady of the house, holding his hat in his hands.

"Needlework? I'm surprised you take up needle and thread any longer, Lanore. Surely you have servants to attend to chores," he said. "Although, it's a good idea to practice your skills. Life with Adair won't always be like this, you know—the big house, servants, riches at your fingertips. There will be lean times when you will need to take care of yourself, if my experience serves me," he said, smiling ruefully.

"Thank you for that piece of advice," I said, icily, making a great show of my tolerance for his presence. "But you see that I am busy—is there a reason you've sought me out?"

"I'll not be imposing on your goodwill any longer, Miss Lanore," he said, almost meekly. "I take my leave today."

"My goodwill? My feelings do not enter into whether you are welcome in this house or not. Adair's wishes are all that matter."

The preacher chuckled at this, dusting his hat against his leg. "Lanore, surely you know that Adair considers your wishes in most things? He is very taken with you. I think you must be quite special to him. I don't mind telling you that I've never seen him act this way before . . . He's never been so smitten by a woman, I daresay." I have to admit, I was flattered by his words, though I kept my head lowered over my sewing and tried not to show it.

Jude then fixed his maniacal glare upon me. "I've come to warn you, too. It's a dangerous game you're playing. There's a reason the rest of us maintain a distance from Adair, and we've learned our lesson the hard way. But now you've shown him love and that's given him the notion that he is deserving of such devotion. Did you ever think that perhaps the only thing that holds the devil in check is that he knows how despised he is? Even the devil longs for sympathy at times, but sympathy for the devil is fuel for the flame. Your love will embolden him—likely in a way that will bring you regret."

His warning rattled and surprised me; it was not something I'd expected from him. But I said nothing, waiting for him to continue.

"I have a question for you and I hope you'll be honest with me. What does a girl like you see in Adair? I have looked into your heart and seen it to be wild and adventurous. He's introduced you to the world of carnal pleasures and you've embraced it as only a child raised by the puritanical will do—to his delight, I might add. Perhaps your wildness is only foolishness, Lanore—have you considered this? Give your lovely body to Adair, if that is your wish, but why would you give your heart over to a man who will only abuse it? He is unworthy of your loyalty, of your love. You are being reckless with your heart, Lanore. I think you are a little too innocent to consort with the likes of him. Forgive me for speaking my mind, but it is for your own good."

I was flabbergasted by his words. Who was he to call me foolish; I was trapped like the rest of them, wasn't I, forced to appease a tyrannical master in order to survive. No, at the time I saw myself as doing the best I could in a terrible situation. I see it differently now, of course; I know I was reckless and unable to speak the truth to myself. I should have been grateful that Jude took the great risk of warning me in Adair's own house, but I was too suspicious to trust him and instead, I tried to bluff him into thinking I knew what I was doing. "Well, I thank you for your advice—I suppose—but you'll forgive me if I say I must decide what is to be done for myself."

"Oh, but it's not just for yourself, is it?" he asked. "You're about to bring your Jonathan into it, too, the man for whom you profess such great love. The eagerness with which you agreed to Adair's proposal makes me wonder if perhaps he wasn't right. You *want* to do as Adair instructs you, don't you? You want your love to be caught in Adair's trap because it means he will be trapped with *you*."

"Do you know what I think?" I nearly shouted, pushing the needlework off my lap as I sprang to my feet. "You're not here to give me advice at all. You're jealous. You wanted to bring Jonathan to Adair yourself but you couldn't. I will succeed where you failed . . ." For all my vehemence, I didn't know what I was talking about; I would certainly have more influence over Jonathan than Jude, but for what purpose? Jude knew, but I didn't.

He shook his head and backed away a step. "I make sure that the people I bring to Adair's attention are deserving in their way. And they go to him of their own free will. What's more, I would never give him someone I claimed to love. Never."

I should have asked him what he meant; but like many a young person, I thought it better to bluff than to reveal that I didn't know what I was doing. And I didn't trust Jude; he was showing me a completely different face and I didn't know what to make of it. Was he hoping to trap me in a moment of disloyalty to Adair, a master he had served far longer than he had known me? Perhaps that was his role among Adair's pack, to be the infiltrator, the informant.

I forced a glower on my face but was trembling, unnerved. Jude had pushed me to the edge of composure. "I've heard enough from you. Leave now before I go to Adair with your deceit."

He drew back in surprise, but only momentarily, then let his shoulders sink. He bowed again in a mock show of respect as he backed out of the room. "I see that I was entirely mistaken about you, Lanore. You're far from reckless with your heart . . . You know exactly what you are doing, don't you? I hope you've made peace with God for what you are about to do."

I tried to calm my breathing and my racing heart, and tell myself that not one of his words was true. "Get out," I repeated, taking a step toward him as though I could drive him out of the house. "And I hope to never see you again."

"Alas, that is not our fate, I fear. The world is a small place, given an eternity, as you will see. Whether you or I wish it or not, our paths will cross again," he said as he swept out of the room.

THIRTY

P reparations for the trip began immediately, my passage booked on a cargo ship departing for Camden in four days. Dona, only too happy to see me go, helped me choose a sturdy pair of traveling trunks from among the dozens and dozens that had made the trip from Europe. In one we put the best of my clothing and in the other, gifts for my family: a bolt of silk from China; a set of collar and cuffs made of Belgian lace, ready to append to a dress; a gold necklace set with faintly pink opals. Adair insisted I take enticements for Jonathan, to show him what delights were available outside the Great North Woods. I explained that my friend had only one weakness, women, and so Dona shuffled through the boxes and unearthed a deck of playing cards, painted with lewdly explicit figures in place of the usual king, queen, jack of the various suits, with the queen of hearts being depicted in an especially remarkable and daring pose; a book of pornographic verse (though Jonathan had never been one for literature; if any book could make a reader out of Jonathan, perhaps this one could); a figurine of carved jade, said to be acquired from the Far East, of a trio having a sexual adventure;

and last, a velvet jewelry roll holding, instead of bracelets or rings, a set of carved dildos, one each made of wood, ivory, and ebony.

I frowned at this last gift. "I'm not sure this would be to his taste," I said, holding up the ebony one, the largest of the triplets, to study its detailing.

"Not for his usage," Dona said, taking the dildo from me and rolling it up with the others in the velvet casing. "You've made his proclivities plain enough. This could be used, say, to entertain his ladies, a novelty to whet their appetites and put them in a playful frame of mind. Would you like me to show you how they are used?" he asked, then cast me a sideways look, incredulous at my lack of sexual sophistication, thinking that perhaps I was not up to the job.

While Dona riffled through the trunks, intent on finding the specific trinket he had in mind, I amused myself by digging through the chests, too, unwrapping mysterious bundles, marveling at the treasure stored within (a bejeweled music box shaped like an egg, a miniature mechanical bird that flapped metal wings and sang a tinny song). Eventually, in a dusty trunk shoved under the eaves in the farthest corner, I found an item that gave me goose bumps. A heavy seal, golden in color (but made of brass, certainly; an object that size made of gold would be worth a fortune), wrapped in velvet and stored in a deerskin pouch. The seal of the long-dead physic of which Adair had spoken? Had he held on to it as a keepsake?

"There you go." Dona's voice called me back and I hastily closed the trunk and pushed it back to its resting place. Dona had wrapped Jonathan's packages in a square of red silk and tied it with a gold cord. He'd wrapped the presents for my family in a length of blue fabric and some white ribbon. "Do not confuse these two packages."

I was perhaps lulled into complacency by these preparations. Adair was being so accommodating with the assortment of gifts, the luxurious travel arrangements. I began to wonder if I didn't have a choice in this, after all, if this wasn't my chance to get out of his grasp. Perhaps I could not trust myself to consider these mutinous possibilities in Adair's presence, lying in bed next to him, but surely hundreds of miles away from him I would be safe. Distance must weaken the link between us.

I was comforted by this thought, maybe even emboldened. I began to see this trip as my chance for escape; perhaps I could even convince Jonathan to leave his family and their expectations behind and escape with me.

That is, until the following afternoon.

Tilde and I were returning from the milliner's with Tilde's new hat when we saw the girl. She stood in an alley, peeking out at the traffic on the street. From what we could see of her, she was thin and gray, a tiny mouse dressed in limp rags. Tilde went over to the girl, causing her to scurry deeper into the alley.

I was wondering why Tilde had gone after the girl in the first place and if I should join them when they started toward me. In the over-cast light of the afternoon, I saw how pitiful the girl was. She looked like a rag that had been crumpled up and discarded, the knowledge that she was disposable stamped everlasting in her eyes.

"This is Patience," Tilde said, holding the girl's small hand in hers. "She needs a place to stay, so I thought we would take her home with us. Give her a meal and a roof over her head for a few nights. You don't imagine Adair will mind, do you?" Her smile was vulpine and triumphant, reminding me immediately of how she and the others had found me on the street a few months earlier. The effect was just as she'd intended. On seeing the alarm on my face, she gave me a sharp, warning look and I knew I was meant to say nothing.

Tilde hailed a carriage and ushered the girl up the steps ahead of us. The little one sat on the edge of the bench, staring out the window with wide eyes, watching Boston spin by. Had I looked like this, so pitiful, nothing more than prey for a predator, practically begging to be eaten?

"Where have you come from, Patience?" I asked.

She regarded me cautiously. "I run away."

"From home?"

She shook her head but offered no further explanation.

"How old are you?"

"Fourteen." She looked no older than twelve and seemed to know it, her eyes darting away from my inquisitive stare.

Tilde took her to an upstairs room as soon as we arrived at the mansion. "I'll send a servant with some water so you can wash up," she said, causing the girl self-consciously to raise her hand to her dirty cheek. "I'll have some food brought up, too. I'm going to find you something warmer to wear. Lanore, why don't you come with me?"

She went straight to my room and began rustling through my clothing without asking permission. "We gave all the small things to you, I think . . . Surely you have something that will fit the girl . . ."

"I don't understand . . ." I cut in front of Tilde and closed the door of the armoire. "Why did you bring her here? What do you intend to do with her?"

Tilde smirked. "Don't pretend to be stupid, Lanore. Of anyone, you should know—"

"She's still a child! You can't hand her over to Adair as though she's a toy." Of all the things I'd known Adair to do, he'd never molested a child. I didn't think I could stomach that.

Tilde went over to a trunk. "She may be on the young side, but she's no innocent. She told me she ran away from a workhouse where she'd been sent to have her baby. Fourteen and with a child. Honestly! We are doing her a favor," she said as she plucked out a narrow set of stays with serviceable cotton laces.

I slumped onto my bed.

"Give these to her and clean her up a little." Tilde shoved the clothing at me. "I'll see about getting her something to eat."

Patience was standing at the window, looking down on the street when I returned to her room. She pushed dirty strands of brown hair from her eyes and looked covetously at the clothing in my arms.

I held it out to her. "Go ahead, put these on." I turned my back as she stripped. "So, Tilde tells me you are from a workhouse . . ."

"Yes, miss."

". . . where you had a baby. Tell me, what happened to your child?" My heart thumped in my throat; surely she didn't run away and leave him behind.

"They took him away from me," she said defensively. "I never seen him, not since he was born."

"I'm sorry."

"That's done and over with. I wish . . ." She stopped, perhaps thinking better of sharing too much with these suspect ladies who had swept her off the street. I knew how she felt. "The other lady tells me there might be a job for me here, as a kitchen girl maybe?"

"Would you like that?"

"But she says I have to meet the master of the house first, to see if he approves of me." She searched my face for some sign that I was in agreement, that a strange trick wasn't being played on her. Tilde was wrong; the girl was still very much an innocent. Like it or not, I heard Jude's words ring in my ears: she was too innocent to consort with the likes of Adair. I could not let what had happened to me happen to her.

I grabbed her hand. "Come with me. Don't say a word or make a sound."

We ran down the back staircase, the servants' stairs, which I knew Tilde never used, and through the kitchen to the back entrance. A handful of coins sat on the corner of the chopping block, waiting no doubt for a deliveryman. I scooped the money up and pressed it into Patience's hand.

"Go. Take this money and keep the clothing."

She looked at me as though I'd lost my mind. "But where am I to go? They'll punish me for sure if I go back to the workhouse, and I can't go home to my family . . ."

"Then take your punishment, or throw yourself on the mercy of your family. For all the wickedness you've already seen, there's more that you have no knowledge of, Patience. Go! It's for your own good," I said as I pushed her out the door, then slammed it shut. The scullery girl entered at this moment and gave me a fishy eye, and I went back up the stairs to the shelter of my room.

I paced wildly. If I'd thrown the girl out for her own safety, what excuse had I for living here? I knew that what I was doing with Adair was wrong, I knew this was a wicked place and yet . . . fear had held me in place. Just as fear now prodded me in the back; it was only a matter of minutes before Tilde realized her catch had been released, then she and Adair would be on me like a pair of lions. I began throwing clothing into a satchel as every nerve in my body told me to flee. Flee or face a terrible wrath.

I was on the street and in a carriage without thinking, counting the money in my purse. Not much but enough to get me away from Boston. The carriage left me at the office for a coach service and I bought fare on the next passenger coach out of Boston, heading for New York City. "The coach don't leave for another hour," the clerk told me. "There's a public house across the street where some people wait until it's time," he said helpfully.

I sat with a pot of tea in front of me, my satchel at my feet, my first chance to catch my breath and think since I'd fled. Even with fear hammering in my heart, I also felt peculiarly optimistic. I was leaving Adair's house. How many times had I wished to do it but lacked the courage? Now I'd done the deed in haste and there were no signs that I'd been discovered. Surely he'd not find me in an hour—Boston was a big place—and then I would be on the road, untraceable. I wrapped my hands around the white china pot for the warmth and allowed myself a tiny sigh of relief. Perhaps Adair's house had all been an illusion, a bad dream that only seemed like reality while in the midst of it. Maybe he had no power to harm me out here. Maybe summoning the courage to run out the door was the only test. The question now, of course, was where to go and what to do with my life.

Then, suddenly, I was aware of the presence of several people at my elbow. Adair, Alejandro, Tilde. Adair crouched next to me and whispered in my ear, "Come with me now, Lanore, and do not think of making a scene. There is jewelry, I'll warrant, in your bag and if you call for help I will tell the authorities that you stole these valuables from my home. The others will swear to it."

His hand nearly crushed my elbow as he pulled me from my seat. I felt his anger radiate like heat from a fire. I couldn't look at any of them in the carriage on the way to the house—I just sat withdrawn into myself, my mouth rusted shut with fear. We'd barely gotten inside the front door when he reached out and slapped me hard across my cheek, knocking me to the floor. Alejandro and Tilde swept hurriedly behind me and out of the hall, like birds lifting from a field ahead of a storm.

From the fury in Adair's eyes, he looked like he wanted to tear me to pieces. "What did you think you were doing? Where were you going?"

No words came to me, but as it turned out, he wanted no answers. He only wanted to hit me, over and over, until I lay in a broken heap at his feet, looking at him through swollen eyes and a haze of blood. His anger hadn't subsided, that was apparent as he nursed his knuckles and paced in front of me.

"Is this how you repay my generosity, my trust?" he roared. "I take you into my house, my family, clothe you, keep you safe . . . In some ways, you are like a child to me. So it is understandable, how disappointed you have made me. I warned you—you are mine, whether you wish it or not. You will never, ever leave me, not until I allow you to go."

Then he lifted me up and carried me to the back part of the house, the kitchen and servants' domain though they'd all disappeared like mice. He carried me down a flight of stairs to the forlorn cellar, past crates of wine, sacks of flour, and unused furniture stored under drapes, through a narrow passage, its walls damp with chill, and finally to an old oak door, heavily scarred. The light in the room was dim. Dona stood by the door in a robe, tightly cinched at his waist, and he hunched over as though sick. Something terrible was about to happen if Dona, who usually delighted in the misfortune of others, was afraid. In his hand dangled a spider's web of leather straps, a harness, but unlike any horse's harness I'd ever seen.

Adair dropped me to the floor. "Get her ready," he said to Dona, who began to peel off my sweaty, bloodied clothing. Behind him, Adair started undressing. Once I was naked, Dona began strapping the harness to me. It was a design of nightmares and began to contort my body in an unnatural position, a pose of utmost vulnerability. It bound my arms behind my back and pulled my head almost to the point of breaking from my neck. Dona let out a whimper as he notched up the straps, but he did not make them any looser. Adair towered over me, his manner menacing and his intent clear.

"The time has come to teach you obedience. I'd hoped, for your sake, it wouldn't be necessary. It seemed that you were destined to be different—" He stopped, catching himself. "Everyone must be punished once, so they *know* what will happen to them if they try again. I told you you'd never leave me and yet you tried to run away. You'll never try to run away again." Adair wove his fingers into my hair and drew his face close to mine. "And remember this while you are back in your village with your family and with your Jonathan—there is nowhere you can go that I can't find you. You can never escape me."

"The girl . . . ," I tried to say through lips sealed with dried blood.

"This is not about the girl, Lanore. Though you should learn to accept what goes on in my house—you *will* accept it, and be a part of it, too. This is about you turning your back on *me*, refusing *me*. I will not allow that. Especially from *you*, I would not have expected that *you*—" He choked off the rest, thinking better of it, but I knew what he meant to say, that he did not want to regret giving a piece of his heart to me.

I won't tell you what happened to me in that room. Allow me this shred of privacy, to keep from you the details of my debasement. It should be enough to know that it was the most horrific ordeal I have ever suffered. It was not just Adair who was my torturer: he enlisted Dona, too, though it was clearly against the Italian's will. It was my taste of the devil's fire that Jude had warned me about, a lesson that tempting the devil's love is a great risk. Such love, if it can be called that, is never sweet. Eventually, you will experience it for what it is. It is vitriol. It is poison. It is acid poured down your throat.

I was barely conscious when they'd finished. I opened my eyes a slit to see Adair picking up his clothing from the ground. He was slick with sweat and his hair was plastered to his neck in dark curls. Dona had gotten his robe on, too, and was crawling on his hands and knees, pale and shaky, as though he might be ill at any second.

Adair raked his hands through his wet hair, then tossed his head in Dona's direction. "Get her upstairs and have someone clean her up," he said before exiting the room.

I winced as Dona undid the leather straps. They had bit into my skin, leaving me with dozens of cuts, the wounds opening again when the straps pulled against the dried blood. He left the horrible contraption on the floor—the straps shaping themselves into a hollow human form—and picked me up in his arms, the tenderest I had ever seen Dona, before or since.

He took me to the room with the copper bathtub, where Alejandro waited with buckets of hot water. Then Alejandro washed me gently, wiping away the blood and the fluids, but I could barely stand his touch and I couldn't stop crying.

"I am in hell, Alejandro. How can I go on?"

He took my hand and daubed it with a cloth. "You have no choice. It might help to know that we have all been through this, each of us. There is no shame in what happened to you, not among us." Even as he washed, my wounds were healing, the tiny slashes disappearing, the bruises yellowing. He dried me and wrapped me in a clean banyan, and we lay together on the bed, Alejandro nestled behind me, not letting me shrink from him.

"So, what happens next?" I asked, my fingers laced with his.

"Nothing. It will go back to as it was before. You must try to forget what was done to you today, but not the lesson. Never forget the lesson."

The night before I was to depart for Boston was a miserable one. I wanted to be left alone with my worries, but Adair insisted on taking me to his bed. I was now terrified of him, needless to say, but he paid no mind to the change in my behavior; I suppose he was used to this from all his minions and expected I would come around again, in time. Or perhaps he didn't care that he'd shattered my trust in him. I remembered Alejandro's advice and behaved as though nothing had happened, trying to be as attentive as ever.

Adair had drunk heavily—perhaps to blot out what he'd done to make me so fearful of him—and puffed on the hookah until clouds of narcotic smoke filled the room. That night in bed I was a distracted, absent partner: all I could think about was what I was going to do to Jonathan. I was about to condemn him to eternity with this madman. Jonathan had done nothing to deserve this.

I had not worked out in my head what I would say to my family on my return to St. Andrew, either. After all, I'd disappeared from their lives when I'd run away from the harbor a year ago. Surely they would have made inquiries of the convent and the shipping master, only to be told that I'd arrived in Boston and promptly vanished. Perhaps they held out hope I was still alive and had run away to keep my baby. Had they checked with the authorities in Boston, harangued the constabulary to search for me until they lost hope and were sure that I had been murdered? I wondered if they'd held a mock funeral for me in St. Andrew—no, my father would not let them display such emotion. Instead, my mother and sisters would carry their grief around with them, heavy stones sewn under their skin, close to their hearts.

And what of Jonathan, for that matter—what did he think had happened to me? Perhaps he had thought of me as deceased—if he thought of me at all. Tears flooded my eyes instantly: surely he thought of me once in a while, the woman who loved him most in the world! But I had to face the fact that I was dead to everyone in St. Andrew. Survivors come to accept a loved one having passed away. They mourn for a while, weeks or months, but eventually the memory is consigned to the past and only visited occasionally, like a once beloved toy stumbled upon in the attic, patted lovingly, but then left behind again.

I woke in the half-lit hours of dawn, sweaty and disheveled from a restless sleep. The ship was to sail on the morning tide and I had to get to the docks before sunrise. As I leaned over to search for my discarded linen under the bedding, I drank in the sight of Adair, his head on the pillow. I guess it's true that even devils look like angels in their sleep, when stillness and contentment are upon them. His eyes were closed, his long lashes brushed his cheeks; his hair tumbled over his shoulders in dark, lustrous curls; and the wisps of hair on his cheeks made him look like a youth, not a man capable of inhuman cruelties.

My head ached from the narcotic I'd breathed all night. If I felt this bad, I figured Adair had to be nearly comatose. I picked up his hand and let it fall, dead weight. He didn't so much as grunt or shift under the covers.

Then a perverse thought came to me. I recalled the tiny silver vial that held the elixir of life, the drop of demonic magic that had changed me forever. *Take it*, the voice said, *that vial is the root of Adair's power. This is your chance to get back at him. Steal his power and take it with you to St. Andrew.*

With the potion, I'd have the ability to bind Jonathan to me, as I was bound to Adair. The thought flashed through my mind, but my stomach went weak. I could never use it—I could never transform someone into what I was now.

Take it to get back at Adair. It's all the magic he has in the world. Think how panicked he'll be when he realizes it's missing!

I wanted revenge for what he'd done to me in the basement. I resented being sent on this errand, being forced to condemn my beloved to an eternity with this monster. More than anything I wanted to get back at Adair.

I prefer to think that I was possessed by a power far stronger than my reason, for I inched cautiously out of bed, dropping my bare feet silently to the floor. As I slipped on one of Adair's banyans, I surveyed the room: where would he hide the vial? I'd only seen it that day, never before or since.

I went to the dressing room. Was it on the tray that held the sewing needles, or in the jewelry case, tucked among the rings and stickpins? Perhaps in the toe of a seldom worn slipper? I was on my knees, feeling my way through a row of his shoes, before I realized Adair would never store such a valuable object where his valet might find it and pocket it. He would either keep it on him at all times—and I'd seen him stark naked on many occasions, with no sign of the vial— or he would secret it away where no one would think to look for it. Where no one would dare look for it.

Candle in hand, I scurried out of the room and took the servants' stairs to the cellar, through the dank subterranean halls that smelled of old standing water, trailing a hand along the thick stone walls. Slowing as I approached the room where no one went and that everyone feared, I pushed back the scarred door and stepped onto the pounded dirt floor where I had recently lain, bleeding.

Holding my breath, I tiptoed to the lone trunk on the other side of the room and lifted the lid. Inside was the hated thing, the nightmarish harness, straps stiff with my sweat, still formed in the shape of my body. I almost dropped the lid at the sight of it, but held my fright in check when I noticed a small bundle in a corner of the trunk. I reached in and lifted out a man's handkerchief, folded into a tiny pillow.

I peeled back a corner of the handkerchief to see . . . the vial. In the light of the candle, the silver vial glimmered like an ornament on a Christmas tree, sparkling with the same kind of faintly tarnished luster. The light seemed to pulse ominously, a warning of some kind. But I'd come this far and was not about to turn back now. The vial was mine. I balled my fist around it, pressed it to my heart, and stole out of the dungeon.

THIRTY-ONE

QUEBEC PROVINCE, PRESENT DAY

Outside the window of the motel room, the sky has gone blue-black, the color of ink from a ballpoint pen. They'd left the blind up as they tumbled into bed together, and now that the rush to discover each other's bodies is over, Lanny and Luke lie side by side, gazing out the window at the northern stars. He runs his fingers down her bare arm, marveling at the luminosity of her skin, how perfect it is, cream with a spattering of faint gold freckles. Her body is a series of smooth, low-rising curves. He wants to skim his hands over her again and again, as if by doing this he can carry off a part of her for himself. He wonders if the magic in her has made her more beautiful, enhanced her natural appearance.

He can't believe his good fortune in having gone to bed with her. He feels faintly like a dirty old man, as he hasn't held a woman this firm since long before he was married. Not since he was in his twenties, but he doesn't remember the sex being as good, perhaps because he and his partners were too self-conscious. He can imagine what his ex-wife or friends would say if they saw Lanny; they would think he was in the clutches of an epic midlife crisis, helping a barely legal woman evade the police in exchange for sex.

She looks him over with a smile on her beautiful face, and he wonders what she can possibly find pleasing about him. He's always thought of himself as an ordinary man: average height, more thin than fat but hardly in any shape worthy of admiration; shaggy, wavy hair on the border between sandy brown and blond. His patients have implied that he's hippieish, like some of the backpackers who descend on St. Andrew in the summer, but Luke thinks they've gotten this impression because he tends toward disarray when there's no one around to tidy him up. What could a woman like her see in a man like him? he wonders.

Before he can ask, however, there's a distraction at the window, a rippling of shadows outside the glass that indicates movement on the walkway. Luke just has time to sit up before banging erupts on the other side of the door and a deep male voice barks, "Open up! This is the police."

Luke holds his breath, unable to think, to react, to *do*, but Lanny is out of the bed in one leap, sheet wrapped around her body, landing noiselessly on cat's feet. She holds a finger to her lips and slips around the corner into the little kitchenette area and then into the bathroom. When she is out of sight, he climbs out of bed, wraps a blanket around his waist, and opens the door.

Two police officers fill the open doorway, shining a flashlight into Luke's face. "We got a call about a man having sex with a minor . . . can you turn on a light, sir?" one of the officers asks, sounding exasperated, as though there is nothing he'd like better than to drive Luke into the wall, a police baton jammed against his throat. Both officers stare at Luke's bare chest and the blanket cinched around his hips. Luke snaps on the closest switch, lighting up the room.

"Where's the girl who registered for the room?"

"What girl?" Luke manages to say, though his throat is dry as desert sand. "There must be a mistake. This is my room."

"So *you* registered for this room?"

Luke nods.

"I don't think so. The desk clerk said there's only one room rented out on this side of the building. To a girl. She told the clerk the room was for her and her father." The police officers crowd the door. "A housekeeper said she heard what sounded like people having sex in here, and since the clerk knew the room was occupied by a father and daughter . . ."

Panic washes over Luke as he tries to recover from his lie. "Oh, yeah, that's what I mean. The girl, we're together, that's why I said this is my room . . . but she's not my daughter. I don't know why she would have told anyone that."

"Right." They look unconvinced. "Do you mind if we come in and look around? We'd like to talk to the girl—is she here?"

Luke freezes, listening—he doesn't hear anything, which makes him think she's slipped out. In the police officers' eyes, Luke sees barely controlled indignation; they would probably like nothing better than to knock him to the ground and kick the shit out of him for all the abused daughters they have seen in their careers. Luke is just about to stammer an excuse when he notices that the policemen are looking at something behind him. He turns, twisting the cheap peach blanket around his legs.

Lanny stands with the sheet still wrapped around her naked body, drinking from a battered red plastic glass, a look of surprise and feigned embarrassment in her eyes. "Oh! I thought I heard someone at the door. Good evening, Officers. Is something wrong?"

The two policemen size her up, head to bare feet, before answering. "Did you register for this room, miss?"

She nods.

"And is this man your father?"

She goes sheepish. "Oh goodness, no. No . . . I don't know why I said that to the guy at the front desk. I was afraid he wouldn't rent us the room, I suppose, since we're not married. He seemed—I dunno— the judgmental type. I just didn't think it was any of his business."

"Uh-huh. We're going to have to see some ID." They are trying to be dispassionate, trying to dispel their righteous anger now that there is no pervert here to bring to justice.

"You have no right to check up on us. It was consensual, what we did," Luke says as he puts an arm around Lanny, drawing her against his side. He wants the police to leave now. He wants this embarrassing, nerve-racking experience behind him.

"We just have to see proof that you're not—you know," the younger of the two policemen says, ducking his head and making an impatient gesture with his flashlight. There is no alternative but to let the officers look over his driver's license and her passport, hoping that any police bulletin from St. Andrew hasn't made it over the border to Canada.

Luke soon realizes that he needn't have worried: the two officers are so flustered and disappointed that they make the most cursory pass over the identification, quite possibly not even reading either document, before shuffling backward out the door with barely audible apologies for the inconvenience. As soon as they've left, Luke pulls the blind over the window that looks onto the walkway.

"Oh my god," Lanny says before collapsing on the bed.

"We should leave. I should get you to a city."

"I can't ask you to take any more chances for me . . ."

"I can't leave you here, can I?" He gets dressed while Lanny is in the bathroom, water running. He runs a hand over his chin, feeling stubble, realizing it has been about twenty-four hours since he last shaved, then he decides to see if the parking lot is clear. He hooks a finger behind the blind and peeks out: the squad car is sitting next to the SUV.

He lets the blind fall back into place. "Damn it. They're still outside."

Lanny looks up from her suitcase. "What?"

"The two cops, they're still out there. Running a check on the license plate, maybe."

"You think?"

"Maybe they're seeing if we have records." He rubs his lower lip, thinking. They probably can't get answers right away on U.S. license plates or drivers' licenses; they probably have to wait for a reply to come back through the system, through police liaison units. There might be a sliver of time before . . .

Luke reaches for Lanny. "We have to go, now."

"Won't they try to stop us?"

"Leave your suitcase, everything. Just get dressed."

They leave the hotel room hand in hand and have started walking to their vehicle when the window of the squad car slides down. "Hey," the police officer on the passenger side calls out, "you can't leave yet."

Luke drops Lanny's hand so she can hang back while he approaches the patrol car. "Why can't we leave? We haven't done anything wrong. We showed you our ID. You don't have any reason to detain us. This is starting to feel like harassment."

The two officers bristle, uncertain but not liking the sound of the word "harassment."

"Look," Luke continues, opening his hands to show that they're empty. "We're just going out to dinner. Do we look like we're going to bolt? We left our luggage in the room; we're paid up for the night. If you still have questions when your background checks come in, you can always catch us after dinner. But if you're not going to arrest me, I believe you can't stop me." Luke speaks calmly and reasonably, arms outstretched, like a man trying to dissuade thieves from robbing him. Lanny climbs into the front seat of the big SUV, giving the police officers a hostile glare. He follows her, starts the engine, and pulls out of the parking space smoothly, checking one last time to be sure the squad car doesn't follow them.

It's not until they're well down the road that Lanny pulls the laptop from under her jacket. "I couldn't leave it behind. It has too much damning information on it, tying me to Jonathan, stuff they could use as evidence if they wanted to," she explains, as though she feels guilty for having taken the risk to save it. After a second, she removes the bag of pot from her pocket, like she's lifting a rabbit from a magician's hat.

Luke's heart warbles in his throat. "The pot, too?"

"I figured after they'd realized we weren't coming back, they'd search the room for sure. This would give them a reason to arrest us . . ." She stuffs the bag back in her jacket pocket. "Do you think we're safe?"

He checks the rearview mirror again. "I dunno . . . they have the license plate number now. If they remember our names, *my* name . . ." They are going to have to abandon the SUV and Luke feels terrible for having borrowed Peter's car. He must take his mind off it. "I don't want to think about it now. Tell me some more of your story."

PART III

THIRTY-TWO

The highway to Quebec City runs two lanes in each direction and is as dark as an abandoned airstrip. The leafless trees and featureless scenery remind Luke of Marquette, the tiny town in the lonely upper corner of Michigan where his ex-wife settled. Luke has been up once to see his girls, right after Tricia moved in with her childhood sweetheart. Tricia and Luke's two children now live in her boyfriend's house, on a cherry farm, and his son and daughter stay with them a couple of nights a week, too.

During the visit, Tricia seemed to Luke no happier with her sweetheart than she had been with him, or maybe she was just embarrassed to be seen by her ex in a run-down house with a twelve-year-old Camaro in the driveway. Not that Luke's house in St. Andrew was much better.

The girls, Winona and Jolene, were unhappy, but that was to be expected; they'd just moved to town and knew no one. It almost broke Luke's heart to sit with them in the pizza place where he'd taken them for lunch. They were silent and too young to know whom to blame or be mad at. They sulked when he tried to draw them out, and he couldn't bear the thought of taking them back to their mother, saying good-bye when all of them were so raw and hurting. He also knew it couldn't be helped: what they were going through couldn't be solved in a weekend.

By the end of his time there, as he was saying his farewells on the cement steps in front of Tricia's front door, things had improved for him and the girls. Their panic had subsided, they had found some solid ground under their tiny feet. They cried when he hugged them good-bye and waved as Luke pulled away in his rental car, but it still tore at his heart to leave them.

"I have two daughters of my own," Luke blurts out, overcome by the urge to share something of his life with her.

Lanny looks over at him. "Was that their picture, at your house? How old are they?"

"Five and six." He feels a tiny glow of pride, all he has left of fatherhood. "They live with their mother. And the guy she's planning to marry." Someone else was taking care of his daughters, now.

She shifts so she faces him. "How long were you married?"

"Six years. We're divorced now," he adds. "It was a mistake to get married, I see it now. I'd just finished my residency in Detroit. My parents' health was starting to fail and I knew I'd be coming back to St. Andrew . . . I guess I didn't want to come back alone. I couldn't imagine finding someone here. I knew everybody, since I had grown up here. I think I saw Tricia as my last chance."

Lanny shrugs, an undercurrent of discomfort in her frown. Uncomfortable with too much honesty, Luke decides, whether she's the one being honest or not. "What about you? Have you ever married?" he asks and his question prompts a laugh from her.

"I didn't hide myself away from the rest of the world all this time, if that's what you think. No, I came to my senses eventually. I saw that Jonathan would never commit to me. I saw it wasn't in him." Luke thinks of the man in the morgue. Women would throw themselves at a man like that. Never-ending come-ons and propositions, so much want and desire, so much temptation. How could you expect a man like that to commit to one woman? It was only natural for Lanny to want Jonathan to be faithful, but could you blame the man for disappointing her?

"So you found someone else and fell in love?" Luke tries to keep the hopefulness out of his voice. She laughs again.

"For a man who married in desperation and ended up divorced, you sound like a hopeless romantic. I said I was married, I didn't say I fell in love." She twists so that she's facing away from him again. "That's not true, exactly. I loved all of my husbands, just not the same way I loved Jonathan."

"*All* of them? How many times have you been married?" Luke again gets the uncomfortable feeling he had in Dunratty's, looking at the mussed bed.

"Four times. A girl gets lonely every fifty years or so," she says, smirking, making fun of herself. "They were all nice, each in their own way. They took care of me. Accepted me for what I am, however much I could share with them."

These glimpses into her life make him wish for more. "How much did you share with them? Did you tell any of them about Jonathan?"

Lanny tosses her head and shakes out her hair, still hiding her face from him. "I've never told anyone the truth about me before, Luke. You're the only one."

Is she just saying that for my benefit? Luke wonders. She's trained herself to know what people want to hear. It's the kind of skill you have to develop if you're going to survive for hundreds of years and not be found out. All part of the subtle art of weaving people into your life, binding them to you, getting them to like you, maybe even to love you.

Luke wants to hear her story, to know all about her, but can he trust her to tell him the truth, or is she just manipulating him until they are safe from the police? As Lanny settles back into thoughtful silence, Luke drives on, wondering what will happen when they arrive in Quebec City, if she will disappear and leave him with only her story.

THIRTY-THREE

BOSTON, 1819

I had planned my trip back to St. Andrew with the enthusiasm customary for a funeral. Using a sack of coins from Adair, I booked passage on a cargo ship sailing from Boston to Camden, and from Camden onward, I would travel in a specially hired coach with a driver. The only transportation to and from St. Andrew had traditionally been the provisioner's wagon, which brought fresh goods for the Watfords' store twice a year. I planned to arrive in style, showing up in a handsome trap complete with cushions softening its hard benches and curtains over the windows, and let them know I was not the same woman who'd left.

It was early fall, and while Boston was only chilly and damp, the passes on the approach to northern Aroostook County would already have snow. I was surprised to be nostalgic for the snow of St. Andrew, the high, deep drifts and landscapes of unbroken white, the scalloped edges of pine trees peeking out from under thick coats of snow. As a child, I'd look out the frosted windowpanes of my parents' cabin and watch the wind blow horizontal sprays of snow as fine as dust, and be grateful to be inside the cabin with the fire and five other bodies keeping me toasty warm.

So that morning, I stood in the Boston harbor, waiting to board the ship that would take me back to Camden in completely different circumstances than when I'd arrived: two trunks of beautiful clothes and gifts, a purse with more currency than the entire village saw in five years, and luxurious travel accommodations. I'd left St. Andrew a disgraced young woman with no prospects and was returning as a refined lady who'd stumbled across a secret provenance and lucked into riches.

Obviously, I owed Adair much. But it did not make me less sad about what I was doing.

While at sea, I hid in my cabin, still overcome with guilt. In an attempt to blunt my emotions, I sat with a bottle of brandy and, with drink after drink, tried to convince myself that I was not a traitor to my former lover. I was coming to present an offer to Jonathan on Adair's behalf, a gift one could only dream of: the ability to live forever. Any man would readily accept such a gift—even pay a fortune for it—if it were presented to him. Jonathan had been chosen for admittance to an unseen world, to learn that life as we knew it was not all there was. He could scarcely complain about what I was bringing him.

Yet *I* knew that this other plane of existence came with a price. I just didn't understand what that price was yet. I didn't feel superior to mortals, as I didn't feel like a god. If anything, I felt I'd left the sphere of mankind and crossed to a realm of shameful secrets and regret, a dark underworld, a place of punishment. But surely I was not entirely lost. Surely there was a chance to make up for one's sins, for atonement.

By the time I'd arrived in Camden, hired the carriage, and started my solitary trip north, the idea of rebelling against Adair began to creep into my head again. After all, my surroundings were so unlike Boston that Adair seemed far away. I bargained with myself: if, after arriving in St. Andrew, I saw that Jonathan was happy in his life with his overbearing family and his child bride, I would spare him. I could take the consequences on myself: I would slip away and make my own way in the world, because I could never go back to Boston without Jonathan. Ironically, Adair himself had given me the means to flee: I had more than enough money to get off to a good start. These fantasies were short lived, however; I couldn't forget Adair's warning to do as I was ordered or suffer at his hand. Adair would never let me leave him.

In this unhappy frame of mind, I steeled myself to roll into St. Andrew that October afternoon, to face the surprise of my family and my acquaintances for being alive, and their eventual disappointment at what I had become.

I arrived on an overcast Sunday. I'd been lucky that the season wasn't as punishing as it could be and the snow along the route had been passable. The trees were bare against a gray flannel sky and the last leaves clinging to the branches were a dead color, shriveled and curled, like bats hanging from their roosts.

The church service had just let out for the day and the townspeople spilled from the broad doors of the congregation hall onto the common. The parishioners stood conversing despite the cold and the wind, reluctant as always to forgo companionship and return home. No sign of my father; perhaps with no one to accompany him, he'd taken to going to the Catholic mass for convenience. But my eyes found Jonathan immediately, and my heart rose on seeing him. He stood on the far edge of the common where the horses and carriages were tethered and was climbing into his family's buggy, his sisters and brother waiting in a row for their turn. Where were his mother and the captain? Their absence made me anxious. On his arm was a young woman, white with fatigue. Jonathan helped her into the front seat of the buggy. There was a bundle in her arms—a baby. The child bride had given Jonathan something I could not. At the sight of the baby, I nearly lost my courage and told the driver to turn around.

But I did not.

My carriage swept into this scene, and was immediately an object of curiosity. At my signal, the driver pulled the horses up and, heart in my throat, I sprang from the carriage into the crowd that had gathered.

My reception was warmer than I'd expected. They recognized me, despite the new clothing and styled hair and hired carriage. I was encircled by people I'd always suspected cared little for me—the Watfords, Tinky Talbot the blacksmith and his soot-smudged brood, Jeremiah Jacobs and his new bride, whose face I recalled but whose name escaped me. Pastor Gilbert bustled down from the congregation hall steps, his vestments twisted by the wind, as my former neighbors whispered around me.

"Lanore McIlvrae, as I live and breathe!"

"Look at her, all fancied up!"

Hands reached from the crowd to offer a handshake, though I saw from the corner of my eye the clucking tongues and shaking heads on the fringe. Then the crowd parted for Pastor Gilbert, who arrived red faced from exertion.

"Dear lord, it is you, Lanore?" he asked, but I scarcely heard him, I was so preoccupied by his appearance. How Gilbert had aged! He'd shrunk and his portly belly had slimmed, but his old face was wrinkled like an apple forgotten in the cold cellar and his eyes were rheumy and red. He clasped my hand with a mixture of affection and trepidation. "Your family will be so happy to see you! We'd given you up for"—he blushed, as though about to let slip the wrong word—"lost. And here you have returned to us—and in such obvious good fortune."

At the mention of my family, the expressions of the onlookers shifted, though no one said a word. Good God, what had happened to my family? And why did everyone seem so much older? Miss Watford had streaks of gray in her hair I did not recall. The Ostergaard boys were fully grown and bursting out of their hand-me-down clothing, wrists protruding from the too short sleeves of their jackets.

The crowd parted again at a commotion in the back, and into the circle stepped Jonathan. Oh, how he'd changed. He'd lost the last of his boyishness, the carefree sparkle in his dark eyes, his swagger. Handsome still, he had an air of sobriety about him. He looked me over, taking in my obvious changes and seeming saddened by them. I wanted to laugh and throw my arms around him to break his somber mood, but I didn't.

He layered my hand between his two. "Lanny, I didn't think we'd see you again!" Why did everyone keep saying this? "By the looks of things, Boston has been good to you."

"It has," I replied, offering nothing yet, wanting to pique his curiosity.

At this point, the young lady holding the infant edged through the crowd and hovered at Jonathan's elbow. He reached back and ushered her forward.

"Lanny, you remember Evangeline McDougal. We married shortly after you left. Though there's been enough time since your departure for us to have our first child, I daresay!" He laughed nervously. "A girl, can you believe my first child would be a girl? No luck, I say, but we'll get it right the next time, won't we?" he said to a red-cheeked Evangeline.

Logically, I knew that Jonathan would be married and that it was possible he'd have a child by now. Seeing his wife and daughter, however, was more difficult than I would have imagined. My lungs felt constricted. I went numb, unable to mumble congratulations. How could everything have moved so fast? I'd been gone only a few months.

"I know it seems so soon, fatherhood and all," Jonathan said, looking down at the hat in his hands, "but old Charles was determined to see me established before he passed away."

My throat tightened. "Your father is dead?"

"Oh yes—I forgot, you haven't heard. Right before my wedding. It would be two years ago, I think." He was dry-eyed and calm. "He'd become ill right after you left."

More than two years since I'd left? How could that be? It was unreal, like something from a fairy tale. Had I fallen under a spell and slept while the rest of the world went about its business? I couldn't speak. Jonathan squeezed my hand, breaking my trance. "We shouldn't keep you from seeing your family. Do plan to come to the house for dinner, soon. I would like to hear what adventures prevented you from returning to us until now."

"Yes, of course." My mind was elsewhere: if all this change had been visited on Jonathan's family, what of my own? What misfortune might have befallen them? And, judging from what Jonathan had said, two years had elapsed since I'd left town, though this made no sense. Did time move more quickly here, or had it passed more slowly in Boston, in the swirl of nightly parties and the languor of Adair's rooms?

I asked the driver to stop the coach up the road from my parents' house. The cabin had changed, there could be no denying it. Modest to begin with, it had grown shabby while I was away. My father had built it himself, like the other first settlers (the only exception being the captain, who'd brought carpenters up from Camden to make his fine house). My father had made a single-room log house designed to be built onto later. And build on he did: an alcove behind the main room to provide sleeping space for Nevin, a loft for us girls, where for many years we'd slept three abreast, like dolls on a shelf.

The house sagged like a good horse that has aged. Chinks of wadding had fallen out from between the logs. The roof was missing a few shakes. Debris had piled up on the narrow porch and the bricks in the chimney had loosened. I saw dots of reddish hide between the trees beyond the house, which meant cattle still grazed in the pastures. My family had retained at least part of the herd, but judging from the condition of the house, something drastic had happened to their fortunes.

I studied the house. The family was home from church—the wagon stood empty by the barn and I could see the ancient chestnut gelding grazing in the pen—but there was no activity around the house, just a ragged plume of smoke rising from the chimney. A mean fire on a cold day. I stole a glance at the woodpile. Neglected. The firewood barely stood three rows high with winter coming on.

Finally, I asked the driver to pull up in front of the house. I waited for a sign of movement within, but getting none, I drew up my courage, climbed out of the carriage, and approached the door.

Maeve answered my knock. Her mouth agape, she took me in from head to foot before shrieking and throwing her arms around my neck. We managed to waltz over the threshold and into the house, her happy voice filling my ears.

"Dear lord, you're alive! Darling Lanore, we thought we'd never see you again!" Maeve wiped tears from her cheeks with the edge of her apron. "When we didn't hear from you . . . the nuns wrote to Mama and Papa and told them you were most likely lost." Maeve blinked.

"Lost?" I asked.

"Dead. Murdered." Maeve gave me a clear-eyed look. "They said it happens all the time in Boston. Newcomers arrive in the city to be spirited off by brigands to their deaths." Her eyes gazed up at me, rapt. "If you were not lost, sister, then what did happen? Where have you been? It's been nearly three years."

Nearly three years! Again, the lost time rattled me. Outside of my time in Adair's company, the rest of the world had been like a train keeping to its own timetable, not about to slow down for me.

I was saved from making an explanation at that moment when my mother shuffled up from the open trap door to the root cellar, her apron gathered to cradle a few potatoes. She dropped everything at the sight of me, turning white as sheeting.

"It can't be!"

My heart squeezed to a standstill. "It is, Mother. It's your daughter."

"Back from the dead!"

"I am no ghost," I said through clenched jaw, trying to hold back tears, and as I hugged her, I felt the reluctance in her wiry old muscles melt away. She hugged me back with all the strength left in her, which was considerably less than I remembered.

As we spoke, she, too, wiped tears from her eyes. She looked over her shoulder at my sister, and nodded. "Fetch Nevin."

My stomach clenched. "Must you, so soon?"

My mother nodded again. "Aye, we must. He's the man of the house now. I'm sorry to have to tell you that your father is gone, Lanore."

You can't predict how you will react to news of that sort. As angry as I'd been with my father and as much as I had begun to suspect that something dire had happened, my mother's news knocked the wind from me. I fell onto a chair. My mother and sister stood around me, hands clasped.

"It happened a year ago," my mother said, soberly. "One of the bulls. A kick to the head. It was very sudden. He didn't suffer."

But they had, every day since: it was apparent in their hardened faces, the shabbiness of their clothes, and the house's disrepair. My mother caught my eye roving discreetly.

"It's been terribly hard on Nevin. He's taken it on himself to run the farm, and you know it's too big a job for one man." My mother's once gentle mouth had developed a hard set, her way of dealing with the merciless circumstances.

"Why don't you hire some help, a boy from one of the other farms. Or rent out the property. Surely someone in town is looking to expand," I said.

"Your brother won't hear of such a thing, so do not be so reckless as to mention it to him. You know how proud he is," she said, turning her head so I wouldn't see the bitterness in her expression. His pride had become their misfortune.

I needed to change the subject. "Where's Glynnis?"

Maeve flushed. "She's working at Watford's now. She's stocking shelves today."

"On the Sabbath?" I raised an eyebrow.

"Working off our debt, truth be told," my mother said, her confession ending in an irritated sigh as she fussed with the potatoes.

Adair's money weighed in my purse. There was no question that

I wouldn't give that money to them, and deal with the consequences later.

The door swung open and Nevin stepped into the dim cabin, a hulking dark figure silhouetted against the overcast sky. It took a few minutes for my eyes to adjust and for me to see Nevin himself. He'd lost weight and gotten hard and sinewy. He'd cut his hair so close to the skull it might as well have been shaved, and his face was filthy and nicked with scars, as were his hands. He had the same scorn for me in his eyes that he'd had the day I left, fueled by his own self-pity at what had befallen them since.

He made a sound in the back of his throat at the sight of me and ducked past to the wash bucket, plunging his hands in.

I stood up. "Hello, Nevin."

He dried his hands on a bit of rag before taking off his battered coat. He smelled of cattle, dirt, and fatigue.

"I'd like to speak to Lanore in private," he said. My mother and sister exchanged looks, then began to head for the door.

"No, wait," I called after them. "Let Nevin and I go outdoors. You stay where it's warm."

My mother shook her head. "No, we have chores that need doing before supper. You have your talk." She shepherded my sister in front of her.

In truth, I was afraid to be left alone with Nevin. His dislike of me was like a sheer rock face; he gave me not an inch in which to begin. I'd be better off walking away, his defiance seemed to say, than to try to find a way into his heart or head.

"So you're back," he said, cocking an eyebrow. "But not to stay."

"No." There was no point in lying to him. "My home is in Boston now."

He gave me a superior look. "I can guess from your fancy clothes what you've been doing. Do you think your mother or me want to know what shameful thing you've done with yourself? Why'd you come back?" The question I'd been dreading.

"To see everyone again," I said, my tone pleading. "To let you know I wasn't dead."

"Such news could have been put in a letter. It's been a long time with no word from you."

"I can only apologize for that."

"Were you in prison? Is that why you could not write?" he asked, mocking.

"I didn't write because I wasn't sure if it would be welcome." What could I have said? I had been certain it was best that they never heard from me again and that was as Alejandro had advised. It's a conceit, or a failing, of the young to think you can excise your past and it will never come looking for you.

He snorted at my excuse. "Did you ever think what effect your silence might have on Mother and Father? It very nearly killed Mother. It was the reason Father died."

"Mother said he was killed by a bull—"

"That was how he died, for certain. His skull split open by a bull, his blood pouring into the mud with no way for us to stop it. But did you ever know Father to let his guard down around the livestock? No. It happened because he was sick at heart. After he got the letter from the nuns, he was not the same. Blamed himself for sending you away—and to think he'd be with us still if you'd let him know you were alive!" He smashed his knuckles into the table.

"I told you I was sorry. There were circumstances that prevented me—"

"I don't want to hear your excuses. You say you weren't in prison. You come back looking like the richest whore in Boston. I've some idea how difficult the years have been for you. I'll hear no more." He swung away from me, nursing his bloodied knuckles. "I forgot to ask—where's the babe? Did you leave it behind with your procurer?"

My cheeks were hot as embers. "You'll be happy to know that the child perished before it was born. A miscarriage."

"Ah. God's will, as they say. Punishment for your wickedness, accommodating that devil St. Andrew." Nevin glowered, pleased with my news, happy to make his judgments. "I never could understand how a smart girl like you could be blind to that bastard. Why didn't you listen to me? I'm a man, same as he, I know how a man thinks . . ." He trailed off, exasperated. I wanted to wipe the smug grimace off Nevin's face, but I couldn't. He might have been right. Maybe he *could* see into Jonathan's mind and understand better than I, and all those years had tried to protect me from temptation. My failure had been his failure.

He wiped his knuckles again. "So, how long are you planning to stay?"

"I don't know. A few weeks."

"Does Mother know you've not returned for good? That you're going to leave us again?" Nevin asked, with pleasure in his voice that I would break our mother's heart again.

I shook my head.

"You can't stay too long," he warned, "or you'll be snowed in till spring."

How long would it take to convince Jonathan to come to Boston with me? Could I stand a winter sequestered in St. Andrew? It made me claustrophobic, the very thought of the long, dark winter days snowbound in the cabin with my brother.

Nevin dipped his bloody fist into the water bucket, tending his self-inflicted wound while he spoke to me. "You can stay with us while you are visiting. I'd rather toss you out on your ear, but I'll not be a source of gossip to the neighbors. But you must behave the entire time, or it's out you go."

"Of course."

"And you'll not bring that bastard St. Andrew around here. I'd say you're not to see him while you're staying under my roof, but I know you'd go to him anyway and lie to me about it."

He was right, of course. For now, though, I had to pretend to be contrite. "Whatever you say, brother. Thank you."

THIRTY-FOUR

That first evening home was difficult. On one hand, I can't recall a more joyful dinner. When Glynnis arrived home from her day at Watford's, we had the opportunity for one more reunion, which sparked our hearts anew (except for Nevin, who would never be forgiving). While the biscuits baked, I brought their presents from my trunk, handing out gifts as though I were Father Christmas. Maeve and Glynnis waltzed around with the Chinese silk held up to their bodices, planning the fancy dresses they would make with it, and my mother nearly wept tears of joy over the shawl. Their delight only made Nevin angrier; thank goodness I'd not brought anything for him (knowing he'd only throw it in the fire) or he probably would have boxed my ears and tossed me out on my ass.

We sat around the table after the plates were scraped clean and the candles drew low, my mother and sisters filling me in on everything that had happened in the village while I was gone: failed crops, illnesses, one or two new arrivals. And, of course, deaths, births, and marriages. They lingered over Jonathan's wedding, expecting I'd want to know all about it, what fancy food was served (not knowing the exotic delicacies I'd consumed), what business associates of the St. Andrews made the arduous trip to attend.

"So sad, the captain didn't live to see it," my mother said.

And the baby! The way my mother and sisters spoke of it, you'd think the baby was a joint product of the town. Everyone, except for Nevin, seemed to have a parochial interest in the infant.

"What did Jonathan name her?" I asked, dipping a last crust into a smear of beef fat.

"Ruth, just like his mother," Glynnis said, eyebrows raised.

"It's a good Christian name," my mother chided. "I'm sure they wanted a name from the Bible."

I waggled a finger around the table. "Not Jonathan, nor Evangeline, I'll wager—it was all his mother's doing. You can quote me."

"Maybe the idea of having a child as soon as possible, maybe that was Mrs. St. Andrew's idea, too." Maeve held her breath momentarily, looking at her sister for encouragement, before she continued. "It was a terribly difficult birth, Lanore. They almost lost Evangeline. She's so wee—"

"And young—"

Nods all around. "So young," Maeve sighed. "I heard the midwife told her not to have any more babies for a while."

"It's true," Glynnis added.

"Enough!" Nevin hammered the end of his knife into the table, making the women jump. "Can't a man eat his evening meal in peace without having to listen to gossip about the town dandy?"

"Nevin—," my mother began, but he cut her off.

"I'll hear no more about this. It's his own fault for marrying the girl. It is scandalous, but I expected no better from him," Nevin grumbled. For a scant moment, I could almost believe that he'd scolded my sisters and mother in order to spare me further talk of babies. He pushed away from the table and headed for the chair by the fire, the place where our father used to sit after dinner. The sight of him in that chair, with Father's pipe, was strange to my eye.

Judging from the position of the moon in the sky, it was near midnight when I climbed down from the loft, unable to sleep. The remains of the fire decorated the walls with a dancing, lambent glow. Restless, I couldn't remain boxed up in the cottage. I needed company. Usually at this time of night, I would be preparing for a night in Adair's bed, and I found, sitting on the settle, that I was hungry—no, ravenous—for physical comfort. I dressed and slipped out as quietly as I could. My driver was sleeping in the barn, kept warm by a mountain of blankets and the heat of a dozen cattle packed with him under the roof. I wasn't about to saddle the family's chestnut gelding, rouse the poor old thing from its deserved rest, so I went off on foot in the only direction that came to mind: to town. For anyone else, even a trip this short on foot would be suicidal. The temperature was below freezing and the wind brisk, but I was impervious to the weather and could walk at a smart clip without fatiguing. I reached the houses on the edge of town in no time.

Where was there to go? St. Andrew was hardly the big city. Few lights were visible through cabin windows. The town was asleep but Daniel Daughtery's public house was still open, light shining through its single window. I hesitated by the door, wondering if it would be wise to be seen about at this hour. Few women went into Daughtery's, and none would go in by herself. Word could easily get back to Nevin and fuel his conviction that I was a common whore. The lure of those warm bodies inside, the low rumble of talk, the occasional bright spark of laughter was strong, however. I knocked the mud from my shoes and went in.

There were only a couple of customers in the small space: a pair of axmen in Jonathan's employ and Tobey Ostergaard, poor Sophia's brutish father, looking like a corpse himself, his skin gone gray and his dead eyes staring at the back wall. Every head turned in my direction as I entered, Daughtery giving me an especially ugly leer.

"A draft," I called out, though it was unnecessary, as there was only one beverage on the bill of fare.

The public room had once been part of Daughtery's home, partitioned off (over the objection of his wife) to accommodate a bar keep, one small table, and assorted stools slapped together from odd pieces of wood, one leg shorter than the other two on each and every one of them. In the warmer months, there were games of chance and sometimes cockfighting in the barn, which was separated by a muddy path from the main house. Most patrons didn't stay but picked up a hogshead of brew to consume at home with meals, as brewing beer was a messy business and Daughtery, it was generally agreed, was the best of anyone in town.

"I heard you was back," Daughtery said as he collected my coin. "From the look of it, Boston has treated you well." He made a naked appraisal of my clothing. "What did a country lass such as yourself do to buy such fine apparel as that?"

Like my brother, Daughtery must have guessed—they must *all* have guessed—what had happened to make a wealthy woman of me. Daughtery was the first to accuse me outright, showing off for his customers. Still, what could I do under the circumstances? I gave him an unreadable smile over the rim of the mug. "I have done what countless others have done to better their lot in life: I have associated myself with people of means, Mr. Daughtery."

One of the axmen left shortly after my arrival but the other came over to ask me to share his table. He'd overheard Daughtery's mention of Boston and was anxious to speak to someone who'd been there recently. He was young, perhaps twenty, sweet-tempered and clean looking, unlike most of the St. Andrew hired hands. He told me he came from a humble family who lived outside of Boston proper. He'd come to Maine for work. He made good pay but the isolation was killing him; he missed the city, he said, and the options for entertainment. His eyes teared as I described the public garden on a sunny Sabbath and the shiny black surface of the Charles River under a full moon.

"I'd hoped to leave here before the snows," he said, gazing into his mug. "But I heard St. Andrew needs hands to stay on through the winter and will pay well. Them that have stayed for the winter shift say it's terrible lonely, though."

"I suppose it's a matter of perspective."

Daughtery banged a mug against the maple counter of the keep, startling us both. "Finish up. Time to go to your respective beds."

We stood outside Daughtery's bolted door, huddled together to cut down the wind. The stranger brought his mouth close to my ear so the heat of his words made the tiny hairs on my cheek stand at attention, like flowers stretching toward the sun. He confided in me that he'd not had the companionship of a woman in a long time. He confessed to having little money, but asked if I might be willing nonetheless. "I hope I'm not being presumptuous about your profession," he said with a nervous smile. "But when you came into Daughtery's by yourself . . ." I couldn't protest: he had me dead to rights.

We stole into Daughtery's barn, the animals so used to nighttime visitors from the bar that they made no fuss. The young axman adjusted his clothing, unbuttoning the fall of his breeches and placing his cock in my hand. He melted at my ministrations, soon lost in his own thick cloud of unbearable pleasure. It must have been the return to St. Andrew and seeing Jonathan again that made my blood rich with passion. The axman's hand might have been on my flesh but it was Jonathan who was on my mind. I was reckless, letting myself think of Jonathan, but that night, the combination of flesh and memory gave me a taste of what it could be like and made me hungry for more. So I pulled the young man to me and settled one foot on a bale of hay, the better to give him access under my petticoats.

The young man rocked into me, sweet firm flesh and gentle hands, and I tried to pretend he was Jonathan, but I could not make the illusion stick. Maybe Adair was right, maybe there was something to be gained in making Jonathan one of us. A terrible hunger told me I had to try or be dissatisfied for the rest of my life—that is to say, eternity.

The axman stuttered a sigh as he came, then drew out a handker-chief and offered it to me. "Pardon my bluntness, miss," he whispered hotly in my ear, "but that was the most amazing fuck I have ever had. You must be the most talented whore in Boston!"

"Courtesan," I corrected him gently.

"And I don't pretend to be able to compensate you in the manner to which you are undoubtedly accustomed . . . ," he said, rooting in a pocket for his money, but I placed a hand on his arm to stop him.

"Never mind. Keep your money. Just promise me you'll not say a word of this to anyone," I said.

"Oh no, ma'am, I won't—though I will remember it for the rest of my life!"

"As shall I," I said, though this sweet-faced boy would be only one of a succession of many—or perhaps the last one, to be re-placed by Jonathan and only Jonathan, if I were lucky. I watched the young axman stumble out into the night, heading toward the road that led to the St. Andrews' property, before I wrapped my coat tightly and started off in the opposite direction. His warmth trickled down the insides of my thighs and I felt a familiar stir-ring in my chest as well, the satisfaction I felt whenever I'd held a man helpless in sexual thrall. I looked forward to experiencing that pleasure with Jonathan and to surprising him with my newly acquired skills.

My route took me by the blacksmith's shop, and by force of habit, I glanced down the path in the direction of Magda's cottage. A brightness was visible behind the shawl she tacked over the one window, so I knew she was awake. Funny how I'd once envied her her cottage—but I suppose I envied it still because I felt a little fil-lip in my heart upon seeing it, remembering the homey treasures that had so impressed me as a girl. Adair's mansion may have been ornate and filled with luxurious things, but once you crossed the threshold, your freedom was gone. Magda was the mistress of her own home and no one could take that away from her.

As I stood at the top of the path, the front door swung open and out popped one of the axmen (thank goodness, for I would have been mortified to see one of my neighbors finish up his business with Magda). The old girl herself came out behind him and for a moment they were caught in the light falling out the open door. The two were laughing, Magda wrapping a cloak around her shoulders as she ushered her customer down the stairs with a wave good-bye. I jumped back into the shadow to spare the axman the embarrassment of being observed, but not before Magda noticed.

"Who's there?" she called out. "Let's have no trouble, now."

I stepped out of the darkness. "None from me, Mistress Magda."

"Lanore? Is that you?" She craned her neck. I trotted past the trundling axman and up the stairs for an embrace from Magda. Her arms felt more fragile than ever.

"Goodness, girl, they told me you were lost to us," she said as she whisked me inside. The room was close because of the heat thrown from the tiny fireplace and the two bodies that had recently been at work (the musk still hung in the air; those axmen weren't too fastidious about bathing and could grow quite rank), so I slipped off my cloak. Magda spun me around by my shoulders to get a better look at my fancy dress.

"Well, Miss McIlvrae, by the sight of you, I'd say you have done well for yourself."

"I can't say it's work I'm proud of," I said.

Magda looked reproachfully at me. "Am I to imagine that you came by your good fortune in the usual way for a young lady . . . ?" When I didn't answer, she shook out her cloak with a snap. "Well, you know where I stand on this subject. It's hardly a crime to take up the only avenue open to you and make a success of it. If God didn't want us to make a living being whores, he'd give us another means to support ourselves. But he doesn't."

"I'm not a whore, exactly." Why did I feel compelled to clarify my situation for her? "There is a man who provides for me . . ."

"Are you married to each other?"

I shook my head.

"Then you are his mistress." She poured gin into two tiny glasses, cloudy with age, and I told her about my life in Boston and Adair. It was a relief to tell someone about him—an adulterated version, of course, omitting the parts of him I would change if I could: his violent fits of temper, the mercurial rise and fall of his moods, the occasional male companion in his bed. I told her he was handsome, wealthy, and taken with me, and she nodded at my good news. "Good for you, Lanore. Make sure you put by some of the money he spends on you."

In the candlelight, I could see Magda's face more clearly. The years of my absence had left their passing on her. Her delicate skin sagged around her mouth and throat, and her black hair was almost half white. Her once pretty stays were now grayed and tattered. Whether she was the only prostitute in town or not, she wouldn't be able to continue in her trade for much longer. The younger axmen would stop frequenting her and the older ones who would still pay for her services were apt to be unkind in their treatment of her. Soon she would be a friendless old woman in a town where life was harsh.

I wore a discreet pearl brooch, a present from Adair. My family knew nothing about jewelry and so I'd worn it openly in their presence, but Magda had to know that it was worth a small fortune. At first I thought that I should give it to my family, they had more right to it than a woman who was only my friend, but I'd resolved to leave them money, and not an insubstantial amount. So I unpinned the brooch from my clothing and held it out to her.

Magda cocked her head. "Oh no, Lanore, you needn't do that. I don't need your charity."

"I want you to have it—"

She waved off my outstretched hand. "I know what you're thinking. And I am planning to retire soon. I've saved quite a bit of money during my time here—Charles St. Andrew should have sent the wages of some of his men straight to me, for all the time they spent in this cottage, and spared them the job of carrying their pay in their pockets for a day or two," she laughed. "No, I'd rather see you save it for yourself. You may not believe me now, since you are young and beautiful and have a man who values your company, but someday all those things will be gone and you may wish for the money that brooch would bring."

Of course I couldn't tell her that that day would never come for me. I forced a little smile as I pinned the brooch back in place.

"No, I am planning to move south in the spring. Somewhere near the coast," she continued. She looked about the room wistfully, as though she planned to leave tomorrow. "Perhaps I will find a nice lonely widower and settle down again."

"I've no doubt fortune will shine on you, Magda, in whatever you choose to do, because you have a generous heart," I said and got to my feet. "I should let you retire for the evening, and I should get back to my family. It was good to see you, Magda."

We embraced again and she rubbed her hand warmly on my back. "Take care of yourself, Lanore. Be careful. And whatever you do, don't fall in love with your gentleman. We women make our worst decisions when we are in love." She escorted me to the door and sent me off with a wave. The truth of her advice weighed on my heart, though, and I headed for the woods less buoyant than before.

The trip home found me even more restless and as I thought on it, I saw that it was because I'd lied to Magda about Adair. It wasn't just that I'd hidden his secret—*our* secret—from her. That was understandable. However, if anyone in St. Andrew would forgive Adair his peculiarities, it would be Magda, and yet I chose to lie to her about him and about my relationship with him. A woman wants above all things to be proud of the man in her life, and obviously I was not. How could I be proud of what Adair had drawn out in me—that he had *known* just by looking at me—that I shared some of his dark appetites. As frightened as I was of him, there was no denying that I'd responded to him, too, that I'd accepted every sexual challenge he proposed. He brought out something in me I could not deny but was not proud of. So perhaps it was not Adair I was ashamed of: perhaps I was ashamed of myself.

These dreadful thoughts filled my mind as I pulled my cloak tight against the wind and hurried down the path to my family's cabin. I couldn't stop from remembering all the terrible things I'd done or thinking how I'd found such delight in dark pleasures—it is no wonder that I questioned whether I hadn't slipped beyond redemption.

THIRTY-FIVE

When I woke the next day, I heard my mother and Maeve whispering to each other in the kitchen so as not to wake me. To them, I must have seemed a lazy layabout, wasting the most productive time of the day, sleeping until noon—though this was still the earliest I'd risen in a long time.

"Aye, look who is up now," my mother called from the fireplace when she heard me groan from above.

"I imagine Nevin had a few words to say about my sleeping habits," I replied as I climbed down the ladder.

"It was all we could do to keep him from dragging you out by your feet," Maeve said, handing me my clothing, which had been laid over a chair by the fire to take off the chill.

"Yes, well, I was restless last night and took a stroll into town," I admitted.

"Lanore!" My mother nearly dropped her knife. "Have you lost your mind? You could have frozen to death! Not to mention that something worse might have happened to you," she said, exchanging a look with my sister—both of them knowing I had little virtue left to protect—which took the sting out of her voice.

"I'd forgotten how cold it is at night this far north," I lied.

"And where did you go?"

"Not to church, I'd wager," Maeve said with a laugh.

"No, not to church. I went to Daughtery's."

"Lanore—"

"A little companionship at a lonely hour, that's all that was wanted. I'm not used to such quiet and early hours. My life is quite different in Boston. You'll have to bear with me." I drew the tape ties of my skirt about my waist before making my way to my mother, and kissed her on the forehead.

"You are not in Boston now, dear," my mother chided.

"Do not let it worry you much," Maeve said. "It's not as though Nevin isn't seen at Daughtery's from time to time. If menfolk get to do it, I don't see why you cannot, at least on occasion"—here she cast a glance at our mother, to see if she would react—"and we shall just get used to it."

So Nevin went to Daughtery's—I would have to be careful. If he found out about my nocturnal dalliances, things would go badly for me.

At that moment, we were interrupted by a knock at the door. One of the St. Andrews' servants extended an ivory-colored envelope with my name written on it. Inside was a note in Jonathan's mother's meticulous handwriting, inviting my family to dinner that evening. The servant waited at the door for our reply.

"What shall I tell him?" I asked, though it was easy enough to guess their response. Maeve and my mother danced about like Cinderella upon learning she was going to the ball.

"What about Nevin? Surely he'll refuse to go," I asked.

"Undoubtedly. On general principle," Maeve said.

"I do wish your brother had a better head for business," my mother muttered. "He could use this opportunity to talk to Jonathan about purchasing more regularly from us. Half the town makes its livelihood off that family. Who else will buy our beef? Them, with all those men to feed . . ." She probably thought the St. Andrews miserly for feeding their hired hands venison caught on the property.

I went back to the door, addressing the servant. "Please tell Mrs. St. Andrew that we would be happy to accept the invitation, and that there will be four for dinner."

Dinner that evening was surreal to me, to be surrounded by both our families. It had never happened in the whole time Jonathan and I had been friends as children, and I would have been happy that evening for dinner to have been limited to just the two of us at a table before the fire in his study. That would not have been proper, though, now that Jonathan had a wife and child.

His sisters had already slipped into early spinsterhood and had developed owlish airs, observing my more lively sisters as though they were monkeys set loose in the house. Poor slow-witted Benjamin sat by his mother, eyes fixed on his plate, lips pursed, willing himself to remain still. Occasionally, his mother took Benjamin's hand and petted it, which seemed to have a calming effect on the poor boy.

And, to Jonathan's left was Evangeline, looking like a child who'd been allowed to sit at the adults' table. Her pink fingers touched each piece of her place setting as though not familiar with the uses of all the pieces of the fine silverware service. And every so often, her gaze would flit to her husband's face, like a dog reassuring itself of its master's presence.

Seeing Jonathan surrounded this way, by the family who would always depend on him, made me feel sorry for him.

After the meal—a rack of venison and a dozen roasted quails, resulting in plates ghoulishly heaped with deer ribs and tiny birds' bones, picked clean—Jonathan looked around the table, nearly all women, and invited me to withdraw to his father's old study, which he'd now claimed for himself. When his mother opened her mouth to object, he said, "There's no man here to join me for a pipe, and I would like to speak to Lanny alone if I may. Besides, I'm sure she would be quite bored otherwise." Ruth's eyebrows shot up, though his sisters did not seem to take offense. Perhaps he was trying to spare them the awkwardness of my company—I'm sure they presumed I was a whore, too, and Jonathan had probably wangled my invitation over their protests.

Once he closed the doors, he poured us whiskeys and packed two pipes with tobacco, and we settled in chairs drawn close to the fire. First, he wanted to know how I'd come to disappear in Boston. I told him a more detailed version of the story I'd given my family, that I was in the employ of a wealthy European, hired to act as his American interlocutor. Jonathan listened skeptically, I'd say, debating whether to question my account or simply enjoy the story.

"You should consider moving to Boston. Life is so much easier," I said, holding a flame to the pipe. "You're a wealthy man. If you lived in a big city, you could avail yourself of the pleasures in life."

He shook his head. "We can't move. There's the timber to harvest, it's our lifeblood. Who would run the logging operations?"

"Mr. Sweet, as he does now. Or another foreman. That's how wealthy men handle their properties. No reason for you and your family to suffer through the deprivation of the terrible winters here."

Jonathan stared into the fire, drawing on his pipe. "You might think my mother would be eager to return to her own family, but we'll never get her out of St. Andrew. She'd not admit it, but she's gotten used to her social position. In Boston, she'd be just another well-off widow. She might even suffer socially for having spent so long in 'the wilderness.' Besides, Lanny, have you thought what would happen to the town if we left?"

"Your business would still be here. You'd still need to pay the townspeople to do whatever it is you pay them for now. The only difference is that you and your family would have the type of life you deserve. There would be physicians to see to Benjamin. You could enjoy Sunday socials with the neighbors, go to parties and card games every night as one of the city's social elite."

Jonathan gave me an incredulous look, dubious enough for me to think that what he'd said about his mother might be an excuse. Perhaps *he* was the one afraid to give up St. Andrew, to leave the only place he'd ever known, and become a small fish in a large, well-stocked pond.

I leaned toward him. "Shouldn't that be your reward, Jonathan? You've worked with your father to build this fortune. You have no idea what is waiting for you outside these woods, these woods as thick as prison walls."

He seemed hurt. "It's not as though I've never left St. Andrew. I've been to Fredericton."

The St. Andrews had business associates in Fredericton as part of the timber trade. Logs were floated down the Allagash to the St. John River and were processed in Fredericton, sawed into boards or burned into charcoal. Charles had taken Jonathan on a trip when Jonathan was still in his teens, but I'd heard little of it. Now that I thought about it, Jonathan seemed to have no curiosity about the world outside our tiny town.

"Fredericton is hardly Boston," I chided. "And besides, if you come to Boston, you would have the opportunity to meet my employer. He is European royalty, practically a prince. But more to the point, he is a true connoisseur of pleasure. A man after your own heart." I tried to smile cunningly. "I guarantee he will change your life forever."

He eyed me. " 'A connoisseur of pleasure'? And how do you know about this, Lanny? I thought you were his interlocutor."

"One can act as an intermediary on another's behalf for many things."

"I admit, you've made me curious," he said, and yet his tone was that of complacence. Part of me mourned Jonathan having been brought to heel by his new responsibilities and not being in the least curious about the temptations I offered him. I was sure, however, that the old Jonathan was in there; I had only to roust him.

Jonathan and I spent most evenings together after that. I quickly saw that he had not cultivated any other friends. I wasn't sure why, since

there couldn't have been any shortage of men willing to enjoy the social status and possible financial benefits that would come with being
Jonathan's closest ally. Still, Jonathan wasn't stupid. These were the
same men who, as boys, had resented his good looks, his position, and
his wealth. Resented that their fathers were beholden to the captain
for wages or rent.

"I shall miss you when you leave," Jonathan said to me on one of
those evenings spent locked behind the study doors, burning good
tobacco. "Would you consider remaining? You don't have to return to
Boston, not if the issue is money. I could give you a job, and then you
would be here to help your family now that your father is gone."

I wondered if Jonathan had given any thought to his offer or if it
had come to him spontaneously. Even if he found some kind of position for me, his mother would object to having a fallen woman working
for her son. He was right about this being an opportunity to do right
by my family, though, and inwardly I squirmed. But I was also riddled
with a nameless fear at the prospect of not obeying Adair's orders.

"I couldn't give up the city now that I know it. You'd feel the same."

"I've already explained to you—"

"You needn't make a decision on the spur of the moment. After
all, to move your entire household to Boston is no small thing. Come
back with me for a visit. Tell your family that you're making a business trip. See if the city suits your taste." I had deftly cleaned the pipe
stem with a wire—a skill picked up from maintaining Adair's water
pipe—and tapped the bowl against a little salver to clear the ash. "It
could be advantageous to you from a business position, as well. Adair
will show you around, introduce you to the men who own the timber
mills and such. He'll take you out in society, too. There's no culture
here in St. Andrew! You have no idea of the things you're missing,
plays, concerts. What I think you'll really find fascinating"—I leaned
forward, our heads bowed close for the utmost secrecy—"is that Adair
is much like you when it comes to a gentleman's pleasure."

"You say." His expression begged me to go on.

"Women throw themselves at him. All types of women. Society women, common women, and, when he tires of such company, there are always the does."

"Does?"

"Prostitutes. Boston teems with prostitutes of all kinds. Fancy brothels. Streetwalkers. Actresses and singers who would gladly be your mistress for the price of handsome rooms and spending money."

"Are you saying I have to go to an actress or a singer to find a woman who would abide my company?" he asked, then glanced aside. "Do all men in Boston pay for a woman's company?"

"If he wants her affections exclusively. These women tend to be better versed in the arts of love than most," I said, hoping to whet his curiosity. It was time to share one of Adair's gifts. "A present from my employer," I said as I handed him a small bundle wrapped in red silk: the deck of ribald cards. "From one gentleman to another."

"Entertaining," he said, as he looked intently at each card in turn. "I'd seen a deck like this when I went to Fredericton, though not as—imaginative." When he went to pick up the red silk to rewrap the cards, a second gift tumbled out, one I'd forgotten I'd brought.

Jonathan drew his breath in sharply. "Good God, Lanny, who is this?" He held a miniature painting of Uzra in his hands, a shimmer of enchantment in his eyes. "Is she a phantasm, the creation of some artist's mind?"

I didn't care for the tone of his voice—no gentleman would speak that way in front of a woman for whom he claimed to care—but what could I do? The portrait was meant to tempt him, and clearly it had done the trick.

"Oh no, I assure you, she exists in flesh and blood. She is my employer's concubine, an odalisque he brought with him from the silk trade route."

"Your employer has a curious domestic arrangement, it would seem. A concubine, kept openly in Boston? I wouldn't think they'd stand for it." Jonathan looked from the painting to me, brows knitted.

"I don't understand . . . why would your employer send gifts to *me*? What is his interest? What in the world did you tell him about me?"

"He is looking for a fit companion and senses you might be a kindred spirit." He was suspicious, perhaps fearing that any interest from a man he didn't know had to be tied to his fortune. "To tell you the truth, I think he is disappointed by the Boston crowd. They are quite a dour lot. He's been unable to find a Bostonian with a spirit similar to his own, a willingness to indulge in whatever fancy intrigues him . . ."

But Jonathan didn't seem to be paying attention to what I'd said. He studied me so closely that I feared I'd inadvertently said something offensive. "Whatever is it?" I asked.

"It's just that you are . . . so much *changed*," he said at last.

"I won't argue with that. I have changed *completely*. The question is, are you disappointed in the change?"

He blinked, a shadow of pain in those dark eyes. "I must say—yes, perhaps a little. I'm not sure how to say this without hurting your feelings, but you are not the girl you were when you left. You are so worldly—you are this man's mistress, aren't you?" he asked hesitantly.

"Not exactly." A term came to me from years earlier. "I am his spiritual wife."

"His 'spiritual wife'?"

"We all are. The odalisque, myself, Tilde . . ." I thought it best to leave out Alejandro and Dona, having no notion how Jonathan would respond to that arrangement.

"He has three wives under one roof?"

"Not to mention the other women he entertains . . ."

"And you do not mind?"

"He may share his affection however he wishes, as may we. What we have is unlike anything you've heard of, but . . . yes, this arrangement suits me fine."

"Goodness, Lanny, I can scarce believe you are the girl I kissed in the church cloakroom those many years ago." He cast a shy look in my direction, as though not quite sure how to behave. "I suppose, given all this talk of freely sharing your affections, it would not be unseemly if I were to ask you for—another kiss? Just to assure myself that you truly are the Lanny I once knew, here with me again?"

It was the opening I'd hoped for. He rose from his chair and leaned over me, grasping my face in his hands, but his kiss was hesitant.

That hesitancy nearly broke my heart. "You must know I thought I'd never see you again, Jonathan, let alone feel your lips on mine. I thought I would die from missing you." As my eyes searched his face, I realized that the hope of seeing Jonathan again was the only thing that had kept me sane. Now we were together and I would not be cheated. I rose and pressed into him and, after a second's hesitation, he drew me into his arms. I was grateful that he still desired me, but everything about him had changed since the last time we'd been together, even the scent of his hair and his skin. The reserve in his hands as he grasped my waist. The taste of him when we kissed. All changed. He was slower, softer, sadder. His lovemaking, though sweet, had lost its ferocity. Maybe it was because we were in his family's house, his wife and his mother just beyond the locked door. Or he might have been consumed with regret for betraying poor Evangeline.

We lay on the settle together after Jonathan had finished, his head lying between my breasts cupped in fine silk stays, beribboned and trimmed with lace. He was still between my legs, lying on a crush of skirts and petticoats hiked to my waist. I stroked his hair while my heart thrummed with bliss. And, yes, I felt the secret thrall of having made him give in to his desire. And as for the wife waiting dutifully on the other side of the door—well, hadn't she stolen Jonathan from me to begin with? And a deed of marriage meant little when he still wanted me, when his heart belonged to me. My body quivered with the proof of his desire. Despite all that had happened to each of us in the years we'd been apart, I was convinced more than ever that the bond between us was unbroken.

THIRTY-SIX

L uke stops at a diner close to the exit from the highway, needing a break from the endless gray ribbon of road. Once they've slid into a booth, he borrows Lanny's laptop to catch up on news and check his email. Besides the usual queue of emails from the hospital administrators ("Employees are reminded not to park in the east parking lot, as this space will be used for snow removal . . ."), no one has written to him. No one seems to have noticed his absence. Luke makes the cursor scurry aimlessly around the desktop in his distraction, but there is nothing to double check. He is about to power down the computer when he hears a chime. Somebody has sent him an email.

He expects it to be spam, another cheerful but impersonal invitation from his bank to open a CD or something similarly worthless, but it's from Peter. Luke feels a pang of discomfort for having taken advantage of his colleague's good nature. Peter is more of an acquaintance than a friend, but since there are few anesthesiologists in the county and Luke is an emergency room physician, they saw more of each other than most of the other doctors. Luke's latest series of misfortunes had made him less friendly than usual, but Peter was one of the few doctors still speaking to him.

"Where are you?" the email reads. "I didn't think you were planning to be gone with the car so long. I tried calling but you're not answering your cell phone. Everything okay? Haven't been in an accident? Not hurt? Worried about you. CALL ME." Then Peter listed all of his phone numbers and his wife's cell phone number.

Luke closes Peter's email, his jaw clenched. *He's afraid I'm cracking up*, Luke realizes. He's aware that his behavior is odd, to say the least, and the people in town hold their breath around him, afraid to mention either Tricia and the divorce or his parents' deaths. They don't think he can handle the abundance of unhappiness in his life. It's not until that moment that Luke realizes that leaving town with this woman has distracted him from his misery. He hasn't *not* been miserable in months. This is the first time he's been able to think of his daughters without wanting to weep.

Luke takes a deep breath and lets it out in a long stream. *Don't jump to conclusions*, he tells himself. Peter is being nice, patient. Hasn't threatened to call the police. Peter is the most well-adjusted person in Luke's life right now, but Luke realizes this is probably because Peter is new to St. Andrew. The young doctor hasn't been infected yet with the town's inherent strangeness, its cold standoffishness, its Puritan addiction to judgment.

For a moment, Luke is tempted to call Peter. Peter is a tether to the real world, the world that existed before he helped Lanny escape from the police, before he listened to her fantastical story, before he slept with a patient. Peter might be able to talk Luke down from this ledge. He takes another deep breath: the question is, does he *want* to be talked down?

He reopens Peter's email and hits Reply. "I'm sorry about your car," he types. "I'll leave it somewhere soon and the police will find it and get it back to you." He considers what he's written and realizes what he's really saying is that he's gone and he won't be coming back. He feels tremendous relief. Before he hits the Send button, he adds to the email, "Keep my truck. It's yours."

Luke stops in the restroom before getting into the SUV and sees that Lanny is already in the front seat, staring straight ahead with a humorless smile. "What's wrong?" Luke asks as he turns the key in the ignition.

"It's nothing . . ." She drops her gaze. "When I went to pay the bill, when you were in the restroom, I saw they had liquor for sale behind the counter, so I asked for a bottle of Glenfiddich. But she wouldn't sell it to me. Said I had to wait for *my father* to come out of the restroom if he wanted to buy a bottle."

Luke starts to reach for the door handle. "I'll go in if you want—"

"Don't. It's not about the scotch; it's just that . . . this happens all the time. I'm sick of it, that's all. Always being mistaken for a teenager, treated like a kid. I may look like a kid but I don't *think* like one and sometimes, I just don't want to be treated like one. I know looking young also helps me get by, but God . . ." She holds her head, shaking it, then throws her shoulders back. "Let's give her a show. Really blow her mind."

Before Luke can answer, Lanny grabs his jacket by the collar and pulls him to her. She locks her mouth over his and gives him a long kiss, grinding against him. The kiss goes on and on, until he gets dizzy. Over Lanny's shoulder, he can see the woman frozen behind the cashier's counter, her mouth formed into a horrified circle and her eyes widening.

Lanny releases him, laughing. She slaps the dashboard. "Come on, *Dad*, let's go find a hotel so I can fuck your brains out."

Luke doesn't laugh with her. Without thinking, he wipes his mouth. "Don't do that. I don't like being mistaken for your father. It makes me feel . . ." *Like I'm a terrible person, and I'm not*, he thinks but doesn't say.

She quiets right down, flushes with shame, and looks helplessly at her hands. "You're right. I'm sorry, I didn't mean to embarrass you," she says. "It won't happen again."

THIRTY-SEVEN

ST. ANDREW, 1819

That blissful reunion on the settle was not to be our last time together. We contrived to meet as best we could, although the circumstances were inconvenient, to say the least—a hay barn on the edge of the pasture, fragrant with dried alfalfa (but then we had to be diligent to brush every seed and stalk from our clothes), or the horse barn off the St. Andrews' house, where we'd lock ourselves in the tack room and quietly grind against each other amid dangling reins and harnesses.

During these times with Jonathan, even as I inhaled his breath and drops of his sweat fell on my face, I was surprised to find Adair creeping into my thoughts. Surprised that I felt guilty, as though I was wronging him, because we were lovers, in our way. There was an undercurrent of fear, too, of the punishment Adair would exact from me, not for swiving another man but for loving another man. Why should I feel guilt and fear if I was only doing what he wanted?

Maybe because in my heart I knew it was Jonathan I loved, only Jonathan. He would win out every time.

"Lanny," Jonathan whispered, kissing my hand as he lay recovering in the hay after an assignation. "You deserve better than this."

"I'd meet you in the woods, in a cave, in a field," I replied, "if that were the only way to see you. It doesn't matter where we are. All that matters is that we are together."

Pretty words, the words of lovers. But as we lay together in the hay and I stroked his cheek, my mind could not help but wander. And it wandered to dangerous places, poking into matters best left undisturbed, such as the circumstances surrounding my abrupt departure years earlier, and Jonathan's silence on the event. Since I'd returned to town he hadn't asked me once about the child. He *wanted* to question me; I sensed it whenever there was a moment of strained silence between us, when I would catch him looking at me sideways. *When you left St. Andrew* . . . but the words remained on his tongue. He must have assumed I'd aborted the babe, as I'd said I would that day in church. But I wanted him to know the truth.

"Jonathan," I said softly, catching and slipping tendrils of his black floss through my fingers, "did you ever wonder why my father sent me out of town?"

I felt him hold his breath, a hesitation in his stillness. After a bit, he replied, "I didn't know you'd gone until it was too late . . . It was wrong of me not to seek you out earlier, to see that you were not in trouble or if something more sinister had happened to you . . ." He began to fiddle absentmindedly with the lacing on my stays.

"What excuse did my family make for my being sent away?" I asked.

"They said you were being sent to care for a sick relative. They were very closed after you'd left and kept to themselves. I asked one of your sisters once if they'd heard from you and if they might give me an address so I could write to you, but she rushed away without responding." He lifted his head from my sternum. "Is that not the case? Were you not caring for someone?"

I could have laughed at his naiveté. "The only one who needed care was myself. They sent me away to have the child. They didn't want anyone here to know about it."

"Lanny!" He pressed a hand against my face, but I shook it off. "And did you—"

"There is no child. I miscarried." I could say those words without emotion now, without a quiver in my voice or a knot in my throat.

"I am so sorry for all you have been through, and by yourself . . ." He sat up, unable to take his eyes off me now. "Does this have anything to do with how you ended up with this man? This Adair?"

I'm sure my expression became very dark. "I don't wish to talk about it."

"What trials have you been through, poor brave Lanny? You should have written me, informed me of your situation. I'd have done anything for you, anything within my means . . ." He went to hold me—for which my body longed—then seemed to think better of it and pulled back. "Have I lost my mind? What—what are we doing? Haven't I wronged you enough? What right have I to start up with you again, as though it's a game of some sort?" Jonathan held his head in his hands. "You must forgive me for my selfishness, my stupidity . . ."

"You didn't force me," I said, trying to calm him. "I wanted this, too." If only I could take my words back; it had been a mistake to bring up the child, dead and gone. I cursed myself for giving in to my petty nature. I had wanted Jonathan to know I had suffered and to acknowledge his part in the ill that had befallen me, but it had backfired.

"We cannot continue like this. This is the last—complication—I need in my life." Jonathan rolled away from me and got to his feet. When he saw my shocked and hurt expression, he continued, "Forgive my frankness, dear Lanny. But you know full well I have a family, a wife, an infant daughter, obligations I cannot forsake. I cannot jeopardize their happiness for the sake of a few stolen moments of pleasure with you . . . And there is no future for us, there cannot be. It would be hurtful and unfair to you for us to continue."

He doesn't love me enough to stay with me—the truth cut my heart like a blade. I gulped for air. Anger flamed up inside me at his words. Could he be realizing this only now, after we had started up our illicit affair again? Or was I hurt because he was forsaking me a second time for Evangeline? I must admit the first thought that came to me, as I sat dumbfounded, was of revenge. I can see how scorned women swear themselves over to the devil; in such a moment, the need for revenge is strong but the ability to extract it insufficient. If Lucifer had appeared before me at that second, promising the means to make Jonathan suffer the everlasting torments of hell in exchange for my soul, I would have accepted it, gladly.

Or perhaps there was no need to summon the devil, to draw up the fiery contract, to sign my name in blood. Perhaps I already had.

I was at a loss, now, for how to carry out Adair's plan, and the realization that I might fail made me sick with fear. I'd thought I'd lure Jonathan to Boston with my love and sexual favors, but I'd failed. Remorse made my lover swear off me, though he promised he would be my friend and benefactor, if need be, forever. I waited to see if Jonathan might change his mind and come back to me, but it became clear as the days progressed that he would not. *A visit*, I begged him; *come to Boston for a visit*, but Jonathan resisted. One day his excuse was that his mother couldn't be trusted not to upset village affairs in his absence, and on another day it was that a complication had arisen that required his attention.

In the end, though, it was always his wife who kept him from agreeing to leave. "Evangeline would never forgive me if I left her alone with my family for a long spell, and she'd never make the trip with the baby," he said to me, as though he really was at the mercy of his wife and an infant—as though he'd never put his own wishes ahead of theirs, dutiful husband and father that he was. Such excuses might have been believable for another man but not for the Jonathan I knew.

The approaching snows were pressing my departure, however. I sensed that if I remained in St. Andrew for the winter, something terrible would happen. Adair, enraged that I'd defied him, might descend on the town with his hellhounds, and who knew what the black-hearted fiend might do to the innocents of St. Andrew, cut off from the rest of the world? I thought of the stories Alejandro and Dona had told me about Adair's barbarian past, leading raids on villages and slaughtering inhabitants who resisted. I thought of the maidens he'd raped and the way he'd drugged me and used me for amusement. Moving within Boston society ensured that Adair's brutal tendencies remained somewhat in check; there was no telling what would happen in an isolated, snowbound town. And I'd be the one responsible for bringing this plague on my neighbors.

I was mulling over my predicament one evening at Daughtery's, hoping to run into the tenderhearted axman I'd met early in my visit, when Jonathan walked in. I'd seen that expression on his face before: he had not come into Daughtery's restless for companionship. He was flush with contentment. He'd come from an assignation.

He started at the sight of me, but, having seen me, could hardly leave without acknowledging my presence. He took the stool across the lone table, his back to the fire. "Lanny, what are you doing here? It's hardly the place for a lady to frequent on her own."

"Oh, but I'm not a lady, am I?" I said, bitingly, though I regretted my bitterness immediately. "Where else can I go? I can hardly drink in the company of my mother and brother; I can't abide their disapproving faces. You, at least, can always go back to your big house for a nightcap. Better quality of drink, at any rate. And anyway—shouldn't you be home at this hour with your wife? You've been up to something this evening, I can smell it on you."

"Considering your position, I wouldn't think you'd be so quick to judge me," he said. "All right—I'll tell you the truth since you demand it from me. I have been with another woman. Someone I was seeing before you returned so unexpectedly. I, too, have a mistress. Anna Kolsted."

"Anna Kolsted is a married woman."

He shrugged.

I quivered with fury. "So you haven't ended your affair with her, even after the pretty speech you gave me the other day?"

"I—I couldn't leave her as abruptly as that without explaining what had happened."

"And will you explain that you've had a moral epiphany? That you've resolved not to see her again?" I demanded, as though I had any right to.

He remained silent.

"Do you never learn, Jonathan? This cannot end well," I said icily.

Jonathan pressed his mouth into a frown, long-simmering resentment bubbling up. "That seems to be what you always tell me, isn't it?" Sophia's name hung in the air between us, unspoken.

"It will end the same. She'll fall in love with you and want you for herself." Fear and sorrow rose up in me as it had the day I'd found Sophia in the river. I wouldn't have thought, after everything I'd been through, that her vision still had the power to affect me—maybe it did because I sometimes wondered if I'd have done well to follow her example. "It's inevitable, Jonathan. Everyone who knows you wants to own you."

"Do you speak from experience?"

His sharpness silenced me for a second, but I couldn't leave it be. I said sarcastically, "Those who have you tend to rue their good fortune. Perhaps you should ask your wife about that. Have you thought how your affair with Mrs. Kolsted will affect Evangeline should she find out?"

Anger overtook Jonathan quickly, like a storm front. He checked over his shoulder to make certain Daughtery was engaged and no one was listening, then gripped my upper arm and drew me close. "For Christ's sake, Lanny, have pity on me. I'm married to a child. When I took her to our conjugal bed, she cried afterward. *Cried.* She is frightened of my mother and dumbstruck around my sisters. I have no need for a child, Lanny. I need a woman."

I pried my arm out of his grip. "Don't you think I know that?"

"I wish to God I'd never given in to my father and married her. He wanted an heir, that's all he cared about. Saw a young girl with many breeding years ahead of her and made a deal with old McDougal, as though she was a broodmare." He ran a hand through his hair. "You've no idea of the life I must live now, Lanny. No one to run the business but me. Benjamin is still as helpless as a four-year-old. My sisters are ninnies. And when my father died, well . . . all his worries were foisted onto my shoulders. This town depends on my family's fortunes. Do you know how many settlers bought their land with loans secured by my father? One harsh winter, or if they've no talent for farming, and they will default on their obligations. I can foreclose, but what use have I for another failing farm? So you'll forgive me, I pray, for taking a mistress and having some small measure of escape from all my responsibilities."

I cast my eyes down.

He continued, wild eyed. "You can't imagine how tempting your offers have been. I'd give up everything to be free of my obligations! But I cannot, and I think you understand why. Not only would my family be lost, but the town, too, would fail. Lives would be ruined. You may have caught me in a moment of weakness when you came back, Lanny, but the past few years have taught me hard lessons. I cannot be so selfish."

Had he forgotten that he'd once told me he wanted to leave them all behind, his family and his fortune, for me? That he once wished his world was just he and I? A more levelheaded woman would have been happy to see that Jonathan had accepted his responsibilities, and was shouldering obligations that might break a weaker man. I cannot say I was happy or proud.

But I understood. I loved the town, in my way, and had no desire to see it falter. Even if my own family was already in difficulty, even if the townspeople had treated me shabbily and gossiped behind my back, I couldn't take away the linchpin holding the town together. I sat opposite Jonathan, grim and sympathetic to the plight he'd just shared with me, yet inside, panic bloomed from my feet to my head. *I was going to fail Adair.* What in the world would I do?

We drank our brew, in dismay. It seemed clear enough that I'd have to give up on Jonathan and needed to concentrate on my own plight: what to do next? Where could I go that Adair wouldn't be able to track me down? I had no desire to reenact the excruciating torture I'd already been subjected to.

We paid for our drink and went out to the path, each of us silent with our own thoughts. The night was again cold, the sky clear and bright from the moon and stars, thin clouds slicing through the silver light.

Jonathan put a hand on my arm. "Forgive my outburst and forget my troubles. You have every right to despise me for what I just said. The last thing I want is for you to take on my burdens. My horse is in Daughtery's barn. Let me give you a ride home." But before I could tell him it was unnecessary and that I preferred to be left with my thoughts, we were interrupted by the crunch of snow at the top of the path.

It was late and near freezing, unlikely for anyone to be about. "Who's there?" I called to a figure in the shadows. Edward Kolsted stepped into a sliver of moonlight, a flintlock in his hands.

"Be on your way, Miss McIlvrae. I've no quarrel with you." Kolsted was a rough young man from one of the poorer families in town and posed no competition to Jonathan for anyone's affections. His long face had been disfigured by smallpox, as many had been in youth, and for a young man, his brown hair was already thinning, his teeth falling out. He leveled the rifle at Jonathan's chest.

"Don't be stupid, Edward. There are witnesses: Lanny and the men inside Daughtery's . . . unless you plan to kill them, too," Jonathan said to his would-be murderer.

"I don't care. You've ruined my Anna and made a laughingstock of me. I will be proud to be known as having avenged myself against you." He lifted the rifle higher. A complete dread chill seized me. "Look at you, you fancy peacock," Edward sneered down his rifle at Jonathan, who, to his credit, stood his ground. "Do you think the town will mourn when you're dead? We'll not, sir. We despise you, the men of this town. Do you think we don't know what you've been up to, bewitching our wives, putting them under your spell? You took up with Anna for a bit of fun, and in the bargain stole the most precious thing I had. You're the very devil, you are, and this town would be better rid of you." Edward's voice climbed, high and defensive, but regardless of his words, I felt sure that Kolsted would not go through with his threat. He meant to frighten Jonathan, to humiliate him and make him beg for forgiveness, and that would give the cuckold a measure of dignity. But he didn't have the resolve to kill his rival.

"Is that what you want of me, to be a devil? That would suit your purpose, exonerate you of blame." Jonathan lowered his arms. "But the truth is, your wife is an unhappy woman, and this has little to do with me and much to do with you."

"Liar!" Kolsted shouted.

Jonathan took a step toward his assailant and my gut twisted, unsure if he had a death wish or if he couldn't let Kolsted hide from the truth. Perhaps he felt he owed it to his lover. Perhaps our argument in Daughtery's had brought about some resolution. But his angry countenance was misleading and Kolsted might be convinced that Jonathan was enraged because he loved Anna. "If your wife were happy, she wouldn't seek my company. She—"

Kolsted's old rifle fired, a blue-white burst of flame at the muzzle, which I caught from the corner of my eye. It went too fast: a crack like thunder, a flash like lightning, and Jonathan staggered backward, then dropped to the ground. Kolsted's face contorted, captured in the moonlight for an instant. "I've shot him," he muttered, as though reassuring himself. "I've shot Jonathan St. Andrew."

I dropped to my knees in the half-frozen mud, pulling Jonathan onto my lap. His clothing was already soaked through with blood, all the way to his greatcoat. It was a deep wound and serious. I wrapped my arms around Jonathan and looked balefully at Kolsted. "If I had a rifle, I would shoot you where you stand. Get out of my sight."

"Is he dead?" Kolsted craned his neck but wasn't brave enough to walk up to the man he had shot.

"They'll be out in a second, and if they find you here they'll lock you up forthwith," I warned, hissing through my teeth. I wanted him to flee: stirring could be heard within Daughtery's and someone would be out shortly to see who had fired the shot. I had to conceal Jonathan before we were discovered.

I didn't have to prompt Kolsted twice; whether it was from fright or sudden remorse, or because he wasn't ready to be taken into custody, Jonathan's assailant drew back like a spooked horse and ran. Locking my arms around Jonathan's chest, I pulled him into Daughtery's barn. I peeled back his greatcoat, then his frock coat, until I found the wound in his chest, blood spilling out from a hole near where his heart should be.

"Lanny," he wheezed, searching for my hand.

"Right here, Jonathan. Be still."

He wheezed again and coughed. There was no help to be had, judging from the distance of the shot and the location of the wound. I recognized the expression on his face: it was the strained look of the dying. He fell into unconsciousness, sinking in my arms.

Voices floated in from the other side of the worm-eaten boards, men from Daughtery's out on the path. Finding no one, they drifted away.

I looked down on Jonathan's beautiful face. His body, still warm, weighed heavily in my lap. My heart clamored in panic. *Keep him alive. Keep him with me at all costs.* I hugged him tighter. I couldn't let him die. And there was only one way to save him.

I eased his body to the ground, spread open his coat and waistcoat. Thank God he was unconscious; frightened as I was, I'd never have been able to do the cursed deed otherwise. Would it even work? Perhaps I remembered it wrong or there were special words I needed to recite to make such potent magic work. I had no time for second guessing, however.

I fumbled at the hem of my bodice, searching for the vial. Once I'd located the tiny silver vial by feel, I ripped out the stitches and pulled it from its hiding place. My hands shook as I pulled the stopper from the vial and separated Jonathan's lips. There was only a drop in there, less than a bead of sweat. I prayed it was enough.

"Don't leave me, Jonathan. I cannot live without you," I whispered in his ear, the only thing I could think to say. But then Alejandro's words came to me, the thing he'd told me that day I'd been transformed—I prayed it would not be too late. "By my hand and intent," I said, feeling foolish even as I spoke, knowing I had no power over anything, not heaven, hell, or earth.

I knelt in the straw, Jonathan propped in my lap, and brushed his hair off his forehead, waiting for a sign. All I remembered from the ordeal was the sensation of falling and a fever sweeping through my body like a fire, then waking much later in the dark.

I hugged Jonathan to me again. He'd stopped breathing and was growing colder. I pulled his coat around him, wondering if I could get him all the way to my family's farm without being noticed. It seemed unlikely, but there was nowhere else to take him, and someone would search Daughtery's barn sooner or later.

I saddled Jonathan's horse, amazed to find I was afraid of the devil stallion no more. With strength I didn't know I had, born of necessity, I threw Jonathan over the horse's withers, swung into the saddle, and sprang out of the open barn doors, streaking through the village. More than one villager would later claim to have seen Jonathan St. Andrew ride out of town that night, throwing theories about his disappearance into disarray, no doubt.

When we reached my family's farm, Jonathan's body cradled in my lap, I went straight to the barn and woke the hired driver. We had to leave St. Andrew that night; I couldn't risk waiting until morning, when Jonathan's family would come looking for him. I told the driver to hitch the horses quickly; we were heading out immediately. When he protested that it was too dark to travel, I told him the moonlight was strong enough to light his way, then added, "I'm paying your wages, so you listen to me. You've fifteen minutes to harness those horses." As for my trunk of clothing and other things, they'd all be left behind. I couldn't risk waking my family by returning to the cabin. My only thoughts at that moment were of spiriting Jonathan out of town.

As the coach rattled down the snow-crusted road, I peeked out the curtained window to see if anyone in the house had heard us, but no one stirred. I imagined them waking to find me gone, wondering—heartbroken—why I would choose to leave this way, my departure as mysterious as my years of silence. I was doing a great injustice to my mother's and sisters' kind hearts, and it struck me to my core, but the truth was, it was easier to disappoint them than to lose Jonathan forever, or to disobey Adair.

Jonathan lay on the bench across from me, wrapped in his coat and a fur lap robe, my cloak balled into a pillow, his head propped at an awkward angle. He made no movement, there was no rise and fall of his chest with breath, nothing. His skin was pale as ice in the moonlight. I kept my eyes trained on his face, waiting for the first sign of life, but he was so still I began to wonder if I had failed.

THIRTY-EIGHT

W e put miles between us and the village in the hours before dawn, the carriage rattling down the rough and lonesome forest trail as I sat vigil over Jonathan. It could have been a funeral trap, with me acting the widow accompanying her husband's body on the journey to his final resting place.

The sun had been out for a while by the time Jonathan stirred. By then, I'd almost come to the conclusion that he was not coming back; I'd sat trembling and sweating for hours, on the verge of vomiting, hating myself. The first sign of life was a twitch of his right cheek, then a flutter of an eyelash. As he was still white as a corpse, I doubted my eyes for a moment, until I heard the low moan, saw his lips part, and then both eyes open.

"Where are we?" he asked in a barely audible rasp.

"In a carriage. Lie still. You'll feel better in a bit."

"A carriage? Where are we going?"

"To Boston." I didn't know what else to tell him.

"Boston! What happened? Did I"—his mind must have gone to

the last thing he could remember, the two of us at Daughtery's—"did I lose a wager? Was I drunk, to agree to go with you—"

"There was no agreement about it," I said, kneeling next to him to tuck the robe around him more tightly. "We are going because we must. You can no longer stay in St. Andrew."

"What are you talking about, Lanny?" Jonathan was vexed and tried to push me away, though he was so weak he couldn't make me budge. I felt something unpleasant under my knee, like a sharp pebble; reaching down, my fingers found a shot of lead.

The shot from Kolsted's flintlock.

I held it up for Jonathan to see. "Do you recognize this?"

He tried hard to focus on the small dark form in my hand. I watched as the memory caught up to him, and he recalled the argument on the footpath and the flash of powder that had ended his life.

"I was shot," he said, his chest heaving up and down. His hand went to his pectoral, the torn layers of shirt and waistcoat, stiff with dried blood. He felt his flesh under the clothing, but it was whole.

"No wound," Jonathan said with relief. "Kolsted must have missed."

"How could that be? You see the blood, the tears in your clothes. Kolsted didn't miss you, Jonathan. He shot you in the heart and killed you."

He squeezed his eyes shut. "You're not making sense. I don't understand."

"It's not something that can be understood," I replied, taking his hand. "It's a miracle."

I tried to explain it all, though God knows I understood precious little myself. I told him my story and Adair's story. I showed him the tiny vial, now empty, and let him sniff its last foul vapors. He listened, the whole time observing me as though I was a madwoman.

"Tell your driver to stop the carriage," he said. "I'm going back to St. Andrew if I have to walk the whole way."

"I can't let you out."

"Stop the carriage!" he thundered, rising to his feet and pounding a fist on the carriage's roof. I tried to make him sit down, but the driver had heard him and pulled the horses up.

Jonathan flung open the tiny door and bounded out into the knee-deep virgin snow. The driver turned, looking down on us doubtfully from his high perch, his mustache frosted with his own breath. The horses shuddered for air, exhausted from pulling the carriage through the snow.

"We'll be back. Melt some snow to water the horses," I said in an attempt to distract the driver. I ran after Jonathan, my skirts slowing me in the snow, and grabbed his arm when I finally caught up to him.

"You've got to listen to me. You can't go back to St. Andrew. You've changed."

He pushed me away. "I don't know what happened to you since you've been away, but I can only surmise that you've lost your mind . . ."

I held on to his cuff fiercely. "I'll prove it to you. If I can make you see that I'm telling the truth, do you promise to come with me?"

He stopped but looked at me as though he expected a trick. "I promise you nothing."

I held up my hand, releasing his sleeve, signaling for him to wait. With my other hand, I found a small but sturdy knife in the pocket of my overcoat. I tore open my bodice, exposing my corset to the frigidly crisp air, and then, grasping the knife's handle in both hands, I plunged it into my chest to the hilt.

Jonathan nearly dropped to his knees, but his hands reached for me reflexively. "Good God! You *are* insane! What in God's name are you doing—"

Blood welled around the hilt, quickly soaked up by my clothing, until a huge sunburst of deep crimson spread across the silk from my belly to my sternum. I pulled the blade out, then grabbed his hand and pressed his fingers to the wound. He tried to pull away but I held him fast.

"Touch it. Feel what is happening and tell me you still don't believe me."

I knew what would happen. It was a parlor trick Dona performed for us when we gathered in the kitchen to wind down after a night on the town. He would sit before the fire, toss his frock coat over the back of a chair and roll up his voluminous sleeves, and then cut deep into his forearms with a knife. Alejandro, Tilde, and I would watch as the two raw ends of red flesh would crawl toward each other, helpless as doomed lovers, and sew up in a seamless embrace. An impossible feat, done over and over, as sure as the sun rises. (Dona would laugh bitterly as he watched his own flesh re-join, but re-creating his trick myself, I saw that it had a sensation all its own. It was pain we sought but couldn't re-create, not exactly. We came to want an approximation of suicide, and in its stead we would have the temporary pleasure of inflicting pain upon ourselves, but even that was denied us. How we hated ourselves, each in our own way!)

Jonathan's face went pale as he felt the pulpy flesh move and shudder and close.

"What is this?" he whispered in horror. "The devil's hand is there, surely."

"I don't know about that. I have no explanation. What's done is done and there's no running away from it. You'll never be the same again and your place is no longer in St. Andrew. Now come with me," I said. He went limp and stark white and he didn't resist when I placed my hand on his arm and guided him back to the carriage.

Jonathan did not recover from shock for the entire trip. It made for an anxious time for me, as I was eager to know if I would get my friend—and my lover—back. Jonathan was always the confident one and it made me ill at ease to be the leader. It was foolish for me to expect anything different; after all, how long had I sulked in Adair's house, withdrawing into myself and refusing to believe what had happened to me?

He kept to the tiny cabin during the sailing to Boston, not stepping on deck once. That whetted the crew's and other passengers' curiosity to be sure, so even though the seas were smooth as well water, I told them that he had taken ill and did not trust his legs to be up and about. I brought him soup from the galley and his ration of beer, though he no longer had the need to eat and his appetite had deserted him. As Jonathan would soon learn, eating was something we did out of habit and for comfort, and to pretend that we were the same as ever.

By the time the ship arrived at the Boston harbor, Jonathan was a strange-looking creature from his many hours in the semidarkness of the cabin. Pale and nervous, with eyes rimmed pink from lack of sleep, he emerged from his cabin dressed in the set of ragtag clothes we had purchased back in Camden from a tiny shop that sold secondhand goods. He stood on the deck, enduring the stares of the other passengers, who doubtless had wondered if the unseen passenger had died in his cabin during the journey. He watched the activity on the pier as the ship was secured in its berth, eyes widening at the crowds. His incredible beauty had been dampened by his ordeal and for a moment, I wished that Adair would not see Jonathan looking so poorly for their first meeting. I wanted Adair to see that Jonathan was everything I'd promised—foolish vanity!

We disembarked and had gone not twenty feet up the pier when I saw Dona waiting for us with a couple of servants. Dona wore a funereal outfit, black ostrich plumes in his hat, and he was bundled in a black cape and leaned on his walking stick, towering over the ordinary people like the grim reaper himself. An evil leer crept over his face as he spied us.

"How did you know I was returning today? On this ship?" I demanded of him. "I sent no letter on ahead to tell you of my plans."

"Oh, Lanore, you are laughably naive. Adair always knows such things. He felt your presence on the horizon and sent me to fetch you," he said, brushing me off. He lavished all his attention on Jonathan, not attempting to disguise that he was inspecting him from head to toe and back again. "So, introduce me to your friend."

"Jonathan, this is Donatello," I said, curtly. Jonathan made no move to acknowledge him or return the greeting, though whether it was because of Dona's bald appraisal or because he was still in shock I couldn't say.

"Doesn't he speak? Has he no manners?" Dona said. When Jonathan didn't rise to the bait, Dona brushed off the snub by turning to me. "Where are your bags? The servants—"

"Would we be dressed like this if we had anything else to wear? I had to leave everything behind. I barely had the money to make it to Boston." In my mind's eye, I saw the trunk I'd left behind in my mother's house, inconspicuously tucked in a corner. When they inspected it—waiting until curiosity got the best of them before they'd violate my privacy, even though they'd know I was not coming back— they would find the doeskin pouch fat with gold and silver coins. I was happy that the money pouch had been left behind; I felt I owed my family that much. I considered it Adair's blood money, paying my family for the loss of me forever, much as he'd assuaged his guilt by leaving money for his family centuries earlier.

"How consistent of you. The first time, you came to us with nothing. Now you bring your friend, both of you with nothing." Dona threw his hands in the air as though I was incorrigible, but I knew why he acted peevishly: even in Jonathan's current state, his exceptional nature was obvious. He would become the apple of Adair's eye, the friend and compatriot against whom Dona could never compete. Dona would fall from grace with Adair; there was nothing to be done for it and that was clear to Dona from the moment he laid eyes on Jonathan.

If only Dona had known, he wouldn't have wasted his envy. Our arrival that day was the beginning of the end for all of us.

Jonathan came back to life on the carriage ride to Adair's mansion. For this was his first trip to a city as big and varied as Boston, and through his eyes, I got to relive my arrival two years earlier: the masses of people on the dusty streets; the proliferation of shops and inns;

the amazing houses made of brick, towering several stories high; the number of carriages on the street drawn by well-groomed horses; the women in fashions of the day, revealing décolletage and long white throats. After a while, Jonathan had to sit back from the window and close his eyes.

Then, of course, Adair's mansion was as overwhelming as a castle, though by this point, Jonathan had grown numb to the novelty of grandeur. He allowed me to lead him up the stairs and into the house, through the foyer with the chandelier swaying overhead and the liveried footmen bowing low enough to inspect Jonathan's crusted shoes. We went through the dining hall with its table set for eighteen to the double-bowed staircase, which led to the bedchambers upstairs.

"Where is Adair?" I demanded of one of the butlers, eager to get this part over.

"Right here." His voice rose behind me, and I whirled around to see him walking in. He'd dressed carefully, with a studied casualness, his hair tied back with a ribbon like a European gentleman. Like Dona, he eyed my Jonathan as though considering a fair price for him, rubbing together the fingers of his right hand. For his part, Jonathan tried to be indifferent, glancing at Adair and then looking away. But I felt a charge in the air and a recognition pass between them. It could have been what mystics claim as the bond between souls destined to travel throughout time together. Or it might have been the dance of rival males in the wild, wondering who will come out on top and how bloody the battle will be. Or it might have been that he was finally meeting the man who kept me.

"So this is the friend you told us about," Adair said, pretending it was as simple as having an old friend down for a visit.

"I am pleased to introduce to you Mr. Jonathan St. Andrew." I did my best impression of a doorman but neither man was amused.

"And you are the . . ." Jonathan fumbled for the word to describe Adair from my fantastic story, for indeed what would you call him? Monster? Ogre? Demon? "Lanny told me about you."

Adair raised an eyebrow. "Did she? I hope Lanny did not make too much of a mess of it. She has such a grand imagination. You shall have to tell me what she said, someday." He snapped his fingers at Dona. "Show our guest up to his room. He must be tired."

"I can take him," I began, but Adair cut me off.

"No, Lanore, stay with me. I'd like to speak to you for a moment." It was then I realized I was in trouble: he simmered with anger, hidden for the sake of our guest. We watched as Dona led a sleepwalking Jonathan up the winding staircase, until they disappeared from view. Then Adair whirled on me, striking me hard across my face.

Knocked to the floor, I held my cheek and glared at him. "What was that for?"

"You *changed* him, didn't you? You stole my elixir and you took him for yourself. Did you think I wouldn't find out what you'd done?" Adair stood over me, huffing, shoulders trembling.

"I had no choice! He had been shot . . . he was dying . . ."

"Do you think I am stupid? You stole the elixir because you had intended from the beginning to bind him to you." Adair reached down and grabbed me by the arm, hoisted me to my feet, and shoved me against the wall. In his hands, I felt the terror of the episode in the basement, strapped in the diabolical harness, helpless in the face of his violence and drowning in panic. Then he hit me again, a stinging backhand that dropped me to the floor a second time. I reached up again to my cheek and found it smeared with blood. He'd split the skin open, and pain was radiating through my face even as the wound's edges began to knit back together.

"If I meant to steal him from you, would I have come back?" Still on the floor, I scrabbled backward like a crab to get out of Adair's reach, slipping on my own silken hem. "I'd have run away and taken him with me. No, it's exactly as I told you . . . I took the vial, yes, but as a precaution. It was a feeling I had, that something bad was going to happen. But of course I came back. I am loyal to you," I said, even though there was murder in my heart, fury at being struck, for being helpless to do anything about it.

Adair glared at me, questioning my declaration, but did not strike me again. Instead, he turned and walked away, his warning to me echoing in the hall. "We will see about your professed loyalty. Do not think this is over, Lanore. I will crush the tie between you and this man so completely that your bond to him will be as nothing. Your thievery and your scheming will come to naught. You are mine, and if you believe I cannot undo what you have done, you are mistaken. Jonathan will be mine, too."

I remained on the floor, holding my cheek, trying not to panic at his words. I couldn't let him take Jonathan away from me. I couldn't let him sever the tie to the only person I cared about. Jonathan was all I had and all I wanted. If I lost him, life would be meaningless, and unfortunately, life would be all that was left to me.

THIRTY-NINE

It is near midnight when they arrive in Quebec City. Lanny directs Luke to what appears to be the best hotel in the old part of town, a tall fortresslike building with parapets for a crown and flags fluttering in the cold night wind. Grateful to be driving the new SUV instead of his old truck, Luke hands the valet the keys and then he and Lanny walk empty-handed into the lobby.

The hotel room is about the most luxurious place he's ever stayed; it puts the hotel where he spent his honeymoon to shame. The bed is a plush affair with feather bed, a half dozen pillows, and Frette sheets, and as he settles into its voluptuousness, he levels a remote at the flat-screen television. The local news programs should be on in a few minutes and he's anxious to see if there is any mention of the disappearance of a murder suspect from a hospital in Maine. Luke hopes that St. Andrew is too far away and inconsequential for the story to be carried in Quebec.

His gaze wanders to Lanny's laptop, at the foot of the bed. He could see if there's anything online, but Luke is struck by a sudden irrational fear that if he searches for their story online, he will give them away somehow, that the authorities will be able to track them down through the combination of an internet connection and the use of suspicious key words. His heart pounds even though he knows this isn't possible. He has made himself almost dizzy with paranoia when he's not sure there is any reason for it.

Lanny comes out of the bathroom on a cloud of warm, damp air. She's swimming in the hotel bathrobe, which is huge on her, and has a towel over her shoulders, her wet hair falling in tendrils over her eyes. She fishes a pack of cigarettes out of her jacket. Before lighting up, she offers one to Luke, but he shakes his head.

"The water pressure is heavenly," she says, sending a stream of smoke toward the sprinkler heads embedded discreetly in the ceiling. "You should take a nice long, hot shower."

"In a minute," he says.

"What's on television? Are you looking for something about us?"

He nods, twitching his stockinged feet at the plasma screen. A flashy logo for the news program flits across, then a serious-looking middle-aged man begins reading headlines while his coanchor nods attentively. Lanny continues to sit with her back to the screen, toweling her hair. Seven minutes into the program, a head shot of Luke flashes behind the anchor. It's the posed personnel photo they took at the hospital that appears every time his name is mentioned in the hospital newsletter.

". . . is missing after treating a murder suspect for the police at Aroostook General Hospital yesterday evening, and the authorities fear that something may have happened to him. The police are asking anyone with information on the doctor's whereabouts to call the crime hotline . . ."

The entire story lasts less than sixty seconds, but it is so alarming to see his face on the television screen that Luke can't absorb what the anchor is saying. Lanny takes the remote out of his hand and turns it off.

"So, they're looking for you," she says, her voice breaking his paralysis.

"Don't they have to wait forty-eight hours before they can consider you a missing person?" he asks, weakly indignant, as though an injustice has been done to him.

"They're not going to wait; they think you're in danger."

Am I? he wonders. *Does Joe Duchesne know something I don't know?* "They read my name on the air. The hotel . . ."

"No reason to worry. We registered in my name, remember? The police back in St. Andrew don't know who I am. No one is going to put two and two together." The girl turns away and blows another long stream of smoke. "It'll be okay. Trust me. I'm an expert at escaping."

It feels as though Luke's brain squeezes against his skull, as if in a panic it is trying to get out. The enormity of what he has done hits him: Duchesne will be waiting to talk to him. Peter undoubtedly has told the police about the SUV and the email, so there's no way they can continue to use it. In order to go back to his home, he will have to lie convincingly to the sheriff and repeat that lie to everyone back in St. Andrew, maybe for the rest of his life. He closes his eyes and fights for breath. His subconscious led him to help Lanny. If he can only fight through the alarm clamoring in his head, his subconscious should tell him what it is he really wants, why he walked out on his life and went tearing down the road with this woman, bridges aflame behind him. "Does that mean I can't go back?" he asks.

"If that's what you want," she says carefully. "They'll have questions, but nothing you wouldn't be able to handle. Do you want to go back to St. Andrew? To your parents' farm, the house full of their belongings, the absence of your kids? Back to the hospital to take care of your ungrateful neighbors?"

Luke's uneasiness grows stronger. "I don't want to talk about it."

"Listen to me, Luke. I know what you're thinking." She slides across the bed to sit next to him, close, so he can't turn away from her. He smells the faint perfume of soap, warmed by her skin, rise from under the bathrobe. "You only want to go back because it's what you know. It's what you have left. The man I saw walk into the ER looked overwhelmed and tired. You've been through a lot with your parents and your former wife, losing your children . . . There's nothing there for you anymore. It's a trap. You go back to St. Andrew and you'll never leave. You'll just grow older, surrounded by people who don't give a damn about you. I know what you're feeling. You're alone and you're afraid you're going to be alone for the rest of your life, rattling around in a big house, no one to talk to. No one to help with the burdens of living—no one to eat dinner with, no one to listen to stories about your day. You're afraid of old age—who will be there for you? Who will take care of you the way you took care of your parents, who will hold your hand when it's your turn to die?" What she's said is brutally true and he can barely stand to listen to it. She puts one arm around Luke's shoulder and when he doesn't push her away, she pulls him closer.

"You're right to be afraid of dying. Death has taken everyone I've known. I've held them in my arms up to their last moment, comforted them, cried when they've gone. Loneliness is a terrible thing." The words are incongruous coming from this young woman, but her sadness is palpable. "I can be here for you always, Luke. I won't go away. I'll be with you for the rest of your life, if you want me to be."

Luke doesn't pull away, but he thinks about her words. She's not proposing love—is she?—no, Luke knows that, he's no fool. Though it's not exactly friendship, either. He doesn't flatter himself into thinking that they have taken to each other like kindred souls: they've known each other for less than thirty-six hours. He thinks he understands what this pretty young woman is offering. She needs a companion. Luke has followed an instinct he didn't know he had and has done well by her. She sees it can work. And in exchange, he can walk away from his old, complicated life without having to do so much as cancel his account with the electric company. And, Luke won't ever be alone again.

He remains in Lanny's arms, letting her stroke his back, enjoying the feel of her hand. It clears his mind and brings Luke peace for the first time since the sheriff escorted her into the emergency room.

He knows that if he thinks too hard, the fog will roll back in. He feels like a character in the middle of a fairy tale, but if he stops to think about what is happening, if he resists the gentle tug of her story, confusion will set in. He's tempted not to question Lanny's unseen world. If he accepts what she says as true, then what he believes about death is a lie. But, as a doctor, Luke has witnessed the end of life, stood by as life dribbled out of a patient. He accepted death as one of his world's absolutes and now he's being told that it's not. Exigencies have been written into the coda of life in invisible ink. If death isn't an absolute, then of the thousands of facts and faiths he's been fed in his life, which *other* ones might be a lie?

That is, *if* this girl's story is true. Even though he's been following her in a compliant fog, Luke still can't shake the suspicion that he's being deceived. She is obviously skilled in manipulation, like many a psychopath. Now is not the time for such thoughts, however. She's right: he is tired and overwhelmed and afraid of coming to the wrong conclusion, making the wrong decision.

He leans back into the pillow, faintly scented of lavender, and nestles against Lanny's warm body. "You don't need to worry. I'm not going anywhere just yet. For one thing, you haven't told me the rest of your story. I want to hear what happened next."

FORTY

BOSTON, 1819

We went out that night, Jonathan's first night in Boston. The event was a sedate one—a musicale, with a piano and a singer of no renown—but still I wouldn't have thought it a good idea to take him out while he was in shock and his mind too unsettled. Secrecy was Adair's byword—he'd impressed that on us all with tales of being suspected of witchcraft and barely escaping violent mobs, fleeing on horseback by moonlight, leaving behind a fortune that had taken decades to amass—and who knew what Jonathan might say in the state he was in. Adair would not be dissuaded, however, and we were dispatched to search through the trunks for a suite of evening clothes for Jonathan. In the end, Adair commandeered Dona's gorgeous French frock coat (Jonathan being as tall as Dona but broader through the shoulders) and had one of the maids slave for a few hours on alterations as the rest of us powdered, perfumed, and dressed to introduce Jonathan to the city.

Only he couldn't go forth as Jonathan, could he? "You must re-member to introduce yourself by another name," Adair explained, as servants helped us don capes and hats under the chandelier in the foyer. "We cannot have word getting back to your little hamlet that Jonathan St. Andrew has been seen in Boston."

The reason was obvious: Jonathan's family would be looking for him. Ruth St. Andrew would refuse to accept that her son had simply disappeared. She'd have the entire town searched, the woods and river, too. When the snow melted in the spring and still no body was found, she would deduce that Jonathan had left on his own and she might cast an even wider net in an attempt to find him. We couldn't leave a trail of crumbs behind, clues that could bring someone to our door.

"Why do you insist on taking him out tonight? Why not let him recover first?" I asked Adair as we clambered into the carriage. He regarded me as he might a simpleton or a noisome child.

"Because I don't want him cloistered in his room, brooding over what he has left behind. I want him to enjoy what the world has to offer." He smiled at Jonathan, though Jonathan only stared moodily out the carriage window, oblivious even to Tilde's hand playing provocatively with his knee. Something about Adair's answer didn't sit right with me, and I'd learned to trust my instincts about when Adair was lying. Adair *wanted* Jonathan to be seen in public, but for what reason, I couldn't determine.

The carriage took us to a tall, stately house not far off the Boston Common, the home of a councilman and attorney whose wife had gone mad for Adair, or I should say, had gone mad for what he represented: European aristocracy and sophistication (if she only knew that, in truth, she was entertaining the son of an itinerant field hand, a peasant with blood as well as mud on his hands). The husband left for their farm to the west of the city whenever the wife hosted one of these parties and it was just as well, as he would have died of apoplexy if he'd known what went on at these events and how she spent his money.

In addition to hanging on Adair's arm for much of the evening, the councilman's wife also tried to interest him in her daughters. Despite the fact that America had recently won its independence and thrown off a monarchy in favor of democracy, some were still enamored of the idea of royalty, and the councilman's wife probably secretly wished to have one of her daughters marry into a title. I expected that when we arrived, she would descend on Adair in a flurry of taffeta skirts and curtsies, ushering in her daughters to stand a little closer to the count, until he could peer down their décolleté with no trouble.

When Jonathan stepped into the ballroom, there was a hush and then a twitter ran through the gathering. It would not be an exaggeration to say all eyes turned to him. Tilde had taken his arm and now ushered him to where Adair stood, speaking with the hostess.

"Allow me to introduce you," Adair began and then gave the councilman's wife a name to remember Jonathan by, Jacob Moore, deceptively common. She looked up, momentarily speechless.

"He's my American cousin, would you believe it?" Adair threw an arm affectionately around Jonathan's neck. "Through family in England on both our mothers' sides. A distant branch of my family . . ." Adair trailed off when it was apparent that no one—for the first time since he'd arrived in America—was listening to him.

"Are you new to Boston?" the hostess asked Jonathan, her eyes never leaving his face. "Because I would remember if I had seen you before."

I stood by the punch table with Alejandro, watching Jonathan stumble through an explanation, needing Adair to rescue him. "I suspect we won't be long here, tonight," I said.

"This will not be as easy as Adair thinks." Alejandro lifted his cup in their direction. "You cannot hide *that face*. Word will get around, maybe even to your wretched village."

There was a more immediate concern, I thought, as I observed Jonathan and Adair together. The women flocked not around the European aristocrat but the tall stranger. They stared at him from behind their fans; they stood blushing at his elbow, waiting to be introduced. I'd seen those expressions before, and I realized at that moment that it would never change. Wherever Jonathan went, women would try to possess him. Even if he didn't encourage it, they would always pursue him. As trying as the competition had been in St. Andrew, now Jonathan would never be mine alone. I would always have to share him.

Tonight, Adair seemed content to let Jonathan be the center of attention; indeed, he appeared to pay close attention to the partygoers' reactions. But I wondered how long that would last. Adair did not seem the type to live in someone else's shadow, and there never was any choice but to let him be the star. Jonathan himself had no choice.

"I fear there will be trouble before too long," I murmured to Alejandro.

"With Adair, there is always trouble. It is just a matter of how bad."

We stayed longer than I thought: the night was starting to surrender to the purple bloom of dawn when we returned to the mansion in quiet exhaustion. I saw that, despite himself, Jonathan appeared to have come out of his shell a little. High spots of color—an excess of drink?—spotted his cheeks and he was definitely less tense.

We climbed the stairs in silence, the sharp report of our heels on the marble floor echoing through the great, hollow house. Tilde tugged at Jonathan's hand, trying to direct him to her room, but he slipped from her grasp with a shake of his head. One by one, the courtiers disappeared behind the gilded doors to their bedchambers until it was only Jonathan, Adair, and myself. I was about to escort Jonathan to his room, to share a few words of reassurance and, with any luck, be invited to keep him warm under the covers, when I was stopped by an arm thrown around my waist. Adair reeled me in close to him and, in full view of Jonathan, ran his free hand over my bodice and my derriere. He kicked open the door to his private chamber.

"Will you join us tonight?" he said with a wink. "We should make this a night to remember, to celebrate your arrival. Lanore is quite capable of pleasing both of us; she's done it many times before. You should see for yourself: she has a gift for loving two men at the same time."

Jonathan blanched and stepped back.

"No? Another time, then. Perhaps when you are more rested. Good night," Adair said, as he pulled me in behind him. There was no mistaking his message: I was a common whore. This was how Adair meant to kill Jonathan's affection for me, and I realized in that instant that I'd been a fool to doubt Adair's ability to make good on it. I barely looked at Jonathan's face—shocked, hurt—before the door slammed shut.

In the morning, I gathered my clothing in my arms, and in my shift and bare feet, stood outside Jonathan's bedchamber, listening for signs that he was awake. I craved in the strongest way to hear the quotidian noises of his morning ritual—the rustle of bed linen, water splashing in the basin—thinking that would make everything right. I had no idea if I could face him. I wanted the kind of reassurance a child gets from a parent's face after he's been punished, but I lacked the courage to knock. It didn't matter: it was completely still within, and given the long, complicated day he'd had, I shouldn't have doubted he'd sleep a full twenty-four hours.

Instead, I washed in my room and dressed in fresh clothing, then made my way downstairs in the hope that, despite the early hour, the servants would have set a pan of coffee brewing. To my surprise, Jonathan sat in the small dining room, steaming milk and dry bread on the table before him. He looked up at me.

"You've risen," I said.

He stood and pulled out the chair opposite his. "I've kept farmer's hours my whole life. Surely you remember that about St. Andrew. If you slept past six in the morning, the entire town would be talking about you by noon. The only thing for it was to be on your deathbed," he said wryly. A sleepy young man carried in a cup and saucer, splashing coffee clumsily over the edge, then set it at my left hand, nodded, and left.

Although I'd thought all evening of how I might explain myself to Jonathan, I'd come up at a loss. I had no idea how to start, so I fumbled with the delicate handle of the cup. "What you saw last night . . ."

Jonathan held up a hand, a strangled look on his face, as though he didn't wish to speak but knew he had to. "I don't know why I reacted the way I did last night . . . You'd told me your circumstances plainly in St. Andrew. If I seemed shocked, it's because, well, I didn't expect this Adair to make the offer he did." Jonathan cleared his throat. "You've always been a good friend to me, Lanny . . ."

"That hasn't changed," I said.

". . . but I would not be speaking the truth if I said his words didn't shake me. He doesn't seem the sort of man a woman should *allow* herself to love." It seemed to bother him greatly, to say that much to me. He kept his gaze on the table. "Do you love him?"

Could Jonathan think I could love anyone but him? He didn't sound jealous, though; he was worried. "It's not about love," I said grimly. "You must understand that."

His face shifted, as though a thought had just come to him. "Tell me that he doesn't—force—you to do these things."

I blushed. "Not exactly."

"Then you *want* to be with him?"

"Not now that you're here," I said, and he squirmed, though I wasn't sure why. At that moment, I wanted to warn Jonathan about Adair's possible intentions toward him. "Look, there's one thing I must tell you about Adair, though you may have guessed it now that you've met Dona and Alejandro. They're—" I hesitated, unsure how much of a shock Jonathan could take after all he'd been through in twenty-four hours.

"They're sodomites," he said plainly. "One doesn't spend one's life around men like the axmen, who have only other men for company, without picking up something about it."

"They consort with Adair. You'll see, Adair has a most peculiar nature," I said. "He is mad for fornication in any form. But there is nothing loving about it, or tender." I stopped short of telling him that Adair used sex as punishment, to exert his will over us, to make us obey him. I said nothing because I was afraid to, just as Alejandro had been afraid to make me aware of the truth.

Jonathan looked at me directly, a frown firmly creased across his mouth. "What have you gotten me into, Lanny?"

I reached for his hand. "I'm sorry, Jonathan, I truly am. You must believe me. But . . . though you may not wish for me to say this, it is a comfort to have you with me. I've been so alone. I've needed you."

He squeezed my hand, though reluctantly.

"Besides," I continued, "what was I to do? Kolsted had shot you. You were bleeding to death in my arms. If I didn't act, you'd be—"

"Dead, I know. It's only that . . . I hope not to be in the position, one day, of wishing that were so."

That morning, Adair sent for the tailor. Jonathan needed a wardrobe, Adair decreed; his new guest could not continue to be seen in public in mismatched, ill-fitting costumes. As every member of the household was a clotheshorse and had enriched the tailor greatly, Mr. Drake rushed over before the breakfast things were even cleared away, bringing with him a train of assistants carrying bolts of fabric. The latest woolens and velvets, silks and brocades, from European warehouses. Tea chests filled with expensive buttons made of mother-of-pearl and bone, pewter buckles for a pair of slippers. I sensed Jonathan did not approve and didn't want to be indebted to Adair for an extravagant wardrobe, but he said nothing. I sat on a stool at the fringes of the activity, ogling the lovely fabrics, hoping to get a dress or two out of the fitting.

"You know, I could use a few new things," I said to Adair, holding a strip of pink satin to my cheek to see if it suited my complexion. "I left my entire wardrobe behind in St. Andrew when we fled. I had to sell my last piece of jewelry to make passage on the ship to Boston."

"Don't remind me," he said drily.

Mr. Drake had Jonathan stand on his tailor's box in front of the biggest mirror in the house and began taking his measurements with a length of string, clucking to himself over Jonathan's impressive proportions. "My, my, you are a tall one," he said, running his hands up the length of Jonathan's back, then over his hips, and finally—nearly causing me to swoon—up his leg to measure an inseam. "The gentle-man dresses left," Drake murmured, almost lovingly, to the assistant scribbling down the numbers.

The order for the tailor was long: three frock coats and a half dozen pairs of breeches, including a pair of the finest doeskin for riding; a dozen shirts, including a very fancy one with lace for gala events; four waistcoats; at least a dozen cravats. A new pair of field boots. Silk and woolen stockings and garters, three pairs of each. And that was just to meet the immediate need; more would be ordered when new ship-ments of fabric arrived. Mr. Drake was still writing up the order when Adair placed a huge ruby on the table in front of the tailor; not a word was spoken but, by the smile on Drake's face, he was more than happy with his compensation. What he didn't know was that the gem was a mere bauble, plucked from a box containing many more, the box itself only one among many. Adair had treasure dating back to the sacking of Vienna. A gemstone that size was as common as a field mushroom to Adair.

"A cloak, too, I think, for my associate. Lined with heavy satin," Adair added, spinning the ruby on its faceted end like a child's wooden top.

The ruby attracted everyone's eye and I was the only one to see Adair take a long, appraising look at Jonathan, from his back down to the graceful dip at the small of his back and over his trim buttocks. The look was so naked and heavy with intent that it froze my heart in fear for what lay ahead for my Jonathan.

As the tailor packed his things, a stranger arrived for Adair. A somber gentleman with two ledgers and a portable writing kit—ink-well, quills—tucked under his arm. The two went immediately to the study without a word to anyone else.

"Do you know who that man is?" I asked Alejandro as I watched the study door close.

"Adair's taken a solicitor while you were gone. It is understandable: now that he is in this country, he has legal matters to attend to regarding his property overseas. These things come up from time to time. It is of no consequence," he answered, as though it was the most boring thing imaginable. And so I paid no more mind to it—at the time.

"It is nonsense," Jonathan said when Adair told him an artist was coming to the house that day to make sketches of him for an oil painting.

"It would be criminal not to have your likeness captured," Adair argued back. "There are far homelier men who have immortalized themselves for posterity, lined the walls of their familial mansions with their sorry likenesses. This very house is a case in point," Adair said, gesturing to the walls of portraits that had been rented with the house to provide a ready-made pedigree. "Besides, Mrs. Warner told me about the artist, quite gifted, and I want to see if he is worth the accolades that are being heaped upon him. He should thank God to get such a subject, I tell you. Your face may well establish this man's career."

"I don't care to make anyone's career," Jonathan retorted, but he knew the battle was lost. He sat for the artist but was not exactly cooperative; he slumped in the chair, leaning with his cheek against his hand, face sullen, like a schoolboy being kept after class. I perched on the window seat for the entire session, seeing his beauty anew through the artist's quick charcoal sketches. The artist clucked to himself throughout, undoubtedly pleased at his good fortune to be working on such a striking figure and getting paid for the privilege.

Dona, once an artist's model, sat with me for an afternoon, ostensibly to study the artist's technique. I noticed that he seemed to observe Jonathan more than he bothered with the artist.

"He's going to become quite the pet, isn't he," Dona said at one point. "You can tell by the portrait—Adair only has likenesses done of his favorite. The odalisque, for instance."

"And what does that mean, to be his favorite?"

He gave me a sly look. "Oh, don't pretend. You have been Adair's favorite for a short while. In some ways, you still are. And so you know, it's onerous. He expects your attention all the time. He's very demanding and easily bored, especially when it comes to sex games," Dona said, lifting a shoulder archly, as though to say he was happy he was no longer pressured to come up with new ways to bring Adair to climax. I looked closely at Dona, studying his features as he spoke: he was a handsome man, too, though his beauty had been forever ruined by some unhappiness he carried inside. A secret malice clouded his eyes and twisted his mouth into a sneer.

"And he's only had portraits done of these two?" I asked, taking up the conversation again. "Only Uzra and Jonathan?"

"Oh, there have been a few others. Only the stunningly beautiful. He's left their paintings in storage in the old country, like the faces of angels locked away in a vault. They've fallen out of favor. Perhaps you'll see them one day." He tilted his head, studying Jonathan with a critical eye. "The paintings, I mean."

"The paintings . . . ," I repeated. "But the fallen ones—what has become of them?"

"Oh, some have left. With Adair's blessing, of course. No one leaves without it. But they're scattered like leaves in the wind . . . We rarely see them again." He paused for a minute. "Though you have met Jude, now that I think of it. No loss, his departure. What a diabolical man, to pass himself off as a preacher. A sinner in saint's clothing." Dona laughed, as though it was the funniest thing he could conceive of, one of the damned masquerading as a preacher.

"You said only *some* have left. What of the others? Has anyone left without Adair's permission?"

Dona gave me a thinly malevolent smile. "Don't pretend to be stupid. If it were possible to leave Adair, would Uzra still be here? You have been around Adair long enough to know that he's neither careless nor sentimental. You either leave in his good graces or, well . . . he's not about to leave someone behind to take revenge on him and reveal him to the wrong people, is he?" But this was the last Dona would say about our mysterious overlord. He glanced down at me and, seeming to think better of divulging anything more, swept out of the room, and left me to ponder all that he'd told me.

About this time, there was a commotion across the room, Jonathan rising abruptly from his chair. "I've had enough of this nonsense. I can bear it no longer," he said, following Dona and leaving the disappointed artist to watch his good fortune walk out of the room. In the end, there never was a painting done of Jonathan, and Adair was forced to settle for a charcoal drawing that was subsequently framed under glass and kept in the study. What Adair didn't know was that Jonathan was to be the last of his favorites to be immortalized in a portrait, that all of Adair's peculiarities and schemes were about to be upended completely.

FORTY-ONE

After the success of the first night, Adair took Jonathan with him everywhere. Besides the usual evening diversions, he began finding things for the two of them to do together, leaving the rest of us on our own. Adair and Jonathan went to horse-racing meets in the country, dinners and debates at a gentlemen's club, and attended lectures at Harvard College. I heard Adair took Jonathan to the most exclusive brothel in the city, where they picked a half dozen girls to attend to them both. The orgy seemed a sort of ritual meant to bind the two together, like a blood oath. Adair impatiently introduced Jonathan to all his favorite things: he piled novels on the nightstand beside Jonathan's bed (the same ones he'd had me read when he'd taken me under his wing), had special meals prepared for him. There was even talk of going back to the old country so Jonathan could experience the great cities. It was as though Adair was determined to create a history for the two of them to share. He would make his life Jonathan's. It was frightening to watch, but it did distract Jonathan. He hadn't spoken of his fears for his family and the town since we left, though it had to be on his mind. Perhaps he was doing me a kindness by not speaking of it, since there was nothing we could do to change our situation.

It was after a little time had passed in this way, the two men spending much of their time in each other's company, when Adair pulled me aside. The household was lounging in the sunroom, the three others teaching Jonathan the intricacies of betting in faro, Adair and I sitting on a divan watching like a contented father and mother admiring their brood at harmonious play.

"Now that I've been in the company of your Jonathan, I've come to form an opinion of him . . . Would you care to know what that is?" Adair said to me in a low voice so he wouldn't be overheard. His gaze did not leave Jonathan as he spoke. "He's not the man you think he is."

"How do you know what I think of him?" I tried to sound confident but could not keep the quaver out of my voice.

"I know you think someday he will come to his senses and devote himself entirely to you," he said sarcastically, indicating how little he cared for the idea.

Forsaking all others . . . Hadn't Jonathan already vowed as much to one woman, for all the good it did? He probably hadn't remained faithful to Evangeline for a month after they were wed. I settled a curdled smile on my lips; I wouldn't give Adair the satisfaction of knowing he'd wounded me.

Adair shifted his weight on the divan, insouciantly crossing one leg over the other. "You shouldn't take his inconstancy to heart. He's not capable of such love, not for any woman. He's not capable of putting anyone else's needs before his own wants and desires. For instance, he told me it troubles him that he makes you so unhappy—"

I dug my fingernails hard into the back of one hand, but there was no pain to divert me.

"—but he is at a loss as to what to do about it. Whereas, to most men, the remedy would be obvious: either give the woman what she desires or break off with her entirely. But he still craves your company and so he cannot be done with you." He sighed, a bit theatrically. "Do not despair. All hope is not lost. The day may come when he will be capable of loving one person, and there is a chance, however slight, that that person may be you." And then he laughed.

I longed to slap him. To throw myself on top of Adair, circle his neck with my two hands, and throttle the life out of him.

"You are angry with me, I can feel it." My impotent anger seemed to amuse him, too. "Angry with me for telling you the truth."

"I'm angry with you," I replied, "but it's because you're lying to me. You're trying to crush my feelings for Jonathan."

"I've managed to make you quite upset, haven't I? Granted, I'll allow that you can usually tell when I'm lying—and you're the only one who seems to have that skill, my dear—but I'm not lying to you this time. I almost wish I was lying. Then you would not be so hurt, would you?"

It was too much to bear, being pitied by Adair at the same moment he was trying to turn me against Jonathan. I looked over at Jonathan as he peered over his cards to the pot in the middle of the table, absorbed in the faro game. I'd begun to find Jonathan's presence a great comfort, like a resonant hum within me. Of late, though, I'd noticed a melancholy undercurrent from Jonathan, which I'd assumed was sadness for having left Evangeline and his daughter. If what Adair said was indeed true, might he not be melancholy for the unhappiness he caused me? It made me wonder for the first time if the obstacle to our love—the defect, as it were—lay with Jonathan and not me. For it seemed almost inhuman to be unable to give yourself over wholly to one person.

A trill of feminine laughter interrupted my thoughts, as Tilde threw down her cards in victory. Jonathan flashed a look back at her, and in that look, I knew that he had slept with her already. Slept with Tilde though he didn't find her particularly alluring, though he knew to be wary of her, though he knew if I found out, I would be devastated. Despair lit up in me like flash paper, despair for what I was helpless to change.

"Such a waste." Adair was at my ear instantaneously, like the serpent in the Garden. "You, Lanore, are capable of such a perfect love, a love like nothing I have ever seen. And why you choose to waste it on someone as unworthy as Jonathan . . ."

His whisper was like perfume on the night air. "What are you saying? Are you offering yourself up as a more worthy object of my love?" I asked, searching for the answer in his wolfish eyes.

"Would that you could love me, Lanore. If you really knew me, you would see I am unworthy of your love. But one day, perhaps you will look on me as you look on Jonathan, with the same favor? Impossible, it would seem, given your devotion to him, but who knows? I've seen the impossible happen, every once in a great long while," he said slyly, but when I tried to ask him to explain himself, he merely wrinkled his nose and laughed. Then he rose from the divan and called to be dealt in on the next round of faro.

Ignored, I went into the study to find a book with which to divert myself. As I passed Adair's desk, the light from my candle fell across a sheaf of papers left on the blotter and my eye went as though by magic to Jonathan's name, written in Adair's hand.

Why in the world would Adair be writing about Jonathan? A letter to a friend? I doubted he had a friend in the world. I held the pages closer to the candle.

Instructions for Pinnerly (the solicitor's name, I'd learned).

Account to be established for Jacob Moore (Jonathan's false name) *with the Bank of England in the sum of eight thousand pounds* (a fortune) *transferred from the account of* . . . (a name I did not recognize).

The instructions called for several other accounts to be set up in Jonathan's false name, drawn from the accounts of other strangers in Amsterdam, Paris, and St. Petersburg. I read it over twice more but could make no sense of it, and left the page as I'd found it on the table.

It appeared Adair was so smitten with Jonathan that he was taking steps to provide for him, as though adopting him. I admit I was slightly jealous and wondered if a fund had been set up for me somewhere. What would be the point, if Adair had never told me as much? I had to wheedle and beg him for spending money, as did the others. It seemed only another sign that Adair had taken a special interest in Jonathan.

Jonathan seemed to accept his new life. At least, he didn't object to being made to share Adair's indulgences and vices, and he didn't bring up St. Andrew. There was only one vice Adair hadn't shared with his new favorite yet, one that Jonathan would not decline if it were offered. That vice was Uzra.

Jonathan had been living with us for three weeks when he was introduced to her. Adair asked Jonathan to wait in the drawing room, as I clung jealously to his side, and then Adair brought Uzra in with a flourish, the odalisque dressed in her usual swath of winding cloth. When he released her hand, the fabric dropped to the floor to reveal Uzra in her glory. Adair even had her dance for Jonathan, swaying her hips and twisting her arms as Adair sang an improvised tune. Afterward, he had the hookah brought down and we reclined on cushions thrown on the floor, taking turns sucking on the carved ivory mouthpiece.

"She's lovely, isn't she? So lovely that I haven't been able to part with her. Not that she hasn't been trouble: she's a devil. Thrown herself out windows and off rooftops. Thinks nothing of giving me fits. Still burns with hatred for me." He traced a finger down her nose, despite the fact that she looked as though she'd bite that finger off if given the chance. "I suppose that's what's kept her interesting to me over the years. Let me tell you how Uzra came to be with me." At the mention of her name, Uzra tensed visibly.

"I met Uzra on a trip to the Moorish states," Adair started, unaffected by Uzra's distress. "I was in the company of a noble who was negotiating for the freedom of his brother, who had foolishly tried to steal some treasure from one of their leaders. I had by that time a fair reputation as a warrior. I had fifty years' experience with the sword, more than most men. I had been bought, as it were, to help this nobleman, my loyalty paid for in coin. That was how I came to be in the East and stumble upon Uzra.

"It was in a large city, in the marketplace; she was following behind her father, and draped as custom demanded. All I could see of her were her eyes, but that was enough: I knew I had to see more. So I followed them to their encampment on the outskirts of the city. Speaking to some of the men tending the camels, I learned that the father was the leader of a nomadic tribe and that the family was in the city so that she could be given to some sultan, some indolent prince, in exchange for her father's life."

Poor Uzra was completely still now. She had even stopped drawing on the hookah. Adair wrapped a tendril of her fiery hair around a finger, gave it a tug as though reprimanding her for her aloofness, then let it fall.

"I found her tent where she was attended by a dozen women servants. They formed a circle around her, and thinking she was hidden from view, helped her out of her robes, slipped the fabric from her cinnamon skin and unfurled her hair, their hands fluttering all over her body . . . Chaos broke out when I burst into the tent," Adair said with a throaty laugh. "The women screamed, ran, fell over each other trying to protect themselves from me. How could they think I would settle for one of them when this mesmerizing jinn stood naked before me? And Uzra knew I'd come for her, from the look in her eye. She barely had time to cover herself with a robe before I swooped down on her and carried her away.

"I took her to a place in the desert where I knew no one would find us. I took her over and over that night, heedless of her crying," he said, as though he had nothing to be ashamed of, as though he had as much right to her as he had to water to slake his thirst. "The sun came up the next morning before my delirium started to subside and I was sated with her beauty. In between our pleasures, I asked her why she was being given to the sultan. It was because her tribe held a superstition about a jinn with green eyes who would bring pestilence and suffering. They were fearful, the idiots, and they petitioned the sultan. The father was ordered to hand her over or be killed himself. You see, to break the curse she had to die.

"I knew that I was not the first man she had been with, so I asked who had taken her virginity. A brother? A male relative, no doubt—who else would be able to get close to her? It turned out to have been her father. Can you believe that?" he asked, incredulous, snorting as though it was the most ridiculous thing he had ever heard. "He was the chief, a patriarch used to having his way. But by Uzra's fifth birthday, he could tell by the girl's coloring that he was not her father. The mother had been unfaithful and, by the green of the child's eyes, had consorted with a foreigner. He said nothing, merely took the mother out into the desert one day and returned without her. By Uzra's twelfth birthday, she had taken her mother's place in his bed; he told her that she was the daughter of a whore and no blood relation to him, so it was not forbidden. She was to tell no one. The servants thought it charming that the girl was so affectionately disposed toward her father that she could not bear to be apart from him.

"I told her none of it mattered. I was not going to give her to that superstitious sultan. Nor would I send her back to her father so he could force himself on her one last time before handing her over, like a coward." Over the course of Adair's story, I had managed to take Uzra's hand and squeezed it, from time to time, to let her know I commiserated with her, but I saw in her dead green eyes that she had taken herself to another place, away from his cruelty. Jonathan, too, was quietly embarrassed for her. Adair continued, heedless of the fact that he was the only one enjoying his tale. "I decided to save her life. Just like the others. I told her that her long ordeal was over. She was to start a new life with me and she would stay with me forever."

Once the opium had had its effect on Adair and he'd fallen asleep, Jonathan and I crept away. "Good God, Lanny, what am I to make of that story? Please tell me he was being fanciful, that he was exaggerating . . ."

"It's odd . . . he said he saved her life, 'just like the others.' But she's not like the others, not from the story he just told."

"How so?"

"He's told me a bit about how the others came to be with him, Alejandro, Tilde, and Dona. They had done horrible things before Adair met them." We slipped into Jonathan's room, which was next to Adair's but smaller, though it did have a good-size dressing room and a view of the garden. And a door that led straight into Adair's chamber. "I think that's why he picked them, because they're capable of doing the bad things he requires. I think that's what he looks for in a companion. A failing."

We shed a few layers of clothing to get more comfortable before lying on the bed, side by side, and Jonathan draped an arm protectively over my waist. The opium was affecting us, too, and I was on the verge of falling asleep. "It makes no sense . . . Why would he choose you, then?" Jonathan asked drowsily. "You've never hurt anyone in your life."

If ever there was an opportune time to bring up Sophia and how I'd driven her to suicide, this was it. I even drew in a breath to ready myself but . . . once again, I could not. Jonathan thought me innocent enough to question my place here. He thought me incapable of evil and I couldn't spoil that.

And, perhaps as telling, he didn't ask why he had been selected, what Adair saw in him. Jonathan knew enough about himself to believe something evil lurked within, something deserving of punishment. Maybe I knew it, too. We were both failed, in our way, and chosen for a punishment that we deserved.

"I meant to tell you," Jonathan muttered, sleepy, eyes already closed. "I will be going on a trip with Adair soon. He told me he wished to take me somewhere . . . I forget where, exactly. Perhaps Philadelphia . . . though after that story I can't say I'm looking forward to going anywhere alone with him . . ."

As I pulled his arm tight against me, I noticed through the thin gauze of his shirt a mark on his arm. There was something sickeningly familiar about the dark mottles veiled by his sleeve, so I pulled the loose garment back to see thin black lines incised on his inner arm.

"Where did you get this?" I asked, sitting up in alarm. "It was Tilde, wasn't it; she did this with her needles?"

Jonathan barely opened his eyes. "Yes, yes . . . the other evening, when we'd been out drinking . . ."

I studied it closely; it was not the heraldic shield, but two spheres with long, fiery tails, interlocked like two fingers hooked together. It might have been different from the one I bore, but I'd seen it before— adorning Adair's back.

"It's the same as Adair's," I managed to say.

"Yes, I know . . . He insisted I wear it. To signify that we are broth- ers, or some such nonsense. I did it only to end his badgering."

Touching my thumb to the tattoo, I felt a coldness ripple through me; that Adair had put his mark on Jonathan signified something, but I could not figure out what that might be. I wanted to beg him not to go away with Adair, to disobey him . . . but I knew the inevitable out- come of that folly. So I said nothing and lay awake a long time listen- ing to the steady, peaceful rhythm of Jonathan's breathing, unable to shake the premonition that our time together was coming to an end.

FORTY-TWO

L uke wakes to the sound of human misery. He is disoriented, as he always is when waking from a nap, and his first thought is that he has overslept and is late for his shift at the hospital. It isn't until he nearly knocks the alarm clock—never mind that it's not ringing—off the nightstand with a wild grope that he realizes he's in a hotel and there is only one person with him, and that person is crying.

The door to the bathroom is closed. Luke knocks gently and, when there is no answer, pushes the door back. Lanny sits hunched in the bathtub, fully clothed. When she looks over her shoulder at him, Luke sees that her eye makeup is streaked down her face in black daggers, like a frightening clown in a movie.

"Hey, you okay?" he asks, reaching for her hand. "What are you doing in here?"

She lets him help her out of the bathtub. "I didn't want to wake you."

"That's what I'm here for." He leads her to the bed and lets her curl up in his arms like a child. "I'm sorry . . . I'm just starting . . . to realize . . . ," she says in ragged bursts between sobs.

"That he's gone," Luke finishes for her so she can continue crying. It makes sense; up until now she has been concentrating on getting away, not being discovered. Now the escape is behind her, the adrenaline subsides, and she remembers how she got here, that she now has to deal with the fact that the most important person in her life is gone.

He thinks of the many times he walked past someone crying in the hall at the hospital, someone who had just been given bad news, a woman hiding her face in her hands and a man standing beside her, numb and struggling. Luke cannot count the times he's stepped out of the operating room, pulling off his gloves and mask, shaking his head as he walks to the waiting spouse, stony in the face of her stubborn expectation of good news. He learned to build a wall between himself and the patients and the next of kin; you couldn't let yourself be drawn into their pain. You could nod your head and share their sorrow, but only for a moment. If you tried to take on their burdens, you wouldn't last a year on the hospital floor.

This girl shaking in his arms, her sorrow is endless. She will fall in her pit of grief for a long time, tumbling down with no way to stop. He supposes there is a formula for how long it takes for the pain to lift, but it's probably tied to how long you've known the deceased. Of course, there is no relief coming for her. How long will it take for Lanny to tolerate the daily pain of Jonathan's absence, let alone live with the fact that she was the one who dispatched him? People have become unhinged over less, carried away by sadness. There's no guarantee of surviving something like this.

He's going to help her. He has to. He thinks he's uniquely equipped for this situation. With his training ("Mrs. Parker? We did everything we could for your son, but I'm afraid . . .") he hopes her sorrow will shed off him like water off Teflon.

She's eased up on her crying and is rubbing her eyes with the back of her hand.

"Better?" Luke asks, lifting her chin. "Want to go out and get some air?" She nods.

Within fifteen minutes they're walking hand in hand into the dusky horizon. Lanny has scrubbed her face clean. She leans into Luke's arm like a girl in love, but on her face is the saddest smile the world has ever seen.

"How about a drink?" he asks. They step off the street into a dark bar and he orders scotch straight up for both of them. "I'll be able to drink you under the table," she warns him and they clink glasses as though they are celebrating. And sure enough, after one shot, Luke feels the warmth that comes at the beginning of drunkenness, but Lanny has had three shots and has only a half-tipsy smile.

"There's something I want to ask you. It's about—him," he says, as though by not speaking the name, the question will hurt less. "After everything he put you through, how could you keep loving him? It doesn't sound like he deserved you . . ."

She picks up her empty shot glass by the rim, like a chess piece. "I could make all kinds of excuses, like how that's the way it was back then, that wives expected their men to fool around. Or that it was just the kind of man Jonathan was and I had to accept it. But that's not the real reason . . . I don't know how to explain it. I've always wanted him to love me the way I loved him. He did love me, I know he did. Just not the way I wanted him to.

"And it's not so different for a lot of people I've known. One partner doesn't love the other enough to stop drinking, or gambling, or running around with other women. One is the giver and one is the taker. The giver wishes the taker would stop."

"But the taker never changes," Luke says, though he wonders if this is always the case.

"Sometimes the giver has to let go, but sometimes you don't. You can't. I couldn't give up on Jonathan. I seemed to be able to forgive him anything."

Luke sees the ocean well up in her eyes and tries to distract her. "What about Adair? From what you've said, it seems that he could have been in love with you . . . ?"

"His love is like the love fire has for wood." She laughs ruefully. "He confused me for a while, I'll give you that. One minute he was charming me, the next minute he'd humiliate me. It was all games and tricks with him. I think . . . he just wanted to see if he could make me love him. Because, I think, no one had ever loved him." She becomes still, hands knotted in her lap, and the glassy surface of her eyes ruptures. "Look what you've done . . . I'm going to start crying again. I don't want to cry in public. I don't want to embarrass you. Let's go back to the hotel room. We can smoke some pot." Luke's face lights up, remembering the big plastic bag, the resinous high. "I'm prepared to smoke that entire bag with you, if that's what it takes to cheer you up."

"My hero," she says as she tucks her arm under his. They weave up the street toward the hotel, a brisk wind slapping their faces. Luke wishes he could give Lanny a shot of morphine to dull her pain. He'd give her a tranquilizer injection to bring her peace daily, if he could. He clears his mind with a shake of his head. He feels like he'd do anything to make her happy again, but he doesn't want to become the valet to her misery.

"What was it about me . . . will you tell me the truth? Am I unworthy of being loved?" she blurts out once they are in bed.

Her question takes Luke aback. "I can't tell you why Jonathan didn't love you back, but for what it's worth, I think he made a huge mistake." Jonathan was an idiot; only a fool would squander such devotion, Luke thinks.

Her look at him is disbelieving, but she smiles. And then she falls asleep. He pulls her against him, wrapping his arms around her sylphlike body, gathering up her elegantly splayed limbs. He can't recall feeling like this, except for that miserable time in the pizza parlor with his daughters, when he wanted to bundle them into his rental car and take them back to Maine. He knows he made the right choice by not giving in to his sadness then—the girls are better off with their mother—but he will be haunted forever by the act of driving away from them. Only a fool squanders such love.

And Lanny. He is willing to do anything to protect this vulnerable woman, to fix her. He wishes he could draw the poison out of her, like a leech with blood. He would take it on himself, if he could, but knows all he can do is be with her.

FORTY-THREE

BOSTON, 1819

An ashy light tugged at my eyelids, waking me from sleep one evening. Uzra appeared next to my bed, a small oil lamp swaying in her hand. It must have been very late, for Adair's house was still as a crypt. Her eyes implored me to get out of bed, so I did.

She glided out of the room in her usual silent way, leaving me to follow behind her. The sound of my slippered feet on the carpets was scarcely a whisper, but in that quiet house, the sound echoed down the halls. Uzra shielded the lamp as we walked past the other bedchambers so we threw as little light as possible, and we were undiscovered by the time we reached the stairs to the attic.

The attic was divided into two sections, one made into the servants' quarters and a smaller, unfinished space for storage. This was the area where Uzra hid. She led me through a maze of trunks that acted as her barrier against the world, and then down an impossibly narrow corridor to a diminutive door. We had to crouch and twist to fit through the door and emerged inside what looked like a whale's belly: rafters for the ribs, a brick chimney instead of a windpipe. Moonlight seeped in from uncovered windows, allowing views onto the un-adorned path to the carriage house. She chose to live in this hollow space to get away from Adair. It was a sad place to live, too hot in the summer and too cold in the winter, and lonely as the moon.

We passed what I assumed was her nest, curtained off by the iri-descent winding sheets of organza she wore as sarongs, hung from the rafters like laundry on a line. The bed itself was made of two blankets from the parlor, twisted together in a circular pattern, not unlike a bed made by a wild animal, frenzied and makeshift. A heap of trin-kets was piled next to the bed, diamonds the size of grapes, a veil of thin gold mesh to wear with a chador. But there was also bric-a-brac, things a child might covet: a cold, lovely dagger, a memento from her birthplace, its serpentine blade like a snake in motion; a bronze hand mirror.

She brought me to a wall, a dead end. Where I saw nothing, though, she dropped to her knees and pried a pair of boards away, re-vealing a crawl space. Taking the oil lamp, she plunged fearlessly into the darkness like a rat used to tunneling between walls. I took a deep breath and followed.

After traveling on hands and knees for about twenty feet, we emerged in a windowless room. Uzra held up the lamp so I could see where we were: it was a small finished space, part of the servants' suite, with a tiny fireplace and a door. I went to the door and tried it, but it was held fast by some means on the outside. The room was dominated by a large table covered with bottles and jars and an array of odds and ends. There was a hutch, and it, too, was stocked with containers of all sizes and shapes, most covered with waxed cloth or stoppered with cork. Baskets tucked under the table were filled with everything from pinecones and branches to inscrutable parts of vari-ous animals' bodies. A few books, ancient and crumbly, were tucked between the jars. Candles stood on plates on the edge of the table.

I inhaled deeply: the room held close myriad smells, spices and forest and dust, and others I couldn't identify. I stood in the center of the space and looked around, slowly. I think I knew immediately what the room was and what its existence meant, but I didn't want to admit it.

I took one of the books down from its shelf. The cover was stretched blue linen embellished with handwritten letters and intricate diagrams of symbols within symbols. Turning the heavy pages, I saw there wasn't a printed page in the entire book: every bit was done in a careful script, annotated with formulas and illustrations—the proper bit of a plant to keep, for instance, or an ornate dissection of a man's internal workings—but all in a language I didn't recognize. The drawings were more telling, for I recognized some of the symbols from childhood as well as from the books in Adair's libraries—pentagrams, the all-seeing eye, that sort of thing. The book was a wondrous piece of work, the product of hundreds of hours of labor, and it reeked of years spent hidden, of secrets and intrigue, and had undoubtedly been coveted by other men, but its contents were a mystery to me.

The second book was older still, with wooden slabs for covers, laced together with a leather thong. Inside, the pages were loose, not stitched together, and by the variety of the papers it seemed to be a collection of notes rather than a tome. The writing appeared to be in Adair's hand, but again in a language I didn't know.

Uzra shifted, restless, shaking the tiny bells on the chain around her ankle. She didn't like being in this room and I didn't blame her. Adair had locked it from the outside for a reason: he didn't want anyone to stumble across it. But as I reached up to return the second book to its place, Uzra stepped forward and grabbed my wrist. She held the lantern close to my arm and when she saw the tattoo—that I'd long since forgotten—she let out a moan like a dying cat.

She thrust her arm under my nose, palm turned up. She bore the same tattoo on the identical place, a slightly larger version but executed more crudely, as though the artist's hand was not as sure as Tilde's. Her look was accusatory, as though I had done this to myself, and yet there was no mistaking her meaning. Adair had chosen to brand us in the same way. His intentions for me could not be far from his treatment of her.

Holding the lantern high, I took in the contents of the room one more time. A description I had heard from Adair's own lips came back to me—that of the room within the physic's keep that had been the prison of his youth. There was only one reason he would need a room like this and hide it away in the farthermost corner of the house. I understood what this place was and why he kept it, and a chilly wave passed through me. The woeful tale Adair had spun of his capture and indentured servitude to the evil physic came rushing back to me. Only . . . now I wondered which of the two men I had been with, these many months; who was the man whose bed I had taken and, indeed, had given the life of the man who meant most to me in the world? Adair wanted his followers to believe that he was a wronged peasant boy who had vindicated himself and was merely enjoying the reward of having deposed a cruel and inhuman tyrant. When in fact, inside that handsome youth was the monster from the story, the collector of power and the despoiler of lives, able to move from body to body. He'd left his own decrepit husk behind, sacrificed it to the villagers—no doubt—with the peasant boy trapped inside, as he spent his last minutes in terror, paying for the physic's cruelties. This lie worked well with his monstrous design and appeared to have hidden him for hundreds of years. Now that the truth was known to me, the question was, what would I do?

It was well and good to suspect Adair's deceit, but I needed proof: to drive home the horrible truth to myself if to no one else. With Uzra tugging at my sleeve to leave, I snatched a page out of one of the ancient books and took a handful of some botanical from one of the dusty jars standing on the table. There could be a terrible penance to pay for stealing these things—I had heard the story from Adair's own lips, hadn't I, the one that ended with a poker wrapped in a blanket and a shower of blows—but I had to know.

*   *   *

I started with a trip to visit a professor at Harvard College who I had met at one of Adair's parties. Not just any afternoon tea party or salon to fete intellectuals; no, I'd met this man at one of Adair's parties of a special variety. I tracked down his office in Wheydon Hall, but he was with a student. When he saw I was waiting in the hall, he dismissed the young man and came out to fetch me, the most charming smile on his devilish old face. Perhaps he was half afraid I'd come to blackmail him, since the last time I'd seen him, he was astride a rent boy even younger than his students and crowing proudly. Or perhaps he was hoping I was delivering an invitation to another party.

"My dear, what brings you here today?" he said, patting my hand as he led me into his office. "I am so seldom blessed with visits from fair young ladies. And how is our mutual friend, the count? I trust he is in good health?"

"As fine as ever," I said truthfully.

"And to what do I owe this happy visit? Perhaps word of another soirée . . . ?" His eyes glinted with the sharpest of hungers, his appetite whetted from too many afternoons gazing over fields of fresh young boys.

"I was hoping I might impose on you for a favor," I said, reaching into my drawstring purse for the page I'd stolen. The paper itself was unlike any other I'd seen, thick and coarse and nearly as brown as butcher's wrap, and now that it was freed from the press of its wooden cover, had begun to curl into a scroll.

"Hmm?" he said, clearly surprised. But he accepted the paper from my hand and brought it close to his face, lifting his eyeglasses to inspect it. "Where did you get this, my dear?"

"From a bookseller," I lied. "A private bookseller who claims to have a trove of ancient books on a subject dear to Adair's heart. I thought I might purchase the books as a present for Adair, but the language is unreadable to me. I wished to verify that the book is as the dealer claims. You can never be too careful."

"No, you cannot," he muttered as he examined the page. "Well, the paper is not of local manufacture. Not bleached. Possibly made by an individual for his own use, as it were. But it is the language you came to me about, isn't it?" He smiled modestly over his spectacles; he was a professor of ancient languages, that much I'd remembered from our fleeting introduction at that party. Exactly what languages, I couldn't recall.

"Prussian, I would think. Similar, at least. Very odd, possibly an archaic form of the language. I've not seen the likes of it before." He reached back to a shelf and pulled down a fat, heavy book and began flipping through its onionskin pages.

"Can you tell me what is being talked about? The subject?"

"What do you *expect* it to be about?" he asked curiously, still flipping pages.

I cleared my throat. "Magic. Of some kind."

He stopped what he was doing and stared at me.

"Alchemy?" I said, more weakly this time. "Something to do with transforming one thing into another?"

"Oh, my dear, it is most certainly about something magical, possibly a spell or incantation of some sort. Exactly what, I can't tell you. Maybe if you left this with me for a few days . . . ?" His smile was coy. I knew enough of the work of scholars to suspect what he might do with this paper left in his care: he might try to stake a career on it, using it as the basis for this or that study, and I'd never see it again. Or, worse yet, if Adair were to find out that it was missing, given over to our randy professor friend, well . . . to say it would go badly for me was an understatement. He lifted an eyebrow in expectation, but I leaned over his desk and snatched the paper back.

"No, I couldn't, but thank you for your kind offer. What you've told me is sufficient," I said, leaping from the chair and opening the door. "And please, do me the favor of not mentioning this to Adair if you should see him? When it comes to gifts, he is a difficult man to please. I do want to surprise him with the books." The old professor looked faintly surprised himself as I bolted from his office.

*   *   *

Next, I went in search of a midwife.

She was hard to find. They were becoming scarcer in cities such as Boston; physicians had almost taken over the job of delivering babies, at least for those who could afford them. Nor was I looking for just any midwife. I needed one like those you'd find in the country, one who knew all about curing and healing with plants and such. The ones who, a hundred years earlier in this very same town, might have been called witches by their neighbors and met their deaths pressed beneath the board or hanged.

Street whores told me where to find the midwife, since she was the only help the prostitutes could afford to cure their clap or help with unwanted pregnancies. I felt a shiver run down my back when I crossed the threshold of this woman's tiny room: it smelled of dust and pollen and old things kept close to rotting, not unlike the secret locked room in Adair's attic.

"Sit down, dearie, and tell my why you've come," she said, motioning to a stool on the other side of the hearth. She was an older woman with a hard, pragmatic cast at the center of her gaze, but an expression of understanding on her face.

"I need to know what this is, ma'am. Have you ever seen it before?" I took a handkerchief from my purse and opened it for her to see. The pinch of botanical I'd stolen had been roughed up in transit, separating into tiny stems and slivers of brittle, broken brown leaves. She held a leaf up to her eye, then crushed it between her fingers and sniffed.

"That is neem, my dear. Used for a great variety of illnesses. Not exactly common in these parts, though, and in this natural state, rarer still. Mostly you see it in tinctures and the like, watered down to its most diluted to make it go as far as possible. How'd you come across it?" she asked, matter-of-factly, as though she might be in the market to purchase some. Perhaps she thought that was why I'd sought her out. She dusted her hands over the fire and let the fragments of leaf fall into the flame.

"I'm afraid I cannot tell you," I said as I pressed a coin into her hand. She shrugged but accepted it, tucking the money into her pocket. "Here is my second request. I have need of an item . . . I need you to fix something to bring on a very heavy sleep. Not necessarily a peaceful one. It must render the person unconscious as quickly as possible."

The midwife gave me a long, silent look, wondering perhaps if I really meant that I wished to poison someone, for how else could you interpret that request? At last, she said, "It can't be coming back to me, if the authorities are called into this matter for some reason."

"You have my word." I put five more coins into her hand, a small fortune. She looked from the coins to me, then closed her fingers around the gold.

In the carriage on the ride back to the mansion, I sat and peeled back the handkerchief from the lump the midwife had given me. The lump was stony hard and white, and though I didn't know it at the time, deadly white phosphorus, probably purchased from a matchstick maker, who in turn had stolen it from her place of employment. The midwife had treated it gingerly, as though she didn't like to handle it, and instructed me to grind it in a mortar and mix it in some wine or spirits, adding laudanum to help the concoction go down. "It's very important to dilute it for medicinal effects. You could use laudanum alone, but it takes a while to be effective. Phos will do the trick quickly, but . . . if a body was to take this amount of phosphorus, the result would be bad indeed," she said with an unmistakable look in her eye.

I'd already settled on a plan, a very dangerous plan, but as I took my leave, I could think only of the true Adair. My mind was full of pity for the unfortunate peasant boy, without even a grave because there was no corpse to give back to the earth. His handsome form was the possession of the man who had overtaken his body through the dark arts.

As for the last bits of the physic's story—well, it was beyond me to know how much was true. Maybe he'd visited Adair's family and left a tribute out of guilt or in thanks for giving him their son, for handing over such a fine body. Or maybe that part was a lie, told to make the story palatable and tragic, to influence the listener's heart in his favor, to deflect suspicion. And the loss of his kingdom? A calculated risk . . . but maybe it was worth it, in the end, to gain a fine new vessel to hold his miserable old soul. But if I didn't stop this terrible man, he would take the dearest thing in the world from me—Jonathan.

Handsome, strong, and able, with a fearsome manhood, the peasant's body must have seemed like a godsend to the physic. But here in the new world, the peasant's body had its limitations. Or rather, the limitations were with the face: it was disconcertingly exotic, olive toned, framed by wild, wiry hair. I saw it in the expressions of the Brahmins when they met Adair, by the wrinkle to their brows, mistrust flitting across their eyes. Here, among descendants of the British, Dutch, and Germans, who had never seen a Turk or an Arab and for whom the hair was not unlike that of their slaves, the peasant's body was a liability. Now I understood Adair's cold, appraising eye as he studied the beautiful but clubfooted scholar Tilde had fetched, and his hungry appreciation for Jonathan's flawless beauty. He'd sent his hellhounds out into the world scouting for the perfect vessel; he even had Jude scouring the countryside for a replacement. But here in Boston, time had run out for Adair and he needed a new body, one that would be amenable to the tastes of the masters of this new environment.

He wanted Jonathan. He wanted to slip on Jonathan like a disguise. People were drawn to Jonathan like bees to sugar, dizzy and powerless with this unknowable attraction. Men wanted to befriend him, orbit him like planets around the sun. Women gave themselves up to him wholly—and none knew this better than I. They would forever crowd around him, open themselves up to him, not realizing that the spirit inside was evil and waiting to exploit them.

And because no one knew Adair's secret, there was no one to stop him. No one except me.

FORTY-FOUR

I arrived at the mansion to find the household in an uproar. The servants were scurrying down the stairs like water rushing downhill, down to the cellar, hiding in storerooms, away from the ruckus coming from above. Fists pounded on doors, latches rattled. The muffled voices of Tilde, Dona, and Alejandro echoed from overhead.

"Adair, what is going on?"

"Let us in!"

I ran up the stairs to find the three huddled helplessly at the foot of the attic stairs, unwilling to interrupt whatever was happening beyond the closed door. We heard terrible noises: Uzra crying out, Adair roaring in response. We heard the flat sound of flesh striking flesh.

"What's this about?" I demanded, whirling on Alejandro.

"Adair went looking for Uzra, that's all I know."

I thought of Adair's story—the physic's fury over things stolen from his table. "We must go up there! He's hurting her." I reached for the doorknob, but it refused to budge. He'd locked the door. "Get an ax, a sledgehammer, anything. We must break this door down," I shouted but they only looked at me as though I'd lost my senses. "You don't understand what he's capable of—"

Then the sounds ceased.

After a few minutes, the key turned in the lock and Adair emerged, pale as milk. Uzra's serpentine blade was in his hand and his cuff was stained bright red. He dropped the knife to the floor and pushed by us, retreating to his room. It was only then that we found her body.

"You had something to do with this, didn't you?" Tilde said to me. "I can see the guilt on your face." I didn't answer. Looking down on Uzra's body, my stomach lurched. He had stabbed her in the chest, and also slit her throat, and that must have been the last thing he did because she'd fallen to the ground with her head thrown back, some hair still twisted where he had held it in his fist. The words "by my hand and intent" echoed in my mind—the same words that had given her eternal life had been uttered again to take it away. Thinking of them now sent a shudder through me, as did spying the tattoo on her arm, thrown carelessly to her side. In the end, his mark upon her body meant nothing. He would retract his troth when it pleased him.

The fight could have been about anything and I would never know for sure, but the timing made it unlikely that it could be about anything other than the secret room. Somehow, Adair must have discovered that things had been taken, and blamed her. And she hadn't disabused him of his assumption. She had either wanted to protect me or—very likely—welcomed this, her best chance at release through death.

I had taken those things knowing what the penalty might be. I just didn't think it would lead back to Uzra. Nor did I think he would kill any of us, least of all her. It was far more in his character to deal out a brutal physical punishment and to keep his victim within his grasp, shivering in terror, wondering when Adair might decide to do it all over again. Never in a million years did I dream he would actually kill her, because I thought that, in his way, he loved her.

I dropped to the floor and held her hand, but it had gone cold already, the soul perhaps fleeing the body more quickly in our cases, so eager for release. The terrible thing was that I had been planning my escape, mine and Jonathan's, but hadn't given a thought to taking Uzra with us. Even though I knew how desperately she wanted to flee, it hadn't entered my mind to help this poor girl who had borne Adair's sick obsession for many years, who had been so kind to me and had tried to help me navigate this house of wolves. I had taken her for granted, and the cold recognition of my selfishness made me wonder if I wasn't Adair's soul mate for sure.

Jonathan had followed the commotion upstairs and, on seeing Uzra's body on the floor, wanted to burst into Adair's chamber and have it out with him. It took both me and Dona to restrain him. "To what end?" I shouted at Jonathan. "You and Adair could pummel each other from here to the end of time and never settle it. However much you might wish to kill each other, it's not within the power of either of you." How I wanted to tell him the truth—that Adair wasn't who we thought he was, that he was far more powerful and dangerous and remorseless than any of us could know—but I could not risk it. I was afraid as it was that Adair would intuit my fear.

Besides, I could not tell Jonathan my true suspicion. I knew it all, now. Those soft looks Adair gave my Jonathan, it wasn't because Adair was planning to bed him. The covetousness he had for Jonathan ran much deeper. Adair wanted to touch that body, to fondle and stroke, to know every dip and bulge and crook not because he wanted to swive Jonathan, but because he wanted to possess him. Possess that perfect body and be known by that perfect face. He was ready to inhabit a body that truly could not be resisted.

Adair sent out instructions: we were to clear out the fireplace in the kitchen and set up a bier. The scullery girl and the cook fled as we commandeered the kitchen, and Dona, Alejandro, and I took the cooking things from the hearth of the huge fireplace. We scrubbed its blackened walls and swept out the ash. The bier was made of wooden

trestles laid with wide planks and we built a pyre in the space between the trestles, dry twigs and pinecones slathered with beef tallow
for kindling, compacted straw and cured firewood for fuel. The body,
wrapped in a white linen shroud, was laid on the planks.

A torch was put to the kindling, which lit easily enough. The logs
took some time to catch and it was almost an hour before it had built
into a great leaping bonfire. The heat in the kitchen was tremendous.
Finally, the body caught fire, the shroud consumed rapidly, the fire
dancing across it in streaks, the fabric curling like skin, black ash
catching on the draft and spiriting up the chimney. The smell, alien
and innately frightening, made everyone in the house restless. Only
Adair could bear it, and he sank into an armchair pulled before the
fireplace and watched the fire devour Uzra in stages: her hair, her
clothing, then the skin of her downy arm before biting into the flesh.
Finally, the body, heavy with moisture, began to sizzle and roast, and
the smell of burning flesh filled the house.

"Imagine the stink rising over the house, out in the street. Does he
not think the neighbors will smell it?" Tilde said tartly, eyes watering.

We huddled in the doorway to the kitchen, but eventually Dona
and Tilde slinked off to their rooms, muttering darkly, while Alejandro and I remained outside the door to the kitchen, sunk to the floor,
watching Adair.

By the time the sky outside started to lighten, the fire had burned
itself out. The house now was filled with a thin gray smoke, which
hung in the air, its perfume the acrid smell of wood ash. Only when
the hearth was cool did Adair rise from his chair, touching Alejandro
on the shoulder as he passed. "Have the ashes swept up, and scatter
them on the water," he commanded in a hollow voice.

Alejandro insisted on doing this himself, crouching inside the
still warm firebox with a small willow broom and dustpan. "So much
ash," he murmured, oblivious to my presence. "All that wood, I suppose. Uzra herself cannot account for more than a handful." At that
moment, the brush touched something solid and he reached down,

searching among the silt. He found a charred nugget, a piece of bone. "Should I save this? For Adair? Someday he may be glad to have it. Such things make powerful talismans," he mused, turning it over like a rare specimen. But then he dropped it in the pail. "I suppose not."

Adair withdrew from the rest of us after that. He stayed in his room and the only visitor he would receive was the solicitor, Mr. Pinnerly, who rushed in the following day with a profusion of papers exploding from his overstuffed satchel. He emerged an hour later, his face as red as though he'd run a country mile. I intercepted him by the door, proclaiming concern for his flushed complexion and offering to fetch him something cool to drink.

"Most kind," he said as he gulped down some lemonade, mopping his forehead. "I'm afraid I cannot stay long. Your master has rather high expectations of what a mere lawyer is capable of accomplishing. It's not as though I can command time and make it dance to my tune," he harrumphed, then noticed the papers threatening to fly out of his satchel and attended to tucking them in place.

"Oh, really? He *is* the demanding sort, but I daresay you seem clever enough to be able to pull off whatever task Adair has set before you," I said, flattering him shamelessly. "So, tell me, what miracle does he expect of you?"

"A series of complicated transfers of money, involving European banks, some in cities I've never heard of before," he said, then seemed to think better of admitting any shortcoming to a member of his client's household. "Oh, it's nothing, pay me no mind. I am merely frazzled, my dear. It shall be done just as requested. Never you worry your pretty head about such matters." He patted my hand in such a patronizing manner that I wished to slap his hand away. But that would not get me what I wanted to know.

"Is that all? Moving money around? I would think a clever man like you would be able to do such a thing with just your little finger." I punctuated my words with an obscene little gesture that involved my own pinkie finger and an insinuation of the mouth, a gesture I had seen made by rent boys that sent an unmistakable message to most men and was certain to capture his attention. Which it did. Discretion seemed to run out of his ears like sawdust from a ruptured child's toy and he gazed at me with his jaw dropped open. If he didn't already suspect this was a household of bum-licking harlots, he knew for sure at that moment.

"My dear, did you just—"

"What else did Adair ask of you? Nothing, I'm sure, that will keep you busy far into the night. Nothing that would keep you from, say, entertaining a visitor . . ."

"Tickets on tomorrow's coach for Philadelphia," he said, hastily, "which I told him was quite impossible. And so I am to rent him a private livery . . ."

"For tomorrow!" I exclaimed. "He is leaving so soon."

"And not taking you with him, my dear. No. Have you ever been to Philadelphia? It is an extraordinary city, much more lively in its way than Boston and not the sort of place that, say, *Mrs. Pinnerly* would be apt to visit. Perhaps I could show it to you—"

"Wait! How do you know I'm not to travel with him? Did he tell you?"

The solicitor grinned at me most salubriously. "Now, don't fret. It's not as though he's running off with another woman. He's going with a man, the happy beneficiary of all these damned money transfers. If your master were to consult me, I would advise him to simply adopt this fellow, for it would be easier in the long run—"

"Jonathan?" I asked, wanting to shake the lawyer by the shoulders to get him to stop his prattling, to pull the name from his mouth like a reticent snail from its shell. "Jacob, I mean. Jacob Moore?"

"Yes, that's the name. Do you know him? He's going to be a very wealthy man, I can tell you that. If you don't mind my saying this to you, perhaps you should consider setting your sights on this Mr. Moore before word gets around . . . umm . . ." With his assumptions of my intentions, Pinnerly had painted himself into a corner and I enjoyed watching him try to extricate himself. He cleared his throat. "That is not to say that I imagine for one second that you . . . and the count's benefactor . . . I apologize. I believe I've overstepped the bounds of my position."

I clasped my hands demurely. "I think you have."

He handed me his glass and picked up his satchel. "Please believe me when I say I spoke in jest, miss. I trust you shan't be going back to the count with any mention of . . . um . . ."

"Your indiscretion? No, Mr. Pinnerly. I am nothing if not discreet."

He hesitated. "And I suppose the question of a midnight visit . . . ?"

I shook my head. "Is out of the question."

He gave me a strangled look, torn between regret and longing, and then sped out of the peculiar house of his most bizarre client, happy (I'm sure) to leave us behind.

It seemed that staggering sums of money were being transferred to accounts in Jonathan's name and the fateful trip to Philadelphia would begin tomorrow. Adair was ready to make his move, which meant that time had run out for me—and Jonathan. I had to act now or spend the rest of eternity in regret.

I went to Edgar, the head butler, the one entrusted with overseeing the other servants and running affairs for the house. Edgar had a suspicious and larcenous heart, like everyone else who found a place in this household, from master through the servants, which is to say he could be depended on not to do his job very well, but only to the minimum degree necessary. It is a terrible trait in a servant if you wish to have a well-run household, but the perfect attitude for one in a house where convention and scruples have been flung out the door.

"Edgar," I said, folding my hands primly before me like the proper lady of the house. "There is a repair needed in the wine cellar that Adair would like attended to in his absence. Please send someone to the mason's and have a wheelbarrow of stones and a wheelbarrow of brick delivered to the basement this afternoon. I've already hired a man to do the job once the count has left on his trip." When Edgar looked at me slyly—the wine cellar had been a crumbling mess the entire time we'd been in the mansion, why the rush now?—I added, "And you needn't trouble Adair about it; he's getting ready for his trip. He's entrusted me with this matter in his absence, and I expect to see it done." I could be high-handed with the servants; Edgar knew better than to cross me. With that, I turned and strode away, to put the next step of my plan in play.

FORTY-FIVE

The next morning, the household was consumed with preparations for Adair's trip. He had spent the morning picking out the clothing he would take with him and then sent the servants to pack for him and load the rented livery. Jonathan had shut himself up in his room, where he was also supposedly packing for the trip, but I sensed that he couldn't bring himself to go and that a fight loomed.

I hid in the pantry with the cook's mortar and methodically ground the phosphorus into dust. As I laid out the things I needed, I was as nervous as I had ever been, sure that Adair would pick up on my emotions and be forewarned. In truth, I didn't know the extent of his powers, if they could truly be called powers. I'd made it this far, though, and had no choice but to gamble with my life and Jonathan's by going the rest of the way.

The house by then was still and it might have been my imagination, but seemed to be tense with unspoken emotions: abandonment, resentment, lingering anger with Adair for what he'd done to Uzra, uncertainty about what lay ahead for all of us. Carrying a tray with the doctored wine, I went past the shut bedroom doors to Adair's room, which had been quiet for the hour since the servants had carted the trunks away. I knocked once and, not waiting for an answer, pushed the door back and slipped inside.

Adair sat in a chair he'd pulled close to the fire, which was unusual in itself as he usually reclined on a bower of cushions. Maybe he sat more formally because he was fully dressed for travel, that is to say, like a proper gentleman of the time and not bare chested as was his habit. He sat stiffly in the armchair in breeches and boots, a waistcoat and high-collared shirt, bound at the neck with a silk cravat, his frock coat hanging over the back of a second chair. His suit was made of dark gray wool with very little embroidery or trim, far more sedate than his usual attire. He wore no periwig, but had brushed his hair back and had it tied trimly. His expression was of sadness, as though he was forced to go on this trip under pressure and that it was not of his own design. He lifted his hand and it was then I noticed the hookah set up next to him, and that the room smelled of sweet opium smoke of the strongest variety. He drew on the mouthpiece, cheeks sucked in, his eyes half closed.

I put the tray on a table near the door and crouched on the floor next to him, gently lacing my fingers into the stray curls on his forehead, brushing them away. "I thought we might spend a minute together before you go. I've brought something to drink."

He slowly opened his eyes. "I'm glad you're here. I've been meaning to explain about this trip to you. You're probably wondering why I'm going with Jonathan and not you." I quashed the urge to tell him I already knew, but waited for him to go on. "I know you can hardly bear to be separated from Jonathan, but I'll take him away from you for only a few days," he said mockingly. "Jonathan will return, but I am going to do some traveling on my own. I may be gone for a while . . . I feel the need to be by myself. This need comes over me from time to time . . . to be alone with my thoughts and my memories."

"How can you leave me like this? Won't you miss me?" I asked, trying to sound coquettish.

He nodded. "Yes, I shall, but it can't be helped. That's why Jonathan is coming with me, so I can explain a few things to him. He will run the household while I am gone. He told me of his duties running his family's business and keeping his neighbors' debts from bankrupting the town; managing one household's accounts should be easy for him. I've had all the money transferred to his name. He will be the one with the authority; you and the others will have no choice but to follow his orders."

It almost sounded plausible and I wondered, for a second, if I had misjudged the situation. But I knew Adair far too well to believe that things were as simple as he made them out to be. "Let me get you a drink," I said, rising to my feet.

I'd selected a heavy brandy, strong enough to mask the taste of the phosphorus. Down in the pantry, I'd carefully poured the powder into the bottle with a paper sleeve, added most of a small bottle of laudanum, corked the mouth, and swished the liquid around gently. The powder had released a few white sparks into the air as I handled it, and I prayed that it would not make itself apparent by sparkling with the residue glowing faintly in the bottom of Adair's glass.

As I poured the concoction now for Adair, I noticed on the dresser a few things laid out, presumably for the trip. There was a scroll of paper tied with a piece of ribbon, the paper old and rough, and I was sure it came from the collection bound between wooden covers in the hidden room. Next to it was a snuffbox and a small flacon, similar to the sort used for perfume, holding about an ounce of a brackish brown liquid.

"Here." I handed a full goblet to Adair. I'd poured a glass for myself, though I had no intention of drinking the entire amount. Just a sip to convince him that nothing was amiss. He seemed heavily sotted by the opium, though I knew the opium alone didn't have the strength to put him to sleep.

I resumed my place near his feet and looked up with what I hoped could be taken for adoration and concern. "You've been upset for days now. It's because of the trouble with Uzra. Don't protest; it's only right that you're upset by what happened, you'd kept her with you for hundreds of years. She *had* to mean something to you." He sighed and let me help him to the mouthpiece again; yes, he was eager for distraction. He seemed ill, slow moving and bloated. Perhaps he was suffering for having killed the odalisque, or perhaps he was afraid of abandoning this body for the next; it had been a long time since he'd done it last, after all. Maybe it was painful to go through. Maybe he was afraid of the consequences for another bad deed, added to the long list of sins he'd already committed, a list for which he would be held accountable someday.

After a couple more puffs, he regarded me through slitted eyes. "Are you afraid of me?"

"For killing Uzra? You have your reasons. It's not for me to question. That's how it is here. You are the master."

He closed his eyes and resettled his head against the high back of the chair. "You have always been the most reasonable one, Lanore. They are impossible to live with, the others. Accusing me with their eyes. They're cold, they hide from me. I should kill the lot of them and start over." By the tone of his voice I could tell it wasn't an idle threat; once upon a time he'd done that very thing to another group of his minions. Wiped them out in a fury. For having a life that would supposedly last an eternity, it was a precarious existence.

I had to keep from shaking as I continued to stroke his forehead. "What had she done to deserve her punishment? Do you want to tell me?"

He pushed my hand aside and sucked again on the mouthpiece. I fetched the bottle and poured another glass for him. I let him stroke my face clumsily with his murdering hands and continued to soothe his conscience with insincere assurances that he was within his rights to have killed the odalisque.

At one point, he took my hand from his temple and began stroking my wrist, tracing my veins. "How would you like to take Uzra's place?" he asked, a bit anxiously.

The notion rattled me, but I tried not to let him see. "Me? I don't deserve you . . . I'm not beautiful like Uzra. I could never give you what she gave you."

"You can give me something she would not. She never gave in to me, never. She despised me every day we were together. From you I sense . . . we have had happy moments together, haven't we? I would almost say there were times you loved me." He put his mouth to my wrist, his fire to my pulse. "I would make it easier for you to love me, if you agree. You would be mine alone. I wouldn't share you with anybody. What do you say?"

He continued to pet my wrist while I tried to think of a response that would not sound false. Eventually, he answered for me. "It's Jonathan, isn't it. I can feel it in your heart. You want to be available for Jonathan, if he should want you. I want you, and you want Jonathan. Well . . . there may yet be a way to make this work, Lanore. There may be a way to get us both what we want." It seemed a confession to all I suspected, and the very idea made my blood freeze.

Adair's keen ability to select damaged souls would be his undoing. You see, he had chosen me well. He had picked me from the masses, known I was the sort of person who, without hesitation, could pour drink after poisonous drink for a man who had just professed love for her. Who knows, perhaps if I had been by myself, if only my future were at stake, I might have chosen differently. But Adair had made Jonathan part of his design. Maybe Adair thought I would be happy, that I was shallow enough to love him and stay with him as long as I had Jonathan's beautiful shell to admire. But Adair's murderous self would be behind my beloved's familiar face and would echo in his every word, and at the thought of that, what else could I do?

He dropped my arm, let the hookah slide from his hand. Adair was slowing, a windup toy that had spent its spring. I could wait no longer. For what I was prepared to do to the man, I had to know. I had to be absolutely certain. I leaned very close to ask, "You are the physic, aren't you? The man you told me about?"

He seemed to need a moment to make sense of my words but then didn't react angrily at all. Instead, a slow smile spread over his lips. "So clever, my Lanore. You have always been the cleverest one, I saw that right away. You were the only one who could tell when I was lying . . . You found the elixir. You found the seal, too . . . oh yes, I knew. I smelled a trace of you on the velvet . . . In all the time I have been alive, you are the first to solve my puzzle, to correctly read the clues. You found me out—as I knew you would."

He was barely lucid and didn't seem to know I was there. I leaned over him now, my hands grasping him by the lapels of his waistcoat, and had to give him a shake to get his attention. "Adair, tell me—what do you plan to do with Jonathan? You're going to take possession of his body, aren't you? That's what you did to your peasant boy, the boy who was your servant, and now you're going to take Jonathan. That is your plan?"

His eyes popped open and that chilling gaze of his settled on me, nearly breaking my composure. "If this were possible . . . if such a thing were to happen . . . you would hate me, Lanore, would you not? And yet I would be no different from the man you have known, the man for whom you have felt affection. You have loved me, Lanore. I have felt it."

"That's true," I said to him, to assure him.

"You would have me still and you would have Jonathan, too. But without his indecisiveness. Without his carelessness for your feelings, without the hurt and selfishness and regret. I would love you, Lanore, and you would be certain of my feelings. That is something you cannot have with Jonathan. That is something you will never get from him." His words jolted me because I knew them to be true. As it turned out, his words were also prophetic; it was like a curse Adair placed on me, dooming me to unhappiness forever.

"I know I shan't. And yet . . . ," I murmured, still stroking his face, trying to gauge his wakefulness. It didn't seem that a body could ingest so much poison and remain conscious.

"And yet, it's Jonathan I choose," I said, finally.

At those words, Adair's glazed eyes lit up with only the faintest spark of recognition deep within them, recognition of what I'd just said. Recognition that something terrible was happening to him, that he was unable to move. His body was shutting down, even though he fought it, struggling in his chair like a stroke victim, spastic and tremulous, drool starting to drip from the corners of his mouth in bubbled threads. I leaped to my feet and stood back, avoiding his hands as they jabbed the air for me—and failed, then froze, then went limp. He grew still suddenly, still as death and gray as clouded water, and tumbled out of the chair onto the floor.

It was time for the final step. Everything had been laid in place earlier, but I couldn't do this part alone. I needed Jonathan. I sprang out of the room and ran down the hall to Jonathan's chamber, bursting in without knocking. He was pacing, but seemed prepared to go out, cloak over his arm and hat in hand.

"Jonathan," I gasped, pressing the door closed, blocking his way.

"Where have you been?" he asked, an angry edge to his voice. "I looked for you but couldn't find you . . . I waited, hoping you would come to me, until I couldn't stand it any longer. I am going to tell him I have no intention of traveling with him. I'm going to tell him that I am breaking with him and then I'm going to leave."

"Wait—I need you, Jonathan. To help me." As angry as Jonathan was, he saw that I was upset and put his things aside to listen to me. I poured out the story, sure that I sounded like a madwoman because I hadn't the time to think of a way to tell him without seeming delusional or paranoid. And inwardly I cringed, because now he would see me for what I was; capable of cunning evil, able to condemn someone to terrible suffering—still the same girl who had sent Sophia to kill herself, cruel and unyielding as steel, even after everything I myself had been through. Surely, Jonathan would denounce me. I expected him to walk out on me, that I would lose him forever.

When I'd told him the entire tale, of how Adair had planned to extinguish his soul and usurp his body, I held my breath, waiting for Jonathan to dismiss me or lash out, for him to call me a madwoman, waiting for the swing of the cape and the slam of the door. But he didn't.

He took my hand and I felt a bond between us that I hadn't known in a while. "You saved me, Lanny. Again," he said, his voice cracking.

Upon seeing Adair on the floor, still as the dead, Jonathan recoiled momentarily, but then he joined me in binding Adair as securely as we could. We tied the monster's hands behind his back, bound his ankles together, and gagged him with a soft cloth. However, when Jonathan went to lash the knots at Adair's wrists to his feet, bowing our prisoner backward in a position of utter vulnerability, I recalled the inhuman harness. The feeling of helplessness came crushing down upon me and I could not do the same to Adair, even though he was my tormentor. Who knew how long he might remain bound like that, before he was found and freed? It seemed too cruel a punishment, even for him.

We then wrapped Adair in his favorite sable blanket, a solitary comfort. I slipped out first so Jonathan, if he ran into one of the others and was questioned, could pass off the bundle in his arms as me. And we planned to meet in the cellar to see my plan to its end.

I rushed ahead, taking the servants' staircase to the cellar. As I waited at the foot of the stairs, resting against the cold stone wall, I worried for Jonathan. I'd let him take all the risk of spiriting Adair out of the room. Though the others had withdrawn, shell-shocked by Uzra's death and the confusion of Adair's departure, it was by no means assured that Jonathan would not cross paths with one of them. He could easily be spied by a servant as well, and one glimpse could undo our plan. I waited tensely until Jonathan appeared with the limp form in his arms. "Did anyone see you?" I asked, to which he shook his head.

I led him through the twisting labyrinth to the very lowest level of the cellar, to the cavelike room where the wine was stored. Here, the cellar was most like a castle's dungeon, sequestered from the rest of the basement rooms, thickly lined with earth and stone to keep the temperature constant for the wine. I'd found a niche in the very back, a tiny windowless cell cut into the mansion's massive stone foundation. It appeared to be an unfinished extension of the wine room, with bricks and wood lying about. Yesterday's deliveries of bricks and stone were piled on the floor along with a bucket of mortar draped with a moistened cloth, nearly dry now. Jonathan looked at the supplies and then at me, surmising instantly the intent of the materials, and then dumped Adair's body on the damp dirt floor. Without a word, he stripped off his frock coat and rolled up his sleeves.

I kept Jonathan company as he closed up the small gap that served as the opening to the cell. First brick, then row upon row of stone to make the opening disappear into the deep-set wall. Jonathan set about his task silently, settling the stones into place with taps of the trowel's handle, drawing on work he had done in childhood, while I kept watch on Adair's dark form, a mere lump of shadow on the cell's floor.

At the hour when Adair had been scheduled to leave, I crept upstairs and sent the livery on its way, telling the driver that the travelers had changed their minds, but wanted the baggage sent ahead to their lodgings as planned. Then I mentioned casually to Edgar that the master had departed on his trip a little ahead of schedule in order to avoid fanfare, wanting to slip away. Adair's and Jonathan's empty rooms seemingly verified what I'd said, and Edgar merely shrugged and went about his duties and would, I suspected, tell the others if asked.

Jonathan continued to work, pausing whenever we heard any movement that sounded like it was coming our way. For the most part, it was exceedingly quiet this deep underground and we heard few stirrings from the occupied floors, but it was unlikely that we would, with storage rooms situated between the first floor and the wine cellar. Still, I was nervous, sure that the others might come looking for me. And I wanted this horrible act behind me. *The man in the cell is a monster*, I kept telling myself to ease my mounting guilt. *He is not the man I knew.*

"Hurry, please," I murmured from my perch on an old cask.

"There's nothing to be done for it, Lanny," Jonathan said over his shoulder, never breaking his rhythm. "Your poisons—"

"Not *mine*, surely! Not mine alone," I cried, jumping off the cask in agitation.

"*The* poison will wear off, eventually. The knots may loosen and the gag come undone, but this wall must not fail. It must be as strong as we can make it."

"Very well," I said, wringing my hands as I paced. I knew that the potion couldn't kill him, even if it had been poison, but hoped that it might make him sleep forever or have caused damage to his brain, so he'd never be aware of what had happened to him. Because he was not a magical being, not a demon or an angel; he could not make the knots untie themselves or fly through walls like a ghost any more than I could. Which meant that eventually he would wake in the dark and not be able to take the gag from his mouth, not be able to scream for help, and who knew how long he might remain there, buried alive.

I waited a moment on our side of the fresh stone wall to see if I felt the familiar electric arc of Adair's presence, but I did not. It was gone. Perhaps it was gone only because Adair was so deeply sedated. Maybe I'd feel him again when he regained consciousness—and what torture that might be, to feel his agony alive in me day after day and not be able to do anything about it. I cannot tell you how many nights I've thought about what I did to Adair, and there have been times when I almost think I would undo what I did to him, if it were possible. But at that time, I could not let myself think about it. It was too late for pity or remorse.

Jonathan slipped out that evening while the others were away at one of their usual pastimes. I had a taste of the struggles that were to come with Jonathan when, once he had stepped outside, he turned to me and asked, "We can return to St. Andrew now, can't we?"

I drew in a breath. "St. Andrew is the last place we can go because there, of all places, we will be most quickly discovered. We'll never grow old, never fall ill. All those people you'd return for, they'll come to look at you with horror. They'll come to fear you. Is that what you want? How would we explain ourselves? We can't, and Pastor Gilbert will have us tried as witches for sure."

His expression clouded over as he listened, but he said nothing.

"We need to disappear. We must go where no one knows us and we must be prepared to leave at any time. You must trust me, Jonathan. You must rely on me. We have only each other, now." He made no argument but kissed my cheek, and started toward the public house where we planned to meet the following day.

The next morning, I told the others that I was leaving to join Adair and Jonathan in Philadelphia. When Tilde raised an eyebrow suspiciously, I used Adair's own words on her, explaining that he had no patience with their accusatory glances for what he'd done to Uzra and that while they might not be able to forgive him, I had. Then I went to see Pinnerly for the list of the accounts that had been set up in Jonathan's name. While the lawyer was reluctant to hand Adair's private papers over to me, a session of no more than ten minutes on my knees in his back room was sufficient to get him to change his mind, and what was ten more minutes of harlotry in exchange for a secure financial future? Jonathan would forgive me, I was sure, and in any case, Jonathan would never know.

The others said nothing outright against me but were clearly skeptical and wary, and gathered in corners and on dark landings to whisper among themselves. Eventually, though, they drifted off to their rooms or about other business, clearing the way for me to creep down to the study. Jonathan and I needed money to flee, at least until we could gain access to the funds that Adair himself had set aside—for his own future use, of course.

To my surprise, Alejandro sat slumped over the table, his head in his hands. He watched indifferently, however, as I socked money from Adair's cash box into a pouch; it would be only natural that I might carry more funds to Adair to use for his trip. But Alejandro cocked his head in curiosity when I pulled the framed charcoal drawing of Jonathan down from the wall. It was the one item I couldn't bear to leave behind. I pried the backing from the frame and, with a piece of tissue over the drawing and a chamois beneath it, I rolled the picture into a tight cylinder and tied it with a red silk cord.

"Why are you taking the drawing?" he asked.

"There's a painter in Philadelphia; Adair plans to introduce him to Jonathan. Jonathan will never agree to sit for his portrait again, and Adair knows it, so he wants the artist to create a painting from the sketch. It seems like a lot of bother, I agree, but you know how Adair is, once he's decided on something . . . ," I said blithely.

"He's never done anything like this," Alejandro said, abandoning his questioning with the despair of one accepting the inevitable. "It's very—unexpected. It is very strange. I'm at a loss to know what to do next."

"All things come to an end," I remarked before slipping out of the study nonchalantly.

I waited in the carriage as servants brought down my trunks, securing them to the back. Then the carriage pulled away with a lurch, and I slipped into the Boston traffic, disappearing completely into the crowds.

PART IV

FORTY-SIX

QUEBEC CITY, PRESENT DAY

They sit at the table in the hotel room, Luke and Lanny, a coffee service of elegant white porcelain spread before them with a plate of croissants, untouched. Four packs of cigarettes, ordered along with the rest of the room service, rest in a silver bowl.

Luke takes another sip of coffee, heavy with cream. Last night was rough, with the drinking and smoking pot, and while the fatigue shows on his face, Lanny's visage reveals nothing except pert, soft, smooth skin. And sadness.

"I suppose you've tried to learn about this spell," Luke says at some length. His question brings a bemused sparkle to Lanny's face.

"Of course I did. It's not easy to find an alchemist, a real one. Every town I went to, I looked for the dark ones, you know, people with a dark inclination. And they are in every town, some out in the open, some driven underground." She shakes her head. "In Zurich, I found a shop on a narrow back street just off the main thoroughfare. It sold rare artifacts, ancient skulls with inscriptions chiseled into the bone, scripts bound in human skin and filled with words no longer understood. I thought if anyone would know the necromancer's true art, it would be the people who owned this shop, who put their lives into tracking down arcane magic. But they only knew rumor. It came to nothing.

"It wasn't until this century, about fifty years ago, that I finally heard something with the slightest ring of truth to it. It was in Rome, at a dinner party. I met a professor, a historian. His specialty was the Renaissance, but his personal avocation was alchemy. When I asked if he'd heard of a potion to confer immortality, he explained that a true alchemist wouldn't need a potion for immortality because the real purpose of alchemy was to transform the *man*, to bring him into a higher state of being. Like the supposed quest to turn base metal into gold; he said that was an allegory, that they sought to turn base *man* into a purer being." She slides her cup away an inch or two, the saucer pushing a minute wake ahead of it in the white damask. "I was frustrated, as you can imagine. But then he went on to say that he had heard of a rare potion with a similar effect to what I'd described. It was supposed to turn an object into an alchemist's—well, *familiar* is the best term, I think. To bring an inanimate object to life, like a golem, to make it the alchemist's servant. The potion could reanimate the dead, bring them back to life, too.

"This professor assumed the spirit that filled the dead person or the object came from the demon world," she says, crackling with self-loathing. "A demon meant to do someone's bidding. That was all I could bear to hear. I haven't gone looking for explanations since then."

They sit quietly and watch the traffic a dozen flights below them. The morning sun is starting to break through clouds, setting the cutlery and silver bowl on fire. Everything is white and silver and glass, clean and sterile, and everything they have been talking about—darkness, death—seems a million miles away.

Luke picks up a cigarette, rolls it between two fingers before putting it aside, unlit. "So you left Adair walled in the mansion. Did you ever go back to see if he got out?"

"I worried about him escaping, of course," she says, nodding almost imperceptibly. "The feeling, our connection, was gone, though. I had nothing to go on. I went back once, twice—I was afraid of what I'd find, you know—to see if the house was still standing. It was. For the longest time it was used as a home. I'd circle the block, trying to feel Adair's presence. Nothing. Then one time I went back and saw that it had been made into a funeral home, if you can believe it. The neighborhood had fallen on hard times . . . I could picture the rooms where they'd work on the bodies, in the basement, steps away from where Adair was entombed. The uncertainty was too much . . ." Lanny tamps out the spent cigarette in her hand and immediately lights another. "So I had my lawyer contact the funeral home with an offer to buy it. As I said, there was a recession; it was a better price than the owners hoped to see in their lifetime . . . They accepted.

"As soon as they moved out, I went in by myself. It was hard to imagine as the house I had known, so much had been changed. The part of the cellar under the front stairs had been updated. Cement floor, furnace, and hot water heaters. But the back half had been left alone. No electricity ran back there. It was left dark and damp.

"I went to the spot where—we'd put Adair. You couldn't tell where the original wall left off and where the part Jonathan built began. It had all aged together by then. Still, no feeling from behind the stone. No presence. I didn't know what to think. I was almost tempted—almost—to have the wall torn down. It's like that perverse voice in your head that tells you to jump off the balcony when you get too close to the edge." She smiles ruefully. "I didn't, of course. As a matter of fact, I had the wall reinforced with rebar and cement. Had to be careful; I didn't want the wall to be damaged during the construction. It's sealed good and tight now. I sleep much better." But she doesn't sleep well; Luke has learned this much in the short time they've been together.

He needs to lead her away from the place he has left her, the dark cellar with the man she condemned. Luke reaches across the table and takes her hand. "Your story . . . it's not finished yet, is it? So you and Jonathan left Adair's house together—what happened next?"

Lanny seems to ignore the question for a moment, studying the nub of the cigarette in her hand. "We remained together for a few more years. At first, we stayed together because it was, ostensibly, the best thing to do. We could look out for each other, watch each other's back, as it were. Those were adventurous times. We traveled constantly because we had to, because we didn't know how to survive. We learned to create new identities for ourselves, how to become anonymous— though it was hard for Jonathan not to attract attention. People were always drawn to his great beauty. But then it became more and more apparent that we remained together because it was what I wanted. An ersatz marriage, only without intimacy. We were like an old couple in a loveless pact, and I'd forced Jonathan into the role of the philandering husband."

"He didn't have to stray," Luke objects.

"It was in his nature. And the women who were interested in him—it was relentless." She knocks ash into the saucer they are using for an ashtray. "We were both miserable. It got to the point where it was painful to be in each other's presence; we had wronged each other so, and said hurtful things to each other. Sometimes I hated him and wished he would just go. I knew he would have to be the one to leave because I would never have the strength to leave him.

"Then one day, I woke up to find a note on the pillow beside me." She smiles ironically, as though used to watching her pain from a distance. "He wrote, 'Forgive me. This is for the best. Promise me you won't come looking for me. If I change my mind, I will find you. Please honor my wish. Your dearest, J.'"

She pauses, crushing the cigarette in the saucer. Her expression is stark and faintly amused as she stares out the tall windows. "He finally found the courage to go. It was as if he'd read my mind. Of course, his leaving was agony. I wanted to die, sure that I would never see him again. But we go on, don't we? Anyway, I had no choice, but it helps to pretend that you do."

Luke remembers how it feels to be exhausted by tension, recalls those days when he and Tricia couldn't stand to be in the same room. When he'd sit in the dark and try to imagine how it would feel if they split up, the peace that would come over him. There was no question that she'd be the one to leave—he couldn't be expected to walk away from his children or his childhood home—but when his family had left and it was just him in the farmhouse, it wasn't like being alone at all. It was as though something had been violently taken away from him, as though a piece of him had been amputated.

He gives her a moment to fold up her pain and tuck it back in its place. "But it wasn't over, was it? Obviously, you saw each other again."

Her expression is inscrutable, light and dark. "Yes, we did."

FORTY-SEVEN

Gray day. I peeked from behind the curtains at the thin sliver of sky visible from the third story of my home, one in a series of ancient row houses in the fifth arrondissement. It was the start of winter in Paris, which meant that almost every day would be gray.

I turned on my computer, then stood by the desk and stirred cream into my coffee while the computer started up. I find the series of whirs and clicks subliminally comforting, like the chirping of birds or some other sign of life external to mine. I cherish normalcy and long for as much routine as I can cram into what is otherwise a free-form existence.

I sipped the coffee. Though I don't really need it the way some people do to pull them into consciousness, I drink it out of habit. I'd barely been asleep, a catnap really; I'd been up until the wee hours as usual, dutifully doing research needed for the book I had been contracted to write but which now bored me to impatience. Then, tiring of that, I resumed cataloging my ceramics collection while watching reruns of American television. I had gotten to the point of thinking

I'd send my ceramics collection off to a university or an art museum, someplace where it would be seen. I'd gotten tired of having so much clutter around all the time, pulling at me like hands clawing from the grave. I felt the need to shed a few things.

My email finished loading and I glanced down the list of the senders' addresses. Business, mostly: my lawyer, my editor at the wonky small press that had published my precious monographs on ancient Asian ceramics, an invitation to a party. What a life I'd made for myself over the past twenty years as a faux expert on Chinese teacups. My false identity was based on a collection of priceless cups my Chinese employer had pressed into my arms as I boarded a British ship to escape the ransacking nationalists. This had happened in *The Jade Pagoda* days, another lifetime ago, another story no one knew.

Then I noticed, in the list of emails, an address I didn't recognize. From Zaire—oh, only it's called the Democratic Republic of Congo now. I could remember when it was the Belgian Congo. I frowned to myself; did I know anyone in Zaire? It was probably a plea for charity or a scam, a con artist claiming to be an African prince who just needed a bit of help out of a temporary pecuniary dilemma. I almost deleted it without opening it but at the last minute changed my mind.

"Dear Lanny"—it read—"Hello from the one person you thought you'd never hear from again. First, let me thank you for honoring my last request by not trying to track me down at any point since we parted . . ."

Damn innocent words, written in flickering pixels on the screen. *Print*, I jabbed at the clicker on the mouse. *Print, damn you, I need to hold these words in my hands.*

". . . I hope you'll forgive me for imposing on you like this. For all its convenience, I've never gotten over the feeling that correspondence by email is somehow less polite and correct than writing a letter. I find using the telephone difficult for the same reason. But I'm pressed for time, so I had to resort to email. I will be in Paris in a few days and would like very much to see you while I am there. I hope your schedule will allow for this. Please write back and let me know if you will see me . . . Fondly, Jonathan."

I scrambled into the seat quickly, fingers poised over the keys. What to say? So much bottled up inside after decades of silence. Of wanting to speak and having no one to speak to. Of talking to the walls, to the heavens, to the pigeons, to the gargoyles clinging to the spires of Notre Dame Cathedral. *Thank God—I thought I'd never hear from you again. I'm sorry. I'm sorry. Does this mean you've forgiven me? I've been waiting for you. You can't imagine how it feels to see your name on my computer screen. Have you forgiven me?*

I hesitated, clenched my hands into two tight fists, shook them, unfurled them, shook them again. Hovered over the keyboard. Finally, typed "Yes."

Waiting for that day to arrive was tortuous. I tried to keep a tight rein on my expectations. I knew better than to get my hopes up, but there was still a small part of me that harbored romantic dreams where Jonathan was concerned. It was impossible not to indulge in a daydream or two, just to feel joy like that again. It had been so long since I'd had anything to look forward to.

Jonathan told me about his life in his second email. He'd picked up a medical degree in the 1930s in Germany, and used it to travel to poor and remote places to deliver medical services. When one had suspect paperwork, it was easier to get past the authorities in isolated areas where a doctor was needed and harried government officials could push your case through. He'd worked with lepers in the Asian Pacific, smallpox victims in the subcontinent. A hemorrhagic fever outbreak took him to central Africa and he had remained to run the medical clinic in a refugee camp near the Rwandan border. It's not open-heart surgery, he'd typed: gunshot wounds, dysentery, and measles vaccinations. Whatever is needed.

What could I say in response, other than to confirm the time and place we were to meet? It thrilled and unsettled me to think Jonathan was a doctor, an angel of mercy. But Jonathan was waiting for me to tell him about my life, and as I sat before the computer I couldn't think what to write. What could I say that wasn't embarrassing? Life had been difficult after we'd parted. I'd done stupid things, which I believed at the time to be necessary for my survival. Now, finally, my life was peaceful, almost a nun's life and not entirely out of choice. But I had come to terms with it.

Jonathan would notice my omission, but I assured myself that he wouldn't harbor any illusion that I'd changed in our time apart—at least not as dramatically as he had. Instead, my first email to Jonathan was full of pleasantries: how I was looking forward to seeing him and the like.

I couldn't sleep at all the night before and sat up, looking into a mirror. Would I look different to him? I examined my reflection fastidiously, worried that there had been changes, as though I was like the women in commercials fretting over laugh lines and crow's-feet. But there were no changes, I knew. I still looked like a college student with a permanently cross expression. I had the same smooth face that Jonathan had looked on the day he left. I still had the smolder of a young woman who could not get enough sex, even if in truth I'd had enough sex to last my multiple lifetimes. I didn't want to look desperate when he saw me, but there was no way to avoid it, I realized, looking into the mirror. I would always be desperate for him.

Still staring in the mirror, I wondered if it would seem strange and maddening, when we met tomorrow. To look at each other, time might as well be standing still. How long had it been since I'd last seen Jonathan? One hundred and sixty years? I couldn't even remember what year he had left me. I was surprised to find that it no longer hurt violently, that it had taken decades but the pain had eased into a dull throb, and was easily outweighed by my eagerness to see him.

I put down the mirror. It was time for a drink. I cracked open a bottle of champagne. What was the use in saving it for tomorrow in the hope that he was coming back to me? Wasn't it enough cause for celebration that Jonathan had contacted me after an eternity of separation? I resolved to nip my hope in the bud before I changed the sheets or put extra towels in the bathroom. He was coming to visit me and nothing more.

Meet me in the lobby at noon, he had instructed in his last email. I could barely wait and considered instead camping out at an earlier hour or going up to Jonathan's room. But wouldn't that be pathetic; better to pretend I could exercise self-control. So instead, I watched the hands of the clock in my study crawl to eleven o'clock before I stepped outside, hailed a taxi, and directed it to the Hotel Prix St. Germain. From the back window of the taxi, I watched my street peel away like the cartoon-painted backdrop to a carousel when the music started up.

I knew of the Hotel Prix St. Germain, but had never been there. It was a quiet place buried on an unfashionable street on the Left Bank, quite in keeping for a bush doctor in Paris for a few days. The air in the lobby was stale, and a professionally dour-looking clerk behind the front desk watched me as I took a seat in one of the leather club chairs in the lobby. Did all hotel lobbies feel like this, like a room holding its breath? The chair I had selected faced the path that ran between the door and the front desk. An ornate old clock suspended over the front door read 11:48. As a young man, Jonathan had made it a rule to keep others waiting. As a bush doctor, I imagined he'd learned to be more punctual.

A discarded morning newspaper sat on the side table. Never one to follow world events, I rarely bothered to get a newspaper these days. Events confused me, they had all become similar. I'd watch the evening news and slip into an uncomfortable feeling of déjà vu. A slaughter in Africa? Was it Rwanda? No, wait, that was 1993. Or the Belgian Congo, or Liberia? A head of state shot? A plummeting stock market? A plague, of polio, smallpox, typhus, or AIDS? I'd lived through all of it from a safe distance and watched as events ravaged and terrorized mankind. It was terrible to see the suffering, and be unable to affect anything. I was a ghost standing in the background.

I could see how it might have appealed to Jonathan to go to medical school, to equip himself to do something about the terrible things going on in the world. To roll up his sleeves and apply himself, even knowing that it would be impossible to eradicate disease, even within a single village, but trying nonetheless. Without realizing it, my eyes had fallen to the newspaper the entire time I'd been thinking.

I looked up abruptly, anticipating Jonathan's entrance.

The front door was pushed open and I leaned forward anxiously at what seemed to be a familiar shape, but relaxed again. The man was wearing wrinkled khakis and an age-worn tweed jacket. A piece of cloth in some ethnic pattern was wrapped around his neck, sunglasses were over his eyes. And his face had grown over, three or more days' worth, scruffy and uneven.

The man walked right up to me, hands in his pockets. He was smiling. Then I knew.

"Is this the welcome I'm to get? Don't you remember what I look like? Maybe I should have sent a recent picture," Jonathan said.

We went outside at Jonathan's suggestion, saying I looked faint. Jonathan took my arm right away and held it tightly as he escorted me out to the sidewalk. We found a quiet corner of a park that was all cement and park benches, only one lone tree bounded by concrete on four sides, but it gave the illusion of nature.

"It's good to see you."

I couldn't answer and my response was unnecessary anyway. It seemed absurd that he had been absent from my life this long and, seeing him again, it seemed no reason on earth should keep us apart. I wanted to touch him and kiss him, to reassure myself that he was there, in the flesh, before me. But as familiar as we were to each other, more than a hundred years of separation stood between us. And, something about his demeanor told me to proceed slowly.

Once I'd regained color, we found a café and ended up staying for hours. Over coffee and tumblers of Lillet and cigarettes (for me—though Jonathan the doctor disapproved), we sat in a booth and caught up on several lifetimes. The bush stories were fascinating and I was amazed that Jonathan could be so happy in a land as dry and sparse as Maine was cool and lush. That he could sit in a tent, patiently filling syringes without a thought to the mosquitoes buzzing around him. Malaria, West Nile, what did it matter to him? He volunteered to trek into a valley gripped by an outbreak of dengue fever. He'd carried antidiarrheals and other medicines on his back when the Land Rover couldn't cross the river. As much as I admired what he did, the stories of putting himself in danger made me uncomfortable, even though such fears were irrational.

"How did you find me, after all this time, in all the world?" I asked him, finally, dying to know. He smiled cryptically, and took another sip of his aperitif.

"It's a funny story. The short answer is technology—and luck. I'd been wanting to look you up for a long time, but struggled with this very question. How in the world could it be done? The answer began with a children's book I happened to see at a colleague's house—"

"*The Jade Pagoda,*" I guessed.

"*The Jade Pagoda,*" he answered, nodding. "Reading the book to the colleague's child, I recognized you in the drawings. With a little research, I found the artist's model—Beryl Fowles, a British expatriate living in Shanghai—"

"I always liked that name. Made it up myself."

"—and hired someone to find out what he could about Beryl. But by then, Beryl Fowles had been gone for decades."

"And yet you still found me."

"I hired an investigator to track down who had inherited Beryl's money, and so on and so on, but the trail ran cold eventually."

"But you didn't give up?"

Jonathan smiled at me again. "Here's where technology comes in. You know about the photo-recognition software they have online these days, so you can try to find photos of yourself or friends on websites? Well, I tried it on one of the pictures in the book and damn if it didn't work. It wasn't easy, and I had to be persistent, but it came up with one match, a thumbnail photograph of the author of a little monograph on ancient Chinese teacups, of all things . . . I never would have thought you'd become an expert on Chinese porcelain. Anyway, your publisher told me how to contact you."

The Chinese teacups entrusted to me by my employer in Shanghai, where I'd gone to work after posing for the children's book. And so my last great adventure in China had led Jonathan back to me.

We ended up at my home by late afternoon, the champagne drunk and a cabernet three-quarters done along with the foie gras and toast. At Jonathan's insistence, I showed him around the house, but I became more and more embarrassed with each room. I amazed even myself with the multitude of things acquired over the years, hoarded as a cushion against the relentless future. Jonathan said kind words, praised my foresight in saving rare and beautiful things for future generations, but he only meant to assuage my guilt. A bush doctor didn't travel with a freighter's worth of bric-a-brac. There was no storehouse of mementoes waiting for Jonathan's return. I came across a box I hadn't seen in nearly two decades, full of precious jewelry that had been given to me by admirers: a ring with a ruby the size of a grape; a stickpin with an heirloom blue diamond. The sight of such excess was sickening and I pushed it back in the forgotten bookcase where it had been moldering.

We came across worse: there was plunder, things I had spirited out of faraway countries during my frantic years. Surely Jonathan recognized them for what they were: beautifully carved Buddhas, handknotted rugs of twenty colors, ceremonial armor. Treasures I'd gotten in trade for long rifles or taken at gunpoint or—in some cases—stripped off the dead. All of it would go, I vowed, closing the doors to these rooms; every stick and statue would be sent off to museums, back to their native lands. How could I have lived so long with these things in my house, without even a thought to them?

The last room we toured was my bedroom on the top floor. It had the sad air of a room no longer used for its intended purpose. There was a Swedish headboard and bedstead beside a set of tall, narrow windows; the windows and the bed were draped in white cotton, an ice blue silk comforter thrown over the mattress. An eighteenth-century French secretary served as a computer table, spindly legs and all, with a Biedermeier chair pulled in front of it. The table was strewn with papers and knickknacks, a gray silk dressing gown was draped over the chair. All gave it the look of a room in which the dustcovers had only recently been pulled off the furniture, as though everything had been in waiting.

Jonathan stood in front of the picture that hung opposite the bed. The artist's name was long lost, but I remembered the day the sketch had been made. Jonathan didn't want to sit for the portrait but Adair had insisted, so he was caught leaning back churlishly in a chair, dark and moody and breathtaking. He thought he would spoil the picture but damn if it hadn't made the drawing better. We both stood in front of it, taken back nearly two centuries.

"Of all the treasures you've amassed in this house . . . I can't believe you kept this stupid drawing," Jonathan said, weakly. When he saw the stricken look on my face, he softened and took my hand. "But of course you would . . . I'm glad you did." We gave it one last look before walking out of the room.

By the time night had fallen, Jonathan was sprawled on a couch in the drawing room and I was on the floor, leaning against an armrest. We'd swapped stories for hours. I'd broken down and told him some of the past I was ashamed of: going out in search of adventure with the madman who'd taken Jonathan's place when he left me. His name was Savva and he was one of us, one of Adair's early companions, the only other one of us I'd ever run across. Savva had the misfortune of being found by Adair, centuries back, near St. Petersburg, stranded in a storm. Savva wouldn't share the details of his falling-out with Adair, but I could guess at them, for Savva had a mercurial temper and a sharp, impatient tongue.

Because Savva couldn't stand to be in any place for long, we'd roamed the continents like exiles. For a man who had been born into ice and snow, Savva was inexplicably drawn to heat and sun, which meant we spent most of our time in northern Africa and central Asia. We'd traveled with nomads across deserts, run guns through the Khyber Pass. Taught Bedouins to shoot the long rifle, even lived with the Mongols for a while (they had been impressed with Savva's extraordinary equestrian skill during the chase to hunt them down). We were together, close as brother and sister until the end of the nineteenth century. We just realized that we had nothing left to say to each other. We probably should have parted decades before, but it had been too easy being with someone who needed no explanations.

"And you." I took the opportunity to change the subject, exhausted from dredging up those memories. "Surely you haven't been alone this whole time. Did you ever marry again?"

He twisted his mouth but offered up nothing.

"Don't tell me you've been lonely all this time? That would be too sad."

"Well, I wouldn't say lonely. You're rarely alone if you're a doctor in these villages, everyone needs your attention and they're so happy that you're there . . . I was always being invited to eat with them, attend their observances. Partake of their lives." His eyes dipped closed for longer and longer instances, and a languor settled on his face. I took a lap robe and spread it over him. He opened his eyes for a brief moment.

"I'm going back to Maine. I want to see it again. That's why I looked you up, Lanny. I want you to go with me. Will you?"

I had to fight back tears at the prospect of returning home with Johnathan. "Of course I will."

FORTY-EIGHT

W e took one of those gigantic Airbus planes for the trip back to America. From New York we took a commuter plane to Bangor, then rented a sport utility vehicle to drive north. I hadn't seen this land for two centuries and, crazy as it may sound, there were stretches that seemed to have changed very little. For the rest of it, there were asphalt roads, Victorian farmhouses, immense fields of neatly tended crops, the spindly towering inchworms of irrigation pipes off on the horizon. Seen from behind the windshield of this big plush vehicle, it was easy to fool myself into thinking that I'd never been there. Then the road would cut off the farming plains, into the Great North Woods. We'd plunge into the cool dark of the forest, flanked by row after row of outsize trunks, the sky obliterated by a blanket of green. The car dipped and climbed to follow the rise and fall of the land and swerved around boulders pushing their way up out of the earth, now mossy with lichen. All this I remembered. I saw the trees and was taken back two hundred years, flooded with the recall of my first life, my true life, the one that had been taken away from me. It had to be the same for Jonathan.

We sensed our home getting closer. The trip passed quickly in an automobile. The last time we had made this trip it was weeks in the carriage, Jonathan in shock from what I'd done to him, barely speaking a word to me.

We were speechless on the approach to town. How everything had changed. We couldn't even be sure that this road, the main road cutting through the middle of town, was the same small dusty wagon trail that led to the fledgling St. Andrew two hundred years ago. Where was the church and the graveyard? Shouldn't we be able to see the meeting hall from here? I rolled the car down the street as slowly as possible so we could try to transpose the town we remembered over the one in front of us.

St. Andrew hadn't become like many towns in America, where every store, restaurant, and hotel is the product of a multinational corporation and generic the world over. At least St. Andrew had some individuality, even if it had lost its original purpose. It was no longer industrious. The sprawling farms were gone and there had been no sign of the logging business for the past ten miles. The business of leisure had taken its place. Wilderness outfitters lined both sides of the main street, businesses where well-scrubbed men in rugged clothing escorted other men and women through the forest or down the Allagash in canoes. Or took them into the middle of the river in hip waders, casting all day for the fish they would release once they had been admired. There were craft stores and inns where once there had been farmhouses and barns, Tinky Talbot's forge and the Watfords' general store. We were amazed to figure out, finally, that the congregation hall must have been demolished and that the center of town was now occupied by a hardware store, an ice-cream shop, and a post office. At least the graveyard had been undisturbed.

This new generation of inhabitants surely thought it pleasant enough, and if I hadn't known what it was like two centuries ago, I wouldn't have objected. But the town now made its living catering to the whims of strangers and seemed degraded, like finding your child-hood home had been turned into a bordello, or worse, a convenience store. St. Andrew had traded its soul for an easier way of life, but who was I to judge?

We checked into a sporting lodge outside town. Dunratty's was like an old motel, shabby from an unavoidable neglect, that catered to the seasonal hunters and fishermen and so a certain austerity was expected. There was a set of ten or so rooms making up one unit, at-tached to the office. We asked for a cabin, the one set farthest into the woods. The caretaker said nothing, merely looked discreetly for the presence of rifles or fishing poles and finding there were none, went back slowly and resignedly to his task. He did ask if we were married, as though he minded that one of his murky cabins would be used as a love shack. The place was empty except for us, we were told; it would be very quiet. He would be available at the house if we needed anything—and he pointed off in some indiscernible direction—but otherwise we could expect to be left alone.

It was dismal, all four walls lined with cheap paneling, the roof merely covered in plywood. The space was dominated by two beds—slightly larger than single beds, neither as large as a double, with Depression-era metal rail frames—set apart by a small dresser put in the place of a nightstand, and topped with a ceramic lamp. Two threadbare upholstered chairs faced what looked to be a thirty-year-old television. To one side was a small, round table accompanied by three armless wooden kitchen chairs. Through a doorway I found a small, functional kitchen, and through a second doorway, a slightly mildewed bathroom. I laughed when Jonathan threw the suitcases on one of the beds. "We're staying?" I asked, incredulous. "There must be someplace nicer. Maybe in town . . ."

Jonathan said nothing but stood before a set of sliding glass doors. Beyond a plain wooden deck were the woods; great thick trunks tow-ering above us, creaking in the wind. We opened the door and stepped into the middle of the forest, and clean air licked over and around us. We stood on the modest square of the deck and looked into the endless forest for an immeasurable amount of time. This was the home we had known. It had found us. "We're staying," Jonathan replied.

We left the cabin about five that afternoon, anxious to look around a little more before the sun set. It was difficult to make our way, though; roads we expected to lead in one direction ended up taking us to another place entirely, as the area had been shaped and reshaped over time. The current grid of roads had been laid down by the modern logging companies and went through mile after mile of forest for no apparent reason, leading straight to a highway, which in turn would take us to the juncture of the Allagash and St. John Rivers. After two false starts, we found a road that reminded us of the carriage trail that had led out to Jonathan's house, and it was with a silent nod from Jonathan that we pursued it to its end.

We burst through a tunnel of overgrown trees onto a cleared swath that had once been hayfields in front of the St. Andrews' house. The road had been moved—it no longer swept through the gully by the icehouse and then up to their big house—but I recognized the shape of the land. Now, a dirt logging road cut to the right of the house, which still stood on the bluff. We sped up a little, anxious to see it again. But as we got closer, I let up on the pedal. The house was still standing, but only someone who had once lived there would have been able to recognize it.

The once glorious house had been left to rot. It was like a corpse that had been exposed to the elements, a skeleton with every feature by which you'd known the person fallen away. The once grand house sagged, stripped of paint, missing slate tiles upon its head, slats from its torso. Even the stand of pines that had formed a windbreak in front were failing, spindly and unloved, the kind of trees you find in a graveyard.

"It's abandoned," Jonathan said.

"Who would have thought," I offered, not knowing what to say. "Oh, well, Jonathan . . . at least they left it in its spot. You saw where my family's house would have been—nothing but a crossroads now. The world moves on, doesn't it?"

Jonathan fell quiet in response to my attempt at cheerfulness. We turned the car around and headed back toward town.

We went to a small restaurant in the center of town that night for dinner. You could call it a restaurant in that it was a place where meals could be purchased, but it didn't resemble the sort of restaurant that I was used to patronizing. It was more like a diner with a dozen laminate-topped tables, each surrounded by four metal-tube chairs. The tablecloths were oilcloth, the napkins paper. The menus were covered in yellowing plastic, and it was a safe bet that the menu had not changed in twenty years. There were five customers, including Jonathan and me. The other three were all men in jeans and flannel shirts and some kind of cap, each sitting at a separate table. The waitress was probably also the cook. She looked at us critically as she passed us menus, as if there was some question of whether she would serve us or not. Country music played sweetly from a radio.

We ordered food that neither of us had seen in a long time, if ever, living abroad: fried catfish fillets, chicken and dumplings, food that was almost exotic in its strangeness. We lingered over bottled beer and spoke little, under the joint impression that the other patrons were watching us. The waitress—hair like coiled wire and determined sags cut into her face—looked pointedly at the half-eaten meals before asking us if we wanted any dessert. "Pie is good," she deadpanned, as if making a general observation.

"Was it disappointing, to visit your home?" I asked, after the waitress had brought over two more beers. Jonathan shook his head.

"I should have expected it. Still, I wasn't prepared."

"It's so different, but in some ways, so much the same. I feel disjointed. If you weren't with me, I'd leave."

We left the diner and walked down the street. Everything was closed, except a tiny bar, the Blue Moon to judge by its neon sign predictably shaped like a crescent moon. It sounded romantic, but through the plate-glass front I saw it was completely full of men, truckers and loggers watching a sporting event on the television. After the commercial part of town had petered out, we came upon the churchyard. There was just enough moonlight to wander among the headstones.

It had become wild and overgrown. Wild berry bushes and nettles had reclaimed the stone wall, shrouded the twin columns that had once flanked the entry, and swallowed up some of the markers. Years of frost heaves had thrown some of the gravestones out of their places; other headstones were eroded by time or had been broken by vandals. I picked my way through the graves quickly, not anxious to visit my former neighbors in this way, while Jonathan made his way from graveside to graveside, trying to read the names and dates, pulling at weeds that had sprung up around the stones. He seemed so sad and wounded that I had to quash the urge to make him leave.

"Look, it's Isaiah Gilbert's marker," Jonathan called out. "He died in . . . 1842."

"A respectable amount of time. A good long life," I called back from the spot where I stood, smoking and weaving from remembrance and vertigo.

By then Jonathan had turned to another tombstone. He was crouching, on the balls of his feet, looking around the churchyard. "I wonder if everyone we knew is here, somewhere."

"It's inevitable that some of them left. Have you found any of my family?"

"Wouldn't they be in the Catholic cemetery on the other side of town?" he asked, walking down an aisle, looking from headstone to headstone. "We can go over there next, if you like."

"No, thanks. I've no curiosity left."

I knew Jonathan had found someone significant when he knelt next to a large double marker. It was rough stone and pitted with age, its broad, flat back to me, so I could not read the inscription. "Whose is it?" I asked as I walked over.

"It's my brother." His hands were running over the engraved words. "Benjamin."

"And Evangeline." I touched the other side of the tombstone. Evangeline St. Andrew, beloved wife. Mother of Ruth.

"So they married."

"Family honor?" I asked, brushing off the letters with my fingertips. "It doesn't look as though she lived long."

"And Benjamin was buried beside her—he never remarried."

In the next hour we found most of Jonathan's family—his mother and eventually the daughter Ruth, too, the last St. Andrew to live in the town. Jonathan's sisters were missing, though, which led Jonathan to hope they'd married and left town, to raise happy and successful families somewhere else and be buried beside their husbands in more cheerful surroundings. He wanted to believe they'd escaped all the melancholy of St. Andrew.

I took Jonathan back to the cabin. I'd smuggled two bottles of an extraordinary cabernet all the way from France in my suitcase. We pulled the cork on one and let it breathe on the counter while we lay in bed together. I held Jonathan against me until the chill had left his body and then I undressed him. We lay in bed between the aged and softened white cotton sheets, sipping the cabernet in tumblers and talking about our childhood, the brothers and sisters, friends, and fools; the closely held long dead, decomposed and inert matter in the ground while we were still inexplicably alive. I could not bear to tell him the truth about Sophia. Instead, we spoke of each cherished one until Jonathan lapsed into sleep—and then I cried for the first of many times.

FORTY-NINE

There were no more excursions to relive the past: no more visits to graveyards, no retracing of paths in the woods at once familiar but now barely evident and ghostly. We walked along the Allagash, sighting moose and deer and admiring the light from the full Maine sun sparkling on the current, rather than reminiscing about events that had transpired on this spot or that. The rest of the time was spent quietly in each other's company.

Time spent together became like a drug I couldn't get enough of, and I began to think maybe we could get lost here, where we had started together. We wouldn't have to live in St. Andrew proper; since the town had changed so much, it might be disconcerting to stay. We could find land in the woods and build a cabin, where we'd live apart from everybody and everything. No newspaper, no clock, no insistent ticking of time tapping us on the shoulder, reverberating in our ears. No running from the past every fifty or sixty years or so, to emerge as another person in another land, or rather pretending to be a new person, as new as a chick just come from the egg, but inwardly feeling like the person I was and could never get away from.

We were out one night on the deck behind the dilapidated cabin, wrapped in our coats, sitting on two folding chairs, drinking wine from glass tumblers and looking up at the flat moon. Jonathan steered our talk to the past and it made me uneasy. He wondered whether Evangeline had had a hard, unhappy life after he disappeared and whether he had been the cause of his mother's early death. I said I was sorry over and over, but Jonathan wouldn't hear any of it, shaking his head and saying no, it had been his fault, he had been terrible to me, taking advantage of my obvious love for him. I shook my head, placing a hand on Jonathan's forearm. "But I had wanted you so much, you see," I told him. "You weren't entirely to blame."

"Let's go out there, again," Jonathan said, "to that place in the woods, where we used to meet, the place with the vault of birch saplings. I've thought of them often, the prettiest spot on earth. Do you think they are still there? I'd hate it if someone has cut them down." Tipsy and warm from drink, we climbed into the SUV, though I had to go back inside the cabin for a blanket and a flashlight. I held the open wine bottle to my chest as Jonathan maneuvered the vehicle through the woods. We had to leave the sport utility on the side of the logging road and travel the last half mile on foot.

We managed to find the glade though it had changed. The saplings had grown but only to a certain size, then stopped. Their tallest branches now touched each other, closing over the hole in the canopy, overshadowing the seedlings that had tried to follow their example. I remembered this glade where we had met as children to laugh and tell each other stories from our lonely lives, but time had taken away its unique beauty. The glade was no longer blessed and graceful; it was as any other patch of forest, no more and no less.

I spread the blanket on the ground and we lay on our backs, trying to see through the foliage canopy to the night sky above, but there were only a few spots where the stars were able to peek through. We tried to believe that it was the same place where we had met but both knew it could have been five paces to the west, or a hundred yards to the left; in short, it was as good as any place in the woods, as long as there was a thinning of the treetops, as long as we could lie on our backs and see stars.

Thinking of our childhood reminded me of the burden I'd been carrying all this time. The time had come to tell Jonathan the truth about Sophia. Old secrets have the greatest strength, though, and I was terrified of how Jonathan would react. Our reunion could be over tonight; he might banish me forever from his life this time. These fears almost made me retreat, again, but I couldn't continue to have this hanging over me. I had to speak.

"Jonathan, there is something I must tell you. It's about Sophia."

"Hmm?" He stirred next to me.

"It was my fault that she killed herself. My fault. I lied to you when you asked if I'd gone to see her. I threatened her. I told her she would be ruined if she had the baby. I said you would never marry her, that you were through with her." I'd always thought I'd burst into tears when I made this confession, but I didn't. My teeth began to chatter, though, and my blood was cold in my veins.

He turned to me, though I couldn't make out his expression in the dark. A long few seconds ticked by before he answered. "You waited all this time to tell me this?"

"Please, please forgive me—"

"It's okay. Really, it is. I've thought about it over the years. Funny how you see things differently with time. Then, I'd never have thought my father and mother would have let me marry Sophia. But what could they have done to stop me? If I'd threatened to leave the family to be with Sophia and the child, they wouldn't have disowned me. They would have given in. I was their only hope to keep the business going, to have someone to take care of Benjamin and the girls after they died. I just didn't see it then. I didn't know what to do, and I turned to you. Unfairly, I see that now. So . . . it's as much my fault as anyone's that Sophia killed herself."

"You would have married her?" I asked.

"I don't know . . . for the sake of the child, possibly."

"Did you love her?"

"It was so long ago, I don't remember my feelings, exactly." He may have been telling the truth but didn't realize he'd drive me mad with that sort of answer. I was sure he saw the women in his life in some kind of priority and I longed to know where I stood, who was on the step ahead of me, who fell below. I wanted our complicated history to be simplified: certainly things had been sorted out with the passage of so many years. Jonathan had to know how he felt by now.

I sat, not touching Jonathan in any way, and that made me nervous. I needed the reassurance of his touch to know he didn't hate me. Even if he didn't blame me for Sophia's death, he might be disgusted by all the terrible things I had done.

"Are you cold?" I said to Jonathan.

"A little. And you?"

"No. But is it okay if I lie next to you?" I took off my jacket and spread it over both of us. Our frosty breaths hovered over us like a specter as we scanned the night sky.

"Your hand is cold." I lifted Jonathan's hand and blew warm breath on it before kissing each finger.

I cupped his cheek. "Your face is chilled." There was no protest, either, as I nuzzled his stubbled face, his handsome nose and his paper-fine eyelids. There was no interruption from there as I peeled back Jonathan's clothing until I'd tunneled a path to his chest and groin. Then I undressed and pressed myself on top of him, the flannel on the inside of my jacket brushing softly against my buttocks.

We made love there on the blanket under the stars. We moved through the sexual act, but it had changed between us. It was slow and tender, almost ceremonial—but how could I complain? The whirlwind of our young passion was gone and in its place was something loving, but that left me sad nonetheless. It was like we were saying good-bye to each other.

When it was over—me leaning over Jonathan like a jockey, Jonathan sighing in my ear, then pulling his trousers up to his waist—I reached into the pocket of my jacket for cigarettes. A contrail of smoke was expelled into the cold air, the warmth in my lungs calming. I continued to draw on the cigarette while Jonathan stroked the top of my head.

I'd wondered what would happen at the end of the trip. Jonathan had never said and I wasn't sure when it was supposed to end. The tickets were open ended and Jonathan had not mentioned when he was expected back at the refugee camp. Not that the trip could drag on much longer; it had been nothing but disappointment (with intermittent wild longings for happily-ever-after), reminders of loss with only the trees and the beautiful sky overhead to welcome us back.

Nor could I throw off the niggling doubt that I was the cause of Jonathan's melancholy. Had I disappointed him, or perhaps Jonathan had still not forgiven me. We hadn't talked about why he'd left me and I assumed I knew the reason: that after years of frustration and recrimination, he had grown sick of disappointing me.

But this time wasn't about being together forever; this was about something else. I just wasn't sure what that was. He wanted to be with me, that much was obvious; otherwise, he wouldn't have asked me to make this trip with him. If he was still angry he never would have contacted me, sent the email, drunk champagne, kissed my face, let me cradle him in bed. I was insecure around him and always would be, the burden of my love like a stone manacled to my neck.

"What would you like to do tomorrow?" I asked, feigning nonchalance, stubbing the cigarette out in the dirt. Jonathan tilted his chin up, toward the stars, and closed his eyes.

"Well, then," I drawled when he didn't answer, "how much longer would you like to stay? Not to rush you, I'll stay as long as you'd like."

He gave a slow smile, but still no answer. I rolled on my side toward Jonathan, propping my head on one hand.

"Have you thought about what we're going to do next? About—us?"

Finally, his eyes opened and blinked up at the sky. "Lanny, I asked you here for a reason. You haven't guessed—?"

I shook my head.

He reached out for the wine bottle, rose up on an elbow and drank, then passed the bottle to me, with just a scant inch or so left on the bottom. "Do you know why I suggested we come back here?" I shook my head. "I did it for you."

"For me?"

"I'd hoped it would make you happy if we came back here together, that it would make up in a small way for when I'd left. This trip hasn't been for me—it's been *hell* for me, coming back. I knew it would be. I've always wished I could have made it up to them, my family, the wife and daughter who thought I deserted them. I'd give anything to have it all back."

How could it shift so suddenly, become so bad? It felt like a cold, invisible barrier was descending between us. "It wasn't your fault," I said, as though we didn't know whose fault it was. I had no stomach for more wine and gave the bottle back to Jonathan. "What's the point of talking about it, Jonathan? There's nothing you or I can do to bring that back. What's past is past."

"What's past is past," he repeated before draining the bottle. He stared into the darkness, careful not to stare at me. "I'm so tired of this, Lanny. I can't continue on this treadmill anymore, this never-ending succession of day after day . . . I've tried everything I could think of to carry on."

"Please, Jonathan, you're drunk. And tired . . ."

The wine bottle sank in the soft earth as Jonathan leaned forward on it. "I know what I'm saying. That's why I asked you to come with me. You're the only one who can help me."

I knew where this was leading: life was circular and even the worst parts of it were guaranteed to come around a second time, begging at your heels. It was the argument we'd had every night for months—years?—before he finally left. He'd hectored, pleaded, threatened. That was the real reason he'd left, it wasn't because he couldn't help disappointing me—it was because I wouldn't give him the only thing he wanted. His one desire would hang in the air between us, the only way for him to escape from everything he wanted to forget: abandoned responsibility, a dead child, betrayal by the person who loved him the most. Only one thing could make it go away.

"You can't ask me to do this. We both agreed it was too terrible a thing to ask of me. You can't leave me all alone with—that."

"Don't you think I deserve release, Lanny? You must help me."

"No. I can't."

"Do you want me to say that you owe it to me?" That stung because he had never, ever said that to me before. Somehow he had managed never to fling those words in my face, words that I fully deserved. *You owe me this because you did this to me. You put this curse on my head.*

"How can you say that"—I wailed, intent on striking back, intent on making him feel as terrible as he had made me feel—"when you walked out and left me to wonder, all those years?"

"But you weren't alone. I was still with you, in a way. No matter where you were, you knew I was there, too, somewhere in the world." Jonathan struggled upright, weary. "Things have changed for me. I have something to tell you. I didn't want to, Lanny. I don't want to hurt you, but you have to understand why I'm asking you again. Why it's important to me now." He took a deep breath. "You see, I fell in love."

He waited, expecting me to react badly to news of the best thing that had ever happened to him. I opened my mouth to congratulate him but, of course, no words came out.

"A Czech woman, a nurse. We met in the camps. She worked for another aid organization. One day, she was called to Nairobi by her home office for a meeting. I got the news over the radio out in the bush that she'd been killed in a car accident in the city. It took me a day to be helicoptered out to recover her body. We'd only been together a few years. I couldn't believe the injustice—here I'd waited so long, lifetimes, to find the one I was meant to be with and we had just a short time together." He spoke quietly, without too much grief, to spare me, I think. Nevertheless, as I listened my insides twisted tighter and tighter.

"Do you see now? I can't go on anymore."

I shook my head, determined to be tough, steely, in the face of his pain.

"I don't want to hurt you," he said. "And I know you know the pain I am going through. Do you want me to tell you how wonderful she was? How I couldn't help but love her? How impossible it is to go on without her?"

"People do it every day," I managed to say. "Time passes, you forget. It gets easier."

"Don't. Not to me. I know better. So do you." Maybe he hated me at that moment. "I can't do this anymore. I can't bear her loss; I can't accept that there is nothing, *nothing* I can do to make this pain stop. I will go insane, insane and trapped forever inside this body. You can't condemn me to that. I resisted for as long as I could because I know— *I know*—it is a terrible thing to ask. I didn't mean to ask you like this. I didn't mean to tell you about her, so abruptly. But you forced my hand, and now that I've told you . . . we can't go back. Here it is, you know what I need from you. You must help me."

He reached out and struck the wine bottle against a rock. The cascade of notes, high and harsh, went through and around us. He clutched the neck and shoulder of the bottle in his fist, serrated peaks of green glass, held in his hand like a bouquet. It was the only weapon at hand; it was crude and violent, and he wanted me to use it on him. He wanted to bleed to death.

You can't leave me all alone, by myself, without you.

I wanted to say that to him, but I couldn't. He had brought me an inarguable reason: he had lost his love and couldn't go on. The time had finally come to let him go.

I couldn't speak and only knew I was crying from the cold ignited on my cheeks by the wind, cold like biting fire. He reached up and touched my tears. "Forgive me, Lanny. Forgive me that it's come to this. I'm sorry I couldn't give you what you wanted. I tried—you don't know how badly I wanted to make you happy, but I couldn't make it work. You deserve to be loved in the way you have always hoped for. I pray that you will find that love."

Slowly, I took the broken bottle from him. Jonathan took his shirt off and offered himself, and I looked from my hand to that pale chest, glowing blue in the moonlight.

We should have had a life of great love.

I couldn't look at him; I simply pushed against him, knowing the edge of the glass would do the rest. The teeth of green sank into his flesh, a perfect circle of a bite, soft and yielding. The broken bottle sank deep and Jonathan's blood welled up to my fingers. He let the quietest gasp escape.

And then a swipe of my hand, and three lines were drawn across the white blankness of his skin. Deep, the wounds split open, letting more blood escape. Jonathan crumpled, falling on his chest and then rolling on his back, hands held limply against the wound, blood gurgling out of him. What stood out to me was that the flesh had given way so easily. I kept expecting the edges of the wound to knit back together but they didn't. "I must've said the words, but my hand and intent, in my head. There was no denying that deed had been done by my hand, but surely this was not my intent. I had made a mistake—this had not been my intent. *Wake up*, I heard my own voice say from far away; *I must wake up*.

And then I did, waking up in the woods with the one I loved rocking, convulsing, in the dirt before me, choking and sputtering, but smiling. His chest rose and fell with deliberation, and I realized I'd seen Jonathan do this once already, in Daughtery's barn. And in an instant I was next to him, pressing his shirt against the wounds, foolishly trying to hold back the flow of blood. And Jonathan shook his head and tried to push the shirt from my hands. In the end, all I could do was hold him.

That was when it hit me, what I had lost. Jonathan had always been there, even during the years when we were apart, and the resonant hum had always been in the back of my mind, a comfort. Now all I had was a great, sucking void. I had lost the only important thing in my life. I had nothing, I was alone, the weight of the world crushing down on me with no one to help me. I'd made a mistake. I wanted Jonathan back. Better to be selfish. Better for him to resent me to the end of time than to feel like this. To feel like this and have no way to make it right or make it go away.

I held his body a very long time, until the blood had gone cold and I was covered with a film of wet slickness. I don't remember letting go of Jonathan. I don't remember leaving the body and running through the woods, screaming to the heavens to take pity on me and let me die. Let it be over for me, too. I could not go on without him. I don't remember ending up at the highway, limping along the logging road to be found by the sheriff and his deputy. It wasn't until I'd been locked in the car with my hands cuffed that it all came back to me, that I realized all I wanted was to be back in the woods with him, to die with him so we could stay together forever.

FIFTY

The narrow front hall of the town house is filled with crates, the wood fresh and prickled with splinters. A hammer, nails, and a pair of work gloves rest on a pedestal table along with a pile of unopened mail. Luke carries a marble bust down the stairs, his face reddening from the exertion. The bust is the second in a pair going to the Bargello, in Florence—one of Italy's many museums, chosen over the Uffizi for its superior collection of Renaissance sculpture—the first piece already packed in its own crate. From the wall, watching the activity, is the one piece of artwork that will never leave the house, the charcoal sketch of Jonathan that Lanny took from Adair's house. The portrait was moved from its original spot—at the foot of Lanny's bed—to the front hall, though Luke had no particular objection to leaving it in place. He is no more capable of being jealous of the man in the picture than he is of hating the golden sunrise or the Notre Dame cathedral.

Lanny comes out from the study with a sealed envelope in her hand. Inside the envelope is a note of apology for having kept the piece of art from its rightful owners, whoever they might be after all this time. The note—which has accompanied every piece shipped so far—is contrite but vague, devoid of any facts relating to how the piece was appropriated, or when, or by whom. Lanny worked on it for days, read several versions aloud to Luke before the two settled on the final wording. They wear latex gloves as they work, so they'll leave no fingerprints. Lanny has arranged for the shipping and the donation of the anonymous gifts to be done through her Parisian lawyer, whom she picked especially for his devotion to his clients and his flexible attitude toward aspects of the legal code. She has no concern that the shipments will be traced back to her, no matter how insistent the various museums and other recipients may become.

As for Luke, he's a little sorry to see all these marvels go so soon after his arrival. He'd like more time to make sense of what must be the most expansive private collection of art and artifacts in the world. Lanny hadn't exaggerated when she told him her house was more amazing than any museum. The upper floors were stuffed with treasures, stored with no rhyme or reason. Each time he dislodges one item to ship, he uncovers eight or ten more. And it's not just paintings and sculpture; there are mountains of books, undoubtedly including many first editions; Oriental carpets made of silk so fine they can pass through a woman's bracelet; Japanese kimonos and Turkish caftans of embroidered silks; all manner of swords and firearms. Grecian vases, Russian samovars, bowls carved from jade, made of beaten gold, chiseled from stone. Several chests filled with fists of crumpled silk and velvet, each one housing a piece of gem-studded jewelry. Then there are the complete surprises: for instance, inside a fan box, he found a note to Lanny written by Lord Byron. Luke can't make out most of the words, but he manages to find "Jonathan" written among the scrawl. Lanny claims she can't remember what the letter was about, but how do you forget a note from one of the world's great poets? It's the house of a mad collector, trying to compensate for an unarticulated, undisclosed lack in her life, a slave to a compulsion to amass beauty. Still, she has generously set aside some pieces to be placed in a trust for Luke's daughters, enough to pay for tuition at a good college when they are older.

Luke discovers that, aside from the collection of ancient Chinese ceramics, no attempt was ever made at an accounting, so he makes Lanny catalog the pieces as they go out: a description, a guess at where she'd acquired it, the name of the person or place that will receive it. He thinks it will be a comfort to her one day; it will give her the ability to remember her distant adventures without being weighed down by the objects themselves.

It's good for her to divest herself of these things, he thinks. It takes her mind off Jonathan, though not entirely; Luke has caught Lanny crying, in a bathroom or in the kitchen while waiting for water to boil for tea. Still, the crying has tapered off of late and their current project, shipping out the contents of her house, has made her visibly happier. She says she feels more at peace, that she's atoning for some of the bad things she's done. Once, she even said she also hoped that if she tried very hard to make amends, she'll be forgiven and the spell will be broken. She'll be able to grow old with Luke, to leave this earth at the same time, more or less. To never suffer that profound loneliness again. That sort of talk—dependency on a magical intervention—makes Luke uncomfortable. Given the circumstances, though, he knows not to doubt (entirely) in improbable interventions.

Lanny tucks the note under the bust and Luke hammers the lid on the wooden box. The courier is coming at two o'clock for the day's delivery and Luke has gotten only the two busts packed up. He'd hoped to have at least a half dozen pieces ready. He'll have to work faster.

When he puts down the hammer to wipe his forehead, he notices the stack of unanswered mail. On the top is a thick envelope from America and, out of reflex, he strains to read the address. It's from a lawyer's office in Boston, the one watching Adair's house—or rather, Adair's crypt. Luke flips through the stack quickly: there are seven letters with the same lawyer's address, going back nearly a year. He opens his mouth to say something about it to Lanny when she rushes by, purse over her shoulder, hunting distractedly for her house key. "I've got a hairdresser's appointment, but I should be back before the courier arrives. Shall I get lunch for us while I'm out? What would you like?"

"Surprise me," he says.

Luke takes delight in how she's fallen back into her routine—a sign that she hasn't been immobilized by depression—and, in particular, how quickly she's incorporated him into her life. He loves that they are so comfortable together. She's given up smoking because he asked, because he can't bear the sight of it even though he knows it poses no health risk to her. She shares everything with him: her favorite bakery, her favorite afternoon walk, the old men she chats with in the park. He is happy to do things for her, to take care of her, and in return she's grateful for every consideration he shows her. Does he love her? He's skeptical, truly skeptical, that love could happen so quickly, especially given who she is and what she has told him, but at the same time there's the giddy sensation that's overtaken him, a feeling he hasn't had since his daughters were born.

Once Lanny has left, he heads back upstairs in search of the next item to be repatriated. He must remember to leave Lanny to deal with the courier because Luke has an appointment later in the afternoon. He's meeting the director of volunteer services at Mercy International, an organization that sends doctors into war zones and refugee camps, clinics for the homeless. It was the last organization that Jonathan worked for; someone had contacted Lanny shortly after she and Luke arrived from Quebec, looking for Jonathan. He'd given the organization her address as a way to get in touch with him during his absence, only he'd never returned and they wanted to know if Lanny knew where he was. She was speechless, momentarily, then collected her wits and said she knew another doctor who might want to donate his services, as long as he could remain in Paris. Luke is glad for the interview, glad that Lanny knows he won't be happy if he can't make use of his medical training, hopes that his rusty French will be good enough to tend to immigrants from Haiti and Morocco.

Luke selects the next item to be shipped, a large tapestry that will go to a textile museum in Brussels. The tapestry has been rolled like a rug and is jammed against a barrister's bookcase that has been packed with all manner of bric-a-brac. Half the glass faces on the bookshelf had been left up and an item falls from a shelf as Luke tries to wrestle the tapestry upright.

He leans over, picks it up. It's a small ball of chamois, and he recognizes by the way the chamois is wadded up—Lanny's haphazard way of packing things—that there's something inside the dusty old cloth. He peels it back carefully—who knows what fragile thing might be inside—to find a tiny metal object. A vial, to be precise, about the size of a child's pinkie finger. Though it is mossy and dark with age, he can tell it's as delicately wrought as a piece of jewelry. Fingers trembling, he tugs off the lid and pulls out the stopper. It's dry.

He sniffs the empty vial. His mind races: it may be dry but there are ways to analyze the residue. They could send it to a lab and find out the elixir's ingredients, the proportions. They could try to make a batch and probably, after some trial and error, they would succeed. Re-creating the potion means he could be with Lanny forever. She wouldn't be alone. And, of course, other people would be interested in immortality. They could sell it for ridiculous sums, dole it out on the tongues of their customers like communion wafers. Or they could be completely charitable—after all, how much money does anyone need?—and give it to great minds to study. Who knows what impact this could have for science and medicine? An elixir that regenerates wounded tissue could revolutionize the treatment of injury and disease.

This could change everything. As would revealing Lanny's condition to the world.

And yet . . . Luke suspects that analysis of the residue would reveal nothing. Some things resist scrutiny, can't be examined in the cold light of day. A tiny fraction of a percent of occurrences can't be explained or reproduced. In his time as a medical student, he'd heard of a few, offered spontaneously by a sage old professor at the end of a lecture, whispered among the students as they filed out of the operating theater after a dissection. There are some physicians and medical researchers who dismiss such stories and would have you believe that life is mechanical, the body no more than a system of systems, like a house. That you will live as long as you eat this, drink that, follow these rules, as though they were a recipe for life; if you fix the plumbing or shore up the frame when they become damaged, because your body is only a vessel for carrying your consciousness.

But Luke knows it's not straightforward like that. Even if a surgeon were to search inside Lanny—and what a nightmare that would be, the body trying to close itself up even as the hands and instruments probed inside—he wouldn't find what part of her had changed to make her eternal. Nor would bloodwork or biopsies or any amount of radiological scans. So, too, you could analyze the potion, give the recipe to a thousand chemists to have them re-create it, but Luke thinks not one would be able to duplicate the result. There is a force at work in Lanny, he can feel it—but whether it is spiritual or magical or chemical or some kind of energy, he has no idea. All he knows is that the grace that is Lanny's existence, like faith and prayer, works better in solitude, protected from skepticism and the brute force of reason, and that, if the facts of her circumstances were made public, she might disintegrate into dust or evaporate like dew in sunlight. That's probably why none of the others—these others Lanny told him of, Alejandro, Dona, and the diabolical Tilde—have gone public, Luke thinks.

He rolls the vial between his fingers like a cigarette and then, quickly, places it under his heel and brings all his weight down on it. It folds as easily as if it were made of paper, squashed flat. He goes to the window, opens it, and throws the chip of metal as far as he can, over the rooftops of his neighbors, deliberately not following its trajectory with his eyes. Immediately, he feels relieved. Perhaps he should have spoken to Lanny before he destroyed the vial, but no—he knows what she would have said. It's done.

ACKNOWLEDGMENTS

While it should be readily apparent that *The Taker* is a work of the imagination, a measure of research went into it, especially regarding the history of the state of Maine. I drew on two volumes in particular: *Maine in the Early Republic,* edited by Charles E. Clark, James S. Leamon, and Karen Bowden (University Press of New England, 1988), and *Liberty Men and Great Proprietors: The Revolutionary Settlement on the Maine Frontier 1760–1820,* written by Alan Taylor (University of North Carolina Press, 1990). Any mistakes or inaccuracies are my own.

It's often said that a writer's life is lonely and that we write in solitude, and while that's mostly true, it would be impossible to make it to publication without relying on the help and good nature of many people along the way. I'd like to thank the readers of previous versions of this novel, including Dolores, Lisa, Randy, Linda, Jill, Kelley, and Kevin; my professors at Johns Hopkins, Tim Wendel, Richard Peabody, Elly Williams, David Everett, and Mark Farrington; Elyse

Cheney and Jeff Kleinman for their early encouragement; and the wonderful organizers of the Squaw Valley Community of Writers.

Enormous thanks go to Tricia Boczkowski, my editor at Gallery Books, for her editorial guidance and boundless good spirits in getting the novel to publication. Also, my thanks to everyone at Gallery for their efforts on my behalf.

Tremendous and undying thanks to Kate Elton, my editor at Century, and her assistant Anna Jean Hughes, for their incredible enthusiasm and support for the novel.

Thanks are also due to Nicki Kennedy, Sam Edenborough, and Katherine West, foreign rights agents at the Intercontinental Literary Agency, and to the publishers of the foreign editions of *The Taker*, for their confidence in taking on this debut work: Giuseppe Strazzeri, publisher, and Fabrizio Cocco, editor, at Longanesi; Cristina Arminana at Mondadori; Katarzyna Rudzka at Proszynski Media; and EKSMO Publishing. Thanks, too, to Matthew Snyder at Creative Artists Agency for seeing promise in *The Taker*.

My deepest thanks must go to Peter Steinberg, my agent, not only for his belief in the novel but for his deft editorial work, which took a wobbly story and transformed it into the novel you have in your hands today.

Thanks to my family for putting up with my insanely writerly ways since I was a humorless little child.

And of course, all my love to my husband, Bruce, who patiently allowed me to sock countless hours into this book and made all my dreams come true.